Praise for *Home*

"To describe this as a good first novel or a good indigenous novel is to undersell it; *Home* is, without qualification, simply a good novel."

Sunday Age

"Behrendt has an extraordinary ability to convey a political message without sacrificing the story."

Australian Bookseller & Publisher

"This novel's greatest strength is its insight into the pain and inherited shame of being Aboriginal in a racist society."

Sydney Morning Herald

"A confident and challenging debut."

Bulletin

"Behrendt brilliantly explores the subtleties of race and identity in a palpable way. It is like getting under another's skin."

The Age

Reading notes for *HOME*
now available on UQP's website
www.uqp.uq.edu.au

Larissa Behrendt is Professor of Law and Indigenous Studies and Director of the Jumbunna Indigenous House of Learning at the University of Technology, Sydney. She is a proud member of the Eualeyai/ Kamilaroi nations of northwest New South Wales. A graduate of the University of New South Wales Law School, she subsequently studied at Harvard University, receiving a Masters and later a Doctorate in Law. She has written two previous books: *Aboriginal Dispute Resolution* and *Achieving Social Justice*.

The idea of writing a novel about Aboriginal lives today came while studying and living abroad. In 2002 the initial manuscript, entitled *Home*, was chosen as the winner of the national David Unaipon literary award.

LARISSA BEHRENDT

UQP

First published 2004 by University of Queensland Press
Box 6042, St Lucia, Queensland 4067 Australia
Reprinted 2004, 2005

www.uqp.uq.edu.au

Typeset by University of Queensland Press
Printed in Australia by McPherson's Printing Group

Distributed in the USA and Canada by
International Specialized Book Services, Inc.,
5824 N.E. Hassalo Street, Portland, Oregon 97213-3640

This project has been assisted by the Commonwealth Government through the Australia Council, its arts funding and advisory body

Sponsored by the Queensland Office of Arts and Cultural Development.

Cataloguing in Publication Data
National Library of Australia

Behrendt, Larissa.
Home.

1. Aboriginal Australians — Fiction. I. Title.

A823.4

ISBN 0 7022 3407 9

Description of cover painting by the artist Bronwyn Bancroft: *Memory* encapsulates an intensity of feeling for the understanding of the past through the mind of the present. The spiral is a visual symbol often related to time and within the painting are figures that signify those who have inhabited our lives and lives before us.

For
Lavinia Boney Dawson
and
Kris Faller

The place where the rivers meet

1

1995

My FATHER TOLD ME that the name of the town meant 'the meeting of the rivers' in the old language. We had set out from Sydney in the fresh hours of the morning, leaving the tame quarters of suburbia, crossing over the mountains, until the landscape bled into undulating black soil plains. The afternoon crept up on us, the distant mountain formation offering a craggy, blue-haze backdrop. Barbed-wire-fenced paddocks held flocks of cotton-wool sheep, undisturbed by our passing.

It is three o'clock in the afternoon as my father parks his car in the main street, bumper pointing at the steps of the well-worn Royal Hotel. The retiring sun sparkles red and gold, the light catching in flashing opal colours. A hot wind blows across the concrete, mortar and wood packing grit in every crevice it brushes over — between bricks, the cracks of window frames, between teeth.

I decide that I will go to the post office. If I send a card today, it will reach my mother by Tuesday. Although that's the day that I'm planning to return, I can see her delivering a trim pink smile of thanks ("Oh, Candy"), and she will be pleased that I have remembered her. I can also see my father dismissing this with an "Oh, Can-deese", as he rolls his eyes.

The air-conditioning in Dad's large sleek car — I can stretch my legs out in front and not touch anything — had protected me from the aggressive heat and light film of swirling dust. I have always preferred the feeling of warmth on my skin to controlled too-frigid temperatures. I enjoy the stifling heat that now clings to my legs, underneath my skirt, embracing my face, as I walk across searing concrete. The post office is built with old burnt-red bricks and garnished with a wide verandah and white flourishes, defying the starching weather and the stretching time.

Inside, the sails of the ceiling fans click slowly, rhythmically. I pick a faded postcard from the wire stand, disappointed that there were none more parochial, less rustic (*Greetings from Big Rig Country* or a flock of sheep: *I miss Ewe*) to send on to my best friend Kate. I look over a display of books laid out on a table, publications of the local Historical Society, mostly photocopies stapled together between colourful cardboard. I decide on a collection of old newspaper articles about the area and a book of one resident family's memoirs. They arrived in 1904, the year my grandmother was born here. I know my father will comment on my impulse-buying. I've bought something at every stop we've made today. Dad loves to dramatise how much money I spend, as though each coin is extracted from his own pocket.

On the back of my postcard of the town centre, sun-scorched and faded, I write — *Hi Mummy, Hot and dusty; lots of sheep. By the time you get this, I'll be home. Love Candy* — and take my purchases to the counter where a homely, wrinkle-faced woman with curled grey hair waits.

"All this way from Sydney?" she asks. I suddenly feel conscious of my suit and my leather shoes that clip confidently across the wooden floor.

"Yes. I guess you can pick a tourist."

"We get to know the faces in here. Are you staying a while or driving through?"

"I'm staying for the weekend."

"Well, there's lots of interesting things to see around here.

There are the fisheries down on the river and there's a pioneers' museum."

"I'm here to visit family," I reply.

"Really?" she answers, her interest piqued. "If they're locals, I probably know them."

"Well, the family names are Lance and Boney."

"Hmmm. Doesn't sound familiar to me. Do they live in town?"

"No, just outside."

"Oh," responds the woman, her mouth making a tight circle as she peers more carefully at me and then, quickly regaining her smile, processes my purchase with renewed efficiency. I have surprised her. She would know "just outside town" means the Aboriginal reserve. She was fooled by my light skin and has mistaken me for exotically Spanish, Brazilian or Italian. I'm used to this reaction but still it annoys me each time, like a distracting hangnail. I don't mind being mistaken for someone from somewhere else, but I mind when the realisation that the dark features are Aboriginal is met with disappointment, confusion or even disgust. I mind when the person observing me feels betrayed by my lightness.

I return to the car and sit with my door open, the stagnant heat still floating against my skin. I know my father will be in the pub for a while. Uncle Henry will convince him to have just one more drink to quench his city thirst. Dad will relish the excited welcome he'll receive as faces, known and unknown, crowd around for a free drink. Only such attention could make my father so flush with generosity.

I'm too shy to enter the bar even though I know Dad will be distracted and detained for a while. He'll be talking about his work at the Department of Aboriginal Affairs and feeding everyone snippets of information about friends and relatives also living in Sydney. I suddenly feel over-dressed and self-conscious in my dark blue cotton suit, something that I would wear to court or for a meeting with a client. I've already attracted the gaze from a group of four locals relaxing on the hotel verandah. I can't be sure whether they're looking at me — so obviously not of this place — or my father's flashy new car. Perhaps both.

I open one of the books I've just bought. The page falls to the writings of a clergyman who, accompanied by a 'black boy', travelled through the area in the late 1880s. He had written:

> *And yet, it was a privilege to be a pioneer, for this is the life that has helped to develop characteristics that make for a real greatness. Friendships, courage, indominatable perseverance in the face of difficulties were the privileges of our pioneers.*

I close the book and think about the woman in the post office and her stagnant, glazed expression that had, for just a moment, rejected me. A glance held only for a split-second, but the message so unmistakable. Perhaps she didn't know what it was that her look revealed, what it was that I saw.

My light cocoa skin wrapped around my mother's European features have allowed me to slip unnoticed into social circles, my presence never enough to make others feel guarded. Not like Kingsley, my brother, who, much darker, can never slip by. There is a price for this free access. I hear the things they assume will pass me by, things that would otherwise be said when I'm not there. I'm treated in these moments as though light skin is different, tougher than the person who wears it. "But you are not a real one," thin pink lips will tell me, to excuse me. "You're different".

But I keep these interactions — these looks, exclamations, excuses and hints of disgust — bottled within me. The words — "not a real one" — work into my skin like splinters, making me feel as though I have Kingsley's own dark skin wrapped around me. It is, of course, easier for me. I have these word-splinters under my flesh but Kingsley is undisguisable, cannot be masked. No one will mistake him as an exotic southern European. I feel guilt about the way I can slip in and out, but I also have a deep envy of Kingsley when dark hands shake his in greeting while darting eyes flit over me with unspoken suspicion.

My father emerges from the pub with a cheerful Uncle Henry by his side, just like veterans on Anzac day, and I am distracted from my brooding. I rise and embrace my gravely handsome uncle, who had, in his youth, been a football player for one of the Sydney teams. Henry's athleticism, all these decades on, still clings to him.

"Ah, Bub, look at you," he exclaims as he pulls me against his chest.

"Oh, Uncle Henry, it is so good to see you."

"Your father's been telling me that you're causing all kinds of trouble in those law courts in Sydney. God only knows we could use your skills around here."

"He exaggerates. I'm just plodding away," I respond, both embarrassed and pleased by my father's boasting.

"I kept all those postcards you sent me from Paris. Showed them to everyone around here who'd listen. Proud of you, I am."

"It's easy to see why you're my favourite uncle." I savour the flushed feeling his attention creates in me.

He holds my arm. "It took your father too long to bring you out here," he glances at his cousin with a reproachful eye.

"Henry is taking us out to dinner. We'll go check into the hotel and rest up before then," my father replies sheepishly.

From the faded floral bedspread in my hotel room I listen to the air-conditioner hum and hiss its secret language. Dad and Uncle Henry have remained at the small hotel bar, which is crowded with furniture but never with people. I excused myself, despite the temptation of Uncle Henry's presence, when the conversation, blurry from alcohol, turned to the knotted web of back-stabbing and double-dealing that make up black politics in the city.

Uncle Henry keeps a distant eye on what is happening in Sydney. He travels there often. On these visits I steal him away for lunch or dinner at white-walled, glass-encased restaurants. I love being escorted by my tall, gentle uncle. He charms me with stories from his tin-box of memories. I listen, captivated. I notice admiring glances thrown his way from blue eyes beneath shy lashes. Other times, looks can be contemptuous, perhaps not meant to be so obvious, and once even accompanied by a shrill, unashamed remark. My uncle dismisses these incidents with a smile. I'm not so forgiving, feeling more protective of him than I do of myself.

"It's the egg trying to protect the chicken," my father would say. You can go on too much about these incidents in the city. I've noticed a short attention span for such things.

In my pastel-flowered hotel room, I begin to sift through the papers I have brought with me. I hate to leave myself without some vestige of work nearby, even if I just carry it, keep it close. I've already redrafted the affidavits and I'm making notes about the next step for the native title claim I'm working on. I have to meet with the representative of the local Land Council on Tuesday and inform him of the progress of the case. Preparing the evidence of witnesses and anthropologists has already taken two years. I also have to make the arrangements to travel out to the peninsula to take another look at the land.

I organise my work by placing it in designated piles, one for each task. I have two more nights in town and curse myself that I haven't brought more to do. I make a mental note to ring Kingsley in the morning to organise further documents to be faxed — provided this hotel has a fax machine. I can trust my brother to be at work on a Saturday. He'll grumble that I'm imposing on him, drawing him away from his own caseload, but he'll at least respect my compulsion to do more, my inability to relax.

Kingsley's temperament has changed over the years. As a child, he was as shy as me, but was always more eager to please and more popular. Somewhere in his travels through this life he lost his amiable nature; I think it fell away once he began university, replaced by a ferocious seriousness. But we have never talked about why this was so. I doubt I could ever bring myself to ask him about it. I'm too afraid of finding out what has taken the most innocent parts of him away.

I pull myself under the stiff covers of my hotel bed and return to my post office purchases. I open the pale lemon cardboard cover and read the introduction of one of my new books, though they are more like pamphlets. It's a small piece written by a Mrs Cynthia Kerrigan-Mullins, the president of the Historical Society. Her great-grandfather owned the first general store in the town so she is well placed, she writes, to narrate the brief history of the little community. She marks the town's development with landmarks that begin with the establishment of her great-grandfather's store. Mrs Kerrigan-Mullins seems to think that the history of the town has been established from that date. It is followed by a postal service and a police station, a drought, a flood and a fire, the arrival of a train line in 1901 and the motor car in 1910. The only details added to the sketch are the refurbishment and extensions to the school and hospital in the middle of the century. In my mind, Cynthia Kerrigan-Mullins looks like the woman in the post office.

The book seems old, written with a tone from the 1950s, but when I look at the copyright date I see that it was printed in 1983; not new, but still thirty years later than I had expected. Well, it is the historical society, I think to myself as I turn to the first chapter titled 'Humble But Strong Beginnings'. This plots the battle of white men against the harsh terrain and unyielding, unsympathetic climate. As for mention of my own people, I find but one. Mrs Cynthia Kerrigan-Mullins has written:

Being troubled by the blacks and living in fear of them, a party was got together who surrounded about three hundred aborigines at the creek and shot down most of them, including men, women and piccaninnies.

I close the book, feeling the same deep chill I get when I find this kind of detached reference in history texts and contemporary media. It freezes me, like ice pressed against my flesh. I read the words, weigh them, over and over again.

"Being troubled by blacks."

"Living in fear of them."

"Three hundred."

"Shot down."

"Men, women and piccaninnies."

Justice Lionel Murphy wrote about this history of frontier violence in the 1979 High Court case of *Coe v. The Commonwealth*. He referred to it as genocide and said that "the aborigines did not give up their lands peacefully, that they were killed or removed forcibly from the land by English forces or colonists in what amounted to attempted, and in Tasmania almost complete, genocide." Genocide. It comes from the Greek *géno*, which means 'race', and from the Latin word *cida*, meaning 'killer'. The word was coined in 1944, a new word for an old concept.

These silent injustices and the unmentionable crimes stain the landscape. I remind myself that these dark happenings occurred because today people are trying to erase them. I remember the little jibes and the answers from back in my childhood. There they laughed at this killing with an innocence that was shocking and shameful ...

"Did they kill the Aborigines?" asked the small, angular, dark- haired boy, his big eyes quizzical.

"Yes," replied the teacher, her brow furrowed with the gravity of the subject, "yes they did."

"Good," squealed the beautifully sculpted lemon-haired girl, sitting at the back of the class, "there are too many of them."

Embarrassed laughter trickled amongst my classmates,

lapping against my burning ears. In silence, I stared at the front of the class, water swimming in my eyes.

I would confide my humiliation and hurt to my closest friend, Kate. Kate is now living in Charmony, France, with a ski instructor she met on a train from Brussels to Amsterdam. Kate would have listened to me explain and complain about Cynthia Kerrigan-Mullins with patient attention.

Kingsley and I were raised in a mostly white suburban neighbourhood on the southern outskirts of Sydney. We were the only dark children in school — kindergarten, primary and high school. I liked to speak out, in my martyr voice, about the dead black voices buried beneath the heroic tales of white men struggling to cross craggy mountain ranges to discover inland treasures — land, gold, caves and lakes: "I hope they let the Aborigines know that the mountain range was there when they *discovered* it." Hateful eyes would aim in my direction, as though I had given away the end of a suspenseful story. I shrugged off their hostility; I felt ashamed for the golden children and said as much to Kate during our soulful talks in the library corner.

Such rebelliousness is liberating but it's also isolating. I didn't mind; I had Kate. And when she wasn't there, I was always able, through books, to be carried to imagined worlds where cruelty lurked in the most sophisticated souls and comfort could be discovered in desolate landscapes. As I slipped into worlds created by Jane Austen, Charles Dickens, Henry James and the Brontë sisters, I had my own retorts and strategies to the restrained or bubbling emotions of the characters I met. None of them, in my mind, mistook me as exotically Other. No mention was made of my skin colour. My romanticism would have surprised anyone who knew my cynical self, except Kate, my sharer of secrets, loves and fears.

I had my own clash of wills with Mr Darcy, Mr Rochester, and Heathcliff — especially Heathcliff, whose wild legacy of malice and revenge inexplicably drew me in. I always felt that if I had known him, if I were there in the house when he arrived, if I were Catherine, I could have made him happy and set his demons free. I understood the meanness that grew out of him, how the crimes of one generation leave a legacy of bitterness and the stigma of prejudice and, for some, the hope of reconciliation. I relished a passionate, epic struggle and a calm hope-filled ending, a triumph.

My brother fared better within the concrete walls and black lace iron of the school. His skill in sports — leading try-scorer in football — provided an effective antidote to unpopularity. The good in him was considered by others to be there "despite his blackness", but not his athleticism, as though his Aboriginality carried a special sporting gene. This magical gene must have skipped me, the lover of words on pages. I would watch Kingsley slam his flesh against other bodies into the soil, his teammates yelling and playfully smacking his strong, broad back, blowing with weighty breaths as together they strode triumphant from the field. I would stand back, watching lovingly, as he won acceptance in the public arena.

As a sensitive child, Kingsley had become quite skilled at avoiding confrontation. If he couldn't forgive, Kingsley could push things to the furthermost regions of his mind, to barren desert plains, a place where things could be abandoned to eventually die. He was uncomfortable with my aggressiveness, my unwillingness to let go, I could tell. He had heard unkind things about me and seen messages scrawled on the toilet doors at school that he hoped were not true. These things he also pushed aside. He wanted a corner for silence, a place for introspective peace. He had wished back then that I would be more like him — less confrontational, less angry — but as we grew older we turned more and more to each other and grudgingly began to appreciate each other's once annoying and puzzling differences and attitudes. We both developed a need to understand the world we lived in — a world of rising deaths in custody and cyclical poverty — and we sought a way to change it.

From high school, we reached for the knowledge of law. I grabbed it with passionate and explosive enthusiasm, Kingsley, my quiet, thoughtful brother, with measured, analytical determination. In just a few years I became disheartened by realities that I had hoped were not possible: ever increasing incarceration rates and police officers caught on videotape at a party parodying the deaths of Aboriginal prisoners.

Kingsley grew more reclusive and secretive; he no longer sought acceptance, just his corner and place of peace. He stopped playing football and would spend his weekends reading, studying and writing. I found it harder to engage him in conversation unless we were talking about work. Our abilities, like our personalities, complemented rather than clashed as we lived within the walls of our shared understanding, as though we were under a protective shell. Joining each other in legal practice seemed inevitable with our shared fervour, complementing skills and dislike of the thought of facing the rough, rarely yielding political arena of Indigenous rights alone.

Law is a language. It becomes less mysterious the more you study it and speak it. You come to understand what the jargon means and how the arguments counter each other. You can understand how power flows through society if you understand the power of legal rhetoric. Legal language is bewildering until it becomes familiar, falling into place, and you then can use the words, get comfortable with them and employ them to show that you belong, that you have mastered the language. Then you rarely, if ever, stop to notice the bewilderment on the faces of others. It is too ambitious to think that you are going to change the world if you understand the language — and you have to be careful that the language does not seduce you — but you are better able to recognise what is going on, to find a name for it. It is just a matter of putting flesh on a skeleton. Justice Brennan put it like that in the *Mabo* case. He said that the court cannot change the principles of law, like the doctrine of *terra nullius*, just so that they fit in with the values that we have in contemporary society, if the change would "fracture the skeleton of principle which gives the body of our laws its shape and consistency". The Court cannot depart from its established principles, he said, where the departure would fracture this "skeleton of principle".

So you have to find a way to put the flesh on while keeping the skeleton intact. Kingsley says that this is not the point of the case, that it is simply a justification for finding native title when it was not recognised before and that I am dwelling too much on the excuses. But I believe you can tell a lot about people from the way they make up an excuse, the way they seek to justify things.

I love Kingsley, my dark, moody counterpart, most in all the world. I had achingly missed him while I was studying in Paris. He could not understand my decision to go away for a year. There was so much to do, he had said simply. He was right, of course, but I needed the time to step back, to think through larger issues, to explore myself, to try to regain my idealism that seemed to have crumpled so quickly when faced with the enormity of the task of law reform ahead. I thrived on the practical, day-to-day litigation but something in me had always wanted to take some time to think about the bigger picture, to return to my youthful ideals and their promised hopes. When I was given the chance to study on an international law program in France, I took it. No one seemed to understand my need to leave except Kate, my confidante, perhaps because she knew my insecurities and fears. She left for London, anxious for the chance to explore the better parts of herself and reinvent the rest, at the same time I left for France.

Paris made me swell with self-assurance. When the Parisians realised I was not Armenian or Algerian, my exoticness was celebrated. And I had met Christoph, whose cobalt eyes would look right into me, whose touch would fall through my skin. He loved me, I confidently knew, and I longed for him in a way that words fail to capture. But I resisted his offer, his insistence, to join me when I returned home. In Sydney I was no longer *la Aborigine*. I was a coon, a boong, a gin. He would hear the taunts about genocide, like, "Good, there are too many of them."

And what of his light white skin and tall Nordic looks? I knew what people would say about me. I was already so light-skinned; he would make me whiter. I feared he would cause me to betray this aspect of my identity that had made me who I was. So I left Christoph and his deep undemanding love for me, as though it was something that could not transcend the winding, cobbled streets of Montmartre or the summer stench of the Seine. My martyrdom seemed almost complete: more scratches, more nails, more needle-jabs.

I fall asleep in the thin shell of the rickety small-town hotel room with a far distant memory of Kingsley's round-moon childhood face, stained with tears, and my attempt at consoling motherly sister words. This merges with one of Kate's witty retorts as we bask in the twinkling sun by her swimming pool, then I am in the sanctuary of Christoph's arms, our bodies press together naked in the dark, leaving nothing between us but skin.

2

1995

I AM SIFTING THROUGH the articles in the *Aboriginal Law Bulletin* when my father rings to tell me we will be leaving in half an hour. I smile as I replace the receiver. He is in the room next door but too lazy to walk over. He's a man who has learnt to enjoy comfort.

I join him in his room at the designated time only to find that we are waiting for Uncle Henry, who will be another hour. I bristle at my father's deceitfulness. I could work in the extra time, finish reading an article on native title extinguishment, but my father wants company and has tricked me. Kingsley, in such circumstances, would just retreat back to his room, but I am held captive by my inability to resist my father's pouts and demands.

"Give your work a break. You don't need to be at it every minute of every day," he snaps.

"Did you sleep well, Dad?" I ask, only to change the subject.

"No. These beds are awful."

"It's hard to believe that this is the best hotel in town."

Dad grins. "Well, we could have stayed with Henry — then you'd think this was the Hilton."

Uncle Henry lives in one of the weatherboard, cardboard-thin houses at the Aboriginal settlement. He has several nieces and nephews staying with him. At the moment they number five. Some are blood, others he just loves and feels responsible for. Since most of the family's time is spent outside, away from the house, there seems to be plenty of room even though two are already permanently settled in the corner of the living room.

I was uneasy at the prospect of staying with Uncle Henry. I'm shy in front of strangers and so many at once seemed overwhelming. I've been rescued by my father's desire for comfort and privacy. "I've had too many years of living like that," he says, his voice a whisper.

"So what's the plan for today?" I ask.

"When Henry gets here we'll pick up Granny from the hospital and she'll take us out to Dungalear."

Dungalear is the place where my grandmother was born. She died many years ago. Granny, who we are to collect, is the eldest member of my Aboriginal family and the last to speak the old language fluently. Granny is the cousin of my grandmother, Elizabeth, and one of the few people living who remember her as a little girl before she was taken away by the Aborigines Protection Board. Granny has been the link to our heritage for me, my father and every other member of our now scattered clan.

Granny is resting in her wheelchair on the back porch of the hospital, looking out over the burnt yellow grass as we arrive. A nurse with brown, neatly clipped hair and a spotless blue uniform accompanies our little party, guiding us to the patient.

"Here she is," chirps the nurse. "She was up early this morning. *Weren't you Mrs Boney?* She had her bath before everyone else. *And you look very nice, Mrs Boney.*"

The nurse speaks louder when addressing Granny as though the older woman is hard of hearing. Granny stares out into the paddock ignoring the perky, prim woman. I don't blame her. Granny is a crumpled, leather-skinned woman with snake-like hands whose presence commands silent respect but she takes this deference with little acknowledgment.

"Well, I'll leave you to her," sings the nurse as she retreats, her rubber soles squeaking against the linoleum.

"Hi, Granny," Henry says as he stoops to kiss her.

"What took you so long to get here?" she asks testily, staring up at his big frame.

"I had some things to sort out this morning," he replies, the gaze of his dark eyes lowered to the floor.

"You were dawdling," she snaps back.

Granny turns to look at Dad. "What took *you* so long?"

"I've been busy in Sydney."

"Huumph," Granny replies, unimpressed, her gaze levelled steadily at him.

I didn't expect such ferocity from the old woman I had heard so much about. I begin to feel intimidated and regret that I have come all this way to meet her.

"So you're Bob Boney's daughter." Granny eyes me.

"Hello, Granny."

"She looks like your mother," Granny remarks to my father and I feel a swell of pride at the connection. Dad has told me of the likeness — around the eyes — but many think I look more like my mother's family than my father's.

"She's come all the way from Sydney, too. She was the one studying in Paris," Uncle Henry offers.

"I know that, " Granny snaps at him. She turns to me again, "What did you want to go there for?"

I don't know whether Granny is referring to Sydney or Paris so I stand mutely, hoping she will ignore me.

Granny decides that the trip to Dungalear can't take place unless we first go to town and fetch Danielle from the Aboriginal Foundation. Danielle is a niece of Henry's, making her a distant cousin of mine. Dad and Uncle Henry think Granny, given the chance to leave the hospital, just wants an excuse to visit the Foundation, which is the meeting place for the town's black community.

It is another hour before Dad and Uncle Henry place Granny and her wheelchair into the car and we arrive at the tin hall, which rests on a slab of concrete. I begin cursing myself for obeying my father and not bringing any work to do, for not even running into my hotel room to grab the *Aboriginal Law Bulletin*. Dad, Uncle Henry and Granny have wasted time in organising medical supplies and chatting with the nursing staff and other patients before we even leave the hospital. I could have read the journal cover to cover by now and done a significant bit on one of the affidavits that await me on the carpet of my hotel room while all this organising and side-tracking takes place. The side trip to the Foundation only increases my frustration.

Dad and I follow Uncle Henry into the Foundation to find Danielle. Henry saunters towards two old men sitting on blue plastic chairs beside a battered wooden table. They greet him with enthusiasm as he pulls up a seat. I hover near the doorway.

"Reggie. Tom. How are you blokes doin'?" Henry is met with nods and grunts. "You blokes know Bob Boney?"

They nod at my slightly built, greying father.

"G'day," Dad returns, taking a place at the table. He shifts his body on the rickety seat to find his balance on a chair that has long ago lost its stability. When he feels safe from falling over he turns to Henry, "Aren't we here to find Danielle?"

"Haven't got that far yet," replies Henry, and turns his attention to the older men. "We've got Granny in the car. We're taking her out to Dungalear station."

"Hey Shirl," yells Reggie. A woman appears from an adjacent kitchen, her hands clasping the hem of her floral dress.

"Yeah? Wha'cha hollerin' for?"

"Granny's out front. Henry and Bob Boney're takin' her outta the hospital for the day."

Shirl leaves the room followed by three other dark, large-bellied women with thin, stick-like legs. They all acknowledge Henry as they pass and he flirts confidently back at them.

"So do you think they'll let you onto Dungalear?" asks Reggie. His eyes are dimmed from working in the mines. His liquorice skin is creased and his pale fingers, which are never far from his face, are twisted and gnarled.

"Dunno. Guess we'll find out when we get there."

The old men smile between themselves as Henry speaks.

"Good luck," replies Tom. His glasses move against his face as he grins. He strokes his white beard with obvious mirth.

"Say, did you hear about Reggie's nephew? Tell him the story Reggie."

Reggie shuffles in his chair and straightens his back.

I return to the car. Granny is sitting with her door open, holding court with Shirl and the other women. They are discussing the nursing staff at the hospital. I sit silently, my irritation gnawing at me, sweat forming on my forehead as the temperature in the car builds. The circle of men and the circle of women are deeply engrossed in conversation and I have the sinking feeling that I'm not going anywhere for a while. I think of my carefully laid out piles of paperwork on the hotel-room floor. I sigh as the clock counts off another hour.

The car slides noiselessly along the road as it leaves the huddle of houses at the edge of the town. The two cousins in the front seat are talking about Reggie's nephew.

"Sometimes kids are just born bad," says Dad.

"Sometimes there's reasons," replies Uncle Henry.

"Sometimes not," Dad answers.

Granny looks out the window as the landscape melts beside the car. She seems to be looking beyond the pastures, fences and houses. I imagine that she can see silhouettes of almost forgotten faces imposed on the curves of the road and long-gone bodies pressed into the branches of trees. I watch her and imagine that the landscape must sing to her with memories — joyful and secret, sinister and sacred.

I sit in the middle of the back seat but the car is large enough for me not to feel cramped. I ignore the *Bob and Henry Show*, as I call it when the two cousins bicker like schoolboys or old women. I look at Danielle, who was the cause of our visit to the Foundation, her strong jaw-line, a defiant chin and thick black hair plaited and pulled back from her face. She is slightly darker than me and without my too-thin European features. I wonder if anyone seeing us side by side would guess we are related, albeit distantly.

As the car passes an old church surrounded by gravestones, Danielle observes, "A cemetery is not a nice place to end up, but if you want to meet God that's the way to go."

"I'm not in a great hurry to get there myself," I reply.

"Do you believe in God?" Danielle asks me.

"Sort of. I mean, I believe in something. Some force. But I do not believe in churches." I hate questions about God and spirituality. I've no comfort with things I cannot articulate.

"Me neither. Reverend Phillips — he's the local Reverend — he comes to the Foundation. He tells me that if I'm smart I'd go to church." Danielle rolls her eyes. "But the older folks seem to like him."

The loyalty to or defense of the church that the older people express puzzles me. The churches were a destructive force that caused irreparable damage to Aboriginal culture through their attempts to Christianise 'the heathens'. Yet even my father, cured of any love of God by many years in a Protestant-run orphanage, will calmly tell me, in the face of my spitting indignation, that the missions provided about the only safe haven from frontier violence. I cannot, however, be appeased on this point, even by conciliatory arguments.

"What do you do around here for fun?" I change the topic.

"I like sports. Basketball and touch footie, anything like that. I'd like to visit Sydney, 'cause sometimes it gets boring here. But I wouldn't want to stay there all the time. This is home."

"The pace in the city is pretty hectic. It's not to everyone's liking."

"Must be cool being a lawyer. I've never met a Murri lawyer before. My brother could have used you a couple of weeks ago."

"I do mostly land claims and heritage protection. I like it but it's not as glamorous as it might seem from the television. It's lots of reading and years of training."

"I never liked school. I was going to do a hairdressing course. I rang the TAFE but they never got back to me. I would like a job taking food around at the hospital, then I could see all the old folks and chat. Now Tamara is in preschool I should think about getting a job again."

"You have a daughter?"

"Tamara is my third." Sensing my astonishment, Danielle adds defensively, "I am twenty-five, you know."

"You're the same age as me," I reply, hoping my surprise won't be construed as rudeness.

"How many kids do you have?" she asks me.

"I don't have any."

"Oh. Oh, well." Danielle pauses before adding consolingly, "Diff'rent strokes for diff'rent folks." It isn't often that I feel as inadequate as her sympathy makes me feel at this moment.

The car turns off the highway on to a gravel road that gives way to dust. A cloud of black dirt follows the car as it trundles along past paddocks of ubiquitous fur-ball sheep.

The outskirts of Dungalear are marked with a wooden sign, painted with thick black letters to read: 'Dungalear Station. Owned by the Baldwins since 1905.'

Danielle opens the gate and waits for the car to pass through before pushing the large metal gate closed. As she steps into the car again she mutters, "*Owned* since 1905. My great–grandfather was the king of the tribe that lived here."

"The king?" I ask with surprise.

"Yeah. We have the plate to prove it. Well, my brother Jason has it."

The king plates, I remembered my father telling me, were given to Aboriginal men the British colonists had chosen to be the leaders of their tribes; there were no 'kings' in traditional societies. So, the naming of 'kings' was a way in which colonists tried to alter Aboriginal practice to suit their own concepts of hierarchy, and I am about to say as much when I notice how proud Danielle's eyes are. I also notice that Dad, Uncle Henry and Granny have all declined to contradict her. I keep quiet as Danielle continues to talk.

"Not that I would like to be back in the Dreamtime. It might have been different if the white people hadn't come. But they did and there's no changing that. Besides, I like it the way it is: basketball, television, CDs. I think it would have been a lot harder back in the old times."

When we arrive at the farmhouse, Dad and Uncle Henry approach the white wooden-framed, tin-roofed structure. Their knock is unanswered so they circle the house for signs of life. The shades are all drawn and there isn't a car anywhere in sight.

"Well, what do you want to do?" asks my father.

"Let's go on anyway. We can leave a note."

"Technically, that's trespassing."

"Technically, I don't give a stuff. Let's not start with accusations of trespassing or the Baldwins will be in trouble," Uncle Henry grins. My father grins back. They return to the car with confident strides and determined, rebellious spirits.

"OK Granny," sings Dad, "which way?"

Granny stares out across the adjoining field directing the car onward.

"Keep going," she mumbles, her hand sweeping in a forward gesture, as though she is chasing away a fly.

Granny's directions form a trail through the scrub. She signals the way over dry waterholes and through thorny bushes, the low tree branches scratching at Dad's new car. He starts to become agitated.

"Are you sure this is the way?" he snaps.

"Keep going," Granny commands, unmoved, gesturing onward.

"I'm sure there must be a better way than this."

"Keep going."

"I hope you know what you're doing."

"Keep going."

My father silently fumes as a branch snaps his car-phone aerial. It hangs limply across the back window.

"She always goes the long way," says Uncle Henry, sensing my father's rising fury. "She avoids Temperance Creek." Granny shoots Uncle Henry a sharp look as he utters the place name, then resumes her vigil at the window. "That's where that massacre was," he continues. "Rounded them up like cattle, old and young, and shot them. About four hundred. And *then* they named it Temperance Creek."

Granny speaks in her stony whisper as the branches continue to thwack the car. "There were only two young ones left, a boy and a girl. The boy they took to Milroy in 1881, and I think the girl was there too."

Dad nods gravely, the aerial long forgotten. I feel the chill crawl up my spine and I move in my seat to shake it off.

The party in the car is silent until Granny speaks again. "Here. Stop here."

Dad stops the car and we open the doors. The breeze drifts through the vehicle. I get out and walk around as Danielle prepares to move Granny from the car to a blanket in the paddock.

As I walk around the field I notice, beneath the tall blades of grass, the scars of the old camp, rust-eaten metal, old tins and broken glass. Everything seems still and silent, even the insects.

"Over here," my father motions to me. I walk to the spot where he is standing and look at the ground where he points.

"This is where your grandmother lived before ..." Dad's voice trails off as thoughts flood his mind.

I stare at the soil, trying to find some sign in the dark blue and emerald-green pieces of glass and the piles of sticks, wanting something that will have meaning, but the ground stands mute. The warm wind sweeps across the knee-length grass, across my legs, like the breath of contented, sleeping children.

Through the years

3

1918

I LIKE THE MORNING BEST of all. The fire is burning. The world seems new. Even the earth and the sky have slept.

Garibooli awoke to the prophetic laughter of the kukughagha, who always announced the dawn. Already there was movement in the camp. She lay in the lean-to, warm under the bundar* skins. She watched the lithe figure of her mother poking at the coals in an attempt to excite the flames, her father and the other men gathering in preparation for a visit to a nearby settlement. In the distance she could hear her aunt's hacking cough. As the camp bustled with its early morning business, Garibooli thought of the festive atmosphere of the night before. There were visitors who had crept on to the property, unbeknownst to the gubbas† who controlled what happened on the land.

"The white man acts as though he is the only one on the land and as if it is *his* ancestors who inhabit the landscape," her baina‡ would mutter, his eyes deep and thoughtful, focused on something distant. Although her parents had wandered freely all over the land when they were children, the family now lived permanently in a small section of

* *bundar* = Kangaroo
† *gubbas* = white people
‡ *baina* = father

Dungalear, confined to an enclosed space. In return, they were given the terror of God, schooling in a tin-roofed hut, clothing they now felt immodest without, and a new language which gave them new names. Garibooli had been given the name Elizabeth by the Reverend's wife, who wrote the new names into a book — making them official in dark blue ink letters.

When Garibooli would ask why they weren't allowed to speak their language, her mother ran out of answers. All Garibooli knew was that it had to be that way because the gubbas said so. The hard thwack of a large wooden ruler across her knuckles, administered by the school mistress whose face knotted with rage at the sound of words that were not the ones that white people would use, reinforced Garibooli's understanding of the way the world worked. The Reverend's wife had tried to explain to her that she was named after an English Queen. But she loved the feel of her real name as it rolled off her tongue, preferring the way that her lips made a ripple, like on the river, to pronounce the third syllable: Ga-ri-boo-li. 'Elizabeth' sounded scratchy and high-pitched, like a bird squawk. She would whisper her real name to herself, over and over again, faster and faster. Garibooli. Garibooli. Garibooli.

Her brother had been given the name Sonny. Garibooli thought of the word 'sunny' from the first time she heard it so began to call him the name 'Euroke', which was the name for the sun in the language they were forbidden to use. He, in return, called her 'Booli', because he knew she liked her real name best.

Yesterday morning the camp had been bustling with soft excitement over the arrival of old Kooradgie*. The men hovered expectantly and the women had been especially diligent in preparing the food. Larger bundar had been killed. There were fewer now with the farmers and the fences. Her

* *Kooradgie* = a wise elder with a gift for healing

father and the other men were gone several days to bring them back.

Kooradgie hobbled with a stick and had an eye missing, the lid in a permanent wink. Garibooli had known him all of her life, almost twelve years, and she now looked forward to the sporadic visits from the hunched-over, strangely shaped man. His skin was marked with deep spots and he might have scared her had he not been so kind. In the afternoon, he had sung to the children and told a story about the biggibilla* man:

> *Long ago, food was scarce and the people were hungry. Even when people had shared what they had managed to catch and find, they were still hungry. Everyone was getting thinner and thinner, except one old man. So one night, after they had shared some small fish that had been all the food that they could find, the other men followed the old man back to his camp. From the bushes, they watched him as he leant over his fire. They could see, just as they smelt the sweet smell of cooking meat in the air, that the old man was eating a big piece of bundar, from one he had killed but kept to himself. The men were angry and beat the old man who had broken the law with his selfishness. As he hobbled off, his legs broken, the men threw spears at him. The old man crawled over the land and his spears turned to spikes, his back legs faced inwards because of the broken bones. You can see them in the footprints of the biggibilla who is forever a reminder of the selfishness of the old man.*

Now, when Garibooli saw the spikey beast she would remember the story and the lesson of sharing.

Earlier in the evening, she had joined her mother in the women's circle, listening to the talk of food. It was ration day tomorrow. The women were complaining about the salted meat that was part of the food provisions. It made the stomach grumble and painfully ache. Although the men

* *biggibilla* = echidna

would work with sweat-drenching effort on Dungalear and the nearby farms, selling wild game or chopping wood, there was very little money and the women would always worry that there was not enough food. The older women wistfully remembered the days when food was plentiful, but that was before the farmers changed the balance of the land forever, leaving the earth incapable of providing the essentials for life.

The talk had turned from the subject of food to hushed whisperings about a more serious and, Garibooli understood from the tone of the voices, a more sinister subject. Tom Kerrigan, the gubba who ran the ration store, had touched one of Garibooli's cousins, Karrwi.

"He's not getting those filthy white hands on my daughter. No. He'll not put a finger on Booli." The evil in the man's touch was conveyed to the young girl by the seething anger in her mother's voice, the set determination in her eyes.

Later in the evening, the women had joined the men in a large circle. Some of the younger children were playing on the outside, behind the adults, but still close enough to see the fire. Garibooli didn't join their games. She liked to listen to the stories the older people would share.

That night, Garibooli had watched the sky, where she had seen the twinkling that formed the Mea-Mei*, until she'd shut her eyes and pretended to be asleep, her head resting on her mother's lap. She could smell the smoke and feel the heat of the fire while her mother stroked her hair.

The talk had moved to the war. There were men among their family who had left to fight, taking valuable manpower away from their camp. For years, the movements of the troops dominated the conversation. It was all going to be over by the first Christmas, they had all said when it began. Now, it was three years on. But this war, on shores far away, seemed less real than the wars in the stories of Kooradgie.

* *Mea-Mei* = the Southern Cross

The Eualeyai and Kamillaroi men who fought in the faraway land had fought by choice, not for survival as their fathers and grandfathers had. Kooradgie had been remembering his ancestors and spoke of the mysterious disease, dunnerh-dunnerh*, caused by the evil magic of the wunda† who lived on the other side of the great mountains. The disease had caused the marks on his face, but he was one of the lucky ones because many had died.

The voices hushed as Kooradgie retold a tale. He cleared his throat and his voice began to hum in the lilting sound of his own language, his eyes never moving from the flickering flames.

It was back in the days when the wunda were scarcer. The ones that were here were the lowest and the meanest of the lot — cattle thieves, convicts and ex-convicts. In those days, we were run down like animals. We lived in constant fear, sometimes only moving at night. Many of the Aboriginal women were captured and abused by the wunda. And you know the punishment for doing that to one of our women. Our law is very strict on that. But they had no respect, the wunda, and when they came they began to run the women down and insult them.

One gubba, a boundary rider, had taken a young bub, not even initiated. He held her captive in his hut. Our men crept to the man's hut in the dark, surrounding it. They started to throw stones on the tin roof. Gubba comes out to see what the noise is. Pssst. Pssst. Pssst. The spears hit him. He laid dead.

When the white fella found out what had happened they were mad. They came in a mob, on horses, and rounded everyone up. Even the old ones, the little ones and the women. And they were shot. You could see the slug marks in the skulls years later.

* *dunnerh- dunnerh* = smallpox

† *wunda* = ghost (a reference to white people)

Garibooli's thoughts of the evening before were interrupted by her brother, Euroke, who had burst into the lean-to and jumped playfully on her.

"Guess where I'm going," he taunted.

"The gilli*?"

"No."

"Where?"

"Over to the fishing grounds. I'm going to catch you a big goodoo."

"You better make sure it's dead. Otherwise it'll eat you with one big bite."

Euroke squealed with pleasure as Garibooli tickled him and made a face like a big fish about to eat him up. Euroke was her only sibling. She had felt an adoring, proud love for him ever since he was a little brown bundle with flapping arms and legs, like a naradarn†, she had thought. Now he was growing and was included more and more with the older men in the lead-up to his Bora‡. The male ceremonies were forbidden to her, as hers were to the men. She had been warned by the older women of the harshness of the penalties for breaching the rules.

Not all the rules had remained. Booli should have been married after her own ceremony. There was a Kamillaroi man picked out for her, but he had been sent away to a prison for spearing cattle and eating it, interrupting the traditional practices. Whether another husband should be found, or she should await his return, was uncertain. The Reverend and his wife had preached against it as they were against all Aboriginal laws no matter how sacred and central they were. Even the Bora had to be done secretly for fear of the wrath of the missionaries.

* *gilli* = the moon

† *naradarn* = bat

‡ *Bora* = initiation ceremony

Garibooli doted on Euroke. She would follow behind him when he went to fish or set traps, letting him lead the way before her watchful eye. She loved the quick way his hands moved when he carved and the slow movements when he painted.

From the tree I can see across the land.
I look at the world from my tree. A sky goddess.
I always come back to this place. My place. Home.

Warm winds swept over the knee-length grass, like the breath of sleeping children. From her perch in the tree Garibooli could see the camp in the distance, the fire's lazy smoke drifting up in to the air until it mixed invisibly with the sky. Noon heat hung with the stillness of the day, as though the whole world were too hot to move. The other children had gone to the river. Garibooli liked to be by herself. She would watch as the silhouettes of the people in her family slipped between trees. She knew all the trees in the area she lived in. She nestled into boughs, straddled branches and climbed up high with graceful agility, ripping the hems and sleeves of her scratchy calico dresses. Or she would sit, still and quiet, in the tree and watch the world around her, then climb down, limb over limb, her brown fingers gripping tan bark.

The sun was melting into her. It was almost in the middle of the sky. Garibooli was thirsty and decided to return to the camp. "Kollo ngai ngin*," she chanted as she ran, as though it was a song. "Kollo ngai ngin."

My favourite thing to do is run through the grass. It softly whips my legs. I can feel the strength in my limbs as I move. I can run fast on my skinny legs. I could surprise you. I am like the wind. My name means whirlwind — Garibooli. Say it. Garibooli. Say it fast. Garibooli. Say it over and over and over again …

* *Kollo ngai ngin* = I want a drink of water

Garibooli returned to an empty camp. Her mother would not be back until the sun was almost set as she had gone with the other women, even the oldest ones, to get the provisions from the ration store. The women would quietly line up, single file, clothes neat, eyes lowered: Yes, sir. No, sir. Thank you, sir. Since Karrwi's budding breasts had been twisted by Tom Kerrigan's large hands, Garibooli's mother, Guadgee (now Thelma Boney), would not let Garibooli join the procession to get the rations. This meant that Guadgee would have to carry the heavy load all on her own, but she was stubbornly determined that her daughter would stay behind.

Garibooli had hoped that Euroke might have returned to the camp with the promised fish. He would have caught one by now, maybe two.

She found the water in the tin amongst the skins and gulped down refreshing mouthfuls. She thought she should walk to the river to fetch some more, gather some food if she could find some, just as her grandmother and aunts had shown her, and find Euroke. But the heat, her running, her climbing, and her late night listening to Kooradgie had meshed together to make her feel deeply tired. She curled up under the lean-to and enjoyed the deliciously heavy sleep. She was so deep in her slumber that she did not hear the birds squawk as they scattered in the distance. She did not wake as the car drove across the paddock, stopping just outside the cluster of trees that lined the camp.

It was the slamming of the car doors that stirred her. The sleep had clouded her head and her limbs felt thick. She heard the voices that she did not recognise and, realising they were strangers, sensed danger.

Euroke had been fishing. He liked the curve of the river where, it was said, an evil water spirit would attack if someone ventured there after dark.

He was carrying his catch on a stick on the way back to the camp. He intended to get his sister to help him prepare the fish for cooking, knowing she would be impressed by his success and flitter around him excitedly. He already felt the warm glow of pride in his stomach.

Euroke had always been aware of his sister's watchful eye. Her presence pulled from him a protecting and caring spirit. Booli would sit quietly and watch him as he worked or played, fascinated by his movements, her big brown eyes focused intently on him. He would suck in the pride he felt at being the centre of the older girl's universe, basking in her gentle adoration.

He passed three younger boys from his camp playing at making a nganda*, nodding at them confidently as he passed, giving them the approval they had sought from him. A short way on, he heard the shrieks of the gila† as they scattered into the sky. Usually there had to be some disturbance to send the birds into such a fit. A car. Gubbas. Gunjies‡. Euroke felt that something was wrong. Something bad. It was always bad when the men in black, in their black cars, came to the camp. Something in his heart told him that he needed to find Booli.

Gariboolí emerged from the lean-to and saw two men in black uniforms walking towards her.

"There's one of them," the taller man shouted as Garibooli stared back at him, a small animal suddenly spying a predator. As the men started to move quickly towards her, she instinctively turned to run. Her mother and father had repeatedly told her: if you see a black car, run the other way; if you see men in black uniforms, the gunjies, run away as fast as you can — hide in the riverbed, climb up high in a tree, be silent until they leave.

Being surprised by their arrival, she had not left herself

* *nganda* = canoe
† *gila* = galah
‡ *gunjies* = police

enough time. In her startled and sleepy state she could not get a head start on them. As she ran to dodge the burning coals of the slumbering fire, thick arms, as strong as a tree branch, pulled at her waist, scooping her thin, tiny frame up. She kicked her legs into the air as she was carried towards the car. She screamed, pressing all the air out of her lungs with fear. When her voice stopped, she gasped hard and fast. She screamed again.

The other gungie — the shorter, rounder, redder man — had opened the door to the back of the car. There was a struggle between the young girl and the man who was trying to put her into the black vehicle. Garibooli heard her name being called distantly. She recognised the cadences and felt almost relief. "Euroke! Euroke! Euroke!" she yelled.

As he approached the camp, Euroke heard the screams. He ran to where the noise came from, his fish and stick long since abandoned. He saw Booli being pushed into the back of a black car by two men dressed in uniforms. He saw the slight figure of his sister turning and kicking wildly at the men.

He ran towards her, yelling her name. "Booli. Booli."

The second uniformed man grabbed her thrashing legs and helped to bundle the small, struggling girl into the car, like a bag of dirty clothing. The door slammed shut behind her. Her skin burned on the sun-heated leather of the seat. She scrambled to the back window. She could see Euroke, could see his mouth open and his arms stretched out to her.

"Euroke! Euroke!" she continued to yell.

"Shut up, girl!" barked the gungie dressed in black, whose hands left red welts on her legs and arms.

Garibooli continued to wail with terror.

"I said shut up! Jeez!" the dark-dressed man hollered.

Garibooli tried to control her sobbing, falling to the leather seat to let the heat scorch her skin. The pain was greater inside her than on her burning face, arms and legs.

She whimpered on the leather, her eyes and nose losing liquids that formed a puddle. Her mind and body froze with an overwhelming fear.

The car door closed and the two men moved quickly into the front seat. Euroke's heart was flooded with fear.

"Booli. Booli."

He ran, but the car started to move away from him. In his desperation, he forgot how much faster it could move than his legs. He saw his sister's face looking at him through the prison of the glass window. She was crying out to him, her eyes enlarged with terror. He held his arms out to her but the car pulled away faster; she moved further and further from him. He did not stop chasing her until the car was too far ahead for him to catch. His sister's face was smaller than the pupil of his eye. He was exhausted but didn't feel his body ache until he sank to the ground, his tears falling into the soil.

The car bumped over paddocks, on to the dirt roads and further into the little town that was still and sleepy on the hot summer afternoon.

If she had sat up, Garibooli would have caught a last glimpse of her mother who, along with the other women in the group, had moved from the centre to the side of the road and was walking with her bundle of rotting rations.

Guadgee walked slowly along the side of the road. The women watched nervously as the police car passed, then looked at each other. The cars were sinister phantoms, symbols of impending doom. Taking away the men to gaol, or — the greatest fear that lurked in the darkest shadows — taking away the children. They had turned, the white people in black uniforms, from horse to cars, turned from killers into thieves still destroying families. Guadgee was already irritated because the flour she'd been given was infested with weevils. She would either have to use it anyway or find food that the bush was less and less willing to yield up to her.

Guadgee could not shake the restless, taunting feeling the car had left her with, even though the back seat appeared to be empty. The black vehicles always made her feel that way, vulnerable, as though she were naked. She would lower her head and hope that she would be left alone. Perhaps it was the heat, and the rotting rations, she thought, that were making her feel unsettled. Perhaps it was the usual feeling of dread she felt when collecting the monthly rations. She hated the indignity of the hand outs. Even more she hated the humiliation of being faced with the man who rationed them out. He never looked at her. Guadgee could not be sure whether the lack of eye contact was because he did not remember her or because he did. His face, his voice, were etched into her being, like heat cracks on a dry waterbed. She would not bring her Booli near this malevolent presence. He was a mi-mi, a stealer of souls, with leather boots and a riding crop.

Guadgee fell silent as the other women around her continued to chatter about the rations, Kooradgie's stories, and the meal from the night before. These lands were not safe for children with dark skin. She lived in constant fear that her children would be hurt, taken from her, or worse. The countryside raced with tales of how the government would send for the children and take them to where the families would never see them again. One woman carried her child in a suitcase when she travelled, she was so afraid of losing him. Others, who had lost one or more, had wailed with grief, willed themselves to die, washed themselves in alcohol. Hopeful that their youthful spriteliness would keep them from harm, Guadgee had told Euroke and Garibooli that they should always be prepared to run and hide. Her children were more precious to her than anything else. They had given her a reason to live again when so many losses and disappointments hardened her. She marvelled at the miracle and mystery of their small hands, delicate fingers and inquiring, thoughtful eyes that seemed to acknowledge her secret.

The buzzing feeling of foreboding was covered by a thick smothering fog of dread when Guadgee saw her son running towards her. He was running from the direction of the camp. She knew before he blurted out the words what he was going to say. Her world had already slowed its time.

"Guni*. They took Booli!" He had reached her, his strong hands clinging to her rubbery waist. "I tried to stop them. I tried. But they were in a car. And I couldn't get there in time. They were going too fast. But I tried, Guni. I tried."

Guadgee held her son's head, holding him tight to her, her rations lying on the ground around her. She could feel his tears dampening her dress, his face hot from grief. The women stood helpless in horror, stunned by the news, overwhelmed by desperate thoughts for the little girl, the little whirlwind they all loved.

"It's not your fault. Hush. Hush. It's not your fault," Guadgee clutched her son as though he were her last breath.

An eerie stillness hung over the camp, engulfing it in a mist. The festivities of Kooradgie's visit seemed to have existed in another dimension. Guadgee wailed inconsolably. Her husband would not be returning until tomorrow but the mothers were too afraid to send any of the younger boys to fetch the men back. Guadgee's grief was flooding over. She beat her chest as she whispered through her tears, "My birrawee†. My birrawee."

She cursed the world and, more bitterly, cursed herself for leaving Garibooli in the camp. In wanting to keep her safe from Tom Kerrigan she had allowed her daughter to be exposed to an even greater danger.

* *guni* = mother

† *birrawee* = child

"I never should have let her stay here on her own," she snuffled.

"You did the right thing, Guadgee. Kerrigan's no good. You did right to keep her at home and protect your little one. After what he did to my Karrwi ..." her sister, Nimmaylee, comforted. After a pause, she quietly added, "And what he did to us."

Guadgee shook with silent, convulsive sobs. "I am so afraid for her. My birrawee. My birrawee."

The sisters held each other in their flooding pain, the same way they had clung together over thirteen years ago on another night in which they had violently been brought to understand what it meant to be a woman wrapped in black skin living amongst the pale, colourless men. Guadgee thought she could see the evil venom flowing though the blue veins in their see-through skin when that evening, all those years ago, the sisters had been down past the graves. It was a place they shouldn't have been in, especially as they were married and old enough to know better.

Guadgee had been walking ahead of Nimmaylee when she heard a scream, then the thud of the older girl's body as it crashed to the ground. Guadgee turned to see a gubba in dirty clothes standing over her sister and then felt an enormous pain as her own body was slammed to the ground. Her back held a searing pain from the force of her fall and was scratched by the fallen branches pressing against her flesh.

She was young, her breasts just having formed. Guadgee began to scream instinctively but was silenced by a hard slap that burnt her face. She closed her eyes tightly and tried to imagine herself as a kukughagha flying high above the earth — untouchable and free — while the man did to her what her husband did, but angry and rough, forceful and mean. Fearing that he would kill her, she remained frozen until the gubba slipped out of her and off her.

"Your go, Jacko," he bellowed, as another figure staggered

from the shadows. The shadow sniggered as he unbuttoned his trousers.

Guadgee never forgot the sound of Tom Kerrigan's voice. That sound and the events of that late afternoon had stained her and she marked all other events in her life against it. She remembered the sickly smell of alcohol on the breath of the white man, of Tom Kerrigan, and felt his humiliation of her every time she went for rations. He never seemed to recognise the hatred that lit her eyes.

But in the late hours of that day, near the graves of her ancestors, when Tom Kerrigan violated her, the world seemed flooded with darkness. She had already lost so much: her mother had been killed, shot dead, just as her father had been; her sister's husband had died in prison hung by a belt that was not his own.* These raw losses and grievings mingled with tales of massacres and mutilations. There were only three lights left — her sister, her daughter, and her son. Each showed her the contentment that could be experienced, even in the most desolate and degraded of environments.

Now her most precious daughter — so much like herself in look, manner and temperament, but fresher and so much more trusting — had been swept away into the harshness of that other world. One of her lights, her hopes, had been extinguished. The pain of loss and its bitterness gnawed at her, devouring her. It would prove to be terminal.

The sound of her pain filled the country. It filled the soil. It filled the trees. It filled the grasses and the empty river beds. It hung in the air for all time.

* In Aboriginal families, the sisters of a person's mother were also called 'mother'. Guadgee and Nimmaylee were sisters; they both would have been mother to Garibooli. Also, Guadgee's husband would have taken Nimmaylee as a second wife when her own husband had died as he would have had responsibility for looking after her.

Euroke cried silently in the shadows, watching his mother as the women surrounded her. His sister had been taken from him and he had been unable to protect, unable to save her. He was unable to console his mother. He longed for something that would bring his sister back, that would fill in the part of him that was missing and making him hurt. He longed for something that would make him feel like he did that very morning, when the dew was new and the world was as he knew it.

"I'll get her back," Euroke swore to himself. "I'll bring her home."

4

1918

GARIBOOLI STOOD AT THE TRAIN STATION in the corner of a small room, looking down at the heavy shoes that had been pinching at her heels. Her crying had ceased, replaced by a numbness that struggled with her anxiety as she thought over what had happened to her in the last day.

Yesterday, when the policemen had brought her to town, she was placed in the police lockup for the night while someone from the government could be organised to take her into their care. Garibooli was kept in the prison cell reserved for drunks and she had almost vomited from the sharp smell of urine and bile. She was not able to eat the bread and water that had been left for her. Nor was she able to sleep. She felt little soothed by being told that she would be collected in the morning by the welfare woman. This turned out to be Mrs Carlyle who now had charge of her.

Instead, Garibooli had sat on the cold iron bench that doubled as a bed for those too drunk or despondent to feel its hardness against their spine. She watched the outside light turn to darkness and, as the shadows drew up the wall, she waited the many hours until the lightness crept back again. All the while she sat alert, certain she would hear a handle's click, that someone would open the door to the cell rooms, that her father and mother would walk in to take her home and put her to sleep among the bundar skins.

When she finally heard the click of the door, it was not her parents but another man in a black uniform. "Well, Poppett, how are you this morning?" he boomed in a thick voice.

Garibooli looked up at him with his bushy eyebrows, hairs peeping out from his nostrils and twinkling brown eyes. The kindness in his voice made her eyes swell with tears.

"Ah, well, I'll fix yer a nice cup o' tea. How's that then, eh?" he continued and she nodded, gratefully.

When he returned, he unlocked her cell and handed her a tin cup hot from the liquid. He watched her as she sipped the tea tentatively. "There's a nice Missers Carlyle here to see you, Poppett, who'll look after yer now. So drink that tea and wipe them eyes. How bout that, eh?" he said with a tender voice and a comforting wink.

He walked with her to the office where one of the policemen who had struggled with her the day before sat writing as a tall, thin woman in a dark blue dress, white gloves and a straw hat looked over his shoulder. She turned and gestured Garibooli to her, "Come here, child." Garibooli walked towards the outstretched hand.

The woman with skin the colour of milk was silent for a moment as she gave Garibooli a penetrating look. Her ice-blue eyes surveyed Garibooli's coffee-coloured face, high forehead, full lips, and deep sorrowful eyes. Garibooli felt as though her whole body was exposed, as though her skin was somehow dirty. But when she looked back into Mrs Carlyle's eyes she could see in the watery blue that there was something inside this woman that wanted to help. To Garibooli, it meant she would assist her in getting home.

"Write: 'Removed at child's own request'." The woman looked at Garibooli again. With a sigh she added, as she adjusted her stiff woollen jacket, "She may not have asked for it now but you can be sure that she will be grateful to be brought up in a Christian home. Now if you will excuse me, I have to put this child in some decent clothes and a pair of shoes before I put her on the train. The filth they live in ... A pity. A real pity." The woman took Garibooli outside and ordered her to wash her feet at a water pump beside the station, then handed her new clothes and told her to change.

"You can burn these," the woman told the officer who had now finished typing. She handed the pile of Garibooli's clothes over, her arm outstretched and her face turned to one side as though they were stained with the urine that had burned Garibooli's nose as she had breathed during the night.

With the paperwork finished, the officers returned to discussing the latest news of the war, ignoring Mrs Carlyle and her young charge. Mrs Carlyle looked to Garibooli's bare feet still caked with black soil. Mrs Carlyle's gaze swept across Garibooli's new clothes and back to her bare feet. "Well, we better get you ready for the train. It's a long way we have to travel." Her tone was gentle, but firm enough that Garibooli could not summon the courage to ask where they were going and how long they would be gone.

Euroke and Garibooli had always marvelled at the trains. The railway was new to the area, slowly replacing the steamships along the river. The two siblings would lie in the long grass by the track and wait for a train to come by. Few came so they had many hours to muse about travelling in the pod-like carriages and imagine the places the tracks would carry them: a circus with magicians like the one that had been to the town and had a man who ate fire, a rodeo with horses that danced with ribbons on them, or a magical place where the rivers tasted like honey.

Now Garibooli was getting to go on the train with the sombrely-dressed, unsmiling white woman whose pursed mouth offered few words. She wondered if her brother would see her pass by. Euroke would know where she went. He would be able to find her or send someone to bring her back. She wished herself to be lying on the ground next to him, looking up at the sky, listening for the distant sound of a passing train.

As the train whisked her forward into the night, all the soil from her home fell away. Gariblooli could not know that she would never again see the place where the rivers meet.

The train journey had been long. Mrs Carlyle had asked Garibooli several questions: How old was she? Could she read? Could she read the following verse from this pocket Bible? The woman noted all the responses in a notebook. The answers never seemed to meet with approval, received by tightened lips and a concerned frown. After the initial questioning, they lapsed into silence. Both looked out the window. Mrs Carlyle thought of a long-ago dance and a sister-in-law that she did not like. Garibooli looked at the landscape, hypnotised as it flashed past. If she didn't focus, it all blurred; if she tried to see the grass or trees, they would disappear as soon as she made them out. Both ways of looking at the world made her dizzy. None of the land looked familiar to her. She tried to remember the countryside and its landmarks — the shape of the landscape, the clusters of houses — so that she could retrace her journey and find her way home.

The train moves fast. It moves as fast as I feel I can run. Like wind. Soon this speed, this breeze, will take me home. Across the grass I love to run through. Home.

"You are a lucky girl, Elizabeth. You have been given a chance, a chance for a better life." The train clicked on. Mrs Carlyle stared out the window again for a moment before returning to stare at the teenaged girl whose head was bent down towards her shiny new shoes.

"*Look* at me when I speak to you, Elizabeth." Garibooli lifted her face and looked across into the blue eyes. She had been taught to look away when an older person addressed her. But then, she realised, Mrs Carlyle was not Eualeyai or Kamillaroi so it must be different for her. She looked at Mrs

Carlyle's sky-coloured eyes, noticed the wrinkles that danced around her tightly wound mouth and the thin layer of powder that clung to her skin.

"You must do *exactly* as you are told in the house and do *everything* that the housekeeper tells you. *Without* complaint. And as *best* you can. The Howards are very kind to let you stay with them and earn your keep so you *must* do everything you're asked. Do you *understand*? And from now on, your name is *Elizabeth*, and Elizabeth *only*."

Elizabeth — once Garibooli, now Elizabeth, and Elizabeth only — nodded, too fearful to ask the one question, the only question, that mattered to her: when was she going home?

It was mid-morning when Elizabeth arrived in the country town whose trees were bursting with pink and white blossoms. The name was written on the station building, in big black letters: PARKES.

They were met by a warm-looking, fleshy young woman in a brown felt hat. Elizabeth felt a surge of relief at the sight of the butter-coloured woman, a contrast to the steeliness of Mrs Carlyle. This was Miss Grainger, the housekeeper.

Mrs Carlyle peered sternly into the young girl's face, "Remember what we spoke about on the train, about you *behaving* and doing your best. Miss Grainger will look after you but you must be obedient and *respectful* to both Miss Grainger and Mrs Howard. Do you *understand*, Elizabeth?"

Elizabeth nodded, even though there was very little she understood about why she was here, sent so far away, to be with Miss Grainger in the home of Mr and Mrs Howard.

The house, with its white Federation accents, was dark against the morning sky as it shielded the rising sun. Massive and ornate, even in shadow it looked mythical. Elizabeth and Miss Grainger entered through the back door and Elizabeth was shown to her room, just off from the kitchen. "You will sleep in here." Miss Grainger pointed to a thin mattress on a wooden bed frame with a blanket on the end. "We'll make some curtains and things and fix this little nook up, and it'll look much more homey then."

Elizabeth didn't quite know what Miss Grainger was talking about but recognised kindness, somewhere in her soft, chubby flesh and her subtle scent of lilac and flour. Elizabeth's "Thank you, Miss Grainger" was for the tone in her voice and the tenderness in her eyes.

Miss Grainger showed Elizabeth the clothes hanging in the closet — two black dresses, two white aprons, two white caps, and a calico nightdress — then left her to settle in.

Elizabeth had cried so much she did not think she could cry again. She lay on the bed and tried to get comfortable. She looked at the sloping ceiling and thought about everything that had just happened to her. It was only two nights since she listened to old Kooradgie's stories and looked up at Mea-Mei, her head in her mother's lap. She closed her eyes and tears slid down her face. She imagined the world as it looked from up in her tree and saw the figure of her baina tending the campfire. She heard her brother calling her name. She saw his face, getting smaller and smaller as she was carried faster and faster, further and further away. Then she saw Euroke's face again, this time larger. It was still distorted, but with laughter as she tickled him, teasing him that he would be eaten by a big fish.

My name is Garibooli. Whisper it. Whisper it over and over again.

5

1918

THE INSIDE OF THE HOWARD'S HOUSE on Hill Street fascinated Elizabeth with its polished wood, sparkling glass and gas lights. It offered a thousand curiosities in the shiny silverware and crystal that danced in the light and in the fine china plates that seemed to be the same white colour as Mrs Howard's skin. The dining room was a mysterious place with heavily embroidered chairs, garland-patterned rugs and a long teak table. Heavy gold-framed pictures of stern men with whiskers and women in stiff, starched garments hung on the wall. Light refracted off every shiny surface. What Elizabeth loved most was the dark wood dining-room table's centrepiece: its silver vine with silver leaves holding real flowers and candles. When the flickering candles were lit, the glass and gold in the room would radiate and she would be hypnotised, her eyes darting to catch every escaping sparkle.

Miss Grainger, plump and neat, her golden hair tied back into her cap, ensured that most of Elizabeth's time in the kitchen was spent usefully and efficiently. Her work was to be that of a kitchen maid, Miss Grainger told her, but she would also do some duties of a house maid, such as sweeping the rugs, washing the linen and the interminable dusting.

Elizabeth's day was more than thirteen long hours of hard work from six in the morning until ten at night, with a half hour for dinner and an hour and a half in the afternoon. This was supposed to be free time, but instead Elizabeth seemed to be required to do needlework. There was a hierarchy of servants: Miss Grainger, as the housekeeper, was on the top, Elizabeth was on the bottom. Other girls from the town were employed in the Howard house, but only Elizabeth and Miss Grainger lived there. Elizabeth often found herself on the receiving end of the teasing of the casual staff, to be saved only when Miss Grainger overheard and intervened. Keeping Elizabeth in her place was a privilege jealously maintained by the housekeeper.

Her first duty of the morning was to clean out the large stove before the cook arrived. She couldn't tend to the ashes without thinking of the fires of the camps. She would be reminded, as she brushed the hearth and arranged freshly cut wood, of the way her mother would stroke her hair, the strength of her father's hands, the way Euroke would lead the younger boys off to fish, her aunt's soft singing and Kooradgie's stories. She would think of these glimpses of the life she wanted to return to before turning her mind to the rigorous schedule of the life she now had.

Elizabeth was shown how to scrub, wash, iron, sew and cook. She would bake bread, make butter and light the copper to wash the clothes. With her skin raw and red, she would scrub with soap she had made until the dirt was lifted from fabric and then she would boil the linen and garments again. She preferred the ironing where, on the cold mornings, she could be close to the heat of the stove. Miss Grainger once told her that making the material for a shirt takes thirty minutes but requires about twelve hours of washing, starching and ironing throughout the years of its use. Although she burnt herself several times at the beginning — once so badly that the cast iron's triangular scar remained — Elizabeth became adept at laundering. She observed closely and learned quickly.

If Miss Grainger told her the proper way to iron a shirt or

instructed her to make the tea a certain way, she would do her best to make sure that she did what she was told. It was a reward to her when Miss Grainger would study what she had done and would announce, "Yes, that's right. Good."

Miss Grainger would dispense sixpence a week pocket money on Fridays, except for the times when Elizabeth broke a dish or damaged her uniform. Elizabeth lived in secret hope that Miss Grainger might show her some affection and that if she were good, if she did as she were told, she would get to see her parents and her brother again. Obedience and respect, instructed Miss Grainger, were important qualities in domestic servants. Elizabeth was instructed to model herself after Christ, the Suffering Servant, and sacrifice her own interests without complaint for those of Mr and Mrs Howard. The lessons from the Bible would remind her of the Reverend who lived near Dungalear Station. The memories of those sermons and the way the children would giggle at the Reverend when his back was turned, brought back memories of the home that she had left behind, of the place where the rivers meet.

Running day and night. Never stopping to catch my breath.
But without the wind in my face.
Without the grass against my legs.
Without the soil under my feet.
Without the pleasure to move free.

Elizabeth slowly became accustomed to the world of the Howards' house; she came to know its rhythm and pace, its rules and routines. She was not allowed to enter the house through the front door and she was not allowed to speak to the tradesmen who came to do work at the house. When Peter, the boy who delivered the mail, came he would try to make jokes with Elizabeth to make her grin. "There's a lot of letters here for you," he would wink. "You must be real popular." He would smile at her and his face, with its crooked nose, would transform and seem almost handsome. Elizabeth couldn't keep from giggling.

"Watch him," Miss Grainger would caution. "He's a Catholic," she would add, as if that were enough said. Despite this stern warning, Elizabeth was always happy when it was she who received the mail.

Miss Grainger was Elizabeth's only ally. It was only when Miss Grainger's own frustrations ran high that she would scold and smack Elizabeth, though remorse and generosity with pocket money followed any cross outburst. Elizabeth came to notice that Miss Grainger's mood swings usually occurred when Mrs Howard was at her worst; it was then that Miss Grainger would withdraw her kind words into a sullenness that would not lift easily.

Elizabeth also learnt to avoid Mrs Howard, who was always uncivil towards her with a briskness that shook her youthful sensitivities. Just as Miss Grainger's comments about how good her work was felt like a pat on the head, Mrs Howard's indifference made her feel scolded. When cleaning or dusting in a room that Mrs Howard was in, Elizabeth would fuss and work harder in the hope of being noticed. This only seemed to irritate Mrs Howard more. She would respond with a frustrated, "Come back and do that later."

The girl noticed that Mrs Howard was bitingly curt if her husband had just left, had just arrived or was about to leave. Elizabeth had been curious yet frightened of Mrs Howard from their first meeting but she was also intrigued by the fine bone features and luminous skin with soft trails of veins, like a fragile flower petal. She was fascinated by the silky flowing floral cloth that hung softly over Mrs Howard's twig-like figure. Elizabeth had been surprised that Mrs Howard was not much older than Miss Grainger; she seemed to be made from a totally different material. For Elizabeth, it was easy to work out; everyone at home was descended from different animals. Elizabeth was dinewan*, and so was her mother. But her father was biggibilla, echidna. Elizabeth thought, even though she was white, that Miss Grainger was like a rabbit and Mr Howard was like a fox and Peter was like a camp dog and Mrs Carlyle had been like a sheep. Mrs Howard didn't seem to be made from anything. It was as though she had come from thin air.

But it was Mr Howard's presence that filled Elizabeth with an anxious anticipation. He was tall and muscular, with tawny features and eyes a colour Elizabeth had never seen before, the stagnant green of slow-moving water. They would sweep past her, sparingly acknowledging her — she could have been painted into the fine patterned wallpaper. Like Miss Grainger, her eyes would follow his figure as he moved past, though Miss Grainger's stare lingered.

Elizabeth had little chance to explore the town, except when doing errands for Miss Grainger. At those times, she enjoyed the walk amongst the banks, stock companies, and hotels housed in wattle and daub with corrugated-iron roofs and plaster surfaces ruled to give the impression of masonry or bricks.

She was, on occasion, sent to the Chinaman's store for forgotten or newly needed provisions. She felt trepidation when face to face with the Chinese shopkeeper. His abrupt speech sounded like a barked order.

Elizabeth would not have been nearly as brave had the shop owner's daughter not been there. Behind the crowded rows of food, the large canvas bags of flour, the large crates of oils and the tins of tea leaves, the girls would talk timidly.

"You're new here," the Chinese girl said to her on Elizabeth's first unaccompanied trip to the store.

"Yes. I'm at the Howard's house. I work there."

* *dinewan* = emu

"It is so big." The Chinese girl said, her eyes widening, "What is it like inside?"

"Well, there are lots of glass and shiny things. A big chandelier and the biggest table decoration you ever saw."

"You're lucky to live there."

"Well, the part I live in is like one of those crates over there. And all those fancy lights and ornaments, they just make for more dusting."

The girls' giggles quickly escalated into laughter.

The Chinese girl had two names, Elizabeth would learn. She was 'Helen Chan' for white people but was born 'Chan Xiao-ying'. Helen's secret name was like music. Xiao-ying, like a soft breath, was much more captivating than Helen, just as 'Garibooli' was to 'Elizabeth'. The language Xiao-ying spoke with her father was Cantonese. When he used the language he knew best, his voice softened and he would appear a calmer man than the one who spoke English.

The physical differences between Xiao-ying's family and her own fascinated Elizabeth. They were as unlike Mrs Carlyle, Mrs Howard and Miss Grainger as her own mother and aunts were. One time, screened behind the shop's crowded stock, Elizabeth had touched Xiao-ying's eyes; their shape captivated her, the skin around them pulling them tight, making them the shape of gum leaves. In response, Xiao-ying felt Elizabeth's skin, rubbing it softly, giving her forearm a tentative caress. Their differences, under their fingertips, were tangible.

"Where do you come from?" Xiao-ying had asked her.

"My family lives far away from here in a place where the rivers meet," Elizabeth explained as clearly as she herself could understand it.

"Did they not want you?" Xiao-ying asked, her voice low and her eyes cast to the ground.

"They made me leave," Elizabeth answered, realising as she spoke that she had not made it clear who "they" were.

The young Cantonese girl's fingers fumbled to unclasp a

small brooch. She placed in on Elizabeth's calloused palm and wrapped Elizabeth's fingers around the small gift. It was all she could think to give a girl whom no one wanted, a girl who caused a flood of feeling inside her, which Xiao-ying hoped could be relieved through this tiny gesture.

Elizabeth studied the carvings in the deep green jewellery that looked like a flower shedding its petals. She felt the coolness of the stone on her fingertips.

"I've never had anything so pretty before. It's even more beautiful than the things that Mrs Howard has."

Elizabeth was awash with guilt for not having explained herself properly but she did not know how to correct the misleading impression she had given, especially after her new friend had shown her the tenderness that she had not been able to elicit from Miss Grainger. She didn't know how to explain that her family — although they loved her — had not been able to stop her from being taken away, and had not come for her, at least not yet.

My name is Gariboolі. Whisper it. Whisper it over and over again.

Elizabeth would sit on the back porch in the dark of the late evening and look at the stars. Other nights she would walk out into the endless back garden and lie on the cool grass, her body pressed against the earth, the blanket of sky above her. The stars were scattered in the same patterns as they were where she came from so, she reasoned to herself, she could not be that far away from her family and the camp. The moon hung above her, an incomplete question mark; the Mea-Mei, the seven sisters, twinkling down over her. She could hear Kooradgie, the old storyteller, his voice rising out of the sounds of the evening.

> *Wurrannah had returned to the camp and was hungry. He asked his mother for some food but she did not have any. He asked other members of his clan for something to eat, but they*

had nothing either. Wurrannah was angry and left the camp saying, "I will leave and live with others since my own family is starving me." So he gathered up his weapons and walked off into new country. Wurrannah travelled a long way until he found a camp. Seven girls were there. They offered him food and invited him to stay and sleep in their camp for the night. They explained that they were sisters from the Mea-Mei clan. Their land was a long way away but they had decided to come and look at this new land.

Wurrannah woke the next morning, thanked the sisters for their kindness and pretended to walk off on his travels. Instead, he hid near the camp and watched. Wurrannah had become lonely and decided that he would steal a wife. So he watched the sisters and followed them as they set out with their yam sticks. He watched as the sisters unearthed the ants and enjoyed their feast.

While the sisters were eating, Wurrannah crept up to where the women had left their yam sticks and stole two. After lunch, when the sisters decided to return to their camp, two sisters discovered that their yam sticks were not where they had left them. The other sisters returned to the camp, believing it would not be long until the two found their sticks and would join them. The two sisters searched everywhere. While they were looking through the grass, Wurrannah stuck the two yam sticks in the ground and hid again. When the sisters saw their sticks, they ran towards them and tried to pull them from the ground, where they were firmly wedged. Wurrannah sprang from his hiding spot and grabbed both girls firmly around their waists. They struggled and screamed but their sisters were too far away to hear them. Wurrannah kept holding them tightly.

When the two sisters had calmed down, Wurrannah told them that they were not to be afraid. He was lonely and wanted wives. If they came quietly with him and did as they were told, he promised to look after them and be good to them. Seeing that they could not escape him, the sisters agreed and followed but they warned Wurrannah that their tribe would come to rescue them. Wurrannah travelled quickly to avoid being caught.

As the weeks passed, the two Mea-Mei women seemed to settle into their life with Wurrannah. When they were alone they talked of their sisters and wondered whether their sisters had begun to look for them, knowing that they would be rescued.

One day, Wurrannah ordered them to go and get bark from some trees so his fire could burn quicker. They refused, telling him that if they did he would never see them again.

Wurrannah became angry. He said to them, "Go and get the bark!"

"But we must not cut bark. If we do, you will never see us again."

"Your talking is not making my fire burn. If you run away, I will catch you and I will beat you."

The two sisters obeyed. Each went to a different tree and as they made the first cut into the bark, each felt her tree getting bigger and bigger, lifting them off the ground. They clung tight as the trees, growing bigger and bigger, lifted them up towards the sky.

Wurrannah could not hear the chopping of wood so he went to see what his wives were doing. As he came closer, he saw that the trees were growing larger and larger. He saw his wives, high up in the air, clinging to the trunks. He called to them to come down but they did not answer him. The trees grew so large that they touched the sky, taking the girls further and further away. As they reached the sky, their five sisters, who had been searching in the sky for them, called out, telling them not to be afraid. The five sisters in the sky stretched their hands out to Warrannah's two wives and drew them up to live with them in the sky, forever.

Elizabeth took comfort from the story of rescue. Looking at the familiar patterns and recalling these stories made her feel as though she was lying only a few feet from her home, as if she could look across and see the fire and the shadows of her family through the trees at the end of the Howards' yard.

Maybe, she thought, the train journey took less time than she had imagined. She had been so afraid, everything was unfamiliar, perhaps it felt longer than it was. A journey always seems longer the first time it is taken, she thought. After all, walking to the store always seemed to take more time than it took to walk back. So maybe, she hoped, she was closer to Euroke, Guni, Baina and Kooradgie and all her family than she had thought. Her family, still Eualeyai. Unlike her, with an altered name. She thought of them as solid and unchanging.

My name is Gariboolí. Whisper it. Whisper it over and over again.

Sometimes, after the work was finished, late at night, with limbs numb from tiredness, Elizabeth would spend time with Miss Grainger. With this feeling of ambient afterglow, Elizabeth felt bravest and the older woman felt affection for the child, more, she reflected, than she ever thought it possible to feel for a little darkie.

Frances Grainger had been of the opinion that the Aborigines were too primitive to be able to adjust to life in the civilised world. She could remember her father's comments that they were all dying out. Mr Howard had explained that the best that could be done was to rescue the children and try to train them. Reflecting on the way in which Elizabeth always tried so hard to do her chores exactly the way she was told, Frances had to concede that on this matter, as with all else, Edward Howard had been right. When the young girl seemed to yearn for her family and her home, Frances would reassure her that what was being done was for her own good and that she ought to adjust to it as best she could.

"I wish I knew when I was going home," Elizabeth would say, as the two sat together on the stone back step.

"You can't always get what you wish for. Sometimes home just doesn't exist anymore." Miss Grainger would offer these observations with such measured sadness that Elizabeth knew that there was sorrow as deep as her own within the woman whose gaze seemed to stare inward rather than out towards the stars.

Elizabeth reflected quietly as she looked out into the darkness. She felt that wherever her mother was, wherever Euroke was, wherever her father was, wherever her tree and her camp was, there was home.

I am running through the grass.
Running further through the grass.
I can feel it whip against my legs.
I can feel the hot sandy soil beneath my feet.

These rare, quiet moments with Miss Grainger came closest to breaking Elizabeth's loneliness, but any intimacy built up in the late evenings had dissipated by morning when an air of friendly formality would fall between the two once more.

Elizabeth would occupy herself with her jobs. Cooking became the duty she enjoyed the most, especially making sweet things. Her favourite was Apple Truelove. She would boil the peeled and cored apples in water and place a dab of fresh churned butter on each. She would then cover each in a sauce of apple stock, sherry, lemon juice and sugar and then place a tablespoonful of apricot jam on the top. It tasted so good that she would be asked to make them when Mrs Howard had a dinner party.

She learnt many little tricks in the kitchen from Miss Grainger. Cauliflower tasted better if it was cooked in milk rather than water. Strong flour, fluffy and light, was better to make bread with because it absorbs moisture. She could tell with a touch of her fingertips when the scone mixture was just right — not too dry so as to create lumpy looking scones and not too wet so as to cause the scones to spread.

Elizabeth also observed the way the adults around her behaved towards each other. Because she was not considered very important in the scheme of things, she was often assumed to be too stupid to see what was really going on. But, she thought, I am smarter than Mrs Howard who does not seem aware of how much Miss Grainger dislikes her. Elizabeth also noticed the way Miss Grainger would repeat everything Mr Howard said, magnifying its insight each time she repeated it. And she saw how, when he was at home, Miss Grainger would make an extra effort with her hair, long and like strings of honey, the prettiest thing about her.

The only person Elizabeth could share these observations with was Xiao-ying, who would giggle as Elizabeth fluttered her eyelashes to imitate Miss Grainger's attention to Mr Howard or walk with exaggerated swinging hips and mouth screwed up tight like a dried plum to show her interpretation of Mrs Howard's walk.

After their giggling subsided the two friends would talk of serious things. Over the early months in which their friendship blossomed, Xiao-ying told Elizabeth the story of how her family came to live in Parkes. Her grandfather on her father's side had left his parents and brothers in China to travel to Australia looking for gold, after promising his cherished wife riches. When she died on the goldfields of Bendigo, he moved to Ballarat. He weathered the resentment directed at the success of the Chinese who extracted much of their wealth from claims that were seen as non-productive by the other miners. The number of Chinese miners, who kept to themselves, weathered the antagonism directed towards them. But fortune did not favour Xiao-ying's grandfather the same way that it had many other Chinese miners who returned to their homeland. Instead, he turned his hand to market-gardening, remarried a younger woman wooed from China, and had seven children.

By the time Xiao-ying's father was born, the market farms were less able to compete with large-area farming. The family moved into the fruit industry and Xiao-ying's father joined the camps in Hay. He worked as a cook until he had enough money to marry Xiao-ying's mother and set up the store in Parkes. Xiao-ying's mother had also been born to market farmers. When farming was no longer lucrative as a small business, her family opened a laundry in Hay. They were married by the time the Immigration Act was passed in 1901 to stop Asians from starting a life in Australia, their family firmly entrenched in an Australian life.

At the end of the day, with the dinner dishes washed and dried, the ironing done, the darning completed, Elizabeth could fall asleep. Her last thoughts were always of Euroke.

He will come and rescue me. He will come and rescue me.

6

1919

THE PACE OF THE HOUSE changed little as the frost-bitten months arrived. The only difference to the routines that governed the house was that Mr Howard was home more often in the colder weather. A principal in a stock company, Edward Howard had acquired all the status he thought he wanted, with his house on Hill Street and his marriage to Lydia Streetland, and was confident in his place in life and society.

It was only Edward's wife who could make him feel as though he did not have command of everything. Lydia Howard harboured more aspirations than he, coming from a family who had thrived in colonial politics, her father a respected politician. Edward was very wealthy, but without her father's influence. Lydia's increasing frustrations at his lack of political ambition would scrape away the comfort from his contentment and, as the years passed, he would resent this, avoiding her company and unspoken accusations.

Lydia Howard, née Streetland, would have objected to the way her husband would have described her if they had a relationship where such inner thoughts could be shared. If they had the type of union where they would speak in the dark hours of the night as they lay in each other's arms, if affection had been an indispensable part of the way they related to each other, she would have told Edward that he was wrong to think that she didn't love him. She had at times wanted to say to him that she cherished him, that she had been irretrievably drawn in, seduced by his reserve and his quiet dignity. But she could never get the words to pass her lips, even when she had rehearsed them.

Lydia first saw Edward Howard in a crowded room at a fundraising dinner for her father's re-election in Sydney. She decided then that they should meet — an encounter he would always believe was fateful chance. Her cunning was no match for his open-faced honesty. The enormity of what she felt for him, the compelling love that grew so quickly within her, was unlike any emotion she had known before. It excited her but made her fearful at the same time. Her heart would beat when she saw him but she reserved her affection so that she would not feel rejected or downcast if the intensity of her feelings were not returned. The uncertainty of her situation, her inability to find security, made her feel she had to push Edward in subtle ways to see if he felt for her as much as she felt for him. What Lydia really wanted, secretly craved, was for him to show her that he felt the storming infatuation inside that she felt for him. When he didn't, when he withdrew further and further, she grew bitter. The betrayal urged on a seeping coldness in her, it increased the aloofness she had armed herself with from the start. His silence, his passiveness and resignation all fed her resentment.

Lydia determined that she and her husband would appear to all others to be perfect in their happiness and ensured that her public persona was one that was socially vivacious and civic-minded. She crowded her house with dinner parties when Edward was home and became involved with as many church and special-events committees as she could when he was away. But it was in her vociferous support for conscription where she found her deepest commitment outside of her home. She was drawn to the nobility of patriotism, the reserve and dignity so evident in displays of duty, bravery and loyalty.

They shall not grow old, as we that are left grow old:
Age shall not weary them, nor the years condemn.
At the going down of the sun and in the morning
We will remember them.

Lydia was unfailingly touched by what she saw as the heroic beauty of self-sacrifice. It motivated her strident belief in conscription and the debate that was still raging as Australia sent more and more young men off to war.

Lydia's father, George Theodore Streetland, was a brisk walrus of a man, whiskered and gruff. He had developed ideals in a young country on old land, felt superiority from the conquering of the continent. Wealth from rum and rebellion were conveniently forgotten in his generation that had edged towards nationhood at Federation. In these moves he was less motivated by a sense of nationalism than the greed of economics. His real drive made him no different to his father who had used alcohol to build a financial empire that was now legitimated on land, stock and agriculture, but G.T. Streetland would never make the link between his own activities and those of his father's. Instead he enveloped himself in the power and privilege of politics in a generation that preferred to ignore the sins of their fathers.

As to Lydia, G.T. was indifferent — tradition needs sons. She was lost behind the heir to the family fortune, William Charles, who had come along when Lydia was still too young to demand any attention in the male realms of a Victorian household. G.T. would engage his son in long conversations about the benefits of free trade between the states, the importance of retaining power from a federal government and the extent to which the interests, especially the economic ones, of a large state like New South Wales might be subsumed by the smaller states. Lydia would hover around the room, pretending to engage in needlework, or playing a game of solitaire until her fidgeting would cause her father to ask her to leave. She would take to her bed and sob, fostering hatred towards her brother, William, and planning her next attempt to win affection from her father. She would imagine how he would look at her, pleased and proud, when he realised how devoted she was to him, how she loved him more than he knew. She hungered for the time when he would acknowledge her.

Her father was often away and she would see him rarely and often then from afar, their time together short and formal before she would be ushered away leaving him in the company of earnest men. She had tried confrontations, petulant tantrums and cutting comments, only to find herself further excluded from the circles she sought to enter and receiving a harsh lecture from her mother about the appropriate behaviour of a young lady.

Until, at one such informal meeting at the fireside, her father's cigar, through inattention and general carelessness, singed her gown. His profuse apology, believing he had hurt her when in fact the damage was only to her dress, compelled her to emphasise an imagined injury to sustain his attention. And from there she studied the subtle art of manipulation. So much easier, was the lesson she learnt, to undertake a conquest through sympathy and guilt than to win it fairly.

She was only a few years older when, at a fundraiser, she had spied a tall, commanding young man with cool green eyes. Upon inquiry she had obtained his name and occupation, and contrived an introduction by persuading her mother to invite him to their next evening party. When Edward Howard was seated beside her at dinner the following week, he was delighted and curious to have found a woman so knowledgeable on all of his interests. Her father was satisfied with the match and Lydia enthusiastically turned her focus and energy from her father to her husband.

To the surprise of her friends and family in Sydney, Lydia Howard set up her house in Parkes. There, however, she had been able to show, through her exile, how much she had sacrificed for Edward. And in Parkes, she was *the* wealthiest woman, not just one of many, and she liked to be without equal.

No one had given more than Frances Grainger to the war effort. To her, the war was summarised by different sentiments than those that Lydia Howard held dear. Frances Grainger knew a different kind of dignity.

But though kind Time may many joys renew
There is one greatest joy I shall not know
Again, because my heart for loss of you
Lies broken, long ago.

Frances had lost her fiancé and her two brothers in the war; the loss of the latter two men destroyed her mother and then her father, dissolving her family and the life she had known before war was declared. Edward, the youngest of the family, had died the first day of the landing at Gallipoli. He did not even reach dry sand. Bernard, the eldest, was shot down a day later. When the third letter came concerning Harold, more fodder for the bullets of the Turks, Frances had almost been expecting it. Words clearly stated in efficient, official type notified her of the erasing of flesh and blood, of bones, tissue and fibre. What she had not anticipated was the loss of her parents, safe as they seemed to be in the home that three young men died believing they were protecting. But her mother, and then her father, slipped away and Frances was alone. These devastating losses had left her without family, without a sense of belonging, without a feeling of security. She had just memories and ghostly companions.

No image of the young men was more vivid to her than the last day all four of them were together on a trip from Summer Hill to Bondi Beach. Her brothers and Harold had raced each other on the sand and in the surf, they had carried her as she squealed with mock rage from her towel to the sea. As she stomped with pretend indignation back from the salty water, she secretly smiled at the pleasure of being surrounded by the three handsome men, the centre of their attention.

With spirits high from their swimming and running, they returned from the beach to news of the war, announced on the radio. The boys jumped joyfully around the house and hollered that they were going to kill the Krauts. The declaration of war seemed to seduce their youthful feelings of immortality and the camaraderie they enjoyed as they had played and rested under the Sydney sun.

Frances remembered that day so clearly, the taste of the bitter water as she was flung into the roaring waves by her spirited companions, the sand that seemed to take days to remove from her hair, the sweetness of the ices that cooled them after their time in the sun. She even remembered the sting of the redness on her pale and delicate skin. It all burnt into her memory like sepia-toned photographs and, from these immortal images, their deaths seemed so impossibly contrasted with their abounding life.

She had looked at a map to find Gallipoli and the Dardanelles but they were just lines, a thin strait that offered no answers to her questions. No explanation of how three men — emerging from waves, covered in sea, salt and sun — could be no more. No sign within the clear crisp lines or the white paper of frostbite, trench foot, and dysentery.

Frances could not explain her ability to sustain herself, her instinctual survival, especially in the face of the fact that she was not enough to compensate her parents for the loss of their boys. Her mother and then her father had chosen to follow their sons to the grave, leaving her alone to ponder black lines on white pages. She looked for her strength in the plain reflection in her mirror each time she brushed her hair. She would also look into her face for that thing in her that was a weakness, the thing that made her not enough. With her father's death, only two weeks after her mother's, she had fled the memories of her family and what she had assumed would be their debts.

The war had caused a shortage of domestic servants. It had meant that women like Frances had more opportunities for work and could command wages unimagined before the war. Demand for domestic help was even greater away from the cities and the Howards paid her well, even by the inflated wartime standards, to run their house in Parkes. She had no skills, having assumed that she would marry Harold and become the mistress of her own home. She thought that work in a factory was unfeminine and that a man would prefer a wife who was domesticated in the way that a woman ought to be rather than made calloused and thick-muscled from menial work with machines. When she had answered the advertisement and met Edward Howard in Sydney on business and determined to find better assistance for his wife before he returned, the decision was made. In Edward she had seen the epitome of her ideal man — strong, reliable, dependable, able to provide, successful, dignified, well bred, good-mannered, with sandy hair and a matching, well-kept beard.

So Frances Grainger had travelled to the kitchen of Lydia Howard, to nurse her grief. There were worse places she could be, she told herself, than in a tidy kitchen in a quiet town, despite the long hours, and the lack of freedom and privacy.

When the heart of winter came, Elizabeth found herself overcome by exhaustion. Tired when she awoke, her eyes struggled to open. Throughout the day, her bones would ache until she eventually, late in the night, fell back into bed, limp and lifeless until, not quite refreshed, she had to rise. She was a sturdy girl and had been used to her share of the work in the camp. Now in the Howards' house, the drudgery and loneliness of a kitchen maid's life and the winter chill highlighted her despair of ever returning home.

All she had was the odd lost word from a distracted Miss Grainger, the sly glances from the men who delivered groceries and wood to the back door, the shy smiles when Peter delivered the mail and the occasional longed-for talks with Xiao-ying.

At night I lie and think about running through the grass.

I am so tired that I only have to imagine that I am running, and sleep finds me.

I run and run towards my dreams, towards my home.

"Come here," Mr Howard one day said to her in the kitchen, a place where Elizabeth had never seen him venture before. She obeyed, just as she had been taught to do. He was home more and had been less distant with her than when she first came to the house. Now that she had settled in, he would watch her as she walked past. He would ask her to come over and take his plate from him as he sat on his own at the big dining table and she would be forced to brush against him. These encounters, brief and innocent, made her feel nervous but also secretly pleased that Mr Howard was paying attention to her. Once she came upon him in his study when she was dusting and he told her she was a good girl with pretty hair and he had stroked it as he told her she must look after it. He had asked how old she was and when she said that she was now almost sixteen, he had told her that it was a lovely age to be but she was very grown-up.

Elizabeth was pleased that he considered her to be as responsible as the others who worked in the house. Too often she was the lowest in the pecking order; everyone got to tell her what to do. It made her happy that someone would notice that she was clever too, especially if that someone was Mr Howard. Miss Grainger always chattered on about how important Mr Howard was, how he was a real gentleman, and she would go quiet as she floated off into her own thoughts. No one has ever noticed my hair before, Elizabeth would think to herself, and began to make an extra effort to make sure it was neat and pretty, just like Miss Grainger did.

Now in the kitchen with her, Mr Howard beckoned her

and as she moved towards him, he leaned in to her and kissed her on the mouth. At first she liked it, the warm-wet touch of his lips, but as his hands moved and grabbed her sides she stood stiff, afraid. He brushed one hand across her breast, down her side, across the curve of her hip and squeezed her, feeling her under her clothes; his other hand held her hard. He was murmuring as though tasting something sweet and melting. Elizabeth was flushed with quivering relief when he stopped, the initial sensual pleasure now erased by her anxiety and the unfamiliarity of being so close to a man. Her whole body was alert with it.

He drew back, studied her lips, and whispered, "Of course, we can't be seen like this, can we?" He turned and exited the room.

Elizabeth stood motionless, her body inert, her mind racing with a flushing guilt. She had liked his touch at first; then she had hated it, that feeling against her skin, his taste and his force. She was fearful of his weight crushing against her, afraid of what he would do next. She felt ashamed of how she had felt both attraction and revulsion, both on her skin and in her body.

She ached to tell Miss Grainger, but she sensed that the older woman would be displeased. She was not even sure how to explain it, what to call it, which words to use. Nor was she sure what it meant. She couldn't even be sure, now that the pot was filling with washed and peeled potatoes, that anything had even really happened, whether Mr Howard had been there at all.

She slipped out after dinner and went to find Xiao-ying. As they lay in the grass in a paddock at the back of town, looking up at the sky, Elizabeth wanted to tell her friend about the strange encounter with Mr Howard. She felt a wariness about revealing it, even to her only friend.

"Do you ever think about boys?" she asked instead.

Xiao-ying laughed. "Do you mean like to kiss and cuddle?"

Elizabeth smiled at Xiao-ying's amusement and nodded.

"Well, I don't think that my father would be very friendly to any boy who came to take me out for a walk or something like that. But," she giggled, "I do think that the boy who delivers the mail, Peter, is very handsome. And," she paused with a cheeky grin, "I think you do too."

Elizabeth felt herself blush and this made Xiao-ying laugh even more. The laughter was contagious and Elizabeth lost herself in it. When their giggles subsided, Elizabeth said to her friend, "Before I was brought here, my family was still trying to figure out who I should be married to. There was one man, but he was taken away by the gunjies for stealing a horse."

"What's 'gunjies'?"

Elizabeth smiled at her mistake, "That's what we called the police back home, in our old language. Sometimes when I am talking I still forget to change some words."

She paused as the thought of the way Miss Grainger would slap her hand when she didn't speak English properly. Then she looked over at Xiao-ying who was still staring at the stars. Elizabeth continued the conversation, "My mother said they used to arrange marriages but all the old ways are hard to follow now and the white people do not like it. Will you marry someone who is Chinese?"

"I guess so. My parents haven't said but I think that's what they want me to do."

"Do you find white-people good looking or do you like Chinese boys better to look at?"

"I like both. I must like white boys because I think that Peter is very handsome." As she made this last remark, Xiao-ying lapsed once more into fits of laughter. Elizabeth, despite her embarrassment that her secret was not so well kept, smiled.

The happiness of spending time with her friend, the teasing and shared wishes, made the encounter with Mr Howard seem far away.

Elizabeth woke to feel pressure on her bed, startled by an intruder. His cold hands were on her warm skin, sending an icy terror through her. His body was heavy, his breath stained with tobacco and whisky as he lifted her nightdress and began stroking her legs. She couldn't move, could only clench her fists as he began to feel between her legs and pressed wet lips against hers. The feel of it made her spine tense up with disgust.

"You are a beautiful girl, Elizabeth," Mr Howard slurred as he lay on top of her. He moved quickly, pushing his hard fleshy part inside her, his voice almost a whine. "I need this. You don't know how much I need this." He kept pushing into her, harder and harder, grabbing her hips and rubbing her breasts. He then made a grunting noise as he shuddered. He released her and fell beside her on the bed. "You must tell no one about this. This will be our secret," he had said, his voice as cold as the night air.

He took some deep breaths, rose, rearranged his nightshirt and stroked her head, "You are a good girl."

She nodded into the darkness, still feeling his sweat and stickiness on her as he closed the door, leaving the smell of their bodies rubbed together. She walked, a little dizzy, to the ceramic basin and washed herself all over, at first gently, then harder and harder, to remove the sweat and smell and the memory of Edward Howard's touch. She remembered how she had been so flattered by his attention, how he had told her she had pretty hair and that she was beautiful. But if the result of that was what he just did to her, she didn't want it. She started to scratch herself, angry at her skin and the body it held. She scratched harder and harder, ripping at her skin.

Mr Howard came to her several times after that, each time with a caress of her hair and a warning not to tell.

Why don't I matter anymore?
Where is Euroke?
Why hasn't he come for me?
Why did he not want me?

7

1919

"*T*HIS SOLEMN MOMENT OF TRIUMPH ... *is going to lift humanity to a higher plane of existence for all the eyes of the future.*"

Lydia Howard and Frances Grainger listened to the crackling voice of David Lloyd George as it echoed through the radio. The war was over. More than three hundred and thirty thousand Australian men sent to fight, over sixty thousand dead in battle, over half injured in some way — a heavy price to pay by a country with a population so small. Lydia Howard was already dreaming of the monument to be erected in the town square: "a higher plane", "for all the eyes of the future", names in gold upon cold granite, immortal and heroic. She held her throat with the overpowering beauty of it.

Frances Grainger thought of three young men, of lines on a map and the taste of the Bondi sea.

One morning, not long after the announcement that the war was over, Miss Grainger had come across Elizabeth hunched over and vomiting on the back verandah. She looked suspiciously at the young girl, noticing the emerging dark circles under her eyes and that her skin was unnaturally lighter. Upon witnessing the same the next morning, Miss Grainger became concerned. She left Elizabeth curled over on the back steps and went to see Mrs Howard in her morning room. "Excuse me, ma'am," she nervously started.

"Yes," Mrs Howard replied, her eyes trained on her letter to emphasise her displeasure at being interrupted.

"I need to speak with you on a matter of some importance ... and delicacy."

Mrs Howard looked up, her expression already communicating deep disapproval.

Miss Grainger continued: "I think the little darkie is ... indisposed."

"The little kitchen girl?"

Miss Grainger nodded, wondering what other 'little darkie' there could be.

"How did this happen?" asked Mrs Howard sharply.

Miss Grainger started to blush but was relieved when she realised that Mrs Howard (who was, after all, a married woman) hadn't really meant for her to answer.

Mrs Howard sighed. "Send for Dr Gilcrest."

Dr Gilcrest examined Elizabeth in the privacy of her room. He ordered her to remove her clothes and lie on the bed. She had shivered at first but reluctantly did as he asked, obeying Mrs Howard's stern instructions that she was to do as she was told. He squeezed her tender breasts, pinched her nipples and inserted cold fingers into her. Then he left the room, making a tart 'tut-tut' sound. Elizabeth felt shamed by the way he touched her, telling herself over and over that he was a doctor, and that the things he had just done to her were what doctors must do, even if they felt too much like the things Mr Howard did to her. She reminded herself that it was her fault, that she must have done something very wrong. She scratched at her arms, her torn nails leaving white marks that slowly rose in pink lines on her skin.

As she buttoned her dress, she could hear voices through the door. She leant against the splintering wood to hear Dr Gilcrest and Mrs Howard talking.

"It is as we suspected," the doctor pronounced.

"I have no idea how this could have happened," puzzled Mrs Howard. After a pause she added, "I wonder who the father could be?"

That was how Elizabeth realised that she was going to have a baby.

When her husband returned, Mrs Howard sat down with Edward and told him about the kitchen girl's pregnancy.

"I was very surprised. I can't think who could have fathered it. So few men come to the house," she had chattered, more to herself than to Edward who was sorting through his mail. "Even deliveries are supervised by Miss Grainger, and rarely is that girl away from her duties."

Lydia had grown accustomed to her husband's indifference to the concerns of her household. Had she looked at Edward, who was looking more intently at his paper than usual, she may have noticed a constriction of his throat and a discernable widening of his eyes.

There was a change in Mr Howard's attitude towards his wife. He was suddenly more attentive to her, as though she were fragile, more easily broken. Lydia initially enjoyed Edward's refocused attention, the sidelong glances when he thought she couldn't see him. But slowly the truth became apparent to her. Lydia Howard could not explain how she pieced it together other than by intuition, which she seldom had; she operated more by calculation than feeling. This time, however, she brought the threads of her suspicions together and they created a tapestry so vivid and clear she could not deny the image it formed. One night, in the privacy of their bedroom, in that intimate interval before sleep, she found the words that had been suffocating her daily thoughts.

"What *do* you know about the girl's condition?" she asked.

He noticeably coloured as he spluttered, "I do not know

what you mean. What would I know of it? I didn't have anything to do with it! Is that what you think of me?"

In the weak glow of the bed-lamp, Edward turned his reddening face away from her, unable to meet her gaze, "Really, Lydia, haven't you got more to fill your day with than coming up with such fanciful ideas?"

He turned his back to her. Lydia felt the white-hot surge of anger and the heat of humiliation creeping through her. She was silent but the overwhelming odour of false indignation hung in the air between them.

As Elizabeth's body started to ripen and burst against her pinafore, Miss Grainger could no longer look her in the eye. She had noticed the flirtation between Elizabeth and the delivery boy and had expressed disapproval even though she had thought that it was a harmless infatuation. She believed Catholics were untrustworthy, but she had never seen him at the house other than to deliver the mail. As the housekeeper, there was little that passed under her nose or was not brought to her attention.

She had noticed Edward Howard's attention towards the young girl, thinking it odd he did not mind that Elizabeth dusted around him when he could have ordered her to come back later when he had finished in his study. Frances had dismissed his attention towards the girl as just part of his concern over the fate of her race, a noble expression of concern for someone so much his inferior. When she had seen the young girl come out of the study smiling, knowing that Edward was also in the room, she presumed that he must have said something kind, given her some little scrap of encouragement. Even now she could not bring herself to imagine that he would act in a scandalous manner. He, with all his dignity and masculine grace, could not have behaved in such an unworthy way with a little darkie. Frances could not even finish the thought, preferring to shudder at the hideousness of it, to suppress her own hungry unanswered longings. But she had also noticed the alteration in the relationship between husband and wife, something she had always observed the nuances of, and she suspected that Lydia shared her suspicions. She no longer saw Edward as the embodiment of perfection, tried not to dream of his lips against hers. And she no longer spoke of him to anyone, especially not Elizabeth.

Elizabeth tried not to be hurt by Miss Grainger's cooler attitude towards her. She had been sick before and had been treated with sympathy and given a lighter load of duties. She knew something was different this time. From Miss Grainger's distance, her unwillingness to engage in conversation, Elizabeth sensed she had done something Miss Grainger found unforgivable.

Xiao-ying remained her only friend, but Elizabeth's movements were now more closely monitored and restricted. Miss Grainger had kept her on an almost impossible schedule and timed her trips to the store. On those occasions, Xiao-ying could only offer consolation in glances and faint smiles.

Rare were the times they could find to meet each other. Once, when the lump in her stomach was only just showing, in the morning cool of spring, she was sent on an errand to the shop. She sat with Xiao-ying on the crates at the back.

"See, there's a lump here how," Elizabeth said, holding the fabric tight over her stomach.

"How will you keep him?" her friend had asked.

"Well," Elizabeth paused, "I don't know. But he can sleep in the bed with me. Back home, everyone just helped each other."

"I can't see Mrs Howard holding the baby while you peel the potatoes."

The thought of Mrs Howard's soft, flowery dresses covered in spit and baby sick made Elizabeth laugh. After a pause, Elizabeth added cautiously, "Maybe they'll let me take the baby home, back to my family."

"That would be good. But," Xiao-ying's voice tapered, "do you think that could really happen?"

Catching the way Elizabeth's face clouded over, she added hastily, "I just mean, have they said anything to you yet about doing that?"

Elizabeth shook her head slowly. "No." Then she said brightly, "But I haven't asked yet."

Xiao-ying left her for a moment and returned with some cloth. "This one was given to me by my mother. I like the blue colour in it," she said, fingering the embroidery on the material. "These other two are just old dresses but there is enough here to make some baby clothes."

She placed the cloth on Elizabeth's lap. Elizabeth touched them, the rough cotton of the discarded floral dresses and the shiny, smooth silk.

"I'll have the best-dressed baby in the world," she said and smiled at Xiao-ying with thanks.

Later that night, when making the tea, Elizabeth ventured to talk to Miss Grainger. The reply was short and sharp. "No. Don't be stupid, girl. If you can't be trusted here, what makes you think you can be trusted there?"

Despite her loneliness in the Howards' house, Elizabeth was excited that she was pregnant. She had her own shame — of being touched in the dark, of being silenced — but her swelling stomach was not part of it. Mr Howard stopped his night-time visits after Dr Gilcrest had looked at her. And now, with the blessing of life growing within her, she couldn't comprehend the coolness of those around her. She sat silently nursing her secret joy — hands on her stomach, soft songs on her breath, kind thoughts and blessings for her belly, her birrawee. It was a boy, she knew, as she stitched together a frock and a bonnet with the material that Xiao-ying had given her. She could feel it. She would name him Euroke. Not Sonny, just Euroke, and she would no longer be all alone.

The Protection Board suggested a new assignment for Elizabeth, to be taken up after the birth. Yet Mrs Howard insisted that the girl stay on, pretending to believe the exterior of her husband's denial.

"I see no reason why she shouldn't," Lydia had said to Edward, daring him to protest against the unstated facts that floated between them. Lydia was holding the pregnancy up to him, trying to break him. She had her triumph over him, had humbled him. She hated him for his weakness, yet some part of her was drawn to him more because she felt that she had beaten him.

Lydia Howard was shrewd enough to ensure that the birth didn't take place in the local hospital. She wanted no speculations, no connections and no contact between her husband and his little half-caste. She would send the kitchen girl to Sydney in the last month of her pregnancy.

For the second time in her life, Elizabeth looked at the world speeding past as the rattle of the train carried her along.

Frances Grainger made the trip with Elizabeth, walking her to the door of a large brick building in East Sydney that was a home for pregnant girls.

"Try not to get into any more trouble," Miss Grainger said curtly before turning on her heel and leaving Elizabeth on her own.

Frances then made her way to Bondi Beach, to her own memorial. So much had changed since she had been there before the war. There were new shops and others had been painted, as though they were all trying to renew themselves and blossom now peace had arrived. She could see the spot on the beach where her brothers and Harold had placed their towels beside her. She imagined the young men as they were that day, running to and from the water, kicking the sand under their feet, splashing in the waves. Back in Parkes, Mrs Howard's charity work on the Country Women's Association Committee, particularly organising the war memorial, had become infuriating. Mr Howard's indiscretion eroded her infatuation for him and he had been one of the main reasons that she had decided to exile herself to the country in the first place. She needed to escape the house and agreed to escort the girl to Sydney and back to Parkes after the birth. She would take the time to look for positions back in the city.

Still, she thought, if only she had felt the touch of Edward's hand on her skin or the sensation of his lips, as she did in her daydreams, she could endure the rest — the rudeness and vindictiveness of Lydia Howard, living in Parkes with only memories from before the war when there was a family in her life. What was the weakness, she asked herself when she looked into the mirror, that made others — Edward, her mother, her father — not want what she had to give?

Frances, who had once felt affection and even pity for Elizabeth, now detached herself from the girl who had done the unforgivable. She would pinch Elizabeth on any slight provocation, enjoying squeezing the young girl's flesh between her own strong fingers. She accompanied such impulses with cruel comments. "No wonder no one wants you," she would say.

Elizabeth's brown skin became tainted for Frances in a way that it had not been before. Before the pregnancy the inferiority of her dark face and arms evoked sympathy. Now the hue would give rise to thoughts that Frances would never have allowed others to express: the darkies were a treacherous race with no morals. Frances felt betrayed by having, at moments in the past, felt a closeness, even an affection, for the traitorous native. She had treated the girl as though she were equal to any other girl on her staff. Now, all concessions and exceptions she had given to Elizabeth were withdrawn. Silence filled the vacuum.

8

1920

WHEN THE BABY ARRIVED, the labour pains drowned out every other feeling Elizabeth carried. The force of life exploding from her, the unswallowing, was a most overwhelming physical punishment. Through her screams she cried for her mother. She cried for Euroke. She cried for escape from her loneliness. She cried for the bird's-eye view of her family's camp from her tree. She cried for a feeling of long-ago innocence, for a feeling so lost to her that she could not give it a name. As the pain ebbed and subsided, she fell into a deep sleep.

In her waking moments she dreamt of her new life with little Euroke, his hands reaching out to her, her heart needing him. As she stitched clothes and booties and a little blanket, her bursting love for her child pulsated through her with each heartbeat. She lay impatiently awaiting her reunion with her son, wishing the door would open so her new life could be carried towards her, his limbs outstretched like a naradarn.

The door did open but it was not the nurse. It was Mrs Carlyle. Elizabeth saw pale skin and a dark linen suit and thought of the terror of the train ride to Parkes, the pungent smell of the police cell and of her brother, her mother, her father. Elizabeth's tightening flesh forewarned her that Mrs

Carlyle's presence was an evil omen. "Euroke," she whispered. The lost brother. Now the lost son.

"Well," began Mrs Carlyle sharply, "I had expected more from you, though I don't know why."

"Where is my son?" Elizabeth demanded, her eyes widening.

"The baby has been sent off to a good home," Mrs Carlyle replied briskly.

"But I want to keep him. He's mine. He's mine," Elizabeth fiercely demanded, clenching her fists.

"How are you going to look after a baby? You have no money, no husband, and you are only sixteen years old."

"He's mine. I want him. Don't touch him!" she leaned towards Mrs Carlyle, who stepped back. Elizabeth saw that Mrs Carlyle was edging towards the door, "No," she began to plead. "I'll look after him. Please, please, please. Give him to me. Please!"

Mrs Carlyle stared at the young girl's face now wrenched with painful urgency. She also saw her clenched fists. She closed the door against Elizabeth's sobbing pleas and comforted herself that she was giving the little boy a better life than the one he would have had with a girl who could behave so violently and irrationally. "How ungrateful. And how little they know."

She reflected on her theory that such children needed to be taken quite young to ensure the best chance of a better life. It was only later she would wonder how the girl could have known she had a son when no one had told her.

Miss Grainger was silent, torn between compassion and self-righteousness, between the living and the dead. She had thought much about Edward Howard in her time away from the oppressive house in Parkes. She had esteemed him in a way that was undeserved and she had made herself subservient to both him and his discourteous and spiteful wife. She felt a bitterness growing within her towards the little darkie, and towards Edward Howard, and her tolerance of the abusive eccentricities of Lydia Howard now seemed exhausted. She felt that she had been used, duped into a situation that she should have found demeaning. Her desire that she would wake to find Edward standing over her bed confessing love had vanished into the same darkness in which she had lost so much already.

Certainly, Edward had made no comments to her that would have led her to believe that he would act in a way that was inappropriate towards her; she had interpreted his distance as confirmation of the strong and immutable values that she had thought he possessed. But, she would also think, he could not be unaware of the way she looked at him, the way she felt, the extra effort she put into everything she did for him. She would, before the developments with the kitchen girl, have been content to have him acknowledge all that she gave to him without expecting anything in return. The awareness that he had longings that she had thought he was above and, even more hurtful to her, that those longings for someone who could not love him as much as she did, sunk her into the most resentful of moods.

Now, accompanying the little darkie back to the Howard household, Frances looked across into the tear-filled, troubled brown eyes and could only see the enemy, the woman, girl actually, who had come between her and Edward. She could see on the dark face the desolate isolation, the abandonment, but she could not offer a touch or a kind word.

The only comfort Elizabeth had on the trip back to Parkes was the rocking of the train. At the home where she had waited for the birth, there had been eight other Aboriginal girls. All, like her, had been taken from their families and placed at a house or cattle station to work as servants. They came from many different places — Kempsey, Junee, Forbes, Newcastle. One girl, Joan Morgan, came from Lightning Ridge and by tracing the limbs of their family tree they discovered that they were cousins. Through their mothers, they were both Eualeyai. With Joan, she could talk about people that they both knew, particularly Kooradgie who had joined Joan's family as often as he had Elizabeth's. Both remembered his permanent wink and his stories about every animal, every part of the landscape and every thing that hung in the sky. What neither of them spoke about was the circumstances by which they came to be carrying children.

As the landscape blurred through Elizabeth's steady gaze, she thought about how much had happened since she was first taken to the Howard house. Mrs Carlyle had been more imposing than Miss Grainger. Mrs Carlyle was pale in expensive dark clothes whereas Miss Grainger was lemon-coloured with her blonde hair and dressed in white cotton. When she had arrived at the Howard house, Elizabeth had thought that Miss Grainger would be kind to her, would offer her friendship and protection. She had worked hard to gain Miss Grainger's favour, was eager to do all that was asked of her, to get the attention, affection and acceptance that would have made the routine of her life more bearable. There were moments where that connection had seemed to be within reach, but it had never been as forthcoming as Elizabeth had initially hoped and with the pregnancy it seemed to evaporate.

Many other things had changed with the pregnancy. Before then, Peter would laugh and do thoughtful things for her. He had given her a shell that curled over itself and had a brown spotted pattern on it, the colour of her eyes, he had said shyly. But, as her stomach began to bloom, coolness seeped in to the way he spoke. When the bulge became visible, he would simply hand her the letters, not even looking her in the eye. His iciness hurt deeply, especially since she was unable to explain why it had happened, that it wasn't her choice. She didn't even like Edward Howard. Once she had, before he began coming to her room to stroke her hair and rub against her. She felt sorry for Miss Grainger, whose gaze still followed him, still thinking of him as a good man.

Mr Howard had taken things from Elizabeth — her friendship with Peter, the trust of Miss Grainger, and the freedom to be with Xiao-ying — and he had done nothing to help her keep her baby. Mrs Howard watched her now in a way that she never had before and it made Elizabeth self-conscious and frightened; as she did her household chores, she felt anxious. Her breasts, full of unneeded milk, ached and reminded her constantly that her child was not with her.

She wanted to lay in the grass with Xiao-ying and look at the sky, to tell someone what she felt. She wanted to be with someone who she would not have to talk to, who would know how she was feeling without having to say it. She wanted to be with Euroke. She wanted to be Garibooli again. And as the train trundled along, she could hear the old language repeating in her head. Euroke. Garibooli, Euroke. Garibooli. Euroke. Euroke. Euroke. Garibooli. Garibooli. Garibooli.

Garibooli. The sound of my name reminds me.
Another time, another place, another me.
I could run fast, through the grass, amongst the trees, like the wind.
Garibooli. My name means whirlwind.
Say it like I say it.
Garibooli. Garibooli. Garibooli.
I say it over and over and over again.

9

1920

ON RETURNING TO THE HOWARD HOUSE, Elizabeth thought of nothing but escaping. She thought of running, through the grass, side by side with the wind. She thought of the train — of moving further and further away with every rumble. She thought of holding her breath until life drained from her. She tried the latter — lying in bed at night trying not to let any more air in — but something, some unknown spark of life, would always make her gasp for air.

Thoughts of a son that she could not nurse and a brother, who seemed her best and only chance to feel protected but whom she could not reach, were with her constantly during the day as she prepared the fire, or made tea or ironed Mrs Howard's tablecloths. At night, when all else in the large house seemed still, she continued to scratch at her skin, harder and harder, the constant motion of her fingernails putting her into a trance. It stopped her thinking about Mr Howard's hands on her.

Edward Howard had gone to Sydney on business for what seemed like a longer than usual period. In his absence, the house was clouded with a thick, expectant atmosphere. Lydia Howard was more bitterly reserved and resentful of her husband's absence now that his presence was focused on her. He would stand behind her, watching as she brushed her hair, as if he wanted to stroke it. He would offer to assist her to close the clasp on her necklace, touching her shoulder when he was finished. He would mutter awkward compliments about her dress and complexion. He withdrew less, begged silent forgiveness and she came to feel closer to him for the acknowledgment of her moral superiority.

Elizabeth had never found affection in the Howard house. Even before the baby, her little Euroke, she was always an outsider and never able to break through to the hearts of the adults around her. But at least before her pregnancy she had human contact that sustained her — Peter and Xiao-ying. Now Peter was as cool towards her as the people she worked with in the Howard house. His change in attitude towards her cut deeply and she felt humiliated and distressed after each encounter with him. Xiao-ying did not withdraw her friendship, but her parents now told Xiao-ying to get back to her chores when Elizabeth would come into the shop. "They say you are a bad influence," Xiao-ying would explain with a sigh.

As Frances Grainger withdrew the hopes she had placed in Edward Howard, she retreated deeper and deeper into the world of the just-ended war. She resented people who treated life as though it could continue on so easily, as though nothing had happened, as though they had slept through the past years. Frances focused much of her resentment on those who had made the war an issue, a campaign and cause while it was taking place, only to move on so easily when it finished. Much of this stewing wrath was directed at Lydia Howard, whose pretence of caring was as easily evaporated as water from a burning log.

But a new threat — communism — became her most consuming fear. Where young men had mowed down the threat of the Hun in the Great War, the communists had sprouted. This spectre had arisen to mock the dead, her dead. She could see its hand reaching over to her with no one left to protect her, everyone either buried or unwilling. There was now no Harold with whom she could build a life. Those dreams had been crushed in crash of surf and gunfire on the shore of Turkey.

There was no Edward Howard either. His handsome face and masculine poise had made her think that he possessed a character to match his looks. That illusion had disappeared as the little darkie's stomach had started to swell. Feeling alone, she was fearful of what she saw as threats to the way of life she had now, simple as it was. She had no sympathy for the Germans, but the communists, she felt, were feeding amongst her. She was overwhelmed by the slow sinking terror that the world was falling in upon her, that she would be crushed.

A change was noticeable in Mrs Howard too. One not related to the end of the war. One that eclipsed her burgeoning civic interest in prohibition (she was excited by the nobility of abstinence, of public denial). Lydia Howard's obsession was with the kitchen girl, "the little darkie" as the housekeeper called her. That she had allowed Elizabeth to stay on was rooted in a need to see the girl more closely and to force this presence onto her husband; the girl was a constant accusation levelled at him, a reminder of the way he had insulted her.

Lydia's vengeful plan to keep Elizabeth in the house did not play out as she had intended. She found herself consuming the poison she had laid out for Edward. Though she pretended distraction, Lydia watched the girl's every movement carefully as quick hands polished silver, dusted, oiled, cleaned. She wanted to find what it was that had attracted Edward, but the only distinctive features were the dark skin and even darker eyes. She concluded that her husband, unable to express himself to her, had used the girl. Her reasoning attempted to account for his actions but settled nothing within her. When he expressed an opinion about the lack of character of the new doctor or criticised an editorial in the newspaper she felt the festering of her inability to forgive him. Lydia concluded that the danger must come from the girl, that the evil must emanate from within her.

Elizabeth had noticed the increased attention she was receiving. She sensed the eyes following her careful movements, could feel the sustained discomfort of having someone reluctantly drawn to her. It made her uneasy and she much preferred the days when she had existed unobserved, when she had wondered if Mrs Howard even remembered she was in the house.

She tried to cope as best she could with the open animosity that lurked everywhere within the house. Late at night she would lie on the ground in the back garden and look into the same sky that covered her home. All that made her happy she tried to find in the lights that sparkled above her: the seven sisters of the Mea-Mei, the shell that Peter gave her, her jade brooch, Euroke. She grew thin from a lack of appetite. Within the damp walls of her room, her thoughts would turn to her troubles and she would lose herself in her late-night ritual of scratching, raising cherry-pink marks across her arms, legs and now empty stomach.

The oppressive humidity of Lydia Howard's antagonism towards Elizabeth began to permeate the house; it stuck to the skin of the women who lived under the same roof. Lydia's glowering became like distant thunder rumbling. Over time it increased with the curtness of her tongue and objects slammed into hard surfaces — a mirror on her dressing table when she thought her face too lined, a book at a wall when she could no longer keep her thoughts on reading, a plate on the floor when the imploding anger within her made eating impossible. She would shriek when she imagined she saw stains on her clothes and demand that they be rewashed. She would push her food away and refuse to eat, complaining about the taste. Her anger was directed at all the staff but fell hardest and swiftest on the kitchen girl and the housekeeper.

One morning, as Elizabeth polished the silver, Mrs Howard approached her. With her face so close that Elizabeth could feel her constrained breathing, Lydia stared into the girl's stunned eyes. Seeing innocence when she wanted to see cunning enraged Lydia beyond her ability to control it. She became infuriated by the fear in the dark eyes before her, the shrinking away. She brought her hand hard across Elizabeth's face in an attempt to expel her resentment. It remained tightly within her. She hit the girl's face again, clipping Elizabeth's skin with her nails.

Elizabeth fled the house and ran to the railway station, believing that the train could take her away. She had no money and did not know where to go, but if she jumped in front of it, with one giant thump, she would be carried somewhere. Perhaps some place with long grass she could run through, some place she could wait for Euroke. Elizabeth stood on the platform, feeling the sting in the graze on her face. It matched the burning sensation she felt across her body as an aftermath of her own silent acts of scratching.

Miss Grainger arrived to bring her home. She did not understand why she had followed Elizabeth to the train station, was surprised that she had any pity left within her.

"You don't want any more trouble," she said with a sigh as she offered Elizabeth a handkerchief. As Elizabeth gratefully took it, she added, "If your family had wanted you, they would have come for you by now."

This last remark, escaping just as Mrs Howard's slap had, came from the part of Frances Grainger that, despite all that had transpired, still coveted Mr Howard and his handsome frame, that part of her that still cursed the fact that he had chosen the little kitchen maid over her.

"I never wanted him to," Elizabeth had blurted, aware of the source of Miss Grainger's hatred.

"You say that again and *I'll* slap you," was all Miss Grainger could offer, grabbing Elizabeth's limp hand and dragging her towards the house. Elizabeth fell into the despair of captivity.

For as long as Elizabeth had been away from the soil she was born on she had wanted to return to it. As the time since she had been taken from the camp stretched from months into years, she began to have doubts about why her family had not come to rescue her. She knew that they could be as unable to find her as she was to get to them, but the seeds that Miss Grainger had sown about her not being wanted had started to grow within her. She would always remember what it felt like to want to leave but not have any money for a ticket, to contemplate escaping from the hollowness she felt inside by lying down before an oncoming train. The suffocating feeling of being chained to an unwanted life left her unaware of the scratch on her face and oblivious to the lone male figure standing in the shadows of the train station.

10

1921

ELIZABETH HAD MET GRIGOR Brecht at the Chinaman's shop, amongst the bags of flour, bins of potatoes, and crates of bottles. It was one of her rare trips there and Elizabeth was happily visiting with Xiao-ying. Grigor was buying provisions from Mr Chan and as they bartered, he kept looking over at the two girls.

"That man's looking at you," Xiao-ying said with a grin.

"No, he's not," Elizabeth blushed and looked at her hands.

When she lifted her eyes, she saw that Grigor was still gazing at her. She quickly turned back to her friend.

"He is nice-looking. Tall and thin. And look how blue his eyes are," said Xiao-ying.

Elizabeth took another glance. He was staring at her, but this time, as he caught her eye, he tipped his hat at her. She turned back to Xiao-ying who was grinning behind her hand.

"You had better go back or Miss Grainger will send a search party for you," Xiao-ying said, gently pushing Elizabeth towards the front of the shop. Elizabeth realised that Miss Grainger would be getting cranky with her for taking so long. She grabbed her packages of pepper and chocolate. Her breath quickened as she walked down the small aisle towards Grigor, who was standing near the door.

"Hello," he ventured, taking his hat off.

Elizabeth's hands felt sweaty and she could feel her heart beating against her breastbone. She had grown taller and thin in this, her seventeenth, year, but still had to look up to meet Grigor's gaze. She was unable to speak.

"How are you today?" he added, turning his hat slowly in his hands.

Elizabeth noticed that he had an accent when he spoke. "You're not from here," she thought to say, her eyes dancing between his face and her feet.

"No. No, I'm not," he said. "I'm from Germany. From a small city called Cologne. I have lots of interesting stories to tell you. And I will if you let me."

"I have to get back to Miss Grainger with these," she said, holding up her parcels.

"I will walk you back then."

"Oh, she will get mad at me if I bring you back," Elizabeth said nervously, knowing that Miss Grainger would be sure to give her that look of disapproval that she so often signalled with these days.

Grigor smiled. "Alright, I will walk with you as far as I can so Miss Grainger will not see. Then she cannot disapprove. My name is Grigor."

Grigor followed her up the steep slope of Church Street towards the corner of Hill Street, carrying her parcels for her. She dawdled as he spun magic around her with his thick voice. She thought Grigor attractive despite being so much older. He had broad shoulders and a strong face with eyes that fascinated her as much as the shape of Xiao-ying's had.

Elizabeth had heard of Germany from Miss Grainger and knew that Germans were less than human, crazed, monster-like devils. They ate children and did other terrible, unspeakable things, so unspeakable that Miss Grainger could never tell her what these things were. Looking into Grigor's face now she couldn't see what she was supposed to be afraid of. She just saw a man. If he had not spoken, there would have been no way to prove that he was not like everyone else in Parkes.

"Do you know what comes from Germany?" he asked as they walked.

"You?" she replied, enjoying the smile that spread slowly across his square jaw as she made her joke.

"Yes," he replied, delighting in the humour in her, "but what else?"

"I don't know."

"Beer."

"But beer comes from everywhere."

"Ah, a common mistake and I shall not hold it against you. But I must clarify something for you. Only German beer comes from Germany. And German beer is very special. It is the best beer in the world. I say this objectively. Do you know why it is the best?"

"No," replied Elizabeth, supressing a laugh at Grigor's enthusiastic seriousness.

"The special nature of German beer dates back to laws made during the sixteenth century which meant that beer in Germany could only be made with hops, malt, yeast, and water. So, you see, all other beer is not real beer."

At the corner of Church and Hill streets, Elizabeth said she had to go. Grigor looked at her wistfully and said, "Meet me again. Let me take you to a moving picture."

She longed to — the chance of escape beckoned her — but she felt it was impossible. Mrs Howard would not let her and Miss Grainger would not help her.

His knowledge of the world charmed her. She knew so little of it, except for Dungalear Station, the Howards' house and that horrible place in Sydney where Miss Grainger had taken her. Within the Howard house she received either cruel words or frosty silence, so to meet a man like Grigor who wanted to talk to her made her feel like she was smiling inside.

"Meet me here then," he suggested. That she knew she

could do. No one noticed as she slipped out under the darkened sky.

She met Grigor at nights, escaping to lie under the stars with him. He made her laugh deeply, in an almost forgotten way, and he seemed to know many things beyond her comprehension. He was unlike anyone from Dungalear and not like anyone in the Howards' home. Yet, like her, he was from faraway, displaced. Grigor told her things he thought she would like, tried to please her. He treated her as though she could think and feel. He showed her that a white man would not always be a Mr Howard. She grasped at Grigor's slow show of affection.

Grigor listened to Elizabeth when she spoke. Though shy at first, she opened up to him with things she held precious to her. She told him about her family, Kooradgie, her parents, and, most sacredly, Euroke.

As more conversations passed between them, she grew closer to him. She would, as they lay in the grass together, lean against his arm, curl her hands around his large muscles, smell his smoke and pepper scent. As she grew more intimate and confident with him, more things fell from her lips, into the air between them, leaving her words for him to inhale.

She would tell him stories of her time at Dungalear, of how her mother would scold her for day dreaming. And how she had overheard her aunt say that the daughter was just like the mother and ever since then when she was told to come down from the tree she would sing back, "No, Mother, I want to be just like you." She spoke proudly about her father whose ability to provide food through the toughest of droughts meant that he was greatly respected and that the family was held in the highest esteem. And she told him of the time she and Euroke were fishing and he fell into the water and dragged her in as he slid. They were both laughing so hard that they couldn't stand up and were at risk of drowning. Kooradgie, who stood watching from the shore, had scolded them for behaving in such a silly manner saying that they didn't need white people to kill them off when they were capable of doing it through their own stupidity. They stood in silent embarrassment as he stormed off until they heard his laughter from behind the trees.

With Grigor, she shared her lost brother, not her lost son. The lost son, who would be over a year old by now. This boy was too secret to speak of and she feared Grigor might react as Miss Grainger, Peter and Xiao-ying's parents had done; he might withdraw his affection and grow cold towards her. Besides, telling of her family, especially Euroke, was hard enough. When she got to the most difficult parts of her story — being taken away from Euroke, her fear on the night she was locked in the gaol, the terror of the train journey with Mrs Carlyle — Grigor would fold her hands into his to let her know that he understood how much she had hurt, how much pain had made its home within her. She would press her head against his chest, feeling the strength of his comforting arms. He loved her most at those moments, this soft, vulnerable thing folded into his arms. No one had recognised this part of her before and she kissed Grigor tenderly for caring. He would respond by touching her until Elizabeth's pleasure turned to fear — the shadow of Mr Howard hanging above them — and Grigor would stop. For Elizabeth, this also distinguished him from the other, omnipresent, white man.

"One day, we will get home, both you and I," he had told her, and she relished his vision for it affirmed her wishes and hopes, made her own dreams seem real and close. He was strong and dependable and could pull her from the circumstances that she found herself trying to survive in; he would not leave her on the train platform unable to return home.

She told him stories, ones she could remember and was not forbidden to tell a man:

Googar was married to two wives, Mutay and Kukughagha. Kukughagha was the mother of three sons. One was grown and lived away from the home; the other two were just babies. They lived in a goolahgool†.*

One day, Googar and his two wives went hunting, leaving the babies at home. They took all the water with them to drink, filling their possum-skin bags with as much as they could carry. They left no water for the babies, who began to get very thirsty under the hot sun. Their tongues began to swell and they could not speak. They saw a man coming towards them and realised that it was their elder brother, named Kukughagha, like his mother. He asked where their mother was but the babies could not answer him. When he asked them what was wrong, they pointed towards the empty goolahgool.

He asked them, "Did your mother leave you without water?"

They nodded.

Kukughagha, the son, told the babies, "I am going to punish them for leaving you here to perish. Go away and wait."

The babies complied, and when they were a safe distance away, Kukughagha, with a mighty hit, split the tree in two, right down the middle. As the tree split, water gushed out in a stream. The babies drank happily and bathed in the water. The pool grew bigger and bigger.

When the hunters were returning to their camp, they reached a stream of water. They realised that their goolahgool must have burst and they tried to make a dam, but the water was rising too fast and the current was too strong. As the three hunters tried to cross the water, the three sons spied them. The eldest brother told the babies to tell the others where to cross the stream. This the babies did, following their elder brother's instructions.

Googar and his wives crossed the river where the babies

* *mutay* = possum

† *goolahgool* = a waterhole in a tree trunk

pointed. Kukughagha, their mother, was getting out of her depth. She cried out "Ku ku gah gah. Ku ku gha gha. Give me a stick. Give me a stick."

Her sons answered from the bank. "Ku ku gha gha. Ku ku gha gha," they laughed.

The three hunters were drowned in the rushing stream.

"You see, we are taught to watch children. And I need to remember that when I wonder why my family has not come for me yet. They are most likely just trying to find a way to reach me."

With each tale Elizabeth told him, Grigor responded tenfold. When he unwrapped his tales of other places she felt lifted out of her surroundings, felt the excitement of escape and the hope it encourages. He told her about the places he had been: London, Paris, Vienna and Venice. He told her about life in Cologne, of his own ceremonies, of Fasching and Oktoberfest, of masked balls and of cross-country skiing.

Grigor had slipped into her life as though falling from the stars that danced above. He would tell her tales just like Kooradgie had. His stories of life in Germany seemed like the other worlds she and Euroke had imagined would greet them at the end of a train journey, each a circus tent containing a different spectacle.

Other times he tried to teach her things about the world, knowing that she had not had much schooling. "On the one hand, the government reforms law at a snail's pace in the interest of the bourgeoisie — that's the middle class — and removes obstacles to industry. It allows workers to be exploited by the rich. On the other hand, the bourgeoisie — that's the middle class remember — leaves all the actual power in the hands of the government. The bourgeoisie buys gradual social emancipation through the immediate renunciation of political power. They find this acceptable because they fear the proletariat — that's the working class, like you and me — more than the government."

When Elizabeth seemed bewildered, Grigor smiled affectionately. He told her that Germans knew more about such things because they had the advantage of being the most theoretical people in Europe. "But I have come to spread the message here. We need to safeguard the true international spirit which allows no nationalism to arise and we need to capture that spirit which welcomes the proletariat movement no matter which nation it comes from." He looked at her earnestly, as though he would consume her. She solemnly nodded without really understanding what he was saying.

"We are outsiders, you and I," Grigor would say, his mind far away, as hers was, but in a different realm, a different geography. Both longing for somewhere else. And lying in the grass, looking up at the Mea-Mei, Elizabeth could almost imagine she was twelve again, Euroke by her side, the smell of the campfire, of roasting bundar. It was the closest she had felt to being home again.

11

1922

SHE WOULD HAVE MARRIED Grigor Brecht to avoid living in the house with Mr Howard who had ignored her since his unwanted violations ended, to avoid the sharp tongue of Mrs Howard, the accusing looks of Miss Grainger, and the ever-present figure of Mrs Carlyle, the angel of dark things. She said "yes" because, along with all these things to flee, all those longed-for escapes, she felt that Grigor really did love her, that when he looked into her face, into her eyes, he saw her; and she felt that he loved what he saw. When he held her hand in his, she felt safe.

Miss Grainger only hardened towards her more. If it wasn't the seduction of Mr Howard and the stealing of her dreams, she could not believe that the little darkie was going to marry a Kraut. That Elizabeth would cohabitate, fornicate and spawn with one who smelt of immorality — the result would be a bastard breed of black Huns. The thought would make her shake with revulsion as she would angrily set the table or count out the silverware. As soon as Elizabeth would enter the room, Miss Grainger would loudly slam down a knife or a spoon, give Elizabeth an accusing stare, and leave the room.

It was Miss Grainger's undisguised loathing that made Elizabeth happiest to get away, more than Mrs Howard's tangible resentment and petty meanness, as much as the constant fear that Mr Howard would resume his night-time visits. Only Xiao-ying, who understood her need to escape, offered a sincere blessing that she find happiness.

"I wish I could come to the ceremony. Why are you not having it here?"

"Grigor says it will be better to do it in our new home, far from here. And except for you, I can't think of anyone here that I would invite. But," she added, touching Xiao-ying's hand, "I will wear the brooch you gave me, so it will be almost like having you there."

Xiao-ying smiled back comfortingly. "Almost. I wonder what your parents would say if they knew. Weren't they looking for someone for you to marry?"

"I guess I found someone on my own," Elizabeth replied softly. "Grigor says that when we are married, he will come with me to find them."

She parted from Xiao-ying with a promise to write, "I'm not very good at it but our letters will help me get better."

Xiao-ying gave her a hug and whispered, "You are my best friend."

"And you're mine," she replied.

As Elizabeth walked slowly back to the Howards', she did wonder what her parents would think if they knew of her plans. While she would never have wanted to disappoint her mother and father, knowing that Grigor had come to save her and was offering to give her a home washed away any fear of their disapproval. And she remembered what Miss Grainger had said so spitefully to her: if they had wanted to get her back, they would have come for her by now. They may not have come for her yet; but Grigor had. With this resolve, she left for a ceremony in a Registry far away from Parkes and for nights she could sleep through without waking once in fear.

I dream that I am home again.

Euroke is near. I can hear him.

I can smell the cooking bundar wafting in the air.

I am home.
I run towards home.
Faster and faster. So fast I fly.
I do not stop until I awake.

Grigor had taken Elizabeth to a thriving town, behind the Blue Mountains, at the end of 1922. There he worked as a photographer on the local newspaper and spent his spare time organising unions and his local branch of the Communist Party. He fulfilled many of the promises that he had made to Elizabeth. He gave her a home where she could run things as she liked and did not have to take orders from anyone else. He did take her to the moving pictures and he continued to tell her stories about his life in Germany and to teach her about the oppression of the working class. But he never took her home to Dungalear.

Grigor Brecht's arrival in Australia had been less romantic and less noble than the way he had described. It was not a principled political exile and it wasn't based on a desire to ensure that the workers of the world unite, as he claimed. Nor was it modelled on Marx's exile from his same country, his same city, as he so often described it.

What Grigor had not told Elizabeth when he lectured her about the exploitation of workers was that he had been born in Cologne to a wealthy family. His family home had a coziness, created by rugs and wallpaper of different colours and patterns, knick-knacks, soft armchairs and overcrowded rustic furniture. This affluent life of privilege was one that did not teach him that there were things he couldn't have and that might be denied to him. He was blessed with opportunity and with strong, clean, clear looks. In his youth, his face and physique opened many doors for him, and he never questioned the opportunities that were given to him, taking it as given: tailored clothes, an excellent education, nannies, hunting in the country, automobiles.

His first interests were not philosophical but aesthetic. Even as a young child he would fix his eye on objects, colours and compositions. He liked drawing and painting and was fascinated by light, texture and form.

From an early age, he felt an affinity with his city, felt connected to the moods of the streets and the feel of the history that hung in the air like a fine mist and coated his body like a second layer of skin. As a young boy he would wander the university and the concert halls. He would sit in the pews of the Cathedral of St Peter and St Mary that had taken over six centuries to finish. He could marvel at what man could achieve with his hands, whether the gothic splendor of a place of worship or the fine ornaments within the church itself: the exquisitely crafted high altar and the Gero cross and its dark Jesus with a pot-belly and man-breasts, the oldest western sculpture. In the grandeur of the cathedral, he could feel not a spiritual awe but a wonder at the capacity of man to create and defy the centuries. Here rested the remains of the ashes of the three kings who visited Jesus. Here the Mailänder Madonna from the thirteenth century lay. Here he sensed a tradition, a heritage, as though Cologne was the beginning of all civilisation. The beauty of what ordinary men could build hypnotised him. He consumed life, experiences and people, moving selfishly, proprietarily, through the streets of a place that felt like a physical manifestation of his persona. He would return home from his adventures with descriptions and sketches, and excitedly describe his discoveries, as though he were the first soul to encounter them.

As he grew into his late teens, he was drawn to the less affluent parts of Cologne, to the Reihenhausers filled with working-class families. He marvelled at the stoic nobility of the poor, was fascinated by those who had to work, those who centuries ago would have had to carve the stone for cathedrals and spend a lifetime making tributes to God. His home had provided seclusion from this part of the world, and once he discovered them he was intrigued by all those outside of his wealthy realm.

Grigor could not express his sense of wonder at the working class until he read the words of Marx and Engels — a language that articulated the principled humanity of oppressed struggle. He found his truth among the well-worn pages: "Communists were the allies and theoretical vanguard of the proletariat." And as he read the text, he knew that this was him, identified and described: a communist — ally and vanguard, friend of the proletariat, unmasker of his own bourgeois culture.

Much to Grigor's frustration, his mother and father were far more tolerant of his ways than he would have liked.

"You are right, of course, Grigor," his mother would sigh. "It is a crime that we have this big, comfortable house and fine food on our table and a library with so many books in it to fill you with ideas. I shall speak to your father and ask him to do something about it."

His mother, who had been a nurse before she married, had seen the face of human misery that Grigor romanticised. Grigor resented her gentle ribbing and its undertone of greater life experiences. His father, a doctor, had a less sarcastic view of Grigor's socialism: "Grigor, we all start out as idealists and end up cynics. It is only natural," he would say with a paternalistic slap on the back.

Amongst his friends, he would rail against his parents, labelling them as part of the problem of class exploitation and disassociate himself from their legacy. While he continued to eat the plentiful food at their table, read the plethora of books in their library and sleep in his comfortable bed, he showed rebellion by dressing in second-hand clothes that were far from fashionable.

"No one looked so poor who lived so well," his mother would call after him as he skulked out the door to meet his friends.

Karl Marx published his first article in a newspaper,

Rheinische Zeitung, in Grigor's home town almost fifty years before Grigor was born. Marx later became an editor of the paper but was forced to resign because of his vocal criticism of political and social conditions. He went to Paris, where he collaborated with Engels but he returned to Cologne and in 1849 was arrested on charges of "incitement to armed insurrection" for his writings in *Neue Rheinische Zeitung*. After his acquittal he was expelled from Germany. The injustice of Marx's persecution infuriated Grigor and he despised the elite of his town even more for the stain he felt this history left on all of them. He felt different and detached from the privileged class he was born into by his understanding of social injustice. His family's comfort began to embarrass him and he began to avoid family events and occasions. He sought to enrage his parents by missing dinner and birthday parties, even one held in his honour, relishing the conflict his behaviour created and savouring their anger.

Grigor embraced the socialist rhetoric as though he were embracing the people themselves. He captured them — with photographs, another luxury his background could afford him. He wanted to document these silently dignified workers, their worn eyes staring blankly back at his open lens. He collected books like John Thomson's *Streetlife in London* with its images of London's working class and Jacob August Riis's studies of the slums in *How the Other Half Lives* and *Children of the Poor*. He was drawn most strongly to the American Lewis Wickes Hine, whose work publicised the poverty of immigrants, miners, ironworkers, steelworkers, and child labourers. That these books had led to social change placed such photographers on the same footing as Marx for Grigor and through them he could see his own future: to document the quiet suffering of the masses.

In his youth, when photography was the domain of only a few because of the cost of large cameras and glass photographic plates, he could pursue his passion without much competition. Even when the introduction of roll film and the box camera brought photography within the reach of more and more people, the freedom to pursue a profession in snapping shots as one felt like it was still only open to few. Grigor found his calling in documenting the disadvantaged and dispossessed; he found a livelihood in the increased demand for photographs to illustrate newspapers and magazines, and for advertising and publicity.

Grigor's fascination with the working classes culminated in his liaison with Esmeralda, a kitchen maid. This lesson ended when Esmeralda became pregnant and named Grigor as the father. Far from keeping his whispered promises to the young coal-eyed girl, his parents gave him money and arranged for him to go abroad. He had been curious about Esmeralda but, faced with having to look after her, realised he did not want to marry her, did not want to be a father and did not want to live in the poverty that would await him if he did.

It was only when he left Cologne, at age twenty-one, and he found himself in another landscape, that he came to realise his sense of self. His Marxism had defined his character but it was shaped around a solid core — the heart of who he was. This would, he realised, carry with him wherever he went, whoever he spoke to, whatever else he chose to be. He was the descendant of Celts, Romans, Gauls, Charlemagne, Teutonic knights, Lutherans, Huns, Visigoths, Saxons, and Carolingians. He had the tradition of Bach, Handel, Herder, Goethe, Musil, Hadyn, Mozart, Beethoven, Hegel, Engels, Marx, and Nietzsche. All that had seemed to merely touch him on the outside as he walked through the intertwined streets of Cologne now seemed embedded in every fibre, hair and skin cell. No matter where he was, this history remained unchanged.

His exile made him long for stability, something solid and reliable; a place to belong. In Australia, a new society still building its traditions, he had floated until he met Elizabeth.

He had seen her before their encounter in the Chinaman's

store. Grigor would have stepped in and saved her that first moment he saw her rushing towards the railway station. A slender, almost nothing figure, she passed him, a bursting rose-coloured welt across her dark cheek. He followed her and stood from a distance, watching as she stood on the station platform, crying and looking down the tracks, as if expecting a train. She, in her distress, did not notice him. He was about to step forward, offer solace and sanctuary, but was cut off by an older woman with honey-coloured hair who led the downcast girl away.

When Elizabeth appeared in the Chinaman's shop, Grigor could not let her slip by him again. His fascination with the shy, sweet-chocolate girl — she was still a girl — was not unlike that which had drawn him to Esmeralda. It was not just her distress that compelled him to intervene; she was the oppressed class he longed to rescue. She was the outcast he wanted to prove he accepted. His intellectual superiority and Elizabeth's peculiar cultural beliefs, her darkness, her solitude, her need for him, gave him the opportunity to be benevolent. He knew that he was her best hope for a better fate and that she knew that too. He had saved her in a way that he now realised he should have saved Esmerelda but for his youth and immaturity. He could look into Elizabeth, almost through her, as though she were smoky glass. She was easily possessed — her acquiescence betrayed her need for him — and, he had to admit, he had, for the first time, found someone whom he loved, albeit in his own private, introverted way.

Grigor found stability and a sense of belonging in his small Lithgow home. He assumed Elizabeth had found it too. His wife, his dusky rescued girl, tugged at something inside him and he could not understand how familial attachments such as Elizabeth professed could not have been supplanted by their own union. He had been so easily able to let his own go, had no need to get back to his parents and a life he had left in shame. As Elizabeth ceased mentioning her family to him, he assumed that she had found her centre elsewhere, just as he had.

At night, into the chilled air, Grigor and Elizabeth would still talk, but rather than reminisce, their conversation was full of the minutiae of their daily lives and their modest hopes for the near future. Grigor was happy with how things had turned out, though anyone who knew him, even saw him passing in the street, would not believe that in his sturdy seriousness he was capable of contentment, let alone joy. He had grown into a man who needed very little and he welcomed the comfort and the ease of Elizabeth: a wife who worked hard, asked for little, and, now that they were married, never said no to his needs.

Over the years that she would share his life, her body would grow soft in places from childbirth and hard in others from the work of motherhood. The children were for her, not him. He hated the noise, the trivialities, and the neediness of the children. He liked that she wanted them, that maternity made her happy. He had promised to give her a home and a family, and he believed when he saw her fussing over the needs and wants of her children that he had been true to his word.

Grigor found his strengths outside the family — within his union meetings, his Party meetings and through the vigilant lens of his camera. He was still, at heart, a man moved by ideas and images. The 35-millimetre camera had arrived — as he liked to note — from Germany. Through his work he explored its compactness and its economy. He experimented with finely powdered magnesium as an artificial illuminant — the powder, sprinkled in a trough and fired with a percussion cap, would throw a brilliant flash of light against the coal-darkened miners, their stunned image preserved amongst a cloud of acrid smoke.

12

1942

THROUGH THE YEARS Elizabeth came to love Grigor deeply, and such faithful affection can forgive character flaws and human failings. She understood him and knew he would feel betrayed by her desire to return to the very life he felt he had saved her from. She had sought escape from the Howards; Grigor had sought to rescue her not just from servitude to the Howards but also from what he perceived to be an earlier life of drudgery. And, with her children around her, she could never say that life with Grigor had not made her happy.

But she never made it back to her family's camp. She was afraid of what she would find, and what she wouldn't, if she returned to the place where the rivers met. And now she had a house full of children to look after and could not imagine how she could leave them to make the journey back to Dungalear Station, even if she felt ready to face what would be waiting for her there. And there was also the spectre of Mrs Carlyle ready to swoop and steal her sons and daughters should Grigor's protection ever falter.

She had given birth to seven children, six to Grigor, and was thirty-five when she had the youngest, now three years old. She had not heard from Thomas, their first child, since he had left on the train to enlist and fight in the war. She tried not to think of him as another lost son — lost in the trenches, lost at sea, lost in the skies. She remembered Miss Grainger, the Howards' housekeeper, and her obsession with the last war and feared she was becoming the same way with this new one. She kept reassuring herself that if anything had happened, if Thomas had been missing, injured or killed, she would have been told. Soldiers couldn't just disappear. He had said he was going to enlist in the Air Force and anyone who knew the young Thomas and his love of airplanes, his obsession with flight, would understand his enthusiasm to join the flying forces.

Despite her assurances to herself, Elizabeth was unnerved by her last image of him, one in which he had disappeared, getting smaller and smaller until he slipped into the distance as she watched the train disappear into the horizon. She knew all too well the transforming power of trains. Her memories held him close while she awaited news of him.

Life with Grigor had the comfort of a shared understanding. Elizabeth had learned to live around his spartan habits. The doors of their house were kept closed and the windows, even in the coldest months, opened to ensure that the rooms were aired. Lights were only on when needed; heating was low at night, whatever the temperature; water was used sparingly. Grigor refused to heat any of the bedrooms, asserting that it was healthy to sleep in an unheated room with the window open. Engrossed in his work in the Communist Party, he left his family much to themselves unless asserting his patriarchal position on the periodic evenings he was home. Affection was reserved, given only when he and Elizabeth were alone. In the day-to-day running of the house, Grigor became an obligation, much like any of her children, but with separate, more binding demands and less obedience.

The world that occurred outside Elizabeth's home, the one that Grigor was fighting to change, evolved without seeming to affect her. The happenings in the wider world never seemed to have the impact and importance of the daily trivialities that filled her every waking hour. The crises of sick children and petty conflicts eclipsed economic forces and the shadows of another European war. It was not until her eldest son, Thomas, left to enlist that Elizabeth would feel that the outside world had entered into her life again. Her family seemed to survive the Depression, even with a growing number of children. Elizabeth's early life had made her resourceful and frugal and Grigor always provided for them, even when it turned out that he had been laid off from the newspaper or his freelance photography work seemed to be drying up. He kept secret the stream of money he received from Germany each month for his pocket — it would dwindle during the years of the war and cease by the time peace was declared — so Elizabeth did not know the full extent of his ability to provide.

Elizabeth's favourite times were when Grigor was out of the house — away at work, drinking at the local pub, attending a union or Party meeting. She kept her children, so precious, close to her; they filled the space around her, relishing the lack of order in the house. She was, by the end of the day, as exhausted as she had felt during her early days in the Howard house, but now the rewards for her aching limbs were unconditional love and soft purring affection — things that she had not known since her days at Dungalear, which was another lifetime, another her.

Elizabeth enjoyed her bulging belly with each pregnancy — continued to whisper and sing to her stomach — and wept with relief and delight each time a child was delivered into her arms. She thrived on the demands of motherhood, her life filled with a special richness and a thousand tiny blessings, and she marvelled that she could experience such joy.

Thomas, her first child with Grigor, was born in the bitter-cold winter of 1924. A shy, gentle boy with acute ideas, he could recall where things were by shutting his eyes and visualising from memory. Her first daughter, Patricia, was born two years later. From their earliest interactions, Patricia would fuss over Thomas, engulf him in her arms, almost suffocate him. Patricia felt most at ease when putting things in order, including her brothers, whom she battled to control. Her relationship with Thomas was one of indulged devotion, one that their mother could not witness without a pang of nostalgia for her own lost brother. William, born in the hottest part of 1928, was, from the start, vivacious and spirited, more adventurous, with the quickest temper. He rebelled against his older sister, resenting any assertion of authority, even if only in the form of affection and mothering. What Thomas would benevolently tolerate, William would try to quench and conquer with his fits. Patricia bore the bruises after attempts to contain him with the belief that he would, over time, grow to love her.

Some years later, in the spring of 1931, another child, a beautiful, bewitching girl called Daisy was added to the family. After Daisy's birth, Elizabeth developed problems bringing a pregnancy to its full term until Bob was born in 1937 and, amid the bushfires of 1939, she delivered Danny. A sense of emergency surrounded the birth of the youngest because of the sombre mood created by the natural disaster and the seventy-five deaths left in the wake of nature's vengeance. The hardest birth, it was the beginning of Elizabeth's frequent bouts of fatigue. By the time Danny came into the family, the elder boys had had their share of play-fathering, with Thomas and William already trying to emulate the aloofness of men several years older than them. It was his mother and Patricia who would fuss over Danny.

The dominating conclave of the eldest three lorded over the youngest children, but Patricia, as eldest daughter, assumed her role as minor matriarch within the ever-expanding cluster of children, especially when their mother was tired. She saw herself as arbitrator of feuds. She could coerce and connive, convince and convict, knew when to bully and when to sweet-talk. She planned adventures, such as an expedition to see the newly opened Harbour Bridge. The younger boys never questioned Patricia's authority. Even Thomas allowed her to have her way. And over the years, William was less violent towards her, begrudgingly giving her the deference she sought in exchange for respect of his privacy.

Elizabeth had always tried to treat her children equally but in her secret heart Thomas, the eldest, was the one she had the most gentle feelings for. He was the first to be placed in her arms and his arrival soothed a little of the pain of having had her firstborn taken from her before she even laid eyes on him. Thomas was a blessing she had clung to when he was the only child. When the house was filled with children, she spent more energy on the demands of the younger ones. She noticed that Thomas was more withdrawn and William more often in trouble at school.

There was also a special bond between the mother and her eldest daughter. Just as her own mother had told her stories to teach her lessons about life and showed her how to prepare food and cure sickness, so too Elizabeth began to teach Patricia the skills needed to run a house. Patricia's natural maternal instincts made her a patient and dedicated student. Elizabeth saw much of her own eagerness to please in her daughter. Patricia would watch earnestly and copy faithfully, and Elizabeth was reminded of her own diligence when she first entered into service in the Howards' house. Patricia would beat butter and sugar to a cream, beat in two eggs, one at a time, then add milk, lemon rind and flour sifted with baking powder and salt. She would leave the mixture to rise, steam for an hour and a half and serve with lemon sauce. Elizabeth would reflect sadly that the legacies she was handing down to her daughter came more from Miss Grainger than from her Guni at Dungalear.

Even in the midst of her domestic joy and contentment, her losses would haunt her, puncturing her bliss with their ghosts of sorrow. In her children — the shape of features, the curve of bone, the hue of skin — Elizabeth could see images of her family who were lost in another lifetime. Euroke, the lost brother, would often seem close to her; his features, so well known to her, scattered and drawn across the faces and movements of her children. It was Thomas, the eldest, who looked most like Euroke. She would look at his born-before eyes and it would cause an irrepressible longing in her. Some of her children were darker — Patricia, William, Danny — and the rest were lighter — Thomas, Bob, Daisy — but Elizabeth could never think of family comparisons without wondering about her missing, oft-remembered child: Euroke, the lost son.

Little Euroke. Whose features were imprinted on his face? What did he see when he looked in the mirror? And what did he think when his thoughts turned to a mother he had never known. She wished that wherever he was, that it was a place where he would know much of love and little of harm, where he would be far from the unspeakable violence of the Mr Howards, the spiteful meanness of the Mrs Howards, and the easily evaporated sympathies of the Miss Graingers. She hoped that he would be far, far away from the evil menace of the Mrs Carlyles.

If your family had wanted you, they would have come for you by now.

Elizabeth felt that she had lived as three different people within her skin. She had been Garibooli during her life by the river with her parents and Euroke. She would remember that life as a time of happiness even though she could still recall the things that made that existence hard. People were often dying, especially the older ones and the babies, food was scarce and there were many dangers. She was warned about the spirits that lived in the waterholes and the spirits that would take her away if she wandered too far from the campfire. She had been warned about the white men. She had heard her parents talking — and the old people too, especially Kooradgie — about the recent killings of her family and neighbours. They spoke of the disease which had spread through them. And they spoke about the way white men had killed off the things that gave them life, the animals and the waterholes. Despite all these things, because Euroke was there, she remembered being happy. She had loved running, across the open country, savoured the freedom to move. Euroke, who called her "Booli" — his playful brown eyes, so gentle and soft, dancing as she tickled him.

Then there came the train ride with Mrs Carlyle that began her life as 'only Elizabeth'. She would remember this miserable time only when it crept, unbeckoned, that wanted to scratch her skin off, to erode every piece of her. That time never left her completely. She could be washing a plate and suddenly see Mrs Howard's hand coming to slap her face, or be tucking a child into bed and hear Mr Howard saying, "No one will believe you," or making a bed and see the doctor and feel his cold fingers inside her. She could not even remember Xiao-ying without the bitterness and loneliness of her time with the Howards and the guilt of a broken promise about writing. These flashes would drag her back into that other world until the signs and sounds of her children rescued her, calling her back to her third life.

This third life also began with a train ride. In this life she was called 'Mum', 'Mummy' and 'Ma'. Even Grigor called her 'Mother', though not when they were alone. Then, she became 'Elizabeth' again. There was a way he looked at her as they talked late into the night, a way in which he seemed to sigh with contentment as he peered into her face, that confirmed he still loved her. Despite this devotion, Grigor seemed, to Elizabeth, to have no interest in their children. He had opinions about them — he always had an opinion — but he did not like to interact with them, preferring them to be scarce when he was at home. This was hard with so many sons and daughters and it was easier when he stayed out late and arrived home when the children were in bed. Still, mothering, she felt, was a woman's job, so she could not be too harsh on Grigor's seeming indifference to child-rearing. Secretly, she preferred that all the parental duties fell to her. She was never happier, never more whole, than when she was 'Mother'. Each of her children, each a part of her, created this being she had become in the third phase of her life. This new her was physically abundant, overflowing. She felt that it was not the different location that had made her different, it was the people around her that brought out different qualities within her.

Elizabeth, when flooded with love for her own children, would see her own mother most clearly. She felt a strengthening attachment to her through the grief and loss created by the theft of a loved child, as though the shared pain enabled her to keep her mother invisibly by her side, allowed her to understand what her mother must have felt and must still be feeling. Six children could not erase the one she had lost; her new family never replaced the one that had been taken from her. At these times, Elizabeth longed to tell her mother — tried to do so by sending her a message from her mind to her mother's — that she had created a new world in which she felt complete and content.

If they had have wanted you, they would have come for you by now.

She remembered Miss Grainger's words, could still hear the voice in which she had said them, but Elizabeth would try to push them away. Her own powerlessness and lack of choice allowed her to understand all that could be beyond a mother's control. She understood the safety that Grigor gave her, that he offered her protection from the Aborigines Protection Board; her children were safe with her while Grigor reigned over the household.

Elizabeth did not feel as though she could talk to Grigor any more about her lost family and her deep wish to see her brother. She feared the dismissiveness that had crept into their conversations about her family, replacing Grigor's previous sympathy on the subject. He seemed to have shaken off his feelings of restlessness, but the end of his time as an emotional nomad had not eliminated her own yearnings, which she now nursed in private.

Grigor never mentioned her skin, as though it did not matter, but Elizabeth came to realise over the years that it did; his silence confirmed how important it was to him. He would never say the things that Miss Grainger thought and would let slip, but she felt acutely his sense of superiority and his pride in rescuing her from the very thing she hungered to find again.

So Elizabeth stayed in the little town behind the Blue Mountains, her swarm of six children around her. Her thoughts in rare moments of peace drifting back to her brother, her head resting in her mother's lap, Kooradgie and his wrinkled face, and the place where the rivers meet.

On nights when the children were asleep, Elizabeth would walk to the back of the yard, sit on the cold grass in the borrowed light of the moon and look at the nocturnal sky. The same unchanging stars looked down at her. She would try to remember the stories, the songs. Here, for a fleeting moment, she was still Garibooli.

Thomas, her eldest, was the only child who would join her. She would not chide him back to bed but allow him to sit beside her on the back verandah or behind the shed at the end of the yard, and stare silently, contemplatively at the sky. In the dimness of the night, she could pretend he was Euroke; in the half-shadows, with the angles of his face, he could have been.

Once, she opened up to him and told him a story she had almost forgotten:

Naradarn wanted honey. He watched until he saw

Wurranunnah[*]. He caught him and stuck a feather in Wurranunnah's *tail so that he could follow him back to his nest. Naradarn told his two wives, who were sisters, that they had to follow him and help him get the honey from Wurranunnah's nest.*

When they reached the tree, Naradarn told one of his wives to go up to the hive and get the honey out. She climbed up to the fork of the tree and slipped her hand into the hive, but could not get the honey out. When Naradarn climbed up to help her, he realised that she was stuck and the only way to get her free was to cut her hand off. He did this quickly. His wife was so shocked that she died instantly. Naradarn brought the body down to the ground. He ordered his other wife up into the tree to chop out the hand and get the honey. When this wife saw that her sister was dead, she was afraid and did not want to go up the tree. She begged Naradarn not to send her up the tree, but Naradarn took a stick and threatened to beat her so she reluctantly climbed up. She slipped her arm into the tree beside her sister's hand. She became stuck and could not move. Naradarn, upon finding her stuck too, chopped her arm off. She died also. Naradarn took his second wife's body down to the ground.

When Naradarn returned to the camp, the other sisters of his dead wives ran to meet him, hoping that he would have honey to share with them. When Naradarn came closer they could see that he was alone and that he was covered in blood. The girls were frightened of him and ran to tell their mother. Their mother went to Naradarn and asked him where her daughters were. Naradarn replied, "Ask Wurranunnah. I do not know where they are." He remained silent in the face of all other questions.

The mother went and told her tribe that her daughters were missing and that Naradarn would not tell her where they were, even though she felt sure he knew what had happened.

An Elder said, "If Naradarn has hurt your daughters, they

* *wurranunnah* = bee

will be revenged. His tracks will be fresh. We will get our best trackers to find out where he has been and see if they can figure out where your daughters are."

The young men with the best eyes and the fastest feet were sent to find the sisters. They found Naradarn's footprints and followed them all the way to Wurranunnah's tree. They could see what Naradarn had done.

That night, a corrobboree was held. The women sat in a half-circle and chanted, hitting two boomerangs together to keep time; others beat possum rugs. Fires were lit, and one burned especially high. Heading the procession of male dancers was Naradarn. The men danced around. The beating grew stronger. The chanting grew louder. The fires were piled higher. The dancers nudged Naradarn towards the brightest burning fire. The mother of the dead girls shrieked loud. Naradarn turned to look at her but was confronted with a wall of men. They seized him and threw him into the fire where he perished in the flames.

"So you see," Elizabeth concluded, "your mother will always know where you are and if something is wrong, Euroke." She looked down at him, trying to shield him from whatever it was that had turned him into a silent and secretive teenager.

Elizabeth didn't realise her mistake until Thomas asked what 'Euroke' meant.

"You remind me of someone I know. Someone I love very much. And 'Euroke' means 'sun' or 'sunny'."

She kissed his head. Thomas was content with the cryptic answer sealed with his mother's lips. Each sat silently, pulled into their own internal worlds. Elizabeth felt for Euroke: her lost brother; her lost son. No, a mother did not always know. She had told Thomas a lie. He might sit comforted by the falsehood that had just fallen so lightly from her lips but she could not help but feel trapped by the truth of what she knew.

Thomas reflected on what his mother had said: *A mother knows. She always knows.* He hoped that this was not true because of the new, secret thoughts that were creeping into his head. Could she see inside him to the feelings and impulses he was suppressing? Could she witness the secret, seductive night-time thoughts that he could not control or understand in the illuminating light of day?

Later, years later, these feelings of shame would not be what he remembered of the warm interaction with his mother. What he remembered was the story. Not its content, for he had forgotten the names by the next morning, but where it had come from, and how that genesis unlocked the mystery of his dark skin. Thomas would try over and over again to remember the name that his mother had mistakenly called him, but it was elusive. Eventually, it was lost.

On the night that Elizabeth had spoken the name 'Euroke' to her son by mistake, whispering the name aloud to her son seemed to awaken a part of her that had been buried under her extra layer of skin. Whispering the name she said so often in her head had made that old life real again. She remembered that part of herself, that girl so free, so spirited. It was like looking at another daughter. The distraction of the memories made her restless.

One afternoon, after Thomas had left, while walking home from the shops, she passed a field. Watching the wind blow the tall grass seemed to transport her to another place and she felt all the layers of her life, all she had experienced since she had left the place where the rivers meet, fall from her, and she felt as she had when she was ten. She placed her bags on the ground and started to walk through the field. The grass hitting her legs brought back the memory and feel of the tall grass of Dungalear Station.

Then she began to lift her pace and go quicker and quicker and faster and faster until she was running, running around the field as though the bulk of her did not exist. The excitement, the adrenalin and the burning breathlessness of having exerted such energy was liberating. But tiredness overcame her. As she walked home, she could not quite catch her breath again. As the day turned over, she could not get rid of the pains in her body. She could not seem to get her breathing or her limbs back to normal.

Elizabeth stood in the dark of a late spring night and hung damp sheets on the line. Although her task could have waited until morning, it was one of those still, peaceful nights in which the stars seemed to expand across the heavens. Elizabeth continued to study the sky. Always it looked familiar to her, just as it had at home.

She finished pegging the clothes on the line and lifted her face to the stars. In the sky she could see the Mea-Mei and — what was his name? — chasing the sisters. Where were they from? Then, amongst the patterns and myths with names that now escaped her, she saw the outline of her brother's face: his childish lips, his brown eyes, his large dark-caramel forehead. "Euroke," she whispered and she remembered her many silent prayers.

He will come and rescue me. He will come and rescue me.

Her heart longed for Euroke. It always had. Sometimes loudly and violently, other times softly and gently, muted by the joys of her children. She had yearned for the gaze of his deep brown eyes and for his infectious laugh, longed for this moment when she could see his face so clearly in the stars. As she looked into the sky, his hand reached down and beckoned her to join him, telling her not to be afraid. Her whole heart seemed to explode with longing. She had been Elizabeth for a time; now she was again Garibooli.

Garibooli. Garibooli. Garibooli. Say it over and over and over again.

13

1929

SONNY BONEY, EUROKE, the lost brother, felt a breeze, soft and gentle, the night that Garibooli died. Walking down the street of the small opal-mining town, he felt a presence drawing close to him, a warm embrace, and he thought of his sister, hovering near but just out of his reach. For him, Garibooli was still alive, just lost, waiting to be found.

Several months after Garibooli had been taken, Sonny's family had been relocated to the mission at Angledool, carried off in trucks. The move took place during a drought but was not driven by lack of water. Sonny's parents were told that if they did not move, their son would be taken too. The family found itself imprisoned by this threat. Aboriginal children had been denied enrolment at the public school near Dungalear and the townspeople had demanded that the Education Department segregate the school, then complained that the Aboriginal children were neglected because they were getting no education. Garibooli's family soon discovered that conditions at Angledool were much worse than they had been at Dungalear.

Within a year, they returned to the place where the rivers meet; Sonny and his father walked the sixty miles back. Only a few months after their return trip, Guni had died of grief and alcohol, the end of her decline that began with the theft of her daughter. Sonny's father and Kooradgie, the great storyteller, followed in the flu epidemic of 1919. Many of the old people were lost during that time. Sonny could still remember the smell of the burning dogwood and sandalwood used to smoke out and cleanse Kooradgie's hut and to burn all of the old man's worldly possessions. This ceremony to honour Kooradgie's passing marked the last observance of this funeral rite and the last performance of the tribal dances. His family had been devastated by the loss of so many of their elders and children, and Sonny had lost both of his parents. Everyone who had known him as 'Euroke' had passed away, moved or disappeared. The need in him to find his sister intensified.

The end of the Great War worsened the inequalities in the small town. A campaign by the white residents had continued to keep Aboriginal people from the town and tied to isolated reserves and camps of tin-sheet tents on the outskirts. At the same time, pressure was also placed on authorities to give more reserve land over to white hands and shift the Aboriginal inhabitants. The contradiction of these two approaches, something that seemed to pass the authorities by, was not lost on Sonny.

Sonny closely watched as the soldiers returned home and he harboured hopes of respect for his people and land returned to those Aboriginal men who had loyally fought for Australia on foreign soil. But the returning black soldiers were shunned by the Australian society they had protected and were excluded from the returned servicemen's clubs. Even the Soldier Settler scheme, which gave farm land to men who had served their country, turned out to be only for white soldiers, and it became clear that the Anzac legend was not going to include the contributions made by Aboriginal soldiers.

Three or four hundred Aborigines had served during the war, though the exact number would never be known as the statistics were not properly recorded. This participation by Aboriginal men came despite laws passed in 1909 which prohibited people who were not 'substantially of European descent' from joining the armed forces. This law was designed specifically to prevent Aborigines, Asians and other non-whites from military service, but this bar was relaxed during the war due to shortages in the number of volunteers, allowing some Aboriginal men to fight, serve and die for their country, which in peacetime would not have wanted them. Aboriginal deaths and acts of heroism on the fields of battle were forgotten by all but the black families who bore them.

Sonny was apprenticed to a sheep station near Tilpa the year after the flu epidemic. Barely a teenager, he began his work in the pastoral industry with four years of building water tanks and windmills and work as a tar-boy in shearing sheds. Along with the scorched-earth scars this work gave him, he was to be paid two shillings a week, with the money to be placed in the care of the manager. He would never see this income. His apprenticeship taught him that he could never complain of unfair treatment, never get mad no matter how provoked, and never strike a white man. He also learnt to take the bad treatment and to live with humility and humiliation. Yet he also knew that he had been lucky. He would later meet men who carried visible scars from the punishments meted out to them during their periods of apprenticeship.

Sonny never trusted white people. His father, familiar with killing times like those that had taken place at Temperance Creek, had advised him of their absolute power over blackfellas. "A blackfella is only acceptable to other blackfellas," he would say before adding, "Stick with your own mob." White people could be polite and kind to him if they wanted, or cruel and mean if they felt that way. The choice was always up to them as to how they would treat him and there was little he could do about it; either way, Sonny was held hostage to the whims of white men. He adapted his life to avoid them, especially the gangs of white boys that 'patrolled' the town's streets. A black man was lucky if these young men stuck only to name-calling.

All his life, Sonny reflected, whitefellas were saying he should be like them, but he knew, just as his father had told him, that they would never accept him. There were a thousand reminders every day to reinforce his outsider status: the young white louts in towns like Walgett and Brewarrina lying in wait in parks and on deserted roads to beat black men like him; having to wait until all the whites were served before getting attention in a shop; constantly enduring hurtful remarks about his supposed inferiority. He would never get used to the way white people tried to strip him of his dignity as a thing of humour and sport.

If life on the ground made him feel broken and barren, especially when all those he loved and who loved him had been taken from him, he was elevated above the world on the back of a horse. Sonny had an intuition for riding — and a skill for riding fast. He felt connected with the beast beneath him as though the flow of the movement, the motion of the gallop, had a life force all its own. Riding at full speed across the terrain, he felt a power over his own destiny that seemed so elusive when he was on the ground.

His other source of escape and comfort came when listening to Bessie Smith on the wireless. Her deep expressive voice, her intense power, went into him, through him, as though he had inhaled her. She seemed to sit in his throat, singing what he couldn't say. Every hurt, pained word suppressed inside him she could squeeze free with her laments:

When it rains five days, and the sky's turned black as night.
I said, When it rains five days, and the sky's turned black as night.

He could feel her arms around him, this dark, fleshy woman from Chatanooga, Tennessee. He had not experienced the strange capacity of a song to touch him since the days he was still with Garibooli and their tribal songs had meanings, messages and stories that resonated with their everyday lives. Bessie Smith expressed the agony of watching his mother, crumpled over from alcohol, her clothes dirty and her hair matted, sobbing between wrenching coughs, "My birrawee. My birrawee."

Trou-ble, trou-ble, I've had it all my days,
It seems that trou-ble's going to fol-low me to my grave.

The teachings of camp life in his youth gave him the confidence that comes with the knowledge that to survive all he needed was his own two hands. When he could find employment he lived in the fringe camps or on the missions. When he couldn't, he sustained himself on the ever-changing land, supplementing the shortfalls in his rations. He would kill possums, especially useful for their meat and their fur that could be made into pliable twine, good for fishing. Their skin was waterproof and made good water bags.

He had tried to keep to as many of the old ways as he could in the midst of the customs and beliefs of the white men, even as the weave of the clan's social and cultural life began to loosen. These rituals he kept hidden and secret, for times when there was no one who could see him but his ancestors. To an outsider, they would seem like superstition. He would not look at a bird flying towards the sunset. He would always look straight ahead when travelling. He would still use a spear to stab the footprints of an animal whilst tracking it to weaken it and would resist the temptation to do the same to a human footprint, no matter what the owner had done to him.

Sonny watched as the landscape he knew by heart changed. His own life was transformed by government regulation and coercion. The Aborigines Protection Board continued to give reserve land away, now to fund the policy that had seen his sister snatched from him. The Board had also leased lands to white farmers for its own revenue, even though Aboriginal men like himself were keen to try their hands at running their own farms instead of working as exploited labour on the properties of white men.

In times when work was scarce, Sonny would return to life on the reserve, a life he loathed — the tyranny of the manager's stock whip, the dirt floors of the shacks and the control over every aspect of his life. He was required to get permission to work, to leave the reserve and move to another. He was told what to eat through the rations assigned to him. This constant monitoring and decision-making on his behalf made him feel the way he had felt when he saw the black car, his sister looking out at him from the back window, moving further and further away from him as he ran faster and faster trying to reach her. There were the inedible, insufficient rations: two pounds of sugar, eight pounds of flour, a quarter of a pound of tea, and a little salt. There were the blankets, one for each family in winter, grey with a red stripe and 'N.S.W Aborigines' in large red letters, to be held up to a camera for a snapshot of white generosity and the forced gratitude of blacks. Sonny continued to catch fish and game to supplement his diet. He would give most of what he caught to the sick children and the old people.

The scene he relived so many times with reflection and regret — "if only I hadn't gone to the river", "if only I had run faster, called her name louder" — had become like so many other stories told by parents and siblings across the years. The terrible conditions on the reserves, caused by government neglect and official corruption, allowed officials to assert that Aboriginal parents were not able to take care of their children and provided an excuse to justify the removal of more of the community's sons and daughters into State 'care'. Distraught parents were powerless to stop these actions. Sonny remembered vividly the scene of a father, George Driver, standing in front of a train in a fruitless attempt to prevent his daughter being taken from him, a daughter he would never see again, a daughter who died five years later while still a State ward.

In 1927 Sonny heard of a petition circulated by a group of Aboriginal people. The men he worked with spoke about this political push and they spoke of a man, Fred Maynard, who was getting people — black and white — to support it. It asked for the dissolution of the Aborigines Protection Board. Sonny could only dream of what that could mean — his freedom, Garibooli's return. He felt awe at the nerve of this Fred Maynard and searched the newspapers for a glimpse of this man who did not seem to be aware of the protocols that governed his own life — that Aborigines had to hold their tongues, accept their lot, and not make white men angry. What would his father, always warning Sonny not to provoke white people, have thought of Fred Maynard? Men like Fred Maynard showed him that it was time to stop relying on the dream of being rescued by well-intentioned white people; it was time to start relying on Aboriginal people. Sonny would have liked to have met this man and often thought of being given the opportunity of shaking his hand and what he would say. What were the words, he pondered, to be said to someone who holds open a promise that life, when one's feet are on the ground, could feel as full of freedom as it does when riding a horse as fast as it can move across the open land?

But these actions of hope did not reach their promise; it seemed to Sonny that it would be a long time before Aboriginal people could start living free from interference from the authorities who would break up their families, tell them where to live and where to work. In scouring the newspapers he came across a news item on November 8, 1928 in the *Sydney Morning Herald*. Seventeen Aboriginal men were killed at Conniston in response to the death of one white man. The killing times that Kooradgie had spoken about were still happening in other parts of the country. And to a man like Sonny, working on the stations in Coonanble and

Brewarrina, the freedom Fred Maynard demanded seemed to be crushed by ever intensified government control over his people's actions and official surveillance of every part of their lives.

Even with this increased control over where they could work and travel, there was more violence and hostility in the towns towards his people, a resentment of their dark skin and searching eyes. White people continued to push black people off their land and to confine them to places beyond the residential areas. Curfews were imposed in the towns to keep Aborigines off the streets after dark. Conditions on the reserves were so bad and government neglect so rampant that poor health continued to be a way of life for Aboriginal people and was used as an excuse for keeping them from entering the towns, creating an intricate segregation in the rural areas.

Even though Sonny had lived through the hard times of the 1920s and the rural recession, the 1929 stock-market crash that, all the way from New York, made headlines in Australian newspapers and heralded the Great Depression, he could never understand the connection between bankers in America and work on the land, other than to reason that if white people lost money, it was bad for him too.

The Depression saw the flourishing of shanty towns, many of them mixed, as dispossessed and destitute white people were forced into the circumstances usually reserved for Aborigines; fringe camps continued to develop as the only alternative to the regimented life on the reserves. Sonny gravitated to the fringe camps in the rare periods he could sustain himself away from the reserve. With so many white men looking for work, Aboriginal men like Sonny had no chance of employment, and the law said they were ineligible for the dole from the Relief Board. On the reserve, men had to work two days for no pay to get rations. This food was worth 3/6 (35c) per week. The dole was 5/9 (58c) per week, rising to 7/— (70c) in 1936, and a white man did not have to work for it. Sonny was too dark-skinned to pass as white, so it was goodoo*, bundar, mutay and such that got him through the worst of these times. He could still get a penny for each rabbit skin and would follow dinewan tracks to find eggs, a delicacy that the old people enjoyed.

In the years Sonny waited out the Depression, he came to admire William Ferguson, an Aboriginal shearer and unionist, who campaigned for full citizenship and equality for Aboriginal people. He also watched from afar as, in 1932, William Cooper established the Aborigines Advancement League urging representations in Parliament and self-sufficiency through the land. Sonny had been impotent when it came to asserting himself, just as he had been at that moment when Garibooli had been taken. He had never dared to live outside of his father's warnings to be subservient to whitefellas who had the power of life and death over him. Maynard, Cooper and Ferguson offered him an alternative to this oppressive, soul-eating subservience. The dream of equality, of fairness, of justice, was something to think about as he was falling asleep, to the voice of Bessie Smith.

I want every bit of it,
Or none at all,
'Cause I don't like it second hand.

In searching for his sister, Sonny had made many inquiries with the Aborigines Protection Board and constantly sent letters that went unanswered, were returned, or were answered with form letters. One, dated 12 May 1920, said that Garibooli's whereabouts were unknown; Garibooli would have been sixteen.

Sonny persisted. Finally, in late 1929 a letter arrived, written from an unknown clerk who was either kind, forgetful or unfamiliar with departmental rules. "Parkes. With a Mr and Mrs Howard. Of Hill Street." Garibooli would be twenty-six.

* *goodoo* = cod

Sonny knew that in all likelihood his sister would no longer be there, but in his heart he clung to his hopes. Sonny used all his hard-earned savings to go to his sister. To Parkes. With the Howards. Of Hill Street. He bought a jacket — second-hand but it looked almost new — on the way, just in case. Even if she wasn't there, he reassured himself, perhaps there would be a clue as to where she was now.

Sonny enjoyed the train trip, buoyed by his hopes and remembering the long, often futile, waiting in the tall grass, with Booli talking of where they could go, wondering where the train would take them. And now, with the gentle jolts and the rhythmic clicks, he was moving closer and closer to her. If she had gone to Parkes — with no answer coming for so long it was hard to place all his faith in the Protection Board letter — she would have travelled on this line. As he looked out over the swaying wheat fields, the farmsteads and the clusters of gum trees, he wondered how it would have looked when his sister saw it through much younger eyes. He knew that she would not have felt the creeping excitement of anticipation he felt as he travelled; he knew that she would have been petrified. He shuddered, too familiar with the pain of the loss and the fear of the unknown, all associated with that day and the men dressed in black in the black car. The gilas bursting through the treetops had warned him. They had been right to be fearful.

He arrived at the tidy, white-painted train station and saw the big black letters: PARKES. His pocket nursed the letter as he looked along the streets for signs of her, imagining Garibooli's girlish figure on the shop verandahs, her shape just as he remembered it. He easily found the street and the imposing house, its dominating posture. Sonny went around to the back door and knocked. An elderly woman, unable to answer his inquiry ("Just new," she had kindly said), had gone to ask the mistress of the house.

Lydia Howard had, through curiosity, come to look at him. She peered into his face, drinking him in. "I'm sorry," she said sharply, "but I have no idea where she is. She left here years ago. Must be almost eight and nine years by now. And she never let us know where she went."

"Do you know anyone who might ...?" he started to ask.

"No," she cut him off. "No, I don't. I don't know anyone who would."

She remained unmoved by the visible disappointment of the man before her, noticed his hands clinging to the folded letter in his hand, relishing the crumbling face with its obvious similarities to another who still haunted her.

The trail was cold. Sonny trudged back to the station. He crushed the letter in his hand, pressing it hard as if it could capture the deep disappointment he felt. Even though he had thought that Booli would have moved on by now, it still came as a blow to find her gone. And he had at least expected to find a clue, the next piece of the puzzle. The stony face of Mrs Howard showed him how cold the trail was. He stopped at the Chinaman's shop to buy some bread and cheese. He looked around at the crowded shelves, the tins and bottles, crates and sacks. He was going to ask the man who wrapped his food and took the last of his money if he had known Garibooli, but he knew if he mentioned his sister's name at that moment he would break open and not be able to control his tears. Sonny waited at the platform for five hours and caught the train home.

He didn't stop looking or hoping that Garibooli would return. He continued to dream that they were never apart. In the songs that filled his head, he continued to find expression for the voids he felt but could not describe.

I ain't got nobody
Nobody
Ain't nobody,
Cares for me.

Lydia Howard had never forgotten Elizabeth. She did not need to be reminded by the man who looked like an older, darker, masculine version of her young, now departed, house maid on the back doorstep. Even when the body of Elizabeth Brecht lay buried under the frozen earth of Lithgow, more than twenty years after she had been in the house, she would be a shadow in Lydia's thoughts.

As the years passed, Lydia developed an all-consuming animosity towards the young girl, still youthfully svelte and freshly beautiful in her aging mind. Lydia had tried to conceive over and over again; each time her body proved stubbornly unyielding. The girl's pregnancy had told her that the barrenness was hers. And Edward had known this too. The knowledge burned inside her. Gripped by her rage she imagined her hands around Elizabeth's unblemished coffee-coloured throat, squeezing the girl as though she were plump fruit, until all her life-juices had gone.

So Lydia Howard, infertile, had lied to the man with those same eyes, same jaw-line, same curves of the lips, saying she knew nothing. Nothing of Elizabeth, of Grigor Brecht, or of the train ride they made to Lithgow. There was no one from that past in her house now to judge the heartlessness of her action.

Miss Frances Grainger was now Mrs Bill Harstead. She cheerfully announced her departure to Mrs Howard, her bags already packed and knowing that there was a dinner party to prepare for that very evening. Frances married a veteran of the Passchendaele and Somme. She had five children, all boys, including an Edward, a Bernard, and a Harold, to substitute for, though never replace, what had been taken from her in the Great War.

Solicitors tracked her down. She had run from the debts of her family, believing them to be poor. Her parents had been frugal and were constantly denying the family things that they claimed they could not afford. Their assets would not have amounted to much, but a wealthy aunt, her mother's sister, had also died in the influenza epidemic just after the war ended.

"Sorry, but with the confusion of the war ..." her Aunt's lawyers had told her. The war: interrupter of lives. Her own sufferings seemed just part of the sacrifice, part of the effort, and not comparable to the sacrifice her brothers and beloved fiancé had made.

Miss Grainger, as Mrs Harstead, ensured that her tables were set properly and decorated in accordance with the latest fashion of the day; she insisted that her sons display impeccable manners. The movements and mannerisms of the secretly despised Lydia Howard were now the models for her household and conduct. The servants were supervised with a sharp eye and a sharper tongue. Rather than teaching compassion, her own experience as housekeeper gave Frances an insight into the way in which the girls under her command might avoid hard work. The introduction of so many modern conveniences — everything was becoming electric now — made work for maids and cooks so much easier than it was during her time at the Howards'. She resented the ease such mechanical advances allowed and was suspicious of the idleness they invited.

Bill Harstead was still living the Great War. He had returned home thin, very nervous, suffering the effects of four years of lost sleep, and tormented by the discovery of an intestinal worm he had caught from drinking the water while fighting in the war. None of this legacy had been evident in lines on maps or names like Gallipolli and Ypres. Somehow, Frances found a macabre comfort in Bill's inability to let the war go. His nightmares woke her but his screams reminded her that the war was not forgotten.

And each cross, the driven stake of tidewood,
Bears the last signature of men,
Written with such perplexity, with such bewildered pity,
The words choke as they begin —

'Unknown seaman' — the ghostly pencil
Wavers and fades, the purple drips
The breath of the wet season has washed their inscriptions
As blue as drowned men's lips.

It was only as the country plunged into another war — again against the Huns — that she questioned what all the waste was for. She hated anything that made her feel as though her brothers and fiancé, the one she still loved most, had died in vain, and despised everything that their absence made her feel vulnerable to. Even amidst the upper-middle-class luxury she was now living in were evocations of the loss that still filled her heart.

14

1946

FOUR YEARS TO THE DAY after Elizabeth died, twenty-six- year-old Neil O'Reilly arrived in Venice.

Little Euroke, the lost son, had been adopted into a family in Gladesville, Sydney, as Neil Padric O'Reilly. He had grown up believing that he was Irish, a dark Celt — black hair and light, tanned skin. He had two other (adopted) siblings: a younger brother, Patrick, and a sister, Katie.

Neil loved the mystery of his salt-of-the-earth Irishman father who seemed to smell of history, a musty rotting-wood-and-lichen scent. His greeting of "Well, son" would cause Neil rippling pride. Neil would sit on a stool at the foot of his father's chair, his eyes wide, as his father talked of their Irish island home, a land once called Hibernia floating on the other side of the world. Even when Patrick and Katie would sit with them, Neil would make sure he sat closest to his father. His mother, a patient, slender woman with straight blonde hair cut with a fringe, folded washing or ironed clothes looking over and smiling as her husband told his stories to their brood.

In medieval Ireland, his father had told him, a bard was part of a respected profession, a literary tradition, strictly trained and serving the Prince. He read tales to Neil from old Irish books — *The Cattle Raid of Cooley*, *The Speckled Book*, *The Yellow Book of Lecan*, *The Book of Ballymote* and *The Book of*

Invasions. Passions and lusts had been faithfully recorded in each old tome and preserved within the walls of the monastery by the monks whose work during the dark ages had been responsible for preserving European histories and literatures within their portable libraries. The poets, his father told him, had plotted revenge on the monks who, for a time, had eclipsed them. Even when Neil couldn't understand the words, he loved the music of the language, the rolling sound of Gaelic names on his father's fluid tongue: Giolla Brighde MacNamee, Gofraidh Fionn O'Dalaigh, Eibhlin Dubh O'Connell, Eiléan Ni Chuilleanáin. Each name evoked a presence as mysteriously ephemeral as his father seemed to be during the storytelling.

His father's tales conjured for Neil a mystical land of mythical ancestors. They also brought home to him the contentment and sanctuary his mother and father gave him, Patrick and Katie. They nourished within Neil a sense of place and a sense of self: real, in Gladesville, and imaginary, in the green velvet land at the end of the sea.

As his father handed down his Irish tales, reading from William Wilde's *Irish Popular Superstitions* and the fairy tales of Oscar Wilde, Neil developed a sense of justice and fairness. Through these stories, Neil learnt that there was a moral to everything:

> *So the swallow flew over the great city, and saw the rich making merry in their beautiful houses, while the beggars were sitting at the gates. He flew into dark lanes, and saw the white faces of starving children looking out listlessly at the black streets. Under the archway of a bridge, two little boys were lying in one another's arms to try and keep themselves warm. "How hungry we are," they said. "You must not lie here," shouted the watchman, and they wandered out into the rain.*

"So, my son, what does this tell you?" would be the question at the end of every reading.

"Well, Father, I think it means that the rich must try to help the poor."

"That's right," his father said, beaming at Neil. "That's what it's saying. It's not right for some people to have lots of things and to give nothing to those who are poorer than them. It's also not right for people who have been fortunate to have no feeling for those who don't have as much as them."

As Neil grew older, his father would talk more and more about the legacy of oppression left by the English on their people: "How many years must you occupy something you have taken illegally before it becomes legitimate? And if it'll be legitimate after, say, three hundred, four hundred years, why not make it legitimate from the start? Take the land now, kill the people now, legally and by force since it is going to be legal in four hundred years?"

Neil did not know how to answer these questions, but came to understand that no answer was required from him.

"During the famine," his father would continue, "starving families would board themselves into their cabins so that their passing away wouldn't be seen. One-quarter of the population disappeared. One-quarter. And it could have been prevented. That, my son, is murder. Calculated murder. Not that the British would own up to it in those terms."

"That's like the story, isn't it father? The one about the rich people in the houses and the beggars outside." Neil would offer.

"That's right," his father would say, patting Neil's head with pride. "You know, after the famine, it was considered bad luck to speak Irish. How's that for killing the spirit of a people? Never forget, my son, that it was Irish resources — our land, labour and blood — that helped to build up England. And this wealth was then used to oppress us. But it's this suffering, my son, that creates people with strength and character."

"So the beggars at the gate are the ones with the character," Neil would add, looking hopefully at his father.

"The English," his father would relate while he stroked his son's head, "believed that everything Irish was inferior. So they tried to destroy it. They tried to destroy this culture" — his father was now clutching the book against his chest — "because, they said, it lacked richness. So the Irish poets began to write in the language of the oppressor. You can only imagine what was lost."

His father looked at the book lovingly and then, shaking it in Neil's direction, continued, "The bind for us Irish was that you were less than nothing if you were one of us, but if you tried to be anything like the English, they'd cut you down. Made people feel ashamed of who they were, it did."

"I'm not ashamed of being Irish," Neil would beam. His father would look at him with a serious face, "No son, I can see you aren't. But there's others were. Look at Emily Brontë. Her Dad was an Irishman as well but he Frenchified their name. As if there's less shame in being French than being Irish," he scoffed. "Made it into Cambridge, became a bleeding Tory and an Anglican to boot. A traitor to his country, he was. They had a secret history, those Brontës, and they were ashamed of it. Just look at *Wuthering Heights*. That Heathcliff was Irish."

His father would thumb through the well-read pages of the faded leather book and read out the phrases that made his argument:

"... I had a peep at a dirty ragged, black-haired child; big enough both to walk and talk ... yet, when it was set on its feet, it only stared round, and repeated over and over again some gibberish that no-one could understand."
"... all I could make out was a tale of his seeing it starving, and houseless, and as good as dumb in the streets of Liverpool ..."

"See, that's the mystery of Heathcliff's childhood. He's Irish. Shiploads of Irish immigrants landed in Liverpool, dying in the cellars and warehouses around the docks. There were many children there, thin as sticks, dressed in rags. That 'gibberish that no-one could understand' was Erse."

Neil would nod diligently in agreement. His father would move closer to him, the musty smell of well-fermented alcohol lurking between the two, and continue his nationalistic reflections.

"But see how the 'dirty, ragged, black-haired child' who spoke 'gibberish' is labelled a savage and a demon. It's suggested that he has a nature that cannot be tamed by kindness and this was simply a way of implying that he was Irish. See how the Lintons' dogs are set on Heathcliff when he dares to venture upon the Grange. Some would say that Heathcliff bit the hand that fed him and that the moral of the story is that if you are kind to savages like the Irish they'll not thank you. To my thinking, the moral would be that if you treat an Irishman like a dog, you'll get what's coming to you."

A curiosity about nature was fostered through the pastoral Irish tales Neil's father told him. He was fascinated with the process of metamorphosis: caterpillar to butterfly, tadpole to frog, eggs to bird, seed to plant. He was curious about how something tiny could create something large — a drop of water becoming an ocean, a grain of sand a desert. It was the hidden mysteries of living things he found most enigmatic — the pulsating cells under a microscope that showed the life within a life. Each blossom, each rock, filled him with one, inescapable demand: "Why?" He would find in the writing of da Vinci his own life motto: *Consistent questioning leads to the truth.*

Neil found in biological science a language for his fascination with nature. He found comfort in discovering clues that led to answers. He took refuge in the fact that the universe was a logical place, governed by laws, and that all could be revealed to him by determined observation and inquiry. In this belief of the ordered rationality of scientific fact he found the perfect counterbalance to the poet's world bequeathed to him by his father.

Neil was a second-year university student, majoring in biology and defining the world in his rational scientific manner, when his parents told him that he was adopted. His dark strain was not Celtic. He was, he was told, Italian. He saw himself become the Star-Child, the boy in Wilde's fairytale who had evoked such sympathy in Neil when his father had read him the story. Unwanted, he had been taken in by the O'Reillys:

> *... but it were an evil thing to leave the child to perish here in the snow, and though I am as poor as thou art, and have many mouths to feed, and but little in the pot, yet will I bring it home with me and my wife will have care of it.*

It was a metamorphosis, one identity inexplicably turning into another. He learned that he had parents who had nurtured him but whose blood and traditions had never been his. Yet he loved them all the more for the gravity and fear they expressed in telling him, their anxiety of losing him when he knew the truth as great as their belief that he should know it. Their love was more sustaining than the existence of a biological mother and father, with eyes like his, with lips like his, who were somewhere in the world. He wondered of them, this unknown man and woman, the sperm and egg, who had made him, who had given him blood but no identity. And, he wondered, like the Star-Child, whether he would also be disappointed if he met them:

> *"If in truth, thou art my mother," he said, "it had been better hadst thou stayed away, and not come here to bring me shame, seeing that I thought I was the child of some star, and not a beggar's child, as thou tellest me that I am. Therefor, get thee hence, and let me see thee no more."*

A thousand scenarios offered themselves: poor, young,

afraid, ashamed, scared, mistress, whore, nun, married, raped, rich, selfish. In "The Star-Child", as in any orphan's dream, the parents turn out to be a king and queen.

> *And the beggar-woman put her hand on his head and said "Rise", and the leper put his hand on his head and said "Rise," also. And he rose from his feet and looked at them and lo! they were a King and a Queen.*

Someone, somewhere had given Neil the genes and cells that determined what he would be. They had not wanted him, but others had. This thought balanced but didn't cancel itself out; the realities of being rejected and accepted co-existed; rationality and irrationality competed for dominance.

The more he thought about it, the more it made sense to Neil that he should be Italian, like da Vinci. This explained his fascination with and empathy for the scientist. Da Vinci had also been illegitimate. Neil would study his copy of *Madonna and Child with St Anne,* the two women, the two mothers, entwined in a warm, maternal benevolence. The Virgin seated in the lap of her mother, reaching out to the child Jesus, the angelic Anne tenderly gazing at Mary's neck, her daughter's arms outstretched, her dreamlike devotional face evident as she extends her hand to the cherubic child for an imminent embrace. Like da Vinci and the young king, Neil was a child with two mothers.

Would his real mother look at him the same way? Or had she never given him a thought? What part of her was now in him? Which genes did he carry? His genes, blood, cells all came from another source, one unknown to him. Yet, the words "My son", from a man not his father and who had given nothing of the organic stuff that made him, was still strong enough to make him feel like a whole person, to make him feel wanted and worthy. This emotion, this love, was hard to place within the structured analytic world of Neil's trusted science.

While the immediate effect of the knowledge of his adoption was a reaffirmation of his love for his adoptive parents and his gratitude for the life they had given him in the Sydney suburbs, the knowledge that he had a different genetic legacy, different parents, was a hairline fracture. Over time, it would shift and separate, rupture and part, pushing him from his stable place of identity, as though loosened from the grips of the family. He was unable to draw himself back together, to feel unbroken. From this divided place, he drifted. A restlessness infected him. Would love conquer, he wondered, or genes determine?

The day after he submitted his doctoral thesis, Neil left the family home in Gladesville and went on a search for himself. Italy, in the aftershock of the war, seemed as dazed, despondent and dislocated as he. Like him, it was trying to rebuild after breaking. Even though nature was more complex than he had supposed when he thought he could find truth in a set of laws, it was, he still believed, only through constant questioning that truth could be found. He travelled to find some connection to his new identity, feeling he would know it if he saw it. The thick voice of his father would often sound in his head:

Where'er I roam, whatever realms to see,
My heart untravell'd fondly turns to thee.

Nature gave strength to species that fitted their niches and were able to adapt to their environment, but he had no such feelings of belonging, could find no such place.

Italy was home to a cultural heritage as rich as the one his adoptive father had sought to hand him. In Venice, Neil felt he was no more stable than the gently rocking gondolas. Looking into the faces of passers-by — he could not even discern the tourists from the locals — and peering at the stones of the Piazza San Marco and the bricks of the Basilica di San Marco, no secrets were revealed, no answers harvested. So he travelled to Verona, home of Romeo and Juliet, a city on the traveller's route from Milan to Venice, with its Romanesque basilica of San Zeno Maggiore dating from the twelfth century and a Roman amphitheatre built in the first century and still used for concerts. He had now realised that "Italian" had more nuance and diversity than his stereotypes had allowed it. This town had been Etruscan, Roman, German, Venetian, French, Austrian and Italian. Like him, finally Italian.

And he went to Florence, the place where da Vinci had worked. If there was something to be found, surely a clue would be evident there. But, as he paced the streets and steps, he still could not find this unnamed thing he was looking for. It was not revealed to him between the Palazzo Vecchio and the Arno, in the Palazzo degli Uffizi, the sixteenth-century former government offices and law courts. It was not trapped in worn, cobbled stones, waiting for his gaze to release it.

As Neil stood on the Ponte Vecchio, standing since 1350 and the only bridge in Florence not destroyed in the recent inferno of Allied bombing, he could sense a certain history, but in all that richness, he could sense nothing of himself. No matter where he went, the buildings and pavements, after all they had borne witness to, refused to deliver the truth, his truth, about how all he was viewing was connected to him. Neil ended his travels just as exhausted and unsatisfied as when he had started. That his journey ended without conclusions only raised a persistent demand: "Di mi. Tell me," he would command the air.

Scientists modify their opinions, even desert their central thesis, if they are presented with sound contrary evidence. That is the way the scientific method is supposed to work. Some, however, cling to their old ideas, making themselves ineffectual, obsolete. They become too afraid to face the humiliating possibility of being wrong, having invested too much emotion and labour in their erroneous results. Creationists cling to their theories in the face of the revelations of Charles Darwin and Alfred Russell Wallace. Darwin had sought the truth; he had often openly acknowledged he was wrong when contrary evidence was presented to him.

Neil's beliefs were constantly challenged by the revelations of his heritage. The rational knowledge that culture was merely an environmental factor could not counter the emotional longings, his need to find "his place". It never conquered his need for something tangible, something that would replace the sound of his father speaking in Gaelic, telling him tales of mythical heroes and a land he had grown to love but had never seen and now had no connection to.

Where'er I roam, whatever realms to see,
My heart untravell'd fondly turns to thee.

Neil returned to his life in Sydney. In 1947, he started work as a lecturer in the same science department he had studied in. While he had chosen a career in the biological sciences, he no longer found comfort in the cold rationality of the scientific method. He watched the developments in his field of genetic biology over the years of his professional life, and the emerging dominant theories told him that his family tree, like all family trees, was rooted in Africa. This meant that Neil had African ancestors dating back two million years — another identity, long encoded in his genes, long running in his blood. The "African Eve theory" placed the ancestors of everyone — Celtic, Italian, Tongan or Chinese — back in Africa only a few thousand years ago. Using that theory, and the broadest definition of 'cousin', every marriage is a marriage between cousins. Neil speculated that, under that hypothesis, his adoptive parents were really just distant relatives.

Scientific reasoning, Neil realised, could not be his sole guide. He knew that even those who discover the rules or write the theories that provide the framework for analysis can't be held captive by the pure rationality of science. Charles Darwin had married his first cousin, Emma Wedgewood, even though he was afraid that his children might suffer from ill-health as products of such close relatives. He worried that his genetic material had not been given proper opportunity to compete with stronger genes in the gene pool. Yet he loved Emma deeply, adored her, admitted that she helped make him a success, and he hated being away from her. His scientific rationality, his understanding of genetics and inter-breeding, could not conquer the love he felt for his wife, did not stop his heart from feeling the way it did.

Where'er I roam, whatever realms to see,
My heart untravell'd fondly turns to thee.

One encounter, one thought, haunted Neil, remaining with him all his adult life. He had been walking through the park opposite Central Station in Sydney in the early afternoon of the last shopping day before Christmas. He was laden with wrapped presents from Mark Foy's department store as he walked the path through the shade that protected him from the summer sun of 1953.

The park always made him feel nervous. He pitied the Aborigines in their drunken clusters, and he thought once more of the tales his father had read to him about the beggars at the gate of the wealthy town. As he strode through the tree-filled park, his eyes locked with one of the men, his dirty grey pants and dark green football socks the only clothes he had on. His hair was long and curly and matted with leaves. He was lying on the ground and looking at a brown paper bag that was wrapped around a bottle. As Neil walked past him, the black man looked up at him and continued to hold his gaze. In that look there was some kind of recognition. Somehow the man, drunk on the grass, seemed to know him, to know his mystery, as though Neil could have been one of them.

This unnerved Neil. The thought was too shocking, too shameful to him. To him, the extinction of the Aborigines was inevitable. With their bottles of acidic wine in brown paper bags and their dirty-rag clothes, they would disappear.

He could see this dwindling race with their lack of flexibility and inability to adapt when unfavourable changes occurred.

Darwin had seen it in South America, in the extermination of the Jews throughout Europe in the centuries before the Holocaust and in colonised people all over the world. He had been disturbed by the brutality of the genocide that he had seen, but he put it in context. Neil, too, believed this evolution to be natural and could no more be mourned than the millions of species that had already disappeared from the earth. The strong devoured the weak; one makes room for the other to grow. It was the natural order, the struggle for life. Neil believed that mild-mannered Darwin could have possessed no desire to do these remnants of a race any harm; he just sought to understand them. It was beyond his control that his ideas were used for cruel purposes: cold, rational, scientific fact.

Even though, as Neil knew from the findings in his field, we are all distant cousins, he needed to show that he was not one of those fading remnants of a dying race. It was as his father had quoted Oscar Wilde: "The only thing that sustains one through life is the consciousness of the immense inferiority of everybody else."

Neil had no proof that he was Italian, that he was heir to da Vinci, Puccini and Etruscan villagers, other than the word of his adoptive mother and father. He wanted something that he could hold up to them, those Aborigines in the park, that drunk lying on the grass, who thought they knew him, and say, "I'm not one of you. I'm not a beggar at the gate."

Later in life, amongst the leafy streets of Paddington, established in his own family home, he would peer into the fair, freckled faces of his children (some so like him, some stamped with the features of his wife, Eliza) to see his Italian lineage. The path to truth, Neil would discover, could be travelled in vain. He found nothing amongst Italian words, food, custom and culture that made him feel the passion and pride that his father's Irish tales and nationalistic reminiscing had given him. And he found nothing that could reconnect him to that Irish tradition once the knowledge he had no blood connection in him severed his ownership of it. From that instability, that question mark, he embraced the nearest thing he did know. He avoided inflicting this pain of the uncertain and irrational onto his children, telling them only of their Irish ancestry as though dark Celtic blood had been passed down to them.

15

1960

CAROLE DYBALL ENJOYED the crisp Canberra mornings. The frosty air bit into her lungs; the leaves had already changed colour. She inhaled the coldness, as though it were life-giving. Carole had been in the small, tree-lined city for only a few months, long enough to find her way around efficiently and to blend into her surroundings. Her attempts at anonymity were undermined by the sharpness of her navy-blue uniform and appealing features. With her creamy, almond-coloured skin and sporty blonde hair, she'd bloomed since she had joined the Women's Royal Australian Navy Service and moved first to Melbourne, then to the national capital. She had embraced the eastern states, preferring the industry, variety and progressiveness to the insular life of Fremantle. The freshness of her new career, surroundings and experiences gave her complexion a soft glow that enhanced the easy kindness of her face.

Carole caught the shuttle bus around the base. She had shifted towards the window when a man, also in a navy uniform, seated himself beside her.

"Cold today," he smiled, crossing his arms with a mock shudder.

Carole was wary of men who grinned at her. She turned her attention to this dark-featured man now sitting next to her. "Quite," she answered, as cool as the air around her. She began to soften with inner warmth as she studied the man's face more closely.

"Where are you off to?"

"That's classified," she replied, smiling shyly.

He grinned back, his eyebrows arched, "You mean that I am not authorised to know? You obviously don't know who I am. I'm Bob. Bob Brecht."

"I'm Carole, Carole Dyball. I'm very pleased to meet you Bob-Bob Brecht." She was unsure why she was so quick to relax with him.

"No. I can assure you that the pleasure is all mine, Carole." He liked the lightness of the sound of her name. "So, do you like dancing?"

"No. I don't like dancing."

"Hmmm. Like to keep off your feet, eh? Well, you must like the pictures then. Don't have to dance through them. Just have to sit."

"Yes, I like the pictures. I like them a lot. But it does depend on what's showing. I don't say yes to just anything."

"No, that's wise," joked Bob, enjoying watching the red blush as it crawled across Carole's face as she realised how he was twisting her remark.

"I just meant," she said quickly, "that *The Grass is Greener* is playing at the moment and I would like to see that."

"Ah, a Cary Grant film. I'm guessing you're a fan."

She smiled, relieved that he was not going to tease her further and returned his gaze, taking in his high forehead and the small dark curls that lapped around it. His mouth was firm, his chin well crafted. "I've been a fan since before I can remember."

"Well, he has been making movies since before you were born."

"Yes, since 1932. *This Is the Night*. Over eight years before I was born. Anyway, Mr Bob-Bob Brecht," Carole rose, "it has been nice talking with you but this is my stop."

"I'm getting off here too."

She shot him a skeptical glance; this time it was she who arched her eyebrow.

"I've missed my stop talking to you," he said with mock indignation, "I should have gotten off two stops ago. It's your fault. You distracted me with all this talk about Cary Grant so now I'll have to walk back and I've already told you that I'm finding it very cold today."

Carole was used to being flirted with and had become quite adept at dodging charming talk and overfriendly gestures in the three years she had been a member of the armed services. This time she felt flattered and enjoyed the attentions of this angelic, dark man with the shy, boyish grin. She sensed a softness in him and so agreed to meet him on Sunday afternoon and go to the matinee to watch the Cary Grant film she'd already seen three times.

Carole should have been a boy, her father had once told her, as should her older sister, Margaret. With Carole, her father had been so sure that he had filled out the registration forms with "Carl Edmund Dyball" before he had seen her. He then had to return to shout abuse at the Registrar for the mistake the next day.

Carole's mother had all her faith in life squeezed out of her by her bullying husband, Reginald, whom she married when she fell pregnant to him. The marriage had never been a happy one for Ruth Dyball. In the early days of her union, after Margaret's birth, she had attempted to run away from him, but without money, family support, or a skill — and with a child to look after — she had to return, defeated. It was a humiliation that hung between her and her husband for the remainder of her life. His taunting of her failure to escape, of her captivity, intensified her suffering. Her isolation and imprisonment would be mocked by her husband's self-congratulatory smirks. She would distract herself with her housework, her children, her thirty-six cats and her Catholicism.

Since Reginald was a butcher, it was never a problem to feed the children and the cats. He had settled them on a large plot of land on the outskirts of Fremantle. The house stood amongst vacant blocks and large open spaces, and this only heightened Ruth's feelings of loneliness and isolation. As the years passed by, and her daughters grew up and left home, the neighbourhood built up. But, rather than feeling connected to its swelling population, she felt increasingly claustrophobic and trapped.

Carole grew up living a double life. There were the times when it was daylight, during which she enjoyed the freedom of the wide fields where bark could be stripped and rocks overturned to reveal tiny creatures. There were the compliant cats in dolls' dresses, whose ears she would peg together so she could put little hats on their heads and pretend that they were attending a tea party. With the cats, cows, chickens, goat, and the usual array of sick birds and ensnared bugs, Carole would make hospital beds and play doctor to real and imagined wounds and illnesses.

Being interested in boys, Margaret disdained Carole's play, but Carole didn't need the companionship of a disapproving sister while she had the world around her to explore, her menagerie of animals — trapped and tamed — to heal. She had her imagination for company.

The other side of Carole's life unfolded in the evenings, after the sun left the sky, when her companion cats were banished from the house and her father was home. He was the only fear she knew as a child. It was a terror that made her stutter. Reginald worked all day at the meatworks and when he was irritated he would come home and relieve his aggression with the slap of his belt. He lashed out when dissatisfied, at furniture, at Carole, her sister and her mother. His anger left red welts and marbled bruises on their arms and legs. Carole quietly hoped she would be ignored, especially when eclipsed by the older, more rebellious Margaret. Most times she could escape detection but would, on occasion, draw her father's ire by not speaking or by stuttering with nervousness.

Carole could not understand Margaret's fascination with boys. To Carole, all men were like her father, who yelled at her and beat her and left her shaking with fear when he shouted at her for being "stupid" and "a fool". When furious, he would grab at his belt with one hand while he held her hair with the other and she would feel the sharp whip of leather against her skin. She would say to herself that the more she knew about men, the more she liked cats.

She would suffer his rage if she failed to complete a chore to his satisfaction or if he was angry with her mother if she cried. And he was so unpredictable. Carole would freeze after accidentally dropping a bottle of milk, expecting him to shout abuse at her, but instead he would say with a laugh, "You know what they say, no use crying over spilt milk." But then when she dropped a glass of juice, he yelled at her for being wasteful and not appreciating the cost of things and sent her out to stand in the cold night air to reflect upon her "selfishness". Instead, she stood in the dark on the back step and puzzled about the difference between spilling milk and spilling squeezed oranges.

Her father embodied the night, her mother the day. If her father's presence in the evenings frightened her, the freedom of her rustic playground and the safety of her mother's presence ensured happiness during her childhood days. Her other escape, her only other point of reference for the wider world, was the moving pictures.

She had first seen Cary Grant in *Every Girl Should Be Married* when she was just eight years old. In the darkened cinema, Carole felt, for the first time, attraction to a man. She was entranced by the way he looked, transfixed by his self-assured manner and acid wit. Her infatuation grew when she saw *Room for One More,* in which Grant played a devoted family man and husband. As the antithesis of her father, Grant was her ideal. She knew that he would never lash at her with a belt or yell at her when she stuttered. Since then, she had seen every new film he'd been in, watching each new feature once a week while it screened at the theatre. Except *An Affair to Remember*, which she saw ten days running, crying at the ending each time.

Carole read everything she could about Cary Grant. She saw him as a man who hid secrets behind the polished sheen of his on-screen charm. Born in Bristol to a working-class family, Grant's father was a trouser-presser given to murderous rages and insisted that his wife never speak to others at parties. Carol could empathise with the image of the cowering child and the silently suffering mother and wife. Even when Hitchcock brought out the brooding, bleak side of Grant's character — as Roger Thornhill in *North by Northwest* (the kind of man who made women who didn't know him fall in love with him) and Devlin in *Notorious* — the strange, shadowy angles of the camera revealed a confident, worldly charm. To Carole, Grant was a man who could understand the split between her own night and day worlds.

Margaret left home when she became pregnant to her boyfriend Darren. When Margaret announced she was departing, her father raged, calling her names that made Carole blush. Margaret had told her that marrying Darren was a way of escaping their father, but to Carole, it seemed like her sister was leaving one prison and entering another. Carole had never liked Darren, finding him too confident, too slick. He winked at her and called her "Doll" while he waited for Margaret to finish getting ready to go out. Carole couldn't keep from staring at his shoes; they were too shiny. Carole, in contrast to her sister, kept her distance from men who tried to court her, fearing that she would be suffocated by marriage just as her mother had been. Having learnt her mother's lesson, Carole didn't wish to have another man standing over her, abusing her and making her feel trapped.

Carole wanted to be a vet. She could then do what made her happy — looking after animals — and be able to escape her father. She planned her High School studies around this goal, but in her second-last year her father stopped her. He had allowed her to begin, believing she would fail. Sensing her success drawing close — with good grades and glowing reports — he forbade her to continue. No pleas, tears or ultimatums could move his iron will and Carole was transferred into the subjects required for secretary school. Not even her school's administration could persuade her father to rethink his actions. Carole knew from the lifetime of sarcastic comments directed at her mother that there was no escape from her father's demands and any opposition to his decisions only made him more unwilling to compromise.

As Carole cried for her lost dream, locked in her room and surrounded by the memorabilia of her childhood, she looked at the photograph of Cary Grant on her mirror taken when he was filming *Destination Tokyo*. Grant was dressed in a naval uniform, his eyes seeming to focus on the inner thoughts that preoccupied him, his hand clasping binoculars. His wedding ring sat prominently on his hand.

Cary Grant had always offered her an escape from her home life, even if it were only for the hours she watched him on the screen. Now he gave Carole an idea of how she could escape permanently. There was something in the reflective resolve of Grant in the naval uniform that drew her in.

Carole had older studio shots in her scrapbook from Grant's earlier films. In three he was dressed in Air Force uniforms. He was a member of the Royal Flying Corp in *The Eagle and the Hawk* in 1932, a blinded pilot in *Wings in the Dark* in 1935 and a French flyer in *Suzy* in 1936. All were made before Carole was born. He had, Carole recalled, had donated his fees for *Philadelphia Story* and *Arsenic and Old Lace* to the war effort. He had flown to London to ask what he could do to help the Allied cause, only to be told that he should return to Hollywood "and carry on doing what you do best". The US government decided that he was more valuable to them as an actor than a soldier. Grant was disappointed, but had said: "Wherever Uncle Sam orders my utilization to the best purposes, there I will willingly go, as should every other man. I feel that Uncle Sam knows best."

Carole applied to join the Women's Royal Australian Navy, the WRANS, in 1957. She passed the admission test and was accepted. It was then she discovered that she would need her parents' consent since she was only seventeen. Her father refused and Carole already knew that it was beyond her power to change his mind.

Then, unexpectedly, her father's sister arrived. Aunt Beatrice saw her brother only on rare occasions. In the quiet of the afternoon, she spoke with her brother behind the closed door of the lounge room. Carole and her mother sat silently in the kitchen and heard the muffled and heated voices.

"How did she know of Father's refusal?" Carole whispered.

"I wrote her," her mother replied, her brow furrowed as she looked at her wedding ring. "I should have thought to do it when he made you change your subjects. I'm sorry."

"Don't be sorry, Mum," Carole said as she touched her mother's hand, knowing how much courage such a secret, subversive act would take. "Thank you."

"Let me make a cup of tea," her mother replied, rising and releasing herself from Carole's touch.

Carole never did discover what transpired in the meeting with Aunt Beatrice to make her father change his mind. She would forever wonder what words were used, what argument presented, that could make him budge from his bullish stance. She marvelled that there might have been magic words or phrases that could have prevented straps across thighs and arms. She would never know that it wasn't the power of language but the power of money that had secured her freedom.

Saying farewell to her mother and father on the docks as she set sail for Victoria, Carole watched as other girls, making the same trip as her, said tearful and loving goodbyes to their families. Her father's parting words, loud enough to cause others to turn and stare, were, "You'll be back in six months, pregnant." Her mother wept for the freedom her daughter had found and with something that bordered on envy.

Carole had scored so highly on her entrance examination that she was to be trained for intelligence work. She was sent to Melbourne where she shared a large house with twelve other girls. Her gentleness made others instantly feel comfortable with her, but her shyness and inexperience in social situations meant she kept aloof and apart from the others and from their jealousies and intrigues. She preferred to read on the nights she did not go out to the pictures.

While other girls struggled with the strict regime of the Navy, Carole found the discipline more relaxed and lacking in the night-time terror of her previous home life. She relished the stimulation, challenge and responsibility of her work, and a financial independence she had never imagined. With a good salary and with the Navy taking care of many of her expenses — accommodation, clothing and food — Carole was able to save most of her pay cheque. She sent money to her mother, but her mother's letters revealed that her father confiscated it; she then reverted to sending gifts, things that her mother could never afford for herself — a velvet coat, French perfume, a floral scarf, leather gloves.

Her mother's fate with an unloving husband remained a warning to Carole and she continued to avoid the attentions of the men around her. She had expected to be constantly repelling the attractions of men in such a male-dominated quarter of a male-dominated world. Instead, she found that her work kept her mainly in the company of other women. They informed her which of her superiors had wandering hands and she felt fortunate that she had been able to avoid any 'incidents'.

In Melbourne, and later in Canberra, Carole still defined men by her experiences with her father. She feared that, underneath the exteriors of the men who took her to dinner and the movies, there lay someone brutal. Each date presented the threat of the trap that had closed around her mother. That was, until the bus trip with Bob Brecht.

There was something in the dark aspect of this Bob Brecht — she had noticed it as soon as her eyes rested on his face — that reminded her of the unassuming gallantry and gentlemanly softness of her matinee idol. He was the kind of man she felt she would be safe with, a man so unlike her father.

As Bob Brecht walked along the edge of the road that threaded through the naval base, he reflected on the woman he had just met, the woman who had agreed, against his expectation, to meet him on Sunday. Her soft, crisp "Quite", her educated accent and tender, gorgeous face had melted him. He felt an exhilaration and anticipation he had not felt since he was a young child in the Boy's Home and was about to kiss Annabel Stewart behind the chicken coop.

16

1943

THE STRONGEST MEMORY Bob Brecht had of his mother was a citrus scent, crisp and tart. Their family home had two large lemon trees in its back yard and his mother had used the fruit for cooking and the juice to clean bench tops and clothes. The odour from the fruit had clung to his mother, lingering in her soft recesses.

Even after she passed away, Elizabeth's lemon scent remained in the air, ghosting her, and through the aroma, her second youngest could sense her close, as though she were about to re-enter the room.

Bob was five when his mother died. His eldest sister, Patricia, then seventeen, was working as a seamstress in a nearby shop. Thomas had left long ago to join the war and not been heard from since. At the funeral, Patricia had clutched Bob, a quiet bundle of a child, pliable in his numbness and confusion at the changes occurring around him. Danny, then four years old, clung to Daisy, a precocious eight, who was trying hard to act as guarded as the older children. William stood aloof, strangely quiet. In the thawing early spring of 1943, all around seemed lifeless and empty.

A large-boned, dark-skinned boy, William started to gather up his shirts, trousers, winter coat and boots. The other children watched him pack and leave; the determined look on his face was enough to keep them silent. They knew this mood of bottled anger all too well. His decision to leave left Patricia an acute sense of abandonment and also a feeling of betrayal. She would now be the eldest child, left to care for the three youngest. She constantly tried but was never able to reach out and connect with William, had been unable to free him from the thoughts that spiralled him into sullen moods. She had seen his tenderness, how docile he could be when he was released, but only Daisy with her smile, her cajoling and her teasing, could bring him back from his thoughts. He would lift her up to carry her on his shoulders or tickle her until she begged him to stop, and his spirits would rise.

"Don't leave us," Daisy pleaded with him as he zipped up his bag with finality.

"Princess, I have to go. I'm no good to you here. I need to do this," he said, pausing to look at her. "I'll do this and then I'll come and get you."

"No. No. You're wrong." She tried again. "I need you."

William hesitated for the shortest moment.

"No," he asserted again. "I must. One day, you'll understand."

William's large frame assisted him in appearing a supposed eighteen years rather than his bare seventeen, and he enrolled to fight in the war. His brothers and sisters could not know that their mother's funeral was a final farewell to their troubled brother too.

To Grigor, the children were a reminder of Elizabeth; their distant murmuring began to grow louder. They haunted his house and formed part of the modest collection of personal belongings his wife had left behind.

He dealt with the loss of his wife the best he could, grieving in his own way. He threw her clothes into the hearth fire. He destroyed her trinkets — cheap glass vases, a polished brown seashell and an imitation ivory brush and mirror set; he threw other possessions away — a jade brooch, a silver hair-clip and a piece of emerald-green and gold Chinese cloth. His anger gave way to the bitterness of losing the focus of his affection and love, the centre of his tenderness. It hardened him against a world that he had already believed to be riddled with callousness and unfairness. He reached for the one thing that he could find solace in: the slow-warming comfort of liquor.

Grigor continued to cast an ominous shadow over the house, crushing everything lemon and light. He would arrive home late at night smelling of the sugary pungency of strong spirits, yelling at any child who was the cause of discomfort or a reminder of his loss. When things were not done as Elizabeth had done them, it was a reminder to him that she was gone. Through his shouting and raging he did not notice his children's terror, did not sense that they grieved as he did nor understand that they too had lost something that intricately and crucially made up their lives.

Patricia, now eighteen, was determined to look after Daisy, Bob and Danny, to make sure they didn't lose anyone else. She juggled the work she did mending and altering clothes for the nearby laundry and the increased domestic duties to try and replace their mother in some small way. She did so until, one day, Mrs Crawford from the Aborigines Protection Board knocked curtly on the front door. The agency had been alerted about the Brecht family by a neighbour who had been concerned about the violent sounds of arguing that came from the house in the late hours of the night. Mrs Crawford would normally have retreated from a family where a white father was in charge, but Grigor, in a sombre hangover of grog, grief and spent rage, stared distractedly at the fire as she spoke.

When she finished, he continued to look at the fire, watching as the logs turned into blackened charcoal. "I cannot look after them. Take them."

"Your eldest daughter is too old ..."

"But you can take the other three."

It was arranged that they would be put in a church-run orphanage.

From the next room, Patricia strained to hear, listening as her father, inert and indifferent, destroyed their family, giving her brothers and sister up without a fight. She clung to the wooden door frame as she heard his words, "I cannot look after them. Take them."

Grigor withdrew into himself, his alcohol and his frayed ideals, becoming obsessed with the propaganda to arouse fears amongst Australians through scare-mongering about socialism. He predicted the upcoming attempts to ban his Party. It was simply history repeating itself, he concluded, seeing himself re-entering a period laced with those same sentiments that had seen Marx's ostracism, vilification and persecution. Grigor had fevered meetings with his comrades at the Lithgow branch of the Communist Party where political discussion focused on the surging tide of hysteria directed toward organised workers. They saw the rise of Robert Menzies as a bad omen. In seeking to hold back the wave of anti-Communist fervour, Grigor found a crusade to distract him from his memories of Elizabeth.

The departure of her family extinguished life in the house for Patricia. She harboured a deep resentment against her father who had given them away so easily and who had made no attempt to prevent her move to the city. She had written in response to advertisements in the Sydney papers and found herself a job as a seamstress.

As she packed her suitcase, she recalled William packing his bags and herself tearfully having to pack bags for Bob and Danny while Daisy chose the dresses and toys that she wanted. Now it was her turn to take what she wanted from this old life and leave her mother's house.

The fury in her brewed and she intended to tell her father how he had abandoned them, how despicable he was to have allowed three of his children to grow up in an institution. But as she faced him sitting in his armchair, her packed case in one hand, the other cradling the jade brooch that she had retrieved from the trash after one of his tantrums had seen it tossed away. Instead of shouting what she felt struggling within her, she could only utter stonily, "Mother told me once that nothing matters more than family. It will be too late when you realise she was right."

17

1943

BOB DID NOT BELIEVE, when he first entered the children's home, that he and Danny would be there for long. At times he thought it was just like in one of his dreams when something bad happened, like a tooth falling out. It felt real, but then he would wake up and realise that it was just imaginary and feel a flood of relief as his tongue touched the teeth firmly planted in his mouth. That, he thought, was what this ward, these sobbing boys, was going to turn out to be. It would disappear when he awoke and be replaced by something strong and reliable, like teeth.

Bob was only six when he was taken from his father's house in Lithgow and placed into the children's home with his younger brother and sister. Although freed from the fear of their volatile father, the younger children missed the attentions of their older siblings, especially Patricia's devotion and her ability to comfort and organise.

Bob and Danny were placed in a large ward that, even with almost thirty boys crowded together, seemed cold. The night air was filled with the sound of muffled sobs. During their first nights in the new surroundings, Bob had crept into Danny's bed when he heard his younger brother sobbing. Danny would cling to him and Bob would wait until he heard Danny's light snoring before slipping out of the warm sheets to cross the cold stone floor to his own bed. As he held his younger brother close, he experienced the gratification that comes with the ability to reassure someone helpless and in need. It eased his own suffering to know that he had to be strong for Danny, who was more frightened and fragile than he.

The adjustment to a new life was hardest for Daisy, placed in the girl's home across the road from Bob and Danny. She had a strict routine like the boys: dress, check beds, help younger ones dress, inspection for school, prayers, church services, meals, duties, lessons, dinner, bed. All announced by the ringing of a bell. No one explained to Daisy what the routine was and she was scolded and ridiculed until she learned the rules and procedures. This was vastly different from the family freedom she had known, from the adoration of her brothers, especially William, who would bounce her on his knee and bring her presents of paper dolls and paste jewellery. He called her "Princess". Daisy saw her father as the lesser evil for when she was living with him at least there were times when she was beyond his gaze and, with her brothers and sister, she could do as she pleased.

Bob and Danny would see Daisy at the nearby school each day. At first, the three huddled in the playground, clinging to the familiarity of each other. But slowly, Daisy, drifted off into her own social circles.

Bob found, over time, that other boys welcomed his good-natured camaraderie. A small group — Thomas Riley, Frank Phillips, Charles Wainwright and Benny Miller — gathered around him. Danny found it hardest to make friends and tagged quietly along after his older brother. He dreaded leaving for class when he would be separated from Bob, and was looking forward to the hour when he would see his brother again.

Bob, always bright, attacked his studies and began to excel at school, but was never more than mediocre with sport. Clumsy at cricket, he never dropped a catch nor hit a century. Playing football, he could score a try as easily as miss a tackle or fumble a pass. He was small-framed and fast, but this was neither asset nor liability. His average ability ensured a stable popularity. Despite their strictness, the discipline of rules appealed to Bob. He felt secure knowing what was good and what was bad, and he developed a dislike for unreliability and irregularity. Against these standards, his father became a disappointment.

Every Sunday, after the church service, all the children would sit on the stone wall that surrounded the orphanage and wait for visitors. It was a way of passing time, time that was slipping away in weeks and months. At first their father came to visit every second weekend, but as the year stretched out his visits became sporadic. As the winter chill arrived, only Danny remained atop the wall waiting as parents or relatives plucked off the luckier children. He was convinced that if he went off to play like Bob and Daisy did, his father would turn up and, unable to find them, leave.

Bob preferred to have no expectations and to just respond to good things when they happened. He thought that Danny set himself up to have his feelings crushed, especially now the weekends of dashed hopes were becoming more and more frequent. He tried to encourage Danny to join him in a game of cards or cricket, but the younger brother was determined to watch for their father. With this new toughness, Bob finally surrendered his dream that his mother would return, walk into his classroom, claiming him as her own for all his classmates to see. He understood; he was not going to wake up to the solid reassurance of teeth. It had been hard to abandon any hope of her return. There was far less to lose if his father never came back — giving up on him was easier.

As their father's visits came further and further apart, their eldest sister, Patricia, began to visit on the odd weekend, rewarding Danny's patience. She would arrive in her neat, fashionable hand-made clothes, bringing small treats of penny candy and sometimes books — *Treasure Island, Robin-*

son Crusoe and *Frankenstein.* Coming from Sydney, it would take her all morning to ride the train and walk from the station. She would have two hours with her family before having to return. Bob loved the smell of her perfume, and her gentleness. He was infatuated with her dark eyes and soft mouth. She gave the whispered promise of a warmth that he thought had died with his mother. Danny would chatter excitedly when she arrived. But as the first hour stretched to the second, he would grow silent and glum. When Patricia would announce it was time to leave, he would cling to her, pleading, "Don't leave me." With Danny's small hands clutching her, Patricia would be reminded of Daisy's last plea to William. She longed to be able to take Danny, Bob and Daisy with her, to have had the money to give them a home again.

During these visits, Daisy remained aloof. Sometimes she only spent an hour with Patricia. She would eye her older sister's clothes accusingly and under her gaze Patricia would feel a flood of guilt. Daisy would make demands — for new shoes, leather gloves, a silk scarf — items Patricia could not afford. And when the elder sister toiled to make or buy something to satisfy Daisy's wishes, her gift would be met with criticism or indifference.

Daisy's anger towards her stung Patricia as much as Danny's pleas. And she could not help but be reminded again of William when she felt the wrath of her sister. Patricia decided that, unlike her missing brother whom she could never reach, she would succeed at getting Daisy to love her, she would lift Daisy's anger and allow her to be happy again.

Bob always knew he was different, that there was a mysterious ingredient he shared with his siblings and mother; he remembered his mother's dark skin and even darker eyes. At first this being different was an instinct. Then it started to take form in teasing words — gentle from friends, harsh from others — and names that made him wince, even when said playfully.

On one of his increasingly rare weekend visits, Bob asked his father why he and his brothers and sisters were dark. His father's face clouded at the question and he was silent as he thought about an answer until asserting firmly, "As far as I am concerned, your mother was as white as everyone else."

Bob never mentioned the subject again to his father and from that moment on he knew there was no easy escape from his ancestry. To those jibes made to his face he would respond, with the same terseness his father had used, "I am as white as you are."

The nagging intuition consolidated into something nameable. His Grade Six teacher had been talking about the bravery of the men who had discovered the Blue Mountains. Lawson, Wentworth, Blaxland were names that still dotted the area in which he lived. It was "the natives" who had tried to stop them. All eyes turned to Bob Brecht. He felt their stares boring into his brown skin with hatred. It was he who had tried to prevent the explorers from crossing the mountains. It was he who had killed white settlers. Bob reddened, he willed himself to disappear, wishing himself as white as thick smoke. He wished that "the natives" had not been troublesome, that they had been helpful, or just disappeared, rather than causing him this public shame.

He came to dread history classes. He would scan through the assigned texts to see what nasty revelations might be made, to find what accusations might be levelled at him: "the natives", "the blacks" and "the Aborigines". When, in Grade Eight, he was issued F.L.W. Wood's *A Concise History of Australia*, he was relieved that it began with the way the Greeks and Romans hypothesised about the existence of a southern land. The text then told of the Dutch who, upon arriving on its shores, declared that there was "no sign of gold or spices or civilized inhabitants" in Australia.

The Aborigines were not mentioned until the landing of

the First Fleet. But, Bob noted with relief, they quickly vanished.

> The *Endeavour* anchored about 2 p.m., and the Englishmen watched the natives cook their fish for dinner. Then a party of 30 or 40 rowed off towards the land. As they drew near, two natives seized their spears and prepared to resist the landing party. After a quarter of an hours fruitless parley, the natives threw their spears at the boats, and the Englishmen fired muskets loaded with small shot. The natives ran away, and the party landed in peace.

Bob found only one other reference in his book to Aborigines, and that was in relation to something called the Tasmanian Black War. Here, too, Aborigines showed their propensity to disappear:

> In 1830, therefor, [Governor Arthur] made an effort to round up the natives, but they slipped through the fingers of soldiers and settlers. The white men complained that a native could run like a dog, and, if he chose, look just like a tree stump. Arthur's black drive cost £30,000, and 3,000 men took part in it. But they caught only a woman and a small boy, who had been asleep under a log. The Governor therefore very sensibly gave the work to men who really understood the natives, in particular George A. Robinson and John Batman. These men collected the remnants of the natives — fewer than 200 — and settled them on Flinders Island. There they rapidly died off, and Tasmania was left to the white men.

His class would not study this "Black War", but the knowledge of it left Bob with one nagging question: if the Aborigines all disappeared, why were his brothers and sisters here? Since his father was white with a German surname, Bob figured, he was only half-Aboriginal. But when the children in his class had stared at him accusingly, the white part of him seemed to have vanished from their view, as though Europeans could disappear like Aborigines were supposed to.

Bob decided that he just needed to make the European

part more prominent, make it reappear, and then he would no longer feel guilty or ashamed. He needed to embrace, he thought, the things that white people seemed to admire so much. Bob found these virtues in the story that had been the source of his embarrassment and ridicule — the crossing of the Blue Mountains. Bob reread the story that his history book told:

> They kept to the right ridge until almost at the end of their journey, and so found a way through the mountain barrier. It was desperately hard work. They had to fight their way through the undergrowth and over rough, dry country ... On the 28th day they were on Mount York. Here they had lost the main ridge, but fortunately, at this particular point, there was a way down into the valley ... They had crossed the region of barren sandstone and found the fertile, well-watered country which lay beyond ... So the little party turned and tramped back towards Sydney. They were tired and ill from hardship, but triumphant, for they had overcome an obstacle which for more than twenty years had defied the bravest and most skilful explorers in the country.

W.C. Wentworth, Bob would learn, had done other things to bring civilisation to Australia. He had advocated trial by jury, established the *Australian* in 1824, promoted freedom of the press, and insisted on self-government. Born in the colony, he was a cattle farmer by the age of eighteen, later a successful lawyer, an orator who could often carry an audience with him and convince them almost against their own will. By 1836, Wentworth was one of the richest squatters in the colony and, to protect the rights of those, like him, who were trying to make the country prosper, had attempted to draw up a "Squatters Constitution", a version of which became law in 1855.

These achievements seemed to be the sorts of deeds that spelt success for white people, for people not stained with black like him. If he'd been the heir of an explorer or a squatter, a descendant of W.C. Wentworth, his classmates would have looked at him admiringly, perhaps enviously.

The recent war, the one that was ending when the Brecht children entered the orphanage, had renewed the hatred of Germans that had been simmering since the Great War. "Brecht" gave Bob the added shame of association with another loathed presence, but irritated him more because the German name meant nothing to him. His father had an accent but never spoke a word of German or talked about his homeland. Bob knew no German other than "Kraut", which he thought was the German word for "German". And although he could not find Germany on a map, he had two brothers who had disappeared to fight the Germans and never returned.

People never noticed Bob's whiteness unless it meant something bad, like Germans. However, his name could be easily forgiven. Thomas, Frank, Charles or Benny would jump to his defence if anyone tried to make an issue or a joke of it. "Leave off, Bob's alright." But they were silent when mention was made of explorers impeded by Aborigines.

At night, however, amongst the sounds of the other boys breathing and snoring, Bob's sense of abandonment would surface. Bob's life, though missing many pieces, was filled with the intrigues of the daily lives of the boys, and eventually the girls, within the home. He even looked forward to the outdoor chores, when it wasn't cold, to tending the vegetables and feeding the chickens. A monthly roster dictated his turns for cleaning toilets, bathrooms or dormitories, or tidying up the yards. Even the cleaning, with the lemon smell of the disinfectant, was tolerable. Bob revelled in the hard work. Vigorously scrubbing, he would breathe in deeply, the citrus fumes permeating his dreams.

From his place in the long line of beds, he would think about his mother, his scented fingers held close to his nose. Although she had died when he was only five, he could still remember his hands grabbing at the loose flesh of her stomach as he stood behind her, his arms around her in a hug. He could see her setting the plate of biscuits in front of him and chiding him when he grabbed a handful. He could see her long dark hair falling around her face as she bent to tie his shoelaces or straighten his collar.

It seemed that things were bigger and slower when the lights were out. What seemed frantic during the routines of the day would stretch out slowly over the empty hours of night. At night he could reflect on the memories of long ago in a boisterous house. He could feel his inconsequential body disappearing and his thoughts and mind growing as large as the whole ward, until he encompassed all within it. It was this Bob, this larger-than- the-physical him, that felt like the real Bob Brecht. At these moments, he was bigger than all the things that trapped him and kept him small.

Not far from the school was an orchard. One day, walking back to the red stone buildings of the home, Bob and Danny ventured there. This was a serious breach of the rules since they were forbidden to leave the school and were now also trespassing. The post-war rationing limited the amount of food the boys received. After a successful but unsatisfying stint of stealing potato peelings from the chickens to satisfy their hunger, Bob had marked out a plan to raid the orchard, enticing Danny with a map drawn in the dirt with a stick.

As the brothers became caught up in their adventure, the thrill of being where they should not have been became intoxicating. To Bob, the feeling of climbing over the orchard fence with a secret purpose reminded him of the feeling he had during the late summer games of cricket with Thomas and William, the cicadas ringing in the light breeze, and his mother calling out to them that it was bedtime.

The rewards for their escapade turned out to be slimmer than their ravenous imaginings. The trees had already been plucked of their fruit, all naked except for one lemon tree.

Danny's disappointment about the size of the bounty was eclipsed by Bob's sensual pleasure: the sweet, acrid smell. Bob had desperately peeled back the skin, enjoying the lemon scent that sprayed him. Bringing the fruit to his lips, he was unprepared for the rebellious reaction of his mouth, repelled by the unsuspected tartness. The comfort of the smell and the sensation of bitterness were irreconcilable.

The citrus spray that lingered on his fingers consoled Bob, even after the smarting cut of the cane was brought swiftly down upon them. Folded against his cheek, the scent on his hands sent him off to a sweet dream.

Apart from the smell of lemons, Bob was discovering other sensual pleasures: Annabel Stewart and a wet first kiss behind the chicken coop. He had asked her to meet him there because he had something to show her, he said. When she arrived, he leaned close to her. A fumbling kiss and a soft giggle proved to him that he could be admired. Annabel Stewart, with her curly brown hair, freckles and hazel eyes, and smelling of rose water, made Bob feel as though he was as good as everyone else.

Annabel Stewart. Bob had thought there was no better creature on God's earth than Annabel Stewart. Bob, would spend eight years in institutional care and one of the few highlights for him was Annabel Stewart. He had been drawn to Annabel. On his ninth birthday, Patricia had given Bob a copy of *Frankenstein*. He remembered reading Victor Frankenstein's description of his beloved Elizabeth; it captured the way he felt about Annabel:

> She was docile and good tempered, yet gay and playful as a summer insect. Although she was lively and animated, her feelings were strong and deep, and her disposition uncommonly affectionate ... her hazel eyes, although as lively as a bird's, possessed an attractive softness. Her figure was light and airy; and, though capable of enduring great fatigue, she appeared the most fragile creature in the world.

He often recalled Frankenstein's monster and his question to his maker: "All men hate the wretched; how then must I be hated, who am miserable beyond all living things." When his classmates had stared at him, blaming him for the impediments of a civilised society, Bob had felt that hatred. And like the monster, he wondered why he had been created in a way that meant that others would not like him. He felt loathsome — "When I looked around, I saw and heard none like me." Bob feared that he may not be able to conquer his blackness, that he might be unlovable and alone. Annabel Stewart had shown him what being accepted felt like, but the fear of rejection fed a dark, recurring nightmare.

Bob found himself facing a presence — more frightening and forbidding than his father. A fire raged between him and the figure. It seemed like a man but the apparition was distorted by the heat and smoke of the fire. He was a black shadow behind the fire. He beckoned Bob, held a hand out to him. Bob stood still. Terrified. Unable to move. Unable to speak.

Bob had long since learnt that it was easier to be popular if you were like everyone else, and this also meant making sure that people didn't know what you were thinking. Words, he thought, had great power. Words spoken aloud could never be taken back. The things that were said to him — the accusations, the facts of history — revealed the magic power of the word. His dreams for his future would have him speak words, as an actor or a lawyer, that would hang in the air forever like a gallery of ghosts.

Bob thought he saw this power of words in another form: photographs were picture-ghosts. There was a picture of Bob taken in an orphanage line-up. In it, he was himself a ghost.

Bob was fascinated with how the pinhole in a camera could invert an image onto film and then, after the film was exposed, create an invisible latent image that remained mysterious until revealed by placing the film in developing fluid.

The negative would show the darkest regions of the image lighter and the lightest darkest, and there he could be white, as white as everyone else. His image was framed in chemicals that darkened in response to light. Only when the negative was placed between a glass plate and light-sensitive paper and then exposed to light would the print appear, re-reversing dark and light, black and white, on paper as proof, undeniable, for all to see. His father, through his photographs, captured people on paper, making them immortal. Disappointingly for Bob, just as his interest in photography blossomed, Grigor's visits stopped altogether.

Bob saw less and less of Daisy as she found her way around the home and the school. She had always been good at making people like her and now Bob saw her using the same charms that had made her so loved by his older brothers. She was able to read people, knew what they needed to hear, exactly the right things to say. By using that art, she had become the favourite of her House mother and father and most of her teachers. As she spent more time talking to adults, she became distant, almost dismissive of Bob and Danny. Sometimes she would pretend not to see Bob in the playground. When he came over to talk to her, she would seem distracted and impatient with him, as though he were keeping her from something more important, or she was embarrassed by him. He would catch her rolling her eyes with exasperation while he was trying to talk to her.

Although Daisy's slights hurt him, Bob felt oddly consoled that his sister had found a place for herself. He fretted about Danny and tried to encourage the other boys to include him in their games. Sometimes his friends would tolerate him, out of deference to Bob, but Danny was more often dismissed as too young, too quiet ... too different. This worried Bob, who understood that being popular with others was something to be cherished, something that eased unhappiness. He wanted this acceptance, this popularity, for

Danny too. Bob could work his way around situations, rules and personalities most of the time. He wasn't one to question or challenge. Daisy was able to do this as well. Danny was more like Frankenstein's monster than he was, Bob thought, especially since Danny was even darker than he or Daisy and so more obvious, more tainted. For this reason, Bob believed, Danny should have been trying the hardest to gain acceptance and to fit in.

When Danny was grudgingly allowed to play games with his brother's friends, because he was the youngest he always batted last and often the school bell would ring before he got his turn. Bob knew that his friends were unfair and tried gentle urging to get them to treat Danny better but, in the face of their taunts and their tricks, Danny would begin to complain or his eyes would swell up with tears. This would only make the older boys delight more in teasing him. In games of touch football, they would never throw the ball to Danny, or they would trip him over or punch him as they fell over in a tackle. "C'mon fellas," Bob would say.

Although Danny would often get upset, only once did he get really angry. In the heat of a summer lunch-time, Danny had been made to fetch the balls that went far afield. He was hot and exhausted. The older boys kept denying him a turn to bat, even letting boys who joined the game late hit before Danny. Bob finally intervened and insisted that his brother have a turn. Frank Phillips, urged on by Benny Miller, threw the ball high so that it almost hit Danny in the face. "Good one," Benny Miller had roared as a second ball whizzed past Danny's head.

A third ball went past, and Charles Wainwright, who was playing wicketkeeper, yelled "Out!"

Danny turned around. "It was not," he said angrily. "You pushed the wicket with your knee. I saw you."

As the other boys began to laugh, Danny got more agitated. Charles Wainwright shrugged his shoulders sheepishly. "You were facing the other way. How could you see me hit the wicket with my knee?"

"You cheated." Danny spat.

"Now, now Blackie," Benny mocked, "don't start telling lies just because you were bowled out."

"I don't tell lies. You do. You all do. You all cheat."

Danny threw his bat to the ground and stomped off the field. As he passed his brother, he glared at him and through gritted teeth said, "I hate you."

Bob felt indignant that Danny would blame him for the behaviour of his friends. He did find it hard when they would use names like "Blackie" because he feared that if he made too much of a fuss, they would call him that too. Danny didn't appreciate how hard he had tried to get them both accepted by other boys. Danny losing his temper and storming off didn't help things. This time, Bob would admit, the boys were pretty cruel and he didn't see how it was funny to tease Danny so much. He remembered Danny clinging to him in the dark hours of cold nights and saying, "Don't leave me." The memory came back to him of the way he had felt on those first nights in the home when Danny had held him close and Bob had felt strong. This memory and the harshness of Danny's angry words began to make Bob feel uneasy and he soon made an excuse so he could go and find his brother. Bob searched their dormitory, the toilet block, and behind the chicken coop but he did not see Danny again until dinner. His younger brother would not look him in the eye. It took days before Bob could get Danny to speak to him again.

When Bob would look back over those years in the home, this period when Danny refused to talk to him was the worst.

18

1946

PATRICIA HAD ALWAYS ENJOYED the time spent in her mother's company with needle and thread, each focused on their own stitching. When they sat together at the kitchen table there was studious silence, but Patricia felt there was also something special at those moments which joined them together in caring for their family whose clothes they made and mended with such devotion. And although Patricia always sensed that her mother kept many secrets inside herself, it was at these times that she felt she came closest to being her confidante.

"That's good, Patsy." her mother would say with an approving smile as Patricia learnt the crafts of dressmaking and embroidering. "You do lovely stitches. It seems a shame the boys don't know how much work goes into repairing their clothes."

"I'm sure it's far from their mind," Patricia laughed, "when they are playing stacks-on-the-mill."

"Well," her mother looked at her with a tender smile, "we know, Patsy."

As Patricia sewed in happy silence with her mother, her thoughts would race through the household goings-on. She would think about how to bring Daisy and Thomas closer, how to convince William that she was only trying to help him, and what toys she might make for Bob and Danny.

Now, as she worked as a junior dressmaker in Madelaine du Pont's shop, a terrace house in Strawberry Hills, her thoughts, as she stitched, would turn to those times she had spent with her mother.

Madelaine du Pont had moved to Sydney from Paris during the war. She had worked for Coco Chanel and spoke of her former employer as though she had been her personal friend rather than just another worker in her large fashion house. Madame du Pont used the same method of dressmaking that she had been taught as a young apprentice in Paris. From her, Patricia learnt the tailoring tradition where, instead of using sketches, she used pins to drape and fit the garment directly on the body.

"Madame Chanel would sometimes insist on up to thirty fittings for one dress," Madelaine would recall airily. The poor models would have to stand for about six or seven hours until we could produce a blueprint from the muslin toile, which we used as a pattern for jersey of finely knitted silk and wool. I will tell you something: I was there when she made jersey fashionable."

Patricia spent most of her time making copies of the clothes Madelaine du Pont selected from fashion magazines. "I am a seamstress, not a designer," Madelaine would say as she stuck the sketches for "ideas" on the wall. But Patricia found that she could look at cloth, its patterns and colour, see it hanging, folded and gathered and begin to imagine it as a dress or coat. She liked blood-red fabrics with gold embroidery or trimmings.

"Ah, Madame liked that too, this red and gold you love so much," Madelaine would reminisce. "I remember we made clothes in the 1920s, loose shift dresses, tunics, crepe de chine blouses, waistcoats and evening coats — dark and neutral colours adorned with Russian peasant designs. I will tell you, we are inspired by what we love and when Madame Chanel fell in love with a Russian Duke you could see it in her clothes. Madame was an artist but she was also a shrewd woman. After the turmoil in Russia, the aristocrats all moved to Paris, and to earn a living the women used their embroidery skills. Madame took advantage of that. We used their work in our clothes."

Patricia noticed that when Madame du Pont talked of her memories of life back in Paris they seemed much dearer to her than anything that occupied her now. Patricia would listen attentively, though as she slid needle through cloth her thoughts would drift back to her own happier times. "Nothing matters more than family," she could hear her mother saying.

"Such fine work," Madelaine would sigh as she examined a jacket perfectly lined with material from which the matching dress was made. "We made them like this for Madame — the lining and dress the same. It was a new thing when we first started making them but it is quite common now." Still looking at the neatness of Patricia's handiwork she would sigh, "Ah, I wish I could pay you more for your work. But," she would add cheerily as she looked from the garment to Patricia, "when we are rich, we will live like queens."

Patricia's arrangement with Madelaine du Pont included her use of the low-ceilinged room at the top of the narrow two-storey brick house from which Madame ran her business. Patricia would work on the clothes from before eight in the morning until well after five. Madelaine would be in the shop from about ten to four. During that time she would show her clientele day dresses of jersey and satin tulle and afternoon and evening dresses of lace and velvet. Madelaine would examine Patricia's work and cautiously encourage her young apprentice to create her own designs.

"I am not sure about this one. It is a little inelegant. But," she would pat Patricia on the arm, "I will show it and see. I do not want to discourage you. I will tell you, I remember so well how it felt to be so dedicated to the craft of making a beautiful dress. When I worked for Madame, I began as one of the *arpètes*, a young apprentice picking up pins and sweeping the floors. Then I became a *petite main* and then a *seconde main* until I became a *première main*. This meant I was responsible for the finished product and directed all of those who were below me. At the time I thought it would be wonderful to be a *vendeuse*, one of the sales people. They were assisted by the ex-models, the *habilleuses*. I didn't get to do that there, but now I have my own little business. It is much better this way."

Patricia found the stretchy nature of the jersey a challenge at first but, with patience, learnt to overcome the difficulties by using a simple shape so the fabric almost moved itself into a dress. Her designs always resulted in more orders. After closing, she would remain downstairs working till late. Madame du Pont was in ever higher spirits as the interest in their clothes increased; her light-hearted playfulness always made Patricia smile. Madelaine would begin their day with a splash of Chanel No.5 on Patricia's wrist. "Five was Madame's lucky number. Perhaps it will bring good fortune to us too," she would chirp as the scent of the perfume filled the salon.

Patricia's pleasure came from thinking about the day when she might, as Madame du Pont often declared, live like a queen. She would buy a big house and bring Daisy and Bob and Danny home to live with her. She would find Thomas and William and they would live there too. They would sit at the dinner table, laughing and talking and teasing each other. She would sit at one end of the table and Thomas would sit at the other. That, she thought, would be better than being a queen.

With these daydreams in her head, Patricia would take the train on a Sunday to visit her brothers and sister. She always felt a mixture of apprehension and anticipation, her stomach unsettled and her mind racing ahead.

She was concerned about Daisy and Danny whose moods could be vivacious or sulky and petulant. On some visits Daisy would be sweet and tender, chatting lightly and admiring Patricia's clothes. Other weeks she was surly and spiteful, passing comments about how fine Patricia's clothes were while her own were so tattered and unfashionable. She would constantly insist on new items — leather gloves, a velvet coat, black shiny shoes with a silver buckle, rose-scented perfume — and sulked if Patricia arrived empty-handed. As Patricia would try to explain that she did not have the money or could not find what she had been asked for, Daisy would pout.

Patricia did not resent Daisy's demands, her ingratitude at the sacrifice and effort made to appease her. When she looked at Daisy she could see the little girl who rode on William's shoulders, the pretty girl she made frilly dresses for, the little girl they called "Princess".

And Danny. He was always so happy to see Patricia that his words tumbled out too quickly, but as her short trip crept closer to its end he would become quiet and hug her arm. His change in mood would pull at her heart.

Bob attempted to make the best of his current circumstances. He was always cheerful and undemanding. Patricia remembered how brave he had tried to be at their mother's funeral, hiding his tears as he put his arm around Danny.

On the way back to Strawberry Hills, she recalled their home in Lithgow and how they had played together in the yard and performed plays, Thomas giving them each a part, or sung Christmas carols, which William refused to join in. Now that the three youngest were shut away and confined to the cold rules of an institution, all she could do was plan how she was going to bring her family together again.

As demand for Madame du Pont's clothes increased, propelled by the popularity of Patricia's designs, she began to talk about bringing on another seamstress. "I have a sister," Patricia ventured.

"Oh," said Madelaine coolly, "can she sew and make dresses as well as you?"

"Well, she is younger than me so she did not get the same

teaching from my mother. She's only fifteen. I can train her."

"Of course, I will have to see her first. Bring her next Tuesday," Madelaine decided.

"I can't. She lives in a home," Patricia explained.

Madelaine looked at her, confused.

"A home, like an orphanage. They won't let her out," Patricia added.

"I tell you, I did not know," said Madelaine, shaking her head. "How very sad. How very sad for you all. I just assumed you had no family around, especially since you are so dark. I thought you probably didn't want to be associated with them. But now I see you have a little sister and two little brothers. Why, you poor girl. Well, we shall see about getting your sister as an apprentice. She will have to share the room with you and I will be forced to pay her less than I pay you. But at least you will be together. That's better than money."

"Nothing matters more than family," Patricia whispered, so quietly that Madame du Pont did not hear.

"Clever girls can always get on in life," Madelaine continued. "Madame Chanel didn't pay her models much. Only a hundred francs a month, a fraction of what one of her dresses would cost. She would say: 'They're beautiful girls. Let them take lovers.'

Patricia tried to sit still and listen to Madelaine's stories but her heart was beating excitedly as she felt that she was finally taking the first step in reuniting her family. She waited eagerly for the next Sunday when she could tell Daisy. She thought over and over again of how excited her sister would be about the prospect of leaving the home and coming to Sydney to live and work with her. She imagined how happy they would be stitching during the day, talking at night, and visiting the boys on Sundays. Patricia remembered how Daisy was always reluctant to do her chores and would prefer the attention of William to sitting at the table sewing with her mother and her sister. But, she reasoned,

Daisy would be pleased to be away from the home so that she would apply herself more diligently now that she was older.

When Patricia finally broke the news to Daisy, she did not receive the excited response she had anticipated.

"What would I have to do?"asked Daisy nonchalantly, looking at her nails.

"You would work on making beautiful clothes, just like I do."

"Would I get to wear them?"she asked petulantly.

"No. You make them for very rich ladies. But Madame du Pont will let you buy the fabric cheap and you can make your own clothes, just like I make them for you."

Daisy screwed her nose up. "How long do I have to work?"

Patricia excitedly explained the routine. "We have to share a room," she said, "but at least we will be together."

"Well," responded Daisy coolly, "I suppose it's better than staying here."

While Patricia could focus on her work and allow Madelaine to chatter and fuss and enjoy her anecdotes about her life in Paris, Daisy would roll her eyes and complain that the conversation was distracting. Her sister's rudeness made Patricia flinch; she found herself having to act as peacemaker.

"Three weeks after Germany invaded Poland, Madame closed her house, saying it was no time for fashion. But she continued to sell her perfume and lived in the Ritz Hotel all through the occupation of Paris. And when it was liberated in 1944, she went to live in Switzerland. I was here by then, having followed my heart. I did not agree with her though. When times are dark, there is even more need for fashion. It cheers us up."

"I'm not sure those killed by the Nazis would agree with you," Daisy said, not looking up from her stitching.

"Madame du Pont used to work in the House of Coco Chanel," offered Patricia. As Madelaine beamed with pride, Daisy asked slyly, "What, as a maid?"

"No," replied Patricia, pretending the confusion was an honest mistake but giving her sister a sharp look, "She was a leading dressmaker. We are very lucky to be working for her."

"Oh. Well. I am sure if I knew who Coco Chanel was, I'd be very impressed," replied Daisy, returning studiously to her work and hiding a smirk.

Where Patricia found Madame du Pont's displays of generosity overwhelming and embarrassing, Daisy seemed to treat them as though they were patronising and cheap.

"Madame would often receive gifts from wealthy lovers but she rarely wore them," Madelaine would reminisce. "She'd wear lots of jewellery in the day or when sailing, even on the beach. And at night, she would wear no jewellery at all. She's the one who made wearing costume jewellery acceptable."

"Did you get that bracelet you are wearing from a lover?" asked Daisy.

"No," blushed Madelaine, "no, I bought it at a market in Bondi."

"Oh," replied Daisy, sounding disappointed.

Madelaine rummaged through a box of jewellery she kept to sell to her clients. She retrieved a pair of red glass earrings that hung on small gold chains. "You may have these. They're very pretty."

"Are they real?" asked Daisy.

"No, of course not," Madelaine replied, trying to sound as though fake rubies were better than real ones.

"Oh. Oh well. Thanks. I guess," replied Daisy in a meek voice.

"Daisy," hissed Patricia. "Where are your manners?"

"Thank you, Madame du Pont," sang Daisy in a mocking tone.

Although their hours were set as nine to five, Patricia would start at eight and Daisy would sail downstairs at about five to ten, just before Madelaine du Pont was expected to waltz through the door. Daisy would put her needle or pins down as soon as Madelaine left at four, leaving Patricia to finish off her own work and then Daisy's as well. The older sister would often work until eight or nine at night.

"You have to be more patient with Madame du Pont, Daisy," she would chide.

"You mean put up with her silliness the way you do. I didn't know that was part of the job. If I did, I would have stayed in the home."

"I know she is ... different. And, as you say, she is a bit silly, but she is letting us work here and we can be together at least."

"*Letting* us work here? You're an idiot. You're making her rich. It's your designs she's selling off to all those rich people who come in here. And each time she says '*One day we will live like queens*' I want to stick pins in her eyes. She already lives like a queen, while we have to share this stupid, stuffy cramped room, and work in a stupid shop making your stupid designs while I get paid a slave wage."

At first Daisy and Patricia had travelled together on Sunday to see their two brothers. But after a few months, Daisy found reasons not to make the trip, saying she would stay at home while Patricia went on her own. Patricia would return to find Daisy in their room and, although she suspected she had been out, Daisy did not confide in her. Several months later, her suspicions were confirmed when she returned from her visit to the home to find the house empty.

Then Daisy began to disappear after work, coming back in the early morning hours. She would sleep in and come down to work at almost midday, well after Madame du Pont had arrived. Patricia would make excuses that Daisy was sick, working extra hours herself to make sure they did not fall behind. Daisy had new fashionable shoes, silk stockings, a watch, a charm bracelet and a pair of pearl earrings — she always seemed to have extra money.

"Where did you get those shoes?" Patricia demanded as she looked at the satin pumps Daisy was putting in the wardrobe.

'From a friend," Daisy said smugly.

"Who?"

"None of your business," Daisy replied sharply, looking Patricia in the eye. "It's alright for you. You were never put in a home like I was. You don't know what I went through there. Bob and Danny have each other, I had no one. No one. And I won't let people walk all over *me*. You might be a Miss Yes-Madame, No-Madame but I'm not."

Patricia sighed, "I don't know what it was like for you. But I am trying to help you now."

"I don't need your help," Daisy hissed. "I can take care of myself like I've had to ever since you let me be taken away to live in an orphanage."

Patricia had always felt sorry for her sister's circumstances and she still felt pity for her now. As Daisy began to stay out at night and miss days of work, Patricia felt unable to confront her. The way her sister was treating her felt exactly the same as the way that her brother William had. He was often so angry with her, no matter how she tried. And the more she tried to understand him and please him, the more he seemed to pull away. Patricia felt she had failed both William and Daisy because she had never found a way to make them trust her and love her. Her attempts to rescue Daisy had only driven her further away.

Then, one frosty winter Sunday after Patricia had returned from her visit with Bob and Danny, she came home once again to an empty house. As she entered the store, she noticed that two of the designs she had finished the day before had been removed from the mannequins and that the lid on the box in which Madame du Pont kept her costume jewellery was unfastened. A feeling of emptiness ran through her as she trudged upstairs. The door to the small wardrobe she shared with her sister was wide open and the best clothes, both Daisy's and her own, were missing. Her mother's jade brooch was gone too. Sitting mockingly on the dressing-table were the red glass earrings.

19

1949

BEFORE MARCEL HAD TOLD HER that she could play at being his mistress, Daisy had kissed a man only once. When Mr Symonds came to tell her she was to leave to be with her sister, he had accepted her hug, then pulled her back, leant down and planted a soft, dewy kiss, like petals, on her lips. He had given her a bunch of purplish-red roses — de la Grifferaie, his favourite. One of them was pressed in her copy of *Little Women*.

Now, as the months of their affair stretched on, Marcel began to suggest that he should look after her all the time. On her eighteenth birthday, he offered to rent a flat for her.

"But you already have a wife and a house," she said, trying not to sound too enthusiastic.

"Yes, *ma belle,*" he replied with a smile. "You are right that I do not need another wife. But," he continued as she straddled his legs, "I need somewhere special to keep a *bijoux* as beautiful as you."

Daisy couldn't understand why Patricia toiled so hard. Her sister seemed to accept the way that Madelaine took her designs and made large amounts of money selling them. It used to grate on her that she and Patricia would be the ones who made the clothes and were paid such small wages while Madelaine was getting rich.

When Madelaine would say cheerily, "When we are rich, we will live like queens", Daisy would feel herself grow cold with rage and felt entitled to take little extras from the business. She began with snippets of cloth that she admired. Then she would take swathes of fabric for her own dresses and scarves. She learnt how to unlock the large jewellery box that held the little pieces that Madelaine collected to sell to her clients. At first Daisy just borrowed the gold pieces that caught her eye, but she decided that a red satin choker with a red velvet rose should adorn no one's neck but her own. After stealing the first piece, the second one was much easier. It didn't seem fair that some women had lots of pretty things and she had none.

It was William she missed every day. When they had been a family, her mother always confided in Patricia in a way that made Daisy feel excluded. But the adoration and loyalty she had received from William encouraged her to feel as though she was entitled to something better. Daisy determined that she was going to be more like Madelaine du Pont — rich and independent — than Patricia, an exploited doormat. It was this restlessness and ambition that made her plan to find a way of living that did not involve making the dresses her sister designed and living in the cramped quarters above the shop.

At first she was curious to see just where Madame du Pont lived, to see the difference between the place where Madelaine slept and the place where she kept Daisy and her sister. She waited one Sunday and made an excuse as to why she could not go and visit Bob and Danny. She went to the address that she had seen on personal correspondence in the shop, catching the bus to Bellevue Hill to see the place where Madelaine du Pont resided.

It was a large white house, two storeys, with a garden with hydrangea bushes and blossoming blush-pink roses. As she studied the windows and their stained-glass patterns, she saw Madelaine, dressed in a smart coat and hat, stride out of the door and drive off in her car. Daisy turned her head and hid her face behind the brim of her hat. As Madelaine's car disappeared down the street, Daisy noticed a curtain being pulled back and a tall man with a dark moustache gazing out of the window. This gave her an idea, and after tidying her hair and pinching her cheeks, she walked down the path to the house and knocked on the front door.

Ever since she was a young girl, Daisy seemed to know how to make a man happy. She could always find the right thing to say to William to break his sullen moods and cheer him up. She understood him, knew he liked to feel she was fragile so that he could protect her. And she loved him because he adored her more than anyone else.

The ability to navigate William, to respond to his needs, had given her skills that helped her survive her time in the home. When Daisy first arrived, the other girls had taunted her, tried to cut her thick black curly hair, and ripped and stolen her clothes. "Daisy Dustbin, ugly little munchkin," Penny Dwyer and Millie Carter used to sing-song as she walked past.

Because the other girls excluded her from their play, Daisy preferred to stay indoors, reading or drawing. This meant she had more contact with her house parents, Mr and Mrs Symonds, particularly Mr Symonds. He would seek out her company. She would listen attentively while he described to her how well he had played in his latest cricket match or how to best prune a rose bush. Regardless of how dull she found the conversation, Daisy would appear interested and ask the right questions in order to keep Mr Symonds's attention. She soon realised that if he did most of the talking he would leave their time together feeling as though it had been very enjoyable.

"I find our little talks very stimulating, Daisy," he would say, as he brushed his greying fringe back off his face, his fingernails lined with grit. He would look down at her, his hands on his hips, the baggy folds of his pants covering his skinny legs. "And you should call me 'John' when we are alone together like this."

Daisy was also astute enough to know that she needed to impress Mrs Symonds as much as she needed to maintain Mr Symonds's favour. So she would assist her House Mother with extra tasks and listen to her frustrations about post-war rationing. But it was with Mr Symonds that she learned to boost esteem and win trust.

"You are blessed with your looks," he would tell her. "Your skin is so light, you can hardly tell that you are a half-caste. It is truly a gift from God that you can pass."

In the environment of the home, she could feel the difference that favouritism from her house parents brought her. The other girls stopped bullying her and no longer stole the pretty things Patricia bought for her. When she did have a fight with Penny or Millie, Mr Symonds would always take her side and she would get what she wanted. It was with this training that she strode confidently to Madelaine du Pont's front door and introduced herself to Monsieur du Pont.

When Marcel du Pont started buying her presents and giving her money in exchange for friendship and favours, Daisy believed that she had suddenly worked out the way life was supposed to work. Marcel du Pont was rich and she was pretty; the bargain seemed fair. At first she would meet him at his home on Sundays while Madame du Pont was attending luncheons with friends and cultivating clients. As she spent more Sunday afternoons with him, he seemed to grow increasingly reluctant to see her leave. They began to meet during the week.

Marcel du Pont had left Paris when the Nazi invasion seemed imminent. Although he was never part of the Orthodox Jewish community, his mother had been before she married his father, and Marcel worried that this would be used against him. The war made ordinary people do the most vindictive things to people that they disliked. So he left his position in a banking firm and with his young wife boarded a ship for England. Eventually he came to Australia with a lucrative business manufacturing filing cabinets.

Daisy listened as Marcel talked about his problems with suppliers, customers, transportation and unions, shaking her head or kissing his forehead when she thought it was required.

"I could never talk to Madelaine about these things," he would sigh. "She's too occupied with her hats, shoes and feathers. It was a mistake to give her a business. I gave it to her as a hobby, you know. To get her out of the house and stop her complaining about being bored. But after your sister came to work for her, she started making money."

"I don't understand it," Daisy would coo. "I have never had someone to look after me. All I have ever wanted was to have a husband who would take care of me."

"Yes, *ma cherie,*" Marcel would say with a twinkle in his eye.

"It's just as well that I keep you occupied here while your wife goes off to sell her wares to all her friends. I should get more money for keeping you off the streets and out of trouble." Daisy looked up at him through her dark lashes.

"Out of trouble?" he would ask with a laugh.

"I think I'm a good influence on you," she said with a smile, stroking his moustache before kissing him gently on the lips.

At first, Daisy understood her arrangement with Marcel in the cold terms of a fair trade, but as their affair became more serious, she found herself feeling affection for him.

"You are a strange little creature," Marcel would say as he cupped her face in his hands. "So young but so old at the same time. So hard but so soft. And so strong-willed, yet so compliant." And then he would playfully slap her on the bottom.

He bought her the presents she had always imagined would be bestowed upon her, making her feel special in the same way William had when he preferred her to the rest of her siblings, or Mr Symonds had when he said he liked their talks. Marcel would smoke a cigar and look at her. Sometimes he would tell her to lie naked on the couch so he could admire her as he sipped his wine. He made Daisy feel that he saw the whole world when he looked at her.

"Do you love me?" she would ask when the depths of her own feelings would overwhelm her.

"What's love between two people like me and you?" he would answer, patting his moustache as though he had given her the reply she hoped for. "Now be a good girl and do that thing you do to me that I like so much."

"Which one?" She smiled at him as she slowly moved to her knees, reminding herself that her role was to not make the sort of demands a wife might.

20

1949

"THE LITTLE BITCH!" Madame du Pont screeched. "Ungrateful little bitch!"

She paced the room, glaring at the naked mannequins that yesterday had displayed expensive dresses due for delivery to her clients.

"I'll make them again," pleaded Patricia, trying to stop Madelaine from calling the police. "I won't stop until they are finished."

Madelaine turned to face Patricia.

"This is your fault. I did this thing for you, gave you this chance. You begged me, I felt sorry for you. Both of you. And this — this! This is my thanks. The little bitch!"

"I'll make replacements. I'll pay for the material from my own money. I'll work on them all day and night until they're done."

"You'd better. It was your idea that she should come here in the first place. I did it as a favour to you. I put a roof over her head, I gave her work, I saved her from the orphanage. And this is what I get." Madelaine swept her arms around the room, from naked mannequins to ransacked jewellery box.

"I'll make the dresses and then, I suppose, you will want me to leave too," Patricia replied quietly.

At this, Madelaine shot her a sharp look. "No, no, you'll not leave. You'll stay here and clean up this mess that you've made. I'll not have you leaving," she said. "But I never want to hear the name of that little bitch again. Ever."

Patricia could tell by the mix of panic and anger in Madelaine's voice that she really did not want her to leave, and that although she would have to weather Madelaine's self-righteous indignation, she had not lost her job or her home.

Patricia worked long hours to complete the dresses and then worked hard to develop more designs to please Madame du Pont. This seemed to lessen Madelaine's anger but it was a long time before she brought another bottle of Chanel No. 5 to the shop. In the meantime, Patricia had to endure Madame's comments to her clients about how ungrateful her little thieving apprentice was. "Of course, it's in their blood, those half-castes," she would hiss, after she had described her woes.

Daisy's departure had left Patricia angry and hurt, but she missed having her younger sister with her. As she laboured to win back Madame du Pont's trust, and as she worked the long hours on her new designs, she thought of Daisy's comments about how Madelaine was taking advantage of her. She had been surprised at how panicked Madelaine seemed when she'd mentioned leaving and was also mindful that Madelaine was using Daisy's behaviour to extract more work from her. She'd taken advantage of Patricia's guilt and had made her work Sundays, which meant she could not see the boys. Patricia thought of Danny, waiting on the stone wall, of how disappointed in her he would be as four o'clock passed and he would head back to his dormitory.

Two months before Bob's fourteenth birthday, Patricia had an idea. She waited for an opportunity to mention it to Madame du Pont. That came when a client wanted her three new dresses completed in just two days.

"Well," Patricia addressed Madelaine, "I would like to do it but I'm afraid it'll have to be my last. I need to find a new job so that I can have my brother with me. I thought, after your experience with Daisy, that you wouldn't be interested in helping me, and, since he is a boy, he does not sew."

Patricia could see the panic spill across Madelaine's face. "But ..." she spluttered, "what about your work?"

"Well, I did think of one way that I could stay here, but I'm not sure you would be happy with it."

When she saw that she had Madelaine's attention, Patricia continued. "Perhaps we could find him a job doing something else, perhaps in your husband's factory."

"Don't talk to me of Monsieur du Pont," Madelaine said with a dismissive wave. "I hardly see him these days and he thinks I'm fool enough to imagine that it is his work that keeps him from home."

"Well, my brother can find work. He's a hard worker, even though he's small. He always helped beat eggs or shell peas at home, any small thing that he could do. And he has the sweetest nature."

"Is he dark like you or light like your sister?"

"He is light, like her, I suppose," replied Patricia, looking at her arm.

"Well, I've found the lighter-skinned ones to be less reliable."

Madelaine simply could not afford to let Patricia go. So it was agreed that Madelaine du Pont would apprentice Bob, but when he arrived he would have to find a job.

At first Patricia thought she should take Danny, as he was the youngest and, much more than Bob, clearly suffering from being institutionalised. She made inquiries but was told he was too young for employment. Bob was fourteen, old enough to work.

Patricia and Bob sat silently on the train, barely able to make eye contact with each other. Patricia's excitement at having Bob with her had been crushed by Danny's reaction to the separation from his brother. She knew that Danny would find it hard to be left alone, but she had not been prepared for the frantic tears and the way Danny's hands desperately clung to her jacket as he screamed, "Don't leave me. Please. Please. Don't leave me." She remembered how he would cry when he was a baby shaking his arms and legs, and their mother would say, "Look, Patsy. He looks like a little bat, a little unhappy bat."

"Don't worry," Patricia said, looking over at Bob whose face was turned to the window to hide the tears falling down his cheeks. Just like at Mum's funeral, she thought. "We'll work hard to get him home with us soon," she said gently.

Bob smiled faintly back at her, but neither were encouraged by the attempt at optimism.

Bob answered a sign at the local post office, finding himself a job as a bicycle messenger delivering telegrams around Strawberry Hills. He would give the meagre amounts he earned to his sister who would pool their money for food. She also made his clothes.

He liked his job at the post office, enjoyed delivering messages as quickly as possible, finding short-cuts and pedalling fast. He also liked the men he worked with — old Mr Booth who showed Bob his wooden leg and told him that he used it to play cricket; Mr Green with his glass eye who studiously counted money and stamps making sure he did not make a mistake; Mr Scott who received and sent the telegrams and grunted more than he spoke; Mr Reed, whose dislike of blood kept him from joining his father's butchery business; and Mr Brown, who sorted the mail and who told Bob he could call him 'Harry'. It was Harry who noticed Bob's hungry response to praise and made a special point of bringing attention to the short time it took Bob to make a delivery.

But there was something about Harry that unsettled Bob. When they first met, their eyes had locked. Harry's brown pupils looked deeply into his. It was as though Harry knew the secret that Bob's father did not want anyone to know, as if he was saying, "me too". Harry, like Bob, did not have dark skin but Bob knew that Harry had the same mysterious essence that had hindered the explorers and held back settlement and civilisation. Bob was unnerved, torn between the embrace that the meeting of eyes gave him and the discomfort that someone else knew his secret. His attempt to blend in, to claim another source of otherness (Greek, Italian, Lebanese) was always at risk of exposure by this kindly old man. It confused Bob that someone could see into him so quickly, render him vulnerable, could also, with just a gaze, offer him acceptance.

As time passed and no words were spoken, Bob relaxed with Harry and came to realise that the old man would keep his secret safe. Bob thought Harry was probably trying to be white like everyone else, just like he was.

Late at night, after ironing Bob's shirt and pants while he polished his shoes, Patricia would lie on her bed and Bob would lie beside her. He had grown since coming to live with her; now, almost sixteen, he was almost as tall as she. Stretching out side by side, they would talk about their day.

"I delivered four telegrams in fifteen minutes. Mr Brown said that I was the fastest person that they have ever had to deliver telegrams," he bubbled proudly.

Sometimes they would speak about their family. "Do you ever think about Thomas?" Patricia asked, and continued before Bob could reply, "I wonder about him all the time."

Bob suspected Thomas and William must have been killed in the war. As time passed it seemed more and more likely that his brothers had met the same deaths as so many others. Patricia's question raised memories of them full of life — chopping wood and playing football — and Bob could understand why Patricia held on, how she clung to the hope they were alive.

It had been months since Daisy had left Patricia and still they had heard nothing from her. "I worry about her, can't stop thinking about whether she's safe. But I'll have to wait to hear from her when she's ready. I keep remembering something Mum said to me once, 'Nothing matters more than family'."

Patricia's voice broke and she turned on her side, propping herself up with one arm and looked at Bob. "I said that to our father once, the day I left Lithgow. You'd already gone and the house was so empty. I had my bags packed and as I walked out the door I said, 'You never deserved Mum, you never deserved us and you will end up old and alone.' "

"What did he say?"

"Nothing. He said nothing. Just kept looking at the fire. So I suppose it's up to us to make sure that Danny is alright."

Patricia lay on her back and looked at the ceiling. She hadn't spoken those words to her father, but they were what she had been thinking in her heart, what she wanted to say. Now that she had told Bob, she had at least said them out loud.

Bob sensed that this was the end of any conversation about their father. He only saw him again once, in the most unanticipated way.

It was several months after Bob began his new job and his new life that he came face to face with his father. There was the slow recognition that comes when you see someone you know unexpectedly, as when your eyes are trying to adjust to the dark; Bob didn't know whether to stop his bike. He sensed his father's shock and hesitation and he slowed his pedals to the same pace that his father slowed his step. His father seemed to be staring at his bike, while Bob sat wondering why he was coming out of a terrace house in Strawberry Hills. After an initial "hello", Bob did not know what to say to his father. The silence stood thick between them until his father finally said to him, "Keep your shoes clean, son."

"Yes, sir," were Bob's parting words.

With Patricia, Bob developed a set routine that gave him the same sense of security that the regime at the boys' home had given him, but he lacked contact with boys his own age.

Sleeping at night on the small balcony of Patricia's attic room without the sounds of other children was the hardest thing for him to get used to, even when he could hear the noise from the street below.

After his sixteenth birthday, his thoughts turned more often to Danny, now approaching fourteen, the age when he could be apprenticed. On Sunday, Bob would travel with Patricia to visit him. Now, when they arrived at the home, Danny would sit sullenly on the wall. During their visit he would be quiet and withdrawn, and instead of crying when they left he would simply slink back to the dormitory with barely a goodbye. The change in Danny unsettled Bob. He still remembered the first night in the large ward and how he had comforted Danny's small, shaking form. The image stabbed into him and now, with the distance of time, he couldn't even remember why they had fought so tenaciously in those final months before Bob left to live with Patricia.

"Not long now until he's fourteen," he would say to his sister as they travelled on the train back to Sydney.

"Soon," she said to him, "soon."

Bob imagined that when Danny came to live with them, it would be just like those early days in the orphanage when his young brother had followed him everywhere — his shadow, as Benny Miller had called him. He would send for his shadow as soon as he had some money, he resolved. He had always thought of him as Frankenstein's monster, the creature who struck fear in others but who desperately wanted acceptance. He could see Danny storming off the cricket oval, taking the bait when the other boys had teased him rather than turning the other cheek and laughing it off. Admittedly, Bob conceded, it was harder for Danny because he was darker — but he should have been more prepared to make an effort to fit in. Maybe when he was back with them, Danny would be happier.

And maybe it was Bob's own aversion to his black heritage, the wish that he was something other than Aboriginal that could not release him from his nightmares.

The man stood over the flames, beckoning to Bob. His face was ashen, his skin peeling. As the flames moved, the face became clearer. It was painted white. The paint was cracking. He motioned to Bob to cross the fire, to come. Bob could not move. He would not move.

Bob jolted awake, breathing heavily and sweating as though the flames in the dream had been licking his body.

21

1949

WHEN PATRICIA NOTICED that there was an increase in Madelaine du Pont's business — with two other dressmakers, one new sales woman and a move to larger premises in Paddington — she knew the time was right to raise the issue of Danny coming to live with her. Patricia knew that she had made Madelaine rich, that Madelaine needed her, or at least her designs. Over the years, she had become more confident with Madelaine and although she didn't stand up to her boss in the way that Daisy had wanted her to, she had used Madelaine's need for her to secure Bob's apprenticeship. Now, with Danny's birthday approaching, Patricia approached Madelaine about him.

"I am not so sure. We have very little room."

"With the new shop, we have two rooms. Danny and Bob can share."

"I don't know …"

"Well, I guess I could always look for employment somewhere else," Patricia said, confidently continuing to sew beads onto emerald satin.

"Oh, alright," Madelaine snapped. "But I will not be able to give you a pay rise if you have him here."

"I'm sure you could find a little something for my pay rise. I'll have two boys to look after now. Otherwise I'd have to find a better-paying job."

After a pause and with the faintest of smiles, Madelaine replied, "I must tell you, Patricia, you were so quiet when you came here but now, with that confidence that is growing inside you, you might make a good business woman. I've taught you well. Perhaps a little too well."

Patricia and Bob made preparations to welcome Danny. Bob tidied his room and made space for his brother. He cleaned the windows and swept the floor. He also used the threepence Harry had given him for the occasion to buy some candy.

Patricia decided to make a soufflé, just like her mother had showed her. As she slowly melted the butter, added the right amount of flour and sugar, then milk and vanilla, stirring until it became a thick sauce, she recalled how Danny liked to stick his fingers in the mixing bowls. As the mixture cooled, she added the yolks of two eggs and beat the whites until they formed peaks. She then placed the mixture in a tin, set a band of paper around the tin to allow the soufflé to rise, and baked it. She couldn't stop fussing over Danny, stroking his hair and kissing his forehead. On this first night, Danny stood quietly, hands by his sides, as Patricia touched him.

Now that Danny had come to stay, he seemed to be folding in on himself. His lively chatter when he was happy seemed to have deserted him. When Patricia reached out to him and asked what was on his mind, he would pull away, unable to look her in the eyes as tears swam in his own.

Bob had found Danny a job working with him in the post office. What would have taken Bob fifteen minutes to deliver would take Danny several hours. He would pretend to work, but hung out with other boys who loitered around the streets of Redfern.

"It was hot," he said to Patricia by way of explanation. "I was thirsty."

Danny was eventually fired, despite Bob's protests, when

he failed to return after a delivery. When he worked as a paper boy, he abandoned his cart and went home. His work at the abattoir and the shoe factory both ended with his being fired for stealing.

Bob fretted about Danny's inability to keep a job. "You just need to apply yourself more. Try harder. I know you can do it," he said to his brother one evening at dinner.

Danny put his fork down and stared at his brother, "Why don't you mind your own business."

"I'm only trying to help you," Bob pleaded.

"Well, don't. When I want your help, I'll ask for it." He stood up, pushing his chair back. His look reminded Bob of the way Danny had looked at him that day he stormed off the cricket ground.

Bob rose and walked around the table towards Danny. "I'm your brother, Danny. I'm here for you."

As he walked closer to Danny, Danny landed a punch squarely in Bob's stomach. Bob curled over from the pain. Danny had left before Bob could recover from the force of the blow.

That night, Bob went into Patricia's room and lay on her bed, watching as she sat in a chair by the open window and embroidered a scarf. "This would look good on our Daisy," she said sadly, holding her handiwork up for Bob to admire.

"Danny doesn't seem very happy," he said, his fingers tracing the flowers on Patricia's bedspread. "I don't understand. He wanted to leave the home so badly and now he seems to hate being here. And everything I do seems to make him more upset, more angry."

"I know how you feel. I tried so hard with Daisy and I still don't know what I did wrong. I keep wondering what I could've done differently. Things were much harder for her than they were for me." She stopped her sewing and looked at Bob. "Danny has always been much quieter than you, a bit more sensitive. And remember, he was so young when Mother ... passed away. And younger than you when he went into the orphanage. You were only six so he can't have been more than four. So little. We have to be patient with him."

Bob nodded in silent agreement, placing a hand on his stomach where it was still throbbing from Danny's punch.

Danny was changing the mood of the household. His absences required as much of their attention and energy with worrying as did fretting over him when he was there. Bob began to believe that it was because of his dark feelings about his brother that he could not shake his bad dreams.

The man beckons, his face of peeling paint intimidating. He is just a man. He cannot hurt him. Bob wants to move forward. He knows he must. It is his fate. There is something waiting for him. But he cannot cross the fire. He is too afraid.

Bob knew that sometimes changes in life happened without notice, and only afterwards is the change recognised. Like being in the orphanage when you are six and believing it will be only for a short while, until one day it's your eleventh birthday and there is no sign that things will change. But other things that change a life occur quickly. Like his mother dying, and his going into the home with Danny and Daisy. Like seeing the sign that changed his life: *See the World and Get Three Meals a Day*.

Bob's eyes stuck to the words: Three Meals a Day.

He circled back and, standing astride his bike, read the ad in full: *Join the Navy. See the World and Get Three Meals a Day*.

On Saturday he presented himself at the recruitment office and signed up for the test. He passed the English component of the entrance examination easily but failed the maths — it had been his worst subject at school. He returned the next week to undertake the test in front of the same officer, to pass the English and fail the maths again. On the third weekend, he arrived at the office and stood in front of the same officer. He passed the English and failed the maths, by one mark. The recruitment officer took the failed exam, moved by the determination and disappointment of the skinny youth, rubbed out an incorrect answer, placed the correct one in its place, and began the process for Bob Brecht's admittance into the armed services in the summer of 1955.

And so he came back into a secure world of institution and routine. He thrived on the order, and after the regimented life in the home, he found the discipline of the Navy easy to adjust to. He was better able to navigate the strict regimen of daily life, and less afraid of the consequences of breaching rules. It was his physique that handicapped Bob. He grew stronger with better feeding and regular meals, but he remained small-framed for his age.

Although he joined the Navy to earn better money, part of the reason was that he could no longer bear the anger that Danny constantly directed towards him.

22

1960

THE PASSAGE OF TIME could never diminish the pleasure that filled Thomas Brecht every time he gently turned an Attic vase in his hands. At thirty-six, he had become an expert on the glossy black pottery. Thomas admired the way the Greeks had created ideal physical and moral types in their art. As Aristotle had written, even if it is impossible for a man to be as perfect as he is in a painting, he should be painted that way so that people have something to aspire to.

Art critic Kenneth Clark wrote something that had also stuck with Thomas. He compared a Greek sculpture of Apollo to an African mask and noted there was no doubt the sculpture embodied a higher state of civilisation. Clark wrote that the mask showed that the Negro imagination was filled with fear and darkness, ready to inflict punishment for the smallest infringement, while the sculpture of Apollo showed that the Greek imagination was a world of light and confidence, governed by reason and the laws of harmony.

Thomas had always had the disadvantage of one skin too few and Clark's characterisation of civilisation against the primitive made him feel raw. It reminded him — seemed to accuse him — of the part of himself he had tried so hard to move away from.

Thomas could still remember the time, before his youngest brothers and sister were born, when he felt like the centre of his mother's world. He loved her tenderness, how she would talk to him while she worked, let him lick the spoons filled with biscuit mixture. As she became distracted with mothering Daisy and Bob and awaiting Danny's arrival, Thomas found more of his life was concerned with the goings-on outside of their family home.

Thomas was tall for his age, handsome with his fresh light tan skin and thick curly hair, and popular with the boys at school. When he was little, he would hold the interest of his friends by talking about planes. "The Halber Stadt CL IV had three machine guns and could fly over a hundred miles an hour. But I'd fly the Fokker DV II. It could go at over a hundred and twenty miles an hour and fly as high as twenty-three thousand feet."

Thomas gained confidence from his popularity and took for granted the easy acceptance of others. He was always happy when he was in the company of other boys, his circle of friends, especially Dennis Walsh.

Thomas's brother, William, was not as tall as he was. William's skin was much darker and he had their mother's nose. He was chubby when he was a baby and as he started to grow became muscular. The brothers, although close in age — with Patricia born between them — seemed so different: different features, different colours. Their frames were so different that William could not wear Thomas's hand-me-downs.

Thomas had been wary of his brother's quick temper. It was more often directed at Patricia, whose attempts to boss both the boys seemed to only antagonise William. "Why don't you ever let her have her way?" he would ask his younger brother after William had ridiculed Patricia's attempts to get them to tidy up their clothes.

"She's not our mother. I don't know why she has to act like she is. I don't like being bossed around."

Thomas would shrug, but William's anger, his unwillingness to do small things to appease others, made Thomas uncomfortable. When he could feel William's mood brewing, his back would get tense and he would try to make himself scarce. When they were young boys, he tried to keep William away from his own friends, afraid that his little brother would be surly and embarrass him. Thomas knew his own easygoing nature was what drew other boys to him.

Thomas had thought himself very different from his brother, as different from himself as his father was from his mother. Although he was in charge of walking William home from school, he encouraged his brother to run ahead so he wouldn't be seen with him.

Walking home from school one cool autumn day, Thomas noticed that William, who had run ahead, was in a field near their house, yelling at other boys. As Thomas approached, he could see his friends — Dennis Walsh, Harry Tanner and Bill Thompson — talking heatedly with William. This is what he had long feared: a display of anger from William towards his friends. He felt rage towards his brother rising in his chest.

"What's going on here?" he yelled at Dennis Walsh.

"And here's the black bastard's black bastard brother," shouted Harry.

"What are you talking about?" Thomas asked Dennis Walsh again. Harry picked up something from the ground and threw it at William. Thomas looked at William's soiled shirt and saw it was covered in cow dung.

"Here's some more stink for you dirty black Abos!" Harry yelled.

"Dennis?" Thomas asked again.

This time the cow dung hit his shirt.

Thomas looked down where it had hit and began to feel tears forming. William ran towards Harry, knocked him to the ground and began to punch him. Thomas was too scared to move. He watched as Dennis and Bill jumped on top of William, hitting and kicking him. William kept punching all three, swinging wildly, throwing Dennis to the ground and kicking him. Harry remained curled over on the ground, nursing his bruises. "You crazy black bastard, dirty crazy Abo," yelled Dennis as William's fist smashed into Bill's face. Bill reeled backwards, crying in pain. William turned and began swinging at Dennis. Dennis backed away from him.

"Get your crazy brother off me, Thomas, you Hun black bastard."

Thomas ran towards his brother. "Come on, Will!" he yelled at him. "Let them go!"

William had caught Dennis, grabbed him by the hair and brought Dennis's head down to smash into his knee. Dennis crumpled to the ground. William walked back over to where Harry was lying on the ground and gave him a kick in the legs. He then leaned over and spat on him.

"Will!" Thomas said. "What are you doing?"

"Giving them what they deserve," William said, looking at his brother.

William was breathing heavily and Thomas grabbed his arm and walked him back towards the house.

"What'll we tell Mum?" Thomas said, looking at the bruises on William's face and arms."

"That I fell out of a tree."

Thomas looked at William's shirt. "That doesn't explain the cow dung."

"I guess it doesn't explain yours either."

William lent on Thomas's arm and limped home. "White bastards," he growled. "I'll beat the crap out of them next time, too."

"I don't know why they called us Abos," Thomas said.

William laughed, then clutched his side in pain. "Look at us, Tom. Look at me. Look at Mum. If we're not Abos, what are we? Anyway, that's what everyone thinks we are."

"But there must be something that we can do?"

"Well, you weren't much help back there. Besides, we can't help that we are Abos. Can't change it."

"We could tell them we're something else. Hawaiian or something," Thomas suggested.

William tried to laugh again. "I don't mind being an Abo. What difference does it make whether we're Abos or something else?"

It was Dennis Walsh's betrayal that hurt Thomas the most. He had always liked Dennis and used to think of him late at night; he liked the blue colour of his eyes and his red hair. Dennis's disgust made him feel ashamed of his mother's darkness. Despite the strong love he had for her, he was shamed by the heritage she had given him. He felt caged by the implication of his family's birthright. No wonder she always looked so sad, he thought, with all that shame heaped upon her. No wonder she never breathed a word about her family. He didn't pry, for he carried his own secrets and knew how uncomfortable too many questions could be.

Even at the age of twelve, he withdrew from his friends and spent most of his time in the library. There he found respite from the taunts of the boys in his class and he also found books about Greek life and art. He liked the clean lines and finely crafted male bodies and copied them faithfully into a notebook, with annotations. He had an outsider's caution and knew that these fascinations should be kept private. If other boys knew what he found fascinating, they would want to throw more cow dung at him. He would be even more despised.

By the time Thomas was close to his seventeenth birthday he felt suffocated by the secrets he kept. His box of treasures contained marbles Dennis Walsh had given him, tattered pages from *The Phaedro*, a secret notebook of his drawings of Greek antiquities, and his attempts to copy the inner pessimism of da Vinci's drawings.

When the war arrived, Thomas turned his eyes to the sky. He wanted to fly, he felt that he could puncture the sky his mother studied so wistfully. Flying wasn't freedom of movement, it was shattering forbidden barriers. He didn't enlist in

Australia. He had heard that Aborigines couldn't enlist and though he would not identify himself as such, he didn't want to suffer the humiliation of being labelled and excluded. His plan was to travel to England, enrol there, and flee his darkness.

On the passage to London he met Mark.

"Tell me something about yourself," Mark had said, smoking a cigarette and stretching back on a steamer chair.

"Well, my parents are dead. They were from Greece, though I've lived in Australia all my life," he said, surprised at how easily the lie slipped from his lips. "I'm off to join the war effort."

"Why not do it in Australia?" Mark asked.

It was a good question and Thomas scrambled to find an answer that would fit in with his falsehoods. "I want to join the Air Force. I thought there would be better training in England."

Mark looked at him suspiciously, then shrugged, "It's the Scouts whose motto is 'Be prepared'. But it is a good idea in other contexts too."

Mark continued to smoke his cigarette and kept his gaze on Thomas. Thomas kept looking back. "It would be a waste to lose you," he said to Thomas.

"We are all certain of death," he told Mark. "It's only the hour of which we are uncertain. Just think of me as carrying on a great Greek tradition."

By the time Thomas arrived in London to make his contribution to the war, he had fallen irreversibly in love with Mark, but he had caught himself in a trap. He'd told Mark that he was Greek, an orphan with no known siblings. He said this lightly when they first met, never imagining the lies would hold him in a trap for the rest of his life.

Thomas trained as a pilot. The ability to integrate himself with a machine, to be subsumed by something larger yet to be an integral piece of it, thrilled him. He loved the incongruency of being in a lump of metal that rationally should not be able to leave the ground, yet could fly with the same mathematical laws that, by appearance, allowed birds to fly. He often thought of how amazed da Vinci, with his passion for understanding the world as it moved towards destruction and decay, would be if he had lived to see such things.

Yet the freedom of flying was laced with the horror of war. He had to shut down feelings about the explosions and ensuing wafts of smoke left in his wake; all he might be destroying with his Hurricane. He tried, without success, to be unfeeling about the loss of men who had become friends.

East and west on fields forgotten
Bleach the bones of comrades slain
Lovely lads are dead and rotten
None that go return again

London life during the war was a desperate time. The Blitz, food shortages and, later, avoiding V-2 rockets put a strain on life that was hard for everyone to bear. The V-2 rockets were referred to as "Bob Hopes" — you had to "Bob" down and "Hope" for the best. One ripped through the Knightsbridge flat of Mark's parents, killing both of them.

The bars that he and Mark frequented — Le Boeuf sur le Toit, The White Room, The Captain's Table — were filled with men in uniform from all ranks. Here, married men preferred to have sex with other men rather than cheat on wives with prostitutes. The late evening raids of these bars were to remind them all that their behaviour was against the law. There was an uneasy tolerance of homosexual activity: dislike of it was pronounced and the enforcement of its illegality often violent.

"We can't be quiet about it. I can't snap shut like you do. Always looking over your shoulder as though it's an embarrassment," Mark would say in frustration at Thomas's attempts to placate him. "It's keeping quiet that allows people to get away with laws that lock us up."

Thomas believed that Mark had no idea of what people really thought, how dangerous people's hatred of what they do not like can be. Thomas always felt the way he did that day when he had been frozen in fear as William attacked their tormentors.

He thought about his hidden darkness when he saw the way the Americans treated their black GIs. There was a saying amongst the English troops: "I don't mind the Yanks, but I can't stand those white chaps they've brought with them." While the English lads seemed happy to mix with 'the coloureds', the US soldiers treated them with contempt and maintained a philosophy of segregation. Thomas knew that the Australian troops would treat their Aboriginal soldiers, sailors and pilots the same way.

As a supposed dark Greek on English soil, he was as close to being a white person as he could be. He played on it, inventing stories of parentage, each more elaborate and unbelievable. It proved as easy to slip into his new identity as into intimate affection with Mark. He had built his life on a lie that had slipped so easily from his lips. His once-upon-a-time family was relegated to oblivion. He felt he had become a da Vinci painting in which the shadow was more powerful than the light.

After the war, Mark took Thomas to Paris, a wonderland where men wore green carnations and danced with other men, unashamed. The death of Mark's parents had left him a large fortune and the freedom to spend it in the company of Thomas. Mark and Thomas stayed at the Hotel d'Alsace and strolled up and down the rue des Beaux Arts, but for all the seductions of this vibrant life, post-war homophobia was becoming more intense.

During the war, some fifteen thousand people wore the pink triangle. Nazi doctors performed barbaric operations in efforts to transform homosexuals into heterosexuals. After the war, the first French anti-homosexual law in a hundred and fifty years was passed and would remain in place until 1981. People freed from the death camps were re-sentenced; many would commit suicide rather than spend more time in prison. In Germany, similar laws saw some homosexual survivors charged after the war — here, too, many preferred suicide to further incarceration.

"They were happy enough to let us fight and be killed in the war," Mark reflected bitterly to Thomas. "But the war won human rights, not rights for our kind."

Mark's activism, his outspokenness, left Thomas feeling anxious. While Mark fought to change anti-homosexual laws, Thomas went to Oxford and earned his doctorate in a study of Attic vases. The ideals of Ancient Greece attracted him. It inspired male values and he preferred this to modern society and its cult of women. In Ancient Greek society, the everyday was ritualistic. Vase paintings told stories about gods and heroes who were greater than mere men.

Some scholars would write that the glory of the Greeks was tarnished by their treatment of women and their participation in slavery. The Greeks labelled all foreigners as 'barbaric' and inferior, well-suited to become slaves. Thomas would reason that there is cruelty and barbarity in every society and that the focus on these uglier aspects of the culture took away what he believed to have been the idealistic strengths of Greek society. Certainly there was a trade in women. The female slaves worked as prostitutes. Their abuse was evident from the same pieces of art that Thomas studied. The men who had the power to do so inflicted humiliation upon the women they owned. They would force their slaves into intercourse openly, whenever the mood took them, in the presence of onlookers. These slaves would be tattooed to show their status and savage origins.

Oscar Wilde once wrote: "For any man of culture to accept the standard of his age is a form of the grossest immorality." He had also said that whatever is modern in our life, we owe to the Greeks, whatever an anachronism to medievalism. The world owed nothing, Thomas thought, to the savage tribes.

These sentiments only reinforced Thomas's feelings about the inferiority of his Aboriginal ancestry and reiterated the sense of shame he knew would attach to it if it were known. His mother would reveal all the lies he had wound around his new life, his new identity. He would remember the link to that dark part of him and the name she had called him. He had now forgotten the word, lost it — Europa? Europe? 'Europe' comes from a Semitic word that simply means 'darkness'. He had known at the time that the word was a door to other things, a special reminder of someone, of something she had held dear.

His mother was a woman with her own secrets, her own thoughts and images locked away in her head. He would recall the closeness of their connection together under the stars when she had finally let the walls slip down and had revealed something secret and special to him. She had beckoned to him and he had responded by abandoning her. It was a time when he guarded himself around her as he was coming to terms with his own private thoughts, but he fled with them rather than trust her to share them. She had said to him once that a mother would always know where her child was. He had doubted her at the time but now, he prayed, he hoped, that she had been telling the truth.

When he would die, at age sixty-five — pilot, expert on Greek antiquities, lover of Mark, eldest brother of five siblings, exile — he would still be ashamed of his secrets. Ashamed of his mother's Aboriginality, ashamed of his father's German name and ashamed that his lifelong love was another man. Death came like a releasing kiss, leaving behind an epitaph, which puzzled everyone who saw it, including those who thought they knew him best: *There shall be wings. If the accomplishment be not for me, 'tis for some other. — Leonardo da Vinci.*

He did rectify one guilt. He left a large bequest to the Lithgow local library to replace the books he had vandalised during his youth.

The earth of Thomas's grave was fresh, but the soil over William's body had been packed tightly for forty years. Like his older brother, William had joined the armed forces. Aborigines had been enlisting since the beginning of the war despite the formal ban on non-white volunteers. Aboriginal men had gained admission by special authorisation, as fifty 'part-Aborigines' did in Darwin in 1939. By 1940, 'full-bloods' were prohibited from signing up; those already enlisted were allowed to stay. But Boards remained confused and recruiting stations signed some 'full-bloods' up. William signed up this way, in an unsuspecting booth in Queensland. He was to remain while others who had been signed up were discharged.

William had gone to Egypt with the 17th Battalion. He was in the offensive in Tobruk, one of the 'rats'. The cohesion within his small combat group was devoid of racism. They were united against a common enemy; internal prejudice could prove deadly. The soldiers on the front were far more accepting of the Aborigine than those higher up the chain of command. Senior Army officers seemed adamant that Australian men should not serve with Aborigines because it would undermine morale in the ranks. However, Aborigines were permitted in the RAAF and could hold commissioned ranks. Each of the services developed their own rules for enlisting Aborigines — or not.

William understood the inequity of being conscripted but not being allowed to vote. He decided that rather than protest about the hypocrisy and demand citizenship rights, he would fight hard, exorcise his rage, and show them all what he was made of. He knew that some were turned away from enlisting, considered 'neither necessary nor desirable'.

By March 1941, there were no Aboriginal officers, but

there were some, like William, serving as corporals and sergeants. Most Aborigines enlisted between mid-1941 and mid-1942. Things had changed after Japan entered the war. William was deployed to New Guinea where he fought along the Kokoda Trail, one of more than 3000 Aborigines who served in the armed service that had not wanted them. In 1944 the Federal Arbitration Court denied Aboriginal pastoral and agricultural workers the award wage. The Aborigines' Progressive Association demanded the release of all Aboriginal servicemen from the Army. William would have supported them in their anger, but by that time it was too late for him to join their fight.

He was killed in a battle at Shaggy Ridge, his grave unmarked. In his pocket was a picture of Daisy and a letter he had begun to write to her but never finished.

Dear Princess,
I won't tell you what it is like here, as I hope you will never know the dark things that men are capable of. Sometimes the only thing that gets me through is knowing that you are safe. I remember when you used to ride around on my shoulders. I remember the way you used to laugh ...

23

1958

WITHIN THREE SHORT MONTHS of joining the Navy, Bob and four of his friends were court-martialled for gambling. Although they had only been playing poker for pennies, they were hauled through disciplinary proceedings. Bob knew it was going badly for him when their assigned advocate addressed the court by saying, "Your Honour, I think you should throw the book at them."

This was the first of many times that Bob and his closest friends, Ernie Gibson, Colin Reid, Geoff Young and Bernie Sinclair, would find themselves relegated to extra duties and marching around the yard. "Being on chooks", they used to call it as they strutted around the parade yard, marching to the directions of a Petty Officer. Bob trained as a radio operator and was assigned to HMAS *Melbourne*. Bob had enlisted eighteen months after the Korean war had ended. Being on an aircraft carrier gave him the regimented life he was used to but, even more than in his youth, he was willing to stretch the rules in the name of having fun.

He was well known for his escapades with Ernie. When they were training in Canberra they had snuck into the women's barracks to visit a girl that Ernie was keen on. Tracey had to hide them in the lockers when an inspection was called. They were almost caught when Ernie — filled with alcohol and oppressed by the heat in the confined space

— vomited. This earned Bob a reputation for being one of the lads, taking orders when he should but still being up for a good time when the opportunity arose. On shore leave, he joined in the social night-time hunts for girls.

Although he loved dancing to Roy Orbison and taking pretty girls to the movies, Bob was nervous in the company of a woman, especially if he liked her. He had affection for the few women he had fleeting relationships with — Penny Sutton, with her green eyes and throaty voice, Charlotte Carter with her long legs and wedding band, and Lily Watson of the jet-black hair and pale skin. But most of the women he met were too unlike the soft and sweet Annabel Stewart to make their way into his heart. Annabel Stewart, when she became his friend, had made him feel as though he was as white as everyone else.

He would provoke the usual male bravado when returning to the ship.

"Did you get any?" Colin would yell out.

"No. And I wouldn't tell you bastards if I did, anyway," was Bob's standard reply.

Bob was always careful to try not to look too clever in front of his friends, a trick he had learnt when trying to win favour with his pals in the home. He loved reading, but would tell his friends he only did it because he had trouble falling asleep; although his buddies did not believe him, they let him be. Within the regimented life of the Navy he found a way to fit in, to be like everyone else. It reminded him of a line that Rudyard Kipling had written in 'Gunga Din':

An' for all 'is dirty 'ide

'E was white, clear white inside

That was him: White, clear white inside — as white as everyone else. "Don't rock the boat, even if you're in the Navy" was his tongue-in-cheek motto. When he looked around, Bob could see there were men who did not fit in, who could not control their tempers or were too awkward — lonely figures who reminded him of Danny. And there was one man who spent all his spare time answering the pile of letters that came for him every week until it was discovered that he sent them to himself.

His shore leave in Sydney was always spent with Patricia. When she was still living in the terrace house with Danny, he would visit with presents for her and Danny from his travels around the Pacific and Asia. Patricia would be delighted with each gift.

"You shouldn't have," she would say as she studied fabric, fluttered fans or opened bottles of perfume. "You should be saving your money for yourself."

Danny was absent from the house more often than he was there, and often Bob would leave without seeing him.

"He's just not able to keep a job," Patricia said forlornly. "It's not the money so much now because I'm being paid more and there is plenty of room here for me and Danny. I've even started to redecorate, to make it seem more cheery." Patricia swept her hand in the direction of the new lavender curtains and matching pillows she had made. She sighed. "More and more of Danny's time is spent with his friends from Redfern and they aren't the sort of people I want him running around the streets with at night. He's gone for days at a time and when he does come home, he sleeps all day."

Patricia did not tell Bob that sometimes Danny would steal money from her purse while other times he would be flush with funds. When she refused the money he offered her, Danny would sneak some crumpled, dirty notes into her handbag.

"When I try to talk to him about it, he tells me to mind my own business. But I'm the closest thing to a mother he has and if it's anyone's business, then surely it's mine," Patricia said, as she and Bob lay side by side on her bed, a warm breeze floating in through the open window.

"Well, I can't see what more you could do for him," Bob would say to comfort her. "He has everything here. Danny's just never happy. He wasn't happy in the home and he isn't happy out of it."

"Bob," Patricia would chide, "You're too harsh on him. He was in that home for a long time on his own. Almost ten years. That's a long time for a little boy, almost his whole life. He probably can't even remember what our life was like before then."

"You're too kind-hearted," Bob said softly, patting her lightly on the hand.

"That's what Daisy would say," Patricia said wryly.

"Still no word from her?"

"No." She paused as a tear formed in the corner of her eye. "I just hope she's alright. I worry about her so much. She's so young and pretty, and although she likes to talk as though she's tough, she's really very gentle."

"As gentle as a snake," Bob said.

When Bob returned to celebrate his twenty-first birthday, a red-eyed Patricia told him that Danny had disappeared. He'd taken a job as a kitchen hand in an Italian restaurant, and had been working there for less than a month when he vanished one night along with the evening's takings. Patricia had gone to the restaurant when Danny had not returned home and found the enraged owner, Pasquale Tramino, about to call the police. She pleaded with him not to press criminal charges and had been so upset that he calmed down and tried to console her. He had since been to call on her several times.

Bob travelled to places that he had seen on the map at school — borders coloured in as though the soil were pastel-pink or lime-green. When he travelled to New Guinea, he read about the war that had started when he was born, a war in which he had lost two brothers. When he travelled to Singapore and Japan, he read about their history and geography. He was overwhelmed by how polite the Japanese were to him and his fellow sailors, even apologising for the war.

"Domo Aragato," thank you, they would say to him and his pals as they walked through the narrow shop-lined streets in their bell-bottomed pants and white sailor hats, Bob buying jade and a carved wooden box for Patricia.

He was treated as an Australian, as a victor, one who had fought on the side of good, not like those Aborigines who had resisted the explorers. Bob felt he was, this time, on the side that was fighting for progress and democracy.

The man stands behind the fire. His face is black but marked with white paint. He holds out his hand to Bob. He stares at Bob. He motions with his hand for Bob to follow. Bob starts to move towards him, frightened but knowing that he must obey the old man. As he tries to step towards the beckoning hand, the flames begin to engulf him.

Bob woke, sitting upright, after the recurring dream. Each time it left him with a feeling of terror. No matter where he travelled, the dream would follow him.

Patricia married Pasquale Tramino in a small ceremony in Madelaine du Point's garden. It was the first time Patricia had been to the house; she thought it the grandest residence she had ever seen. Madelaine arranged for a caterer, decorated her yard with white lilies and had fitted Patricia's dress: ivory satin with scalloped lace sleeves and an ivory train. Patricia would not have spent her own money on such extravagance. Even though Madelaine paid her more and she did not have anyone but herself to support, her frugality through the years when she struggled to feed and clothe Daisy, Bob and Danny made it hard for her to spend money on something frivolous like flowers and fancy food. Madelaine, however, was used to spending money on luxuries and took charge.

"I have no daughter. You are the closest thing I have to that," she said matter-of-factly, and proceeded to organise the entire event to her own taste. Patricia didn't mind that she didn't seem to have much choice in the details. She enjoyed seeing Madelaine so animated and merrily preoccupied. At least, Patricia thought to herself with a smile, I got to pick the groom. She also persuaded Pasquale to have Bob as his best man. Patricia thought of her mother and her brothers and sisters as she walked down Madelaine's path to exchange her vows, allowing herself that one moment of sadness before the joy of the wedding.

Bob was happy for his sister. So long she had seemed to devote too much energy to a family that kept slipping through her hands like water. And Bob liked Pasquale, who had arrived in Australia after the war and worked hard to start his restaurant in East Sydney. Bob loved eating in his little restaurant that was frequented by a regular band of good-humoured Italians, mostly workers from the wharves at Woolloomooloo, who would sit all evening drinking coffee as though they had no other place to go.

Patricia would work for Madelaine during the day and at three in the afternoon would leave to walk down Crown Street and over Oxford Street, to help Pasquale with his restaurant. She had negotiated a higher wage along with fewer hours with Madelaine and dedicated most of her time to designing and directing the younger seamstresses. Madelaine now had a staff of ten, and although she would still not let Patricia deal with the clients, there was little else in which Madelaine did not involve her.

Between the extra income she was now bringing in from Madelaine and her husband's increasingly profitable restaurant, Patricia and Pasquale were able to afford a modest little house in East Sydney, near the restaurant. Finally Patricia had a home of her own, something she would never have dreamed of if she had not met and agreed to marry Pasquale.

"I got what most girls dream of — a husband and a home — but I do not have what most girls take for granted: a family," she told Bob one day. Now, instead of lying on the bed they sat talking; they sat at Patricia's kitchen table and confided in each other.

It was after Patricia became pregnant with her first child that she answered a knock on the door to find Daisy standing before her, in expensive clothes and with two large suitcases in her hands.

"I have nowhere else to go," she said. "And if you ask me where I've been I'll leave now and never come back."

Bob warned Patricia to be careful.

"How can you say such things? She's my sister. Our sister."

"You do not even know where she has been all these years, what she has been up to, what she has done, who she's been with."

"She'll tell me when she's ready. We can't know what she suffered in the home."

"I was there too, remember."

"I know. I remember," she said, patting his arm. "But you are much stronger than she is."

Before he could interject Patricia continued: "Bob, I'm so happy she's here. I've missed her so much and here she is, back again, and me about to have a baby. It's just as though we are going to start to be a family again."

Bob let his concerns drop, knowing that he would never change Patricia's mind. He hoped he was wrong that the distrust he felt was not as accurate as Patricia's faith. But he had met too many women like Daisy, women who saw men as a resource and other women as competition. He knew how vulnerable Patricia's sense of duty had made her to the demands of Daisy and Danny. And he never forgot how Daisy had treated him when she was in the home, ignoring him when he came to speak with her as though he were an embarrassment. Unlike Patricia, he could not forget the feeling of being rejected by his sister. And neither of them, he thought to himself, had ever forgiven their father.

Bob often remembered the last time he had seen their father, that chance encounter in Strawberry Hills. His father, descending the steps of the tidy, yellow-painted terrace house, had looked so surprised to see Bob. Months later Bob was sent to deliver a telegram to that address. When the telegram was handed to him, Mr Scott seemed to smirk with his grunt and Mr Green gave him a wink with his good eye. "Well, Bob," said Mr Reed, "I don't think we will blame you if you take longer than usual at that stop." Then Bob realised that the house he'd seen his father walk out of was a place where men paid women to do things to them, the sort of things he still imagined doing with Annabel Stewart.

He realised that the family would always mean something different for Patricia than it did for him. She was always looking back and trying to recreate it the way it was when their mother was alive. He knew that it was gone irrevocably, that what had been lost — Thomas, William, their mother — could never be regained and that what had changed Daisy and Danny meant they would never be the same as they were as children in Lithgow. If he wanted a family again, he would have to create one himself. He was pleased when Patricia finally married after so many years of putting all her energy into bringing them together under one roof. Pasquale had given her a chance to start her own family, to begin again.

The first time Bob looked into Carole Dyball's face he knew that there was something about her that made him feel that if she were with him, he would find a home. She was like Annabel Stewart who had given him confidence and acceptance; similar to his sister, Patricia, who had given him a place in the world, a feeling of stability and warmth that he had yearned for ever since those days when he could grab his mother's flesh in his tiny hands.

24

1970

BOB BRECHT'S GOOD FORTUNE was to marry a woman very much like his mother. The tragedy for Carole Dyball was that she had married a man who shared too many of the views held by her father. The wedding was intimate and simple: Carole's mother was the only one of her family to attend, Patricia the only one of Bob's. Their Navy friends filled the small church. Carole's father had refused to attend. She had travelled home to introduce Bob to him. He'd taken one look at Bob, rebuffed his outstretched hand and said to her: "You are not going to marry him."

Carole could only imagine what battles her mother must have fought with her father to get to the wedding in Sydney. "He is much easier to get around in his old age," she said when Carole asked her about it.

Bob felt the sting of his father-in-law's rejection. He had tried all his life to fit in, to be accepted. He had a job and could provide a home; he was aggrieved to find that seemingly this was not enough.

"It makes no difference to me," Carole said of her father's refusal to wish them well. "I don't like him much anyway."

"Even so, it would be nice to have him happy for you," Bob said sulkily.

"Well, if he'd asked my permission to marry my mother, I

would have told him he wasn't good enough for her and boycotted their wedding."

Bob kissed her affectionately.

Carole, aware of how much Bob liked to read, encouraged him to continue his education. He took a correspondence course to finish his High School equivalent and resumed his studies in Australian history, but found, with the eyes and experience of an adult, that he was no longer unquestioning of what he read. Where once he had accepted words on pages as absolute truths, he was becoming sceptical of the receding lines and the curves, the ideas and assertions. He began to ask himself: What is this history, this silence that could be broken by whispering.

Drawn to travel tales now that he had sailed to foreign lands, he read Darwin's diaries and could see what Darwin had seen in South America: *Everyone is fully convinced that this is the next just war, because it is against the barbarians. Who would believe in this age that such atrocities could be committed in a Christian civilized country*.

Darwin was not surprised by what he saw when he arrived in Australia in 1832. Tasmania, in 1803, had a community of twenty-four prisoners, eight soldiers and twelve volunteers, including six women. 1804 saw the first massacre of Aboriginal people by members of the new colony. In 1827, the *London Times* reported that sixty Aborigines had been killed in revenge for the murder of one settler. Two years later the colonial government decided to concentrate the natives in a barren area on the west coast. Prisoners were sent out to hunt down the natives and given £5 for every Aborigine that they brought back to the white settlement. Nine died for every one that was delivered. In 1830, as part of a further attempt to eradicate the natives, a human line spread out across the vast island with forty-yard gaps between them. No Aborigines were caught but by the end of the exercise there were only three hundred left.

Darwin wrote in his diary in 1836: "there is no doubt that

this train of evil and its consequences originated in the infamous conduct of some of our countrymen." Darwin had also written that, in some landscapes, weeds take over most tenaciously and the only constant in nature is superior force. His observations fascinated Bob and helped to explain the reason why history was told to him the way it was.

Bob also read George Orwell, whose *Animal Farm* detailed the easy corruption of power, and whose *Burmese Days* recounted the infectious corruption of colonisation. With these new insights, he returned to the telling of Australian history, concluding that might did not always equal right, but it did equal victory and the privilege of writing the winner's version of history.

In his correspondence course, the assigned text was A.G.L. Shaw's *The Story of Australia*. There, Bob read:

> In India, South Africa and New Zealand, English colonists were opposed by native peoples, vigorous and often highly civilized; in Australia there could be no serious resistance from the aborigines with their primitive culture.

It was still there, the inevitable assertions of his inferiority and the continual accusations that he was the descendant of savages, primitive tribes. He realised that he was not seen as equal to white people. He saw also the continual attempt to tell the story that he and his family had simply vanished into the mists of time, inevitably overcome by the superiority of the whites.

As he started to question the conclusions of historians Bob also began to question other things he had been taught. He recalled how, in his youth, explorers like Wentworth seemed to embody all that was noble, good and civilised. Wentworth represented the economic development of the colony, which the blacks had threatened to prevent. He also represented the push to take sheep farming further west where the land was considered uninhabited. Wentworth crossed the Blue Mountains with Lawson and Blaxland, propelled by their desire to find any good pastures beyond the existing limits of settlements — Bob had thought these actions heroic. Keeping to the mountain ridges, instead of seeking the valley pathways, the party took fourteen days to reach the western edge of range. In doing so it was proclaimed that they opened up an area "equal to every demand which this country may have for an extension of tillage and pasture lands for a century to come". Until he read Conrad and Orwell, Bob had loved the accounts of the conquest.

There was also the contribution of Wentworth to the government of the time. Here the history books seemed to tell a different story to the one Bob remembered from childhood history lessons. Wentworth had dominated the constitutional debates in New South Wales and fought vigorously for local self-government and colonial control of land policy. When the push began to wrest political control from the squatters, whom Wentworth represented, and hand it to the people, he fought hard against it. He feared that if greater democracy were allowed, "all property and intelligence" would leave the colony, for "who would stay, while selfishness, ignorance and democracy hold sway?" To check it, he proposed that the distribution of seats should be weighted against the towns and there should be an hereditary upper house.

Through this reading of history Bob began to realise that the truths taught to him in his youth could be challenged by looking from a different perspective. As a young boy he'd aspired to be like the explorers who had forged their way across Australia and had daydreamed of a lineage going back to W.C. Wentworth, who, he thought then, embodied the excitement of the taming of a wild country. The story was now being rewritten, particularly with the work of historians like Henry Reynolds whose books *Frontier* and *The Other Side of the Frontier* included accounts of massacres and exploitation as well as evidence of subversion and resistance by Indigenous people. They had a new way of telling history, from the viewpoint the local Aboriginal people whose ancestors had been travelling across the mountain range for thousands of years and had aided Blaxland, Lawson and Wentworth in their crossing. His people had also been explorers, even if they were eclipsed by the Wentworths of recorded history.

Bob's faith in the indoctrination received at school was further fractured when he read that his boyhood hero had said, while arguing in 1844 against a proposal to allow Aborigines to give evidence in courts, that it would be "quite as defensible to receive as evidence in a Court of Justice the chattering of the orang-outang as of this savage race". The explorer who had conquered the Blue Mountains was not interested in extending his notion of rights to everyone. His notion of government would not have included Bob. No matter what Bob did, no matter how he tried to fit in, he would never have been acceptable to W.C. Wentworth. Just as he would never meet with approval from Carole's father.

Formerly, Bob had been frustrated that Danny would not make the effort to fit in. But, Bob now realised, Danny had always known that it didn't matter how hard they tried, that some people would consider their blackness a barrier they could not break through, that they would never be white enough. Bob had tried to make himself into an image, to turn himself into a white person. That, he had believed, was what was expected of him. Now he was to find there were those who would never truly accept him as being white: in that sense he had been set up to fail. But, he was also to learn, that to some he had never been Frankenstein's monster at all.

He'd been sitting in a pub on a Sunday afternoon with his old Navy buddies, Ernie Gibson and Colin Reid, all former radio operators now working for the Department of Civil Aviation. They would meet and reminisce about their times together in uniform and keep up with news from Geoff Young, who'd married a girl he had asked out for a bet, and Bernie Sinclair, who was now running the airport at Cooma.

"Ain't that Neville Bonner something," Ernie said.

Bob felt the familiar instinctive twinge, dreading a conversation about Aborigines and their inferiority.

"You know," Ernie continued, "I think it's really something that he's made it all the way into parliament. That's a first we can all be proud of. An Aboriginal Senator. And in the Liberal Party. We've come a long way."

Ernie then turned to Colin, telling him that he'd decided to buy one of those new Japanese cars, a Mazda. As Bob listened to their banter he thought about Ernie's words. His remarks hadn't been directed at him, as an accusation or patronising observation as if to say, "You can be white like everyone else." It was, instead, an honest feeling of pride and at that moment Bob started to think that maybe the reason his mates never mentioned his dark skin was not because they were being polite but because it really didn't matter to them. He sat back while Ernie and Colin went on to argue about patriotism and the Japanese, and he realised that Ernie's remark was the first positive thing he'd heard about an Aboriginal person. Ernie thought it was the most normal thing in the world for them to succeed. Carole was always trying to tell him this, but Bob had dismissed her consolations because he felt she could never understand what it was that he was going through. Now, hearing Ernie speak on this lazy Sunday afternoon, he began to realise that perhaps she was right.

Carole had always loved a happy ending. Her favourite movie was still *An Affair to Remember* — when Nickie Farrente swept Terry McKay up in his arms, realising that she was paralysed, it seemed as though their life together was just beginning. But films rarely focused on what happens after the wedding, and after four months as Mrs Bob Brecht, she knew why.

She was required to resign from her position from the Women's Royal Australian Navy upon marriage, and Bob had insisted that she should anyway. "I want my wife to stay at home. I can support you and look after you. Trust me."

Having his wife stay at home was an important status symbol to him; it showed he was a good provider. But there was not enough to keep Carole occupied in the house, and after preparing breakfast for Bob she spent the rest of the day thinking up chores. She found herself vacuuming the entire house daily and cleaning the curtains once a week. She missed the financial independence a job had given her. Now she relied on the money that Bob gave her and had to economise.

"We could use the extra money," she would say to him.

"I don't want you working. It'll look like I can't support you."

"Why do you care what people think?"

"It matters to *me*. That's the end of it. That ought to be reason enough."

"But Patricia works ..."

"I don't care what Patricia does. It's not how I want things to be in my house. I can take care of you. It might be tough now but things will get better. Trust me."

Carole had not spoken to her father and sister since her engagement, but she wrote her mother a long letter every Sunday night, and would receive a response the following week. Their letters were full of housekeeping details, new products to try, a trick for getting red-wine stains out of the carpet, and comments on the latest gossip about the royal family. Although Carole could write to her mother about the trivialities of their life — the new towels she had bought, planting pansies for the summer, her latest haircut — she could not write about how suffocated she felt with Bob, how she felt as though the walls in the house were beginning to close in on her. With a slow panic she began to realise that she was in exactly the same position as her mother.

This did not stop her from loving Bob. Rather, she felt trapped by her love for him. Much like the small birds and injured marsupials she had nursed as a child, she discovered there was something lost and broken within him. For all his fun-loving, outgoing attitude and his desire to be one of the boys, there was a large part of him that felt unworthy and self-conscious.

Carole had sensed the way he prickled when anyone spoke of his skin colour, or when they passed an Aboriginal person in the street or when anything about Aboriginal people came up in conversation. She had not understood this self-consciousness when they met. Now she tried to reassure him.

"Do you know what I would change about you?" she would ask him as they sat together on the porch of their modest weatherboard home in Sydney's southern suburbs, watching the sun drift below the skyline.

He would look at her expectantly.

"Nothing," she would say with a smile.

Silently he reflected that given the chance, she probably would change his skin colour to win her father's approval.

Secretly Carole thought to herself, if she were given the chance, she would take away his increasingly bad temper. It was as though he never trusted her to really love him because he didn't believe he was worthy of it. He would be jovial and relaxed with his friends, light-hearted and playful, but alone with Carole he would delve into his books, his mood becoming serious and agitated as he read. If she asked him if he would like a cup of tea, he would snap at her curtly to leave him alone. But if he felt his needs were not being met he would snarl that it was obviously too much trouble for her to get him just one lousy cup of tea.

Carole would merrily ask him about his day when he came home and fuss to get his dinner ready for him as she engaged him in conversation about the stresses of his work at the airport. He would grumble about the shift-work roster, sitting at the table while he waited for Carole to serve his dinner. She would listen patiently, but when she would begin to tell him about her day he would snap. "I'm too tired to listen to chatter."

Some nights he'd look at the plate she put before him. "What is it?" he would ask as he poked the food with a fork.

"It's a fish curry."

"I don't feel like fish. What else do you have?"

"You haven't even tried it yet."

"This looks too runny and I had an upset stomach today. Haven't you got a steak?"

"I'll see what I can find," she sighed as she rose to look in the fridge.

"What do you do around here all day that you can't have a decent bloody meal ready for me?" he would ask irritably. Inside him, dark and light seemed to live side by side.

He seemed resentful of any contact she had with people who might not accept him. About her letters to her mother he would snipe, "I suppose you are going to write to complain about me and tell her what a lousy husband I am."

"I'm just telling her about what I've been up to, that's all. I don't complain about you."

"It shouldn't take too long to tell her that you sit around here all day. I bet your father's glad that you seem so miserable all the time. Does he say 'I told you so'?"

"I don't speak to him, as you well know. And remember that my mother did come to the wedding. *She* was happy for me when I married you."

Feeling that the arguments were not worth the hassle, Carole did not write her letters when Bob was around and she kept the ones that arrived hidden from him. She believed that if she could appease him, show him that she could make an effort for him and just be patient, he would realise how much she loved him and be happier with her.

She read an interview in the *Women's Weekly* with Dyan Cannon, who had been married to Cary Grant: "I couldn't please him, no matter what I would say. He criticised everything I did." That described exactly how she felt with Bob.

She had tried so many things to occupy the hours that stretched out her days — embroidery, knitting, painting furniture, crocheting, baking, macramé — but her husband would always make a comment about how she must have too much time on her hands. He belittled her crafts to his Navy friends saying, "That is the result of a small amount of talent and too much time." In the mix of outrage and stinging betrayal, she wanted to remind him that of the two of them, she had held the higher position in the Navy.

Throughout the many frustrations and disappointments she met with in married life, Carole clung to the way Bob had looked at her when they first met. She could not let go of the way that he would watch adoringly as she brushed her hair or put cream on her face. And she could sustain herself during the daylight hours by the way he would, with tenderness, say to her in the dark, "I love you, Carole. You are the best thing that has ever happened to me." She continued to believe that if she were patient, if she nursed him through his insecurities and showed him how much she loved him, he would be released from his dark side and become the man she thought she had married.

The troubles in her relationship with Bob drew her closer to her sister-in-law, Patricia. Although she would never tell Patricia the details of the conversations that had passed between herself and Bob, would never betray his bitter side or reveal the humiliation she suffered, she would say that she found him difficult and that his refusal to let her work was frustrating.

"He would never dream of misbehaving in front of you," she'd say laughingly to Patricia as she watched her preparing the tea. "He would never repeat the things he says to me about women working for fear that he'd get a word or two from you."

Patricia placed a cup and saucer in front of Carole, then sat down at the kitchen table, facing her. She picked up her cup, holding it between her two hands. She blew on the liquid to cool it. "I don't understand it, really. I suppose that Mother always stayed at home. She took in washing but he was too young to know she did all that extra work. It would have just seemed like more of her usual chores to him."

"Maybe it's not so much that he compares me to you and his mother as that he cares what his friends think. You know — he'll feel less of a man if his wife has to work. I don't understand it. He has so much to be proud of but he seems trapped by what other people think of him."

"He always seemed so able to fit into different situations," Patricia said, watching as Carole took a delicate sip from her cup. "He seemed to cope better than Daisy and Danny in the home. He was quick to make friends and didn't complain. I suppose because he seemed to be handling what was happening to him, I never gave him the same attention, forgot to make sure that he was adapting to life in the orphanage." Patricia paused. "He was young too when he lost Mother, and I suppose that just because he seemed brave at the time, that didn't mean he wasn't affected by it."

While Carole could confide in Patricia, taking her flowers from her garden and talking about the clothes she was designing, she found Daisy dismissive of her attempts to start conversation, making it clear that there was no place for Carole in her scheme of things. Daisy would take a cigarette from her silver cigarette case, snap it shut and tap her cigarette firmly on the lid. She'd tilt her head slightly as she lit the cigarette, flicking her hair back when it was lit. Often when Carole would call by to see Patricia, to help with the new babies, Daisy would make a quick exit. "Well, I'll let you two housewives talk about baby poo and cleaning products. I'm off to see if Pasquale needs a hand in the restaurant."

"She never seems to have the stomach for the children," sighed Patricia as she watched her sister leave. "She's much better at helping in the restaurant. She's so outgoing that the customers all love her, and I don't know what Pasquale would do without her. I get so caught up here with Thomas and Robert. We're lucky that she can help out. But that new dress I made looks lovely on her. This new fashion for mini skirts and cropped jackets suits her figure. I could never get this pudge into an outfit like that." Patricia patted her stomach where childbirth had left padding.

Carole thought that Daisy's manner of taking leave when she arrived, and her snide comments about the trivial and unpleasant tasks associated with motherhood, revealed Daisy's disdain for her sister. She did not say anything. Patricia was so protective of Daisy that nothing could be said against her. And Carole wondered if perhaps her own view of Daisy had been influenced by Bob's dislike of her.

When Carole had Candice and Kingsley to occupy her days, she didn't feel the sting of Bob's frustrations with her as much as she did before. Caring for and nurturing a small child gave her back the feeling that she was doing something purposeful with her life. When she held the first small bundle in her arms and looked at Candice's face, crinkled and red, eyes tightly shut, and touched her tiny hands, Carole felt the surging love that comes from being needed.

Bob had shown a mix of trepidation and enthusiasm about the arrival of Candice. He seemed to be fascinated and frightened of her at the same time. He would leave the chores of child-rearing to Carole — changing of nappies, toilet-training, the teething and the nursing through childhood ailments. When Candice or Kingsley cried during the night, Bob would shake Carole awake and say, "Honey, your baby is crying."

But at other times, when he was stopped on the street and told that his children were beautiful and well dressed, or when Candice won a prize at school for her finger-painting or Kingsley said his first word — "Dad" — he seemed to lose his distance and flush with joy.

Bob seemed willing to participate in the responsibilities of parenthood when Candice and Kingsley were well dressed and well behaved, or when others praised or rewarded them, Carole preferred it this way. She liked to be the one who wiped noses, tied shoes, lulled them into eating their greens and taught them how to write letters and colour between the lines.

When she first became a mother, Carole's bond with Patricia became stronger. She could talk with Patricia about childcare — healing rashes, teaching a child to walk, and later to read and then to write, how to stop a child from wetting the bed and sucking their thumb. Patricia doted on Candice, whose arrival coincided with the birth of Patricia's third son. She made dresses and matching hats of pink gingham and white lace or orange and brown velvet for Carole's daughter and little pants and matching shirts of navy cotton with white or tartan trim for her son.

Carole worried that Candice and Kingsley would feel ashamed of their tan-coloured skin, just as their father did. She would tell them that they were special and gifted, and could do anything they chose to. She would tell them their darkness was beautiful. "Look how pretty this red dress is with your dark hair and dark eyes, Candice."

She tried to find Candice dolls with dark hair and dark eyes. When Candice came home from school crying because she had been teased, Carole sat her down with a chocolate-chip biscuit and a glass of milk and explained: "They're just jealous because they know that you are pretty. Besides, brown skin is better because you won't turn red in the sun, the way I do."

The growing bond that Carole developed with Patricia only sent Daisy further away. She would turn silent when their chatter focused on the children and before too long would be making her excuses to leave and work at the restaurant.

When misfortune befell Patricia, Carole lost her best friend. She needed one more than ever then, because with the loss of his sister Bob lost control of himself.

25

1970

WHEN GRIGOR BRECHT PASSED AWAY, making a widow of his second wife, only two of his children, those from that second marriage, attended his funeral.

Until his last days, he had been haunted by what his eldest daughter had prophetically said as she walked out of their Lithgow home — that it would be too late when he would finally realise — nothing was more important than family.

As Patricia spoke, Grigor could see in her face her resemblance to her mother. He realised that she was now the same age as Elizabeth had been when he first saw her on the railway platform at Parkes. It worried him that Elizabeth, somewhere above, would be watching him. Although he went to sleep every night hoping that, by some miracle, he would wake to find her beside him, he sensed her fury that he had let their children slip from his home; he knew she would have hated him for losing them, the same way Patricia seemed to despise him.

Without her children in his house, Grigor felt as though Elizabeth was further from him. When she had first left him, the presence of his children taunted him, but after they left the house was still and silent. Discarded clothes, old toys and school assignments lay around like skeletons.

When he visited the home, he found it difficult to make conversation, particularly with Danny who seemed to swing from elation to distress in the course of an hour. Yet even over the distance that he felt between the children and himself, he could recognise himself in them. And he was desperate to try and establish some sense that they were his as much as they were Elizabeth's. When Bob asked why his skin was dark, Grigor wanted his son to know that his mother was every bit as good as a white person; as white as everyone else.

About a year after Patricia had departed, Grigor met Dawn Phillips. He had come to Sydney for a Communist Party meeting. It was late evening but he could not sleep. Once he would have stayed with his comrades in the bar of the pub in the Rocks where he had his room for the night, but on this night he was restless with his inner thoughts of Elizabeth, so he walked the windy, stone-stepped streets. He was crossing the Harbour Bridge when he saw a thin woman looking over the bars of the walkway to the water below as she hugged her cardigan tightly around her body. She seemed in a daze, lost. He approached her and asked, "Are you alright, young lady?"

At first, the petite caramel-haired woman was startled then accusation flashed in her eyes. She pulled her hands to her face and started to sob. Grigor handed her his handkerchief, when she ignored it and continued to cry he took off his jacket and placed it around her shoulders. She leant into him. With Dawn's fragile frame heaving against his tall embrace, Grigor was overcome with the desire to rescue her. She poured out the tale of her pregnancy to her boyfriend, Freddy. He had promised to marry her but when his parents discovered their plans — and the fact that she was Catholic — they forbade it. Freddy succumbed to their pressure and had since become engaged to Charlotte Winter, a Protestant girl.

Grigor saw more than a passing resemblance in Dawn's pale, translucent skin and green eyes to Esmeralda, the long-lost servant girl back in Germany who, in his later years, had begun to drift into his thoughts more and more.

"Come now, a cry will do you good. You'll feel better in the morning."

Dawn flashed back at him, "What do you know? I have nowhere to go. Nowhere to sleep. No money. No one to look after me. And if I do wake up tomorrow, I am sure I would not feel any better than I feel now." She burst into tears again.

"I will find you a room. You can have a nice bath and something to eat and a sleep. If you still feel this way in the morning, I will walk you back here and toss you off this bridge myself."

At this, Dawn's sobs seemed to subside. Sensing a break in her mood, Grigor added seriously, "Think. If you jump over this bridge, you just make life easier for this — what was his name?"

"Freddy."

"Yes, Freddy. You would just allow him and his family to ruin you and your child. Why should your child be the loser and this Freddy the winner? There is more of you in this little child than Freddy."

"But who will want me now?" Dawn sobbed again. "Who will look after me?"

"There are always solutions, my dear," Grigor said, guiding her by the arm as they walked towards his pub. "They may not be apparent when you're standing on a big bridge like this, contemplating a swim after midnight but after a good sleep and breakfast, they will become clearer."

He paid for her hotel room, met with her the next morning, and then, as a result of their discussion over sausages, steak and eggs, escorted her home to Lithgow with a promise to look after her and her child. They were married before he ever mentioned that he already had six children — seven, if he included the child he had fathered long ago with Esmeralda.

Dawn Phillips, now Dawn Brecht, followed Grigor's reassuring words from the harbour to the mountains. A way out with dignity was what she was praying for and Grigor's sanctuary was all she could have hoped for at that moment when she was prepared to take her own life. She liked his home with its four bedrooms and large parlour. None too pleased that she was a second wife, Dawn began her efforts to erase all signs of her predecessor from the house.

She had mistaken Grigor's concern for her for love, and did not understand that when he stopped to talk to her on the bridge he was searching for stability and homely comfort. She did not realise he expected her to provide that for him. With his new marriage, he planned to retrieve his children from the orphanage.

He often thought about the night that Mrs Crawford knocked on the door. As he looked around his ill-kept house, his head throbbing from the alcohol that was still in his system, his throat sore from yelling, Mrs Crawford had asked questions he did not know how to answer; he believed that there must be better places for these children than with him. Grigor knew in his heart that he was not a bad man.

Mrs Crawford started talking about "care", "responsibility", "standards" and "education". "They need special attention before they are able to adjust to life in our society," she had told him. "There is much of the savagery still left in the half-breeds and they are better off with concentrated care."

As Mrs Crawford made her case to Grigor for his handing his younger children into state care, he thought about the scene in the house the night before, the one that felt foggy in his already thick head. He had stumbled home when the pub closed. He could recall falling on the front steps, banging his knee hard. He cursed as he lay there and he could hear voices and movement in the house. If Elizabeth had been there, the children would have been asleep, not making noise and scurrying around like rats. She would have heard him fall, as the children had, and would have rushed to see if he was alright, would have tended to his injury and fussed over him as though the accident were the step's fault instead of his. As he opened the door he yelled at the children to get to their beds.

He stumbled down the hallway to the lounge room and sank into his chair. He felt something hard snap under his weight. He pulled himself out of the chair and looked down to see a doll, its face broken. He grabbed the pieces and threw them into the fire as he yelled, "Who in bloody hell left that damned thing there?"

Above the fireplace, his favourite photograph of Elizabeth looked back at him from the frame, her hair thick and black, her eyes sparkling as she held her newborn child, Thomas, up to the lens, blossoming with motherhood. Seeing it made him ache. He grabbed it and threw it in the fire.

In the morning, he felt remorseful. The children avoided eye contact, left the room when he entered. In each of them he could see his Elizabeth; could feel her disappointment.

When Mrs Crawford reasoned with him, Grigor decided that if they were gone he would not be constantly reminded of Elizabeth. So he let Mrs Crawford make the arrangements she had urged on him.

But without the children around him, he felt strangely empty and began to lose his passion for everything else in his life. Elizabeth's death, the loss of her affection and tenderness, seemed to harden him against the rest of the world.

Grigor's failure to renew a family life with Dawn seemed a part of the disillusion he felt in life more generally. The bickering within the Australian Communist Party about the wording of resolutions and the tenacious battles that preceded the voting started to feel petty and tiring. He kept fighting for the cause, kept repeating the rhetoric and dogma that he believed offered the only way for a better life, but the dwindling attendance at meetings extinguished the enthusiasm. What had once seemed inevitable — a socialist world — was now losing its appeal to the general public. The ideals by which he had defined himself were almost forgotten and all he had fought for was unravelling.

A negative attitude towards communism had been building up ever since the Bolsheviks had shown that revolution was possible. In Australia, he had seen the increase of deportations of aliens and had avoided this danger by going bush. It was on such travels that he met Elizabeth. When he brought her to his mountain town, Grigor was heavily involved with his local branch of the Communist Party. The Lithgow branch attracted men from the coalmines and steelworks, the coke ovens and blast furnaces. He worked with Charlie Nelson, Jock Lindop, Jock Jamieson, and Harry den Hartog. It was a small group but, driven by Charlie's passion, there was dedication to spreading the word to the workers. Together they organised May Day parades with bunting and platforms and rousing speeches. In the pub, amongst his comrades Grigor would condemn the continual surveillance of the party and its members.

But when Stalin made his pact with Hitler, Grigor had to find excuses for him. But by this time, Grigor's ideals had been shattered. For the first time he began to feel that he was reciting Russian propaganda rather than building a universal Marxist dream. He watched the escalating violence directed against communists and socialists in Australia. They became the target of Catholic antagonism through the Catholic Social Studies Movement propelled by the likes of B.A. Santamaria.

He would leave the house for meetings he didn't attend, instead walking the streets or slinking into the bar to drink to memories of lost ideals. It was with profound disillusionment that he had embarked on his trip to Sydney and came across Dawn Brecht. He had thought that Dawn would enable him to get his children back, that he could start again and do better this time. But when Dawn entered his home she saw the portraits — the children around the Christmas tree, the older children laughing as Bob knelt over his present wildly pulling off the wrapping paper; the children lining up in their best attire ready for a trip to Katoomba, with William caught glancing sideways as though intent on travelling in an opposite direction; and Grigor's last birthday gift to Elizabeth, a portrait with Thomas holding Bob, William with his hands on Patricia's shoulders as she beams at the camera and Patricia cradling baby Danny. This photograph, the first of all her children together, had been the one Elizabeth liked the most. Dawn eyed the pictures carefully. Her new husband's children were 'half-breeds': she saw in the darker three the inferiority of savages and she felt disgust choking her.

"Where are they now?" she demanded.

"My two eldest boys went missing in the war. The eldest girl is in Sydney. But the youngest three, they are in an orphanage." He added, after a careful pause, "Dawn, I would like to get them back."

"When?"

"We could ..." he began.

"We?" Dawn interrupted, "if you think I am taking on more children with this one not even born yet, you are clearly trying to push me over the edge." She began sobbing. "I came here to have this baby. I'm not ready for anything else."

"Of course you must settle in first," Grigor said. "We will talk about my children later."

Every time he tried to bring the subject up, Dawn would cry, working herself into a fit. It was never the right time, and eventually, after Dawn gave birth to her second child, he stopped bringing up the subject altogether.

Grigor had thought that all women had maternal feelings, and it shocked him that Dawn didn't feel anything but hostility towards his other children.

Dawn, Grigor discovered after their hasty wedding, suffered from bouts of hysteria — uncontrollable crying and shouting. At first he thought she was distressed about the pregnancy, but over their first months together he came to believe that she was damaged and unstable. He liked a woman with vulnerabilities who, with his help, could learn to bear up to hardship with determination and fortitude, as

Elizabeth had done. Dawn's problems seemed so complicated and deep, Grigor felt unable to ease them.

Grigor withdrew from family life, immersing himself in photography. Light meters and other technology had long ago replaced the materials he had begun his career with. He spent his time developing portraits of football teams and families, but he preferred his portraits of the miners, returning to the surface, blackened faces and widened eyes. For Grigor, they held more truth than the contrived pictures of parents and children dressed in Sunday best.

He resented Dawn for the way in which she had assumed his acceptance of her child, Dalia, though she had rejected his. He knew that she had thought less of him because his children and first wife were dark. "They are as white as you are," he would lash back at her before he came to realise that her resultant hysterics were not worth the faint satisfaction of such a comment.

Dawn Brecht was already bitter when Grigor stopped to talk to her. Freddy had used her. He had refused to marry her. She had thought the pregnancy would change his mind. It didn't. In fact, there was no disapproval from his family, no Charlotte Winter. Dawn had made that up because it was too hard to say that Freddy just did not want her and that her attempts to bend him to her will had failed.

She found it difficult to keep control of herself. There was always some trial that was hers to bear. Her first child was forever sick and crying. The second was even worse, the noise thundering in her ears, her space shrinking.

"I should have jumped," she would sob, trying to remind him of the role he was to continue to play with her.

"I should have let you," he would reply, showing her how far they had fallen away from each other.

Grigor was not what she would have settled for if life had been fairer to her. She set about making his home hers by erasing the belongings in it from his former life and imprinting her own taste on the décor. The pictures of his children and his first wife had shocked her, made her feel superior both to his first family and to Grigor himself. It released her from the debt she felt she owed him when he talked her out of jumping from the bridge, and gave her a sense of having saved him by giving him respectability and white children. Grigor's inability to see what she offered hardened her against him. By the time he seemed to concede her position, she no longer felt enough affection for him to feel victorious.

As an old man, with nine children — only two of whom he had contact with — and two wives, one he mourned and one he detested, Grigor would concede that Patricia's parting words had been right. He experienced their truth the day he had seen his son on a sunny afternoon in Strawberry Hills. During that encounter Elizabeth's ghost seemed to be pointing an accusing finger at him.

Grigor looked at his young son, so full of youthful enterprise. He wanted to tell him about Marx, the nobility of the workers, the streets of Cologne, of exile, of Esmeralda, of Elizabeth crying at the train station. If he had some vocabulary or dialogue to build upon with the boy, some ability to express what he felt inside, he would, at that moment, have reached out to his son. But the silence was too thick to break.

When he closed his weary eyes for the final time, Grigor Brecht thought to himself that perhaps, at last, he would see his Elizabeth again, and this time she would rescue him.

26

1970

WHEN PASQUALE HAD ASKED Patricia to marry him she answered, "I want a big family. At least five children."

Pasquale had smiled at her and promised, "We will do whatever you want when you are my wife." She could see the smile in the soft lines at the side of his eyes and was flushed with the pleasure of being adored, a new and overwhelming sensation.

She liked the way he spoke, with a soft and unassuming voice. He struggled with English, but she found his turn of phrase musical. She liked his solidness, the large muscles in his arms and his thick chest, the grey that lapped his curls and the rough skin on his hands. It felt honest to her. He would lift his chest high when she held his hand as they walked down the street and he would gently bring her hand to his lips and kiss it tenderly.

The attention that Pasquale showered on her was something Patricia had never expected. He was the first man to ask her out, the first who had ever touched her skin. That first time he ran his hand slowly down her arm as he looked into her eyes, she felt his touch sweep through her whole body, felt a part of her merge into him. She would have said 'yes' to anything he asked.

When they moved into their own home, Patricia felt a renewed happiness with life. Not since the times when she had sat with her mother, fussing over her brothers and sisters, had she had such a feeling of tranquil completeness. All the disappointments and failures she had felt in the past seemed to evaporate. She scrubbed, painted, stitched and hammered to turn his shabby flat into a cosy home. Pasquale would marvel at the little changes she made and she could see the pride he had in her and their home. When he introduced her at the restaurant as his wife, he always paused slightly after he said the word 'wife' as if to savour the sound of the word.

She was also able to help Pasquale at the restaurant, decorating the place to make it more attractive. The old regulars teased her husband, who grinned back sheepishly. To her own surprise, she also seemed to have a knack for making small improvements to the way Pasquale ran his business. She had watched Madelaine build her little business into a profitable one and had absorbed more than she realised. "Every penny you can squeeze out of the supplier is one for your pocket; every penny you can squeeze out of the buyer is one for your purse," Madelaine had often said.

Patricia negotiated better prices from the grocers and told the regulars who ate on credit that if they paid half their debts Pasquale would erase the rest. This gave them the incentive to finally pay up, and Patricia used the money to buy new tables and chairs. She put plants in the window, made curtains and matching tablecloths and cushions for the chairs. It added to the charm of the restaurant and attracted more customers. She ensured that the regulars still felt welcome, aware that the tables of cantankerous old Italian men added to the atmosphere. In a short time, the success enabled them to move to a bigger house.

Patricia was pregnant with her first child when Daisy came to live with her. She was overjoyed when she opened the door and saw her sister standing before her. She had long imagined Daisy returning; she would be remorseful, tearful and apologetic for leaving the way she did, for not saying goodbye, for stealing those things she took. But Daisy was not contrite — she was defensive and guarded.

Patricia thought that Daisy's defiance was masking wounds. She looked at her sister, so beautiful with her thick black hair, her high cheeks, and saw in her hazel eyes loneliness and despair. Daisy was turning to her for support and Patricia could not help but open her heart to her and let her into her home.

It seemed right that, at the moment in her life when she was starting her own family with Pasquale, her sister should come back. Although the table would not be crowded with the faces of her brothers and sisters as she had long imagined, now there would be her own children there, Pasquale, and Bob and Carole. And now Daisy as well.

It had been eleven years since Daisy left, and she never did explain where she had been. Although Patricia often wondered about the jade brooch Daisy had stolen from her that day she left, Patricia resisted her longing to ask if Daisy still had it and would never have asked for it to be returned. Patiently she waited for Daisy to talk when the time was right.

During his visits, Bob would chide her for her generosity in bringing Daisy into her house. "You don't even know where she has been all these years, what she has been up to, what she has done, who she has been with," he had said when he was alone with Patricia. She tried to explain to him that he was being too hard on Daisy, that he did not understand how for all her tough exterior, she was more fragile than she wanted anyone to know.

She thought Bob's attitude towards Daisy and Carole were odd. With Daisy, he could never see past the question mark about her disappearance. As for Carole, Patricia could see that the way he treated her was killing something in his wife. "You should realise how lucky you are to have Carole," she would say to him.

"I do," he would reply sulkily. "I look after her and make

sure that she doesn't have to work. She has what every woman wants. There are plenty of women who would be very happy with an arrangement like that."

At this, Patricia would laugh. "Bob, you are a man, and men are not best placed to know what every woman wants. In fact, your idea of what women really want is suspiciously like what men really want. Seriously, you shouldn't worry so much about what other people think. It's not worth hurting the people you love." Patricia realised as Bob looked at her stonily, that she would not be able to change his attitude towards Carole. Her own life soon settled around the routine of child-rearing, first one child, then two and then three. When Thomas was born, as Patricia looked down at him nestled in her arms, she often thought of her mother and her words of advice — nothing is more important than family. She had lost her brothers, Thomas and William, long ago and now she had lost Danny too. As she looked down at her first child, perfect in his features, she could feel the pounding of her heart and knew that if anything happened to her child it would not continue beating.

With her second son, William, and her first daughter, Elizabeth, Patricia felt the strings that tied her heart together tightening, strengthened by the way that Thomas would play with his little green soldiers, William draw pictures for her to stick on the fridge and her little Elizabeth arrange flowers in a vase with such earnest concentration. Elizabeth's birth had been difficult and Patricia had almost died. This, she thought, made her daughter even more precious.

She had to juggle the demands of child care and was less able to assist Pasquale in the restaurant. She could barely find time to design clothes for Madelaine. But she was happy, and when Bob and Carole had their two she would often have all five children playing through her house.

With the arrival of her niece and nephew coming along, Patricia began to long for another child. The restaurant was going well and, with Daisy so eager to help, she was rarely needed. But when she said to Pasquale that she thought it was time for them to have another child, Pasquale asked her to wait a while.

"Why? The restaurant is making more money than ever and I am ready for another child. When Candice and Kingsley are here and there are five little ones, I feel the place is emptier when they go."

"I hardly see you any more. You are never in the restaurant. Always here with the children."

"But you see me here. I don't understand. I thought we agreed that we would have five. You told me when we got married that if I was your wife I could have anything I wanted. This is what I want. Five children. Nothing is as important as this."

"You are more important than this. You know what the doctor told you after Elizabeth was born. He said you shouldn't have more — it's too dangerous."

"He said it *might be* dangerous. And it is a risk worth taking."

Pasquale remained silent. He could never argue with her when she wanted something. She had considered his complaint about seeing less of her, and it was true that they were really together only when he came home from the restaurant, late at night when she was exhausted. The feel of his hand sliding slowly down her arm still stirred her, but she was less and less able to summon the energy to respond to him. But her yearning for another child was taunting her and it was with delight that she confirmed with her doctor that she was pregnant again. His concern that her heart was weak did not dampen her spirits.

At first she headed for home but, enjoying the sunshine dancing on her skin, her feeling of elation drew her towards the restaurant to share the news with Pasquale. She would promise him that she would make sure she spent more time with him; she even thought, with all the money the restaurant was making, that perhaps he could hire someone to manage the place. Daisy seemed to know how the place ran and, although Pasquale would insist there needed to be a man in charge, Patricia was confident that her sister could ensure that everything ran smoothly. In fact, she thought, it would be good to give Daisy the extra responsibility. And Pasquale would see that she was right about having another child. He loved her. Even now, he would cradle her in his arms through the night as they slept.

As she walked in the back door of the restaurant, into the kitchen, she noticed Pasquale stepping back from Daisy, turning to look at her. She saw the shock on their faces at her unexpected visit.

Patricia laughed, "I know you think I don't come here often enough, Pasquale, but you don't need to look so surprised."

"What are you doing here?" he sputtered.

"I have some good news and I thought I would come straight here and tell you. I'm glad you're here too, Daisy. I've just come from the doctor's, and guess what?" Patricia looked at Pasquale's still surprised face. "I'm pregnant," she said with a smile.

Pasquale and Daisy continued to stare at her.

"I know you said you weren't sure whether the time was right, but it looks like God decided for us."

Patricia began to feel confused about the silence. When she had told him she was pregnant with Thomas, Pasquale had grabbed her up in his arms and danced her around the room with glee.

"Tell her," Daisy said as she took a step back towards Pasquale.

Pasquale still looked at Patricia, unable to say anything.

"Tell her," Daisy repeated as she placed her hand on Pasquale's arm.

In response to Pasquale's continued silence, Daisy said coldly, "I'm pregnant, too."

As she saw the look of fear cross Pasquale's face, Patricia

realised the truth. She suddenly felt dizzy, as though time had slipped into some other hour. She turned and walked out, heading towards her home, where her children were and where everything made sense.

She entered her house and sat down in the armchair where she would sit to sew. With the children at school, the house was empty. She kept thinking that she had to go to pick the children up. She thought of Thomas, and the image of her brother and her son seemed to interchange. She was trying to catch her breath, to ease the sharp pain running down her arm. The pain heralded a thick wall of blackness.

Daisy could never see the self-satisfied way that Patricia would pat her pregnant stomach without being reminded of Marcel. When she began living in the apartment he had rented for her, she thought that this would be a stepping-stone to a better life. As her life began to revolve around Marcel, she felt herself becoming more deeply attached to him, waiting to hear the click of his key in the lock, sitting close to the phone expecting his call. She would run to him when he opened the door, then cling to him, kissing his face and neck, drawing him close.

"*Cherie,*" he would laugh, "I was here but yesterday."

The more she longed for Marcel to be with her and dreaded his going, the more she wished that instead of being his mistress she could be his wife. "I would love to be married to you," she said to him shyly one day as she lay naked across his trouser-clad lap. The sun was streaming through the window, dancing on Daisy's light brown skin.

"If we were married, you would not be so pleased to see me when I came to visit," he said, playfully slapping her thigh.

For five years he had dismissed her hints as light-hearted teasing. He would, Daisy thought, take her demands more seriously if she fell pregnant, if she could give him the child that Madelaine had never managed to.

Although she had been on the pill, she stopped taking it.

Three months later, she went to Marcel, bubbling with enthusiasm.

He looked at her coolly. "I thought you were taking precautions," he said, looking at her questioningly.

"I've been sick. I mean, I was sick before, about a month ago. And when you vomit you can accidently throw the pill back up. Anyway, it's not one hundred per cent safe. The doctor said it wasn't. So, it's a miracle, a little miracle."

"Well, this miracle is inconvenient. We will have to fix it."

"But I want to keep it, Marcel. I want to have your child. I want us to be a family." She was expecting him to embrace her, to be delighted that she had given him this gift, not want to leave her.

Instead, he stood back from her and laughed. "*Cherie*. A man does not want his mistress to turn into a wife. I already have one of those. I don't want another. Where is the fun in that?"

"But what about our baby, *your* baby?" she pleaded.

"What would I do with one of those? I do not know why you think that I would want something around me that does nothing but cry and shit. I would rather have a puppy. They don't need nappies."

Daisy felt cold, she pulled her arms around her body and she looked at Marcel. She could see in his eyes that he was displeased. It was a look she saw when he spoke of Madelaine and the things she did that he did not like — buying a new car without asking him, expanding her business in some way. She hoped his reaction was just due to surprise and that once he got used to the idea, he would change his mind. Marcel sat in his chair and opened his cigarette case.

"Darling," she began, "I know this is a shock, not what we expected, but think about it."

He looked at her and lit a cigarette. He said, "Oh, Daisy. I hope you did not think that this little trick would get me to leave my wife and marry you? *Cherie*, you are a lovely little woman, beautiful and sexy, but I have a wife."

"But you don't love her. You love me. You say all the time that she is not a good wife. I would be. I would do anything for you, Marcel. I do everything you say."

"Ah, my sweet girl, you do not understand. I couldn't have you as my wife. There are some women who are made to be wives and some who are made to be mistresses. You, my darling, are not wife material. You are like an exotic flower and should be savoured. You are not one for the kitchen and for child-bearing." He drew on his cigarette and levelled his gaze at her.

"Well, I am going to have this baby anyway, whether you like it or not."

Marcel laughed at her again. "And what will you live on?"

He kept smoking, waiting for her to answer. When she started to cry, he remained unmoved.

"I will not support you. And you do not have a job. You could get one, but you are a little too used to a comfortable apartment, fine clothes and your life of luxury, I think."

Daisy had no means to support herself when she became Marcel's mistress and she realised she had less ability to do so now. She had expected Marcel to bend to her will and was shocked by his coldness. She also realised for the first time that no matter what she did, Marcel would never take her as his wife.

He did not visit her for two weeks, the longest time he had stayed away since she moved into the apartment. She ran out of money after ten days and began to panic, remembering Marcel's taunts. On the twelfth day, she rang him at home. When Madelaine answered she hung up. She rang again several hours later and this time Marcel answered. He was furious with her for calling. "I will come and see you tomorrow", he said through gritted teeth.

"When?" she begged.

"When I get there. Don't call here again."

He was still fuming when he arrived the following day.

"Oh Marcel, I'm sorry. I'm so sorry," she said, running to

him as he entered. She began kissing him on his lips and cheeks. "I was so worried that you weren't coming back. Please forgive me."

He stood coldly still while she wept. "Really, Daisy. These theatrics are tiring."

Marcel — and his money — arranged for a car to drive her from her apartment to a small terrace house in Kings Cross, then back to her apartment. There were roses waiting for her when she returned, but no Marcel to greet her. He did not come until two days later, and by that time she was not able to do anything but cry.

"This will get very boring soon, my love," Marcel said. "If I wanted a dull time, I could stay at home with Madelaine."

Daisy had thought that by doing what Marcel wanted and getting rid of the baby their relationship would be as before. She could live with not being his wife, she reasoned, so long as she was still his mistress. It was a better life than working. But she knew now that she was faced with the possibility that he might not want her any more. That she did love Marcel.

She also noticed he was no longer playful and indulgent. He did not visit her every day, sometimes visiting her only once a week. He did not stay for long and was not interested in caressing her.

Daisy, trying even harder to please him, spent more time on her hair and skin before he arrived. She would lie naked on the couch for him, but he would barely look at her.

"Daisy," he would sigh, "you are too old for that now. It was charming when you were eighteen. You will be thirty in a few years."

"Marcel, don't you love me any more?" she whispered.

"*Cherie*, the time has come for us to part," he continued, his eyes on his shoes. "I know that you will need some time to get a new life, find a new boyfriend. So I will pay for the lease for six more months, but then no more."

"No!" she yelled, crossing the room and kneeling before him, clinging to his legs. "No, Marcel. Don't leave me. I love you. I love you so much. I'll do anything for you. Anything. I am sorry that I got pregnant but I did what you wanted — I got rid of it, just like you said. Please. Oh, please."

Marcel sighed, stroking his moustache. "You are a clever girl, Daisy. You will find a way. Just like the day you marched up to my front door and found me."

"But I am not like that any more. I love you," she pleaded.

"Girls like you don't change, Daisy." He stood to leave. "You will fall on your feet, my dear. Now get up off the floor."

Daisy stayed in her apartment for most of the six months. She did not have Marcel's money to keep her going, so she started pawning the gifts he had given her to buy food, gin and cigarettes. Although she ate very little, she drank and smoked quite a lot. She would drink herself to sleep on the couch where she had once posed for Marcel. When she awoke in the morning, she would look in the mirror at the wrinkles that had begun to cross her forehead and creep around the corners of her eyes.

Who would want me now? she thought to herself. She had spent over ten years with Marcel. He had been the focus of her life. Without him, she was helpless. *What will I do*? she asked herself into the misty hours of the night.

With three weeks before her lease ran out, and no further visits from Marcel, Daisy had to plan. She could get herself a job, but she had no skills. She had looked through the paper, but the only jobs she could have applied for — shop assistant, seamstress, waitress — all paid so little she would have to give up her apartment. She would not be able to afford much at all.

She remembered that Marcel had spoken about Patricia's wedding. It had been held at his house; Madelaine had gone overboard with the arrangements, he had grumbled, and teased her about not being invited. Daisy felt a mixture of contempt — that Patricia would be marrying some old Italian at Madelaine's home — and jealousy that Patricia was getting married at all. Marcel had also mentioned that Patricia was finally living in her own place, much to Madelaine's delight, as she now had extra room in the shop. Patricia, Daisy knew, would look after her and not make her get a job.

Daisy couldn't bring herself to feel grateful that Patricia had taken her back in; her sister's good nature only irritated her. Daisy thought that it was unfair that Patricia, with her innocence about the world, her inability to stand up to anyone, should end up with a house of her own, a husband who was making a reasonable income and a family on the way. Prettier, smarter and more sophisticated than her sister, Daisy thought she was the one who should have been mistress of her own home. Patricia seemed to have obtained all these things without even trying.

Pasquale was not the sort of man that Daisy would have chosen for herself. He was too old and unattractive, without Marcel's smoothed hair and tailored clothes. But, she observed, he was devoted to Patricia, would follow her around the kitchen with his eyes as she made his breakfast and he pretended to read the paper. He had stability and a soundness that she knew now was more valuable than gold bracelets, shiny earrings and pretty dresses.

As she watched Pasquale's affection for her sister, Daisy remembered Marcel's words to her: that she was the sort of woman who a man would want as a mistress, not a wife. She had fallen in love with Marcel's worldliness, his urbanity. But, now she was older, she began to think that instead of a man like Marcel, what she really wanted was a warm, kind man like Pasquale, someone who would adore her. Yes, Pasquale, who rubbed Patricia's feet when she was pregnant and who thought she was beautiful even when she was fat.

As the children came along, Patricia seemed more interested in motherhood than in her husband, and Daisy could see Pasquale becoming frustrated with his place at the periphery of his wife's attention.

"Oh, Pasquale," she would coo to him. "If I had a husband

like you, I would give him all the attention he wanted. But Patricia is different to me, so you'll just have to accept it and hope she stops taking you for granted."

Daisy spent more and more time in the restaurant, assisting Pasquale with the orders for the kitchen, with the books and customers. She would float around the tables, cigarette in hand, standing with her figure at its best advantage, talking cheerfully and flirtatiously to the diners, looking over to Pasquale to see if he noticed the attention she was getting. Although all the regulars had lost their hearts to her, it was Pasquale who had captured hers.

"You know if you ever need to talk, I am here for you," she would say to him, patting his arm as he tried to count the night's takings. "I know how lonely you are."

Patricia had been the one their mother had spent the most time with, cosily sewing at the kitchen table or cooking the evening meal. "When you are older," they would say to Daisy, "you can help too." But that time never came. Instead, Patricia was able to live and work in Sydney while she was placed in a home with other girls who were spiteful and mean. If it had not been for Mr Spencer taking her side against everyone else, her life would have been unbearable. And now she was the one who did not have a man to love her and who had to give up her baby while Patricia had a man who loved her, her own home and children.

Some days Daisy wondered why she had decided that staying with Patricia was the best way to get back on her feet. She knew that Patricia would always welcome her back, but her focus on her children made Daisy think that she'd paid a high price for this salvation. She was further irritated by the smugness of Bob's wife, who came over with her two spoiled and overdressed children. The five children would run and scream through the house, thundering up stairs and under tables while their mothers chatted on as though the world was full of silence.

"I can't stand it," Daisy would say to Patricia as she saw

Carole and her two children walking up the front path. Grabbing her cigarettes she would declare: "I'm not staying to listen to you two talk about your little brats. And if I have to listen to Bob's wife complain one more time about how she would like to go back to work, I'm going to throw a glass at her." She stubbed her cigarette out in an ashtray on the mantelpiece. "I hate women like that, always whinging when they have everything."

"Oh, Daisy," Patricia would say, removing the dirty ashtray. "You'll feel differently when you have children of your own."

Daisy would roll her eyes, toss her cigarette case into her handbag, then turn on her heel and leave the house for the restaurant. She would nod at Carole as they passed at the door, a tight, forced smile on her face.

Despite her efforts to distract Pasquale's attention from Patricia by offering him a sympathetic ear or a shoulder to cry on, Daisy had not succeeded. Even though she was prettier, slimmer, more stylish and younger, Pasquale did not try to touch her, did not flirt with her, did not even seem to look at her. So she tried a different tactic.

At the end of the evening, when Pasquale had finished stacking the chairs on the tables and was about to start counting the money in the till, Daisy burst into tears, sobbing in the kitchen. At first he did not seem to hear, so she sobbed louder. This time he heard and asked, "What is wrong, little Daisy?"

She continued crying, ignoring his question.

"Please tell me. You are always try so hard to help me, let me help you if I can."

"I can't tell you. It's too horrible." He searched in his pants pocket and found his handkerchief. He unfolded it and handed it to her. "Do not be sad, Daisy. And you can tell me. I am your friend."

She sobbed into his handkerchief before she continued,

"Oh, Pasquale, I can't keep anything from you. I'm just so upset about something Patricia said."

Daisy leaned on his shoulder as she continued to sob. "She said she didn't need you any more, that her children were enough. I told her how selfish she was and how much you loved her. How lucky she was to have you."

"There, there. You are so kind, so sweet to worry about me. I know she is busy with the children and has not so much time for me now." He patted her arm. "Do not worry for me. I am getting used to things being this way."

"It just makes me feel so bad. I see how hard you work here." Daisy took his hands and held them in hers. "Especially after you stayed so long by her side after she had Elizabeth and was so sick."

"You should not upset yourself like this, little Daisy. Always you try to help me. Please, please, stop crying."

"I'd do anything to help you." She looked at Pasquale, tears still in her eyes, and said, "Could you please just give me a hug?"

Awkwardly, he stepped towards her and she pulled him tightly to her, crying against his chest.

Daisy knew that when he had first come to her, first made love to her, it was his loneliness that drove him to her. She felt confident, though, that over time, he would begin to love her back. But as Pasquale's eyes continued to follow Patricia, Daisy would rub up against him in the restaurant during the night so that when the door was locked, the staff gone and the money counted, he would bend her back over the kitchen counter and start to unbutton her dress.

"It was your fault," she would say to Pasquale after Patricia died. "If you had told her the way I said, it wouldn't have turned out the way it did. But don't worry, my darling. You have me to look after you now."

Pasquale was too heartbroken to argue when Daisy moved into the bedroom he had shared with Patricia.

Nor did he argue as she packed his three children off to boarding school while she had their daughter, Rose.

Daisy had seen the disbelief on Patricia's face before she walked out of the restaurant. Daisy had expected her to be upset, but thought that the logical conclusion was for Pasquale to leave Patricia and buy Daisy a home of her own. She had never intended to cause her sister's heart attack. *I never wanted her dead*, she thought to herself, as she looked at the jade brooch that had been locked in the bottom of her jewellery box. She felt the stone in her hand as she looked at the pattern, like a rose blossoming.

Patricia had always been fond of the brooch because it had been their mother's. When Daisy had packed her bags to go and live with Marcel, she'd seen it amongst Patricia's things and taken it. Daisy never wore it, she did not even like it, but it was a piece of their mother that she, not Patricia, now had. Even though she knew her sister valued it, Daisy never gave it back. She thought of Patricia now, of the attempts to make her happy, how she would sew dresses for her and admire her looks. *There is no one now who will forgive me and love me despite my faults*, Daisy thought, clutching the brooch in her hand. She took it to Pasquale. "Here," she said, handing it to him. He looked at it, puzzled. "Patricia would want to be buried with this. It was our mother's." She pulled Pasquale's hand towards her and pressed the brooch into his fleshy palm.

27

1982

THE ONLY CONSOLATION, Bob thought to himself, was that Patricia did not know about Pasquale's infidelity before she died. "That would have killed her if her weak heart hadn't," he said to Carole.

Patricia's death was the most painful loss that he had experienced in his life. There would be no more talks in her kitchen, no more goodbye hugs when she would squeeze him tightly. She had always been there for him — when he was in the home, when he was on shore leave, when he felt frustrated with Carole.

His connection to Daisy had been severed when her pregnancy was discovered. He had not known at the time of Patricia's funeral that Daisy had become Pasquale's mistress — only the timing of Rose's birth revealed the sins of the parents. That Daisy had so quickly taken over Patricia's home confirmed Bob's misgivings about his younger sister and he could not bring himself to speak to her. Her betrayal of Patricia was something Bob thought he had to punish her for.

Bob tormented himself over not having been more forthright with Patricia about the dangers of letting Daisy into her home. He should have taken the same firm line with his sister as he did with his wife.

Patricia left a void in his life that he was unable to come to terms with. He worked more, slept less, took on extra shifts at the airport, became increasingly irritable and ate irregularly. The more Carole tried to console him, the less he wanted her to help him. The anger inside him seemed always to be just below the surface. The world was turning against him — the people who cut him off in the traffic, the woman at the cash register who insisted on counting out one-cent pieces, the bank that failed to credit the last payment on his home loan. Each thing seemed intentionally directed at him, making his heart and head pound. When his anger subsided, it left a pain in his chest.

By the time Bob turned forty-five, the pain was relentless. It made him short of breath. It became so unbearable that he went to see a doctor who, concerned, ran some tests and ordered him to hospital for treatment of a suspected heart condition.

There, under the anaesthetic, an old dream returned to him.

The old man stood on the other side of the fire, beckoning to him with his hand.

Through the heat haze, he could see the man's dark features and the white paint in thick lines on his body. His hand was held out to Bob. Bob did not feel afraid. He wanted to cross the fire. The man spoke to him. "No matter which way you turn, there is something that you are not facing."

New, experimental open-heart surgery saved Bob from the medical condition that had taken his mother and eldest sister. He awoke to the months of recuperation with the same restlessness he had felt since Patricia died, but now he seemed to have lost something of himself. He constantly wondered about Danny — what had happened to him, where he was now? Danny, who would not have known that Bob had married Carole and was a father of two, nor that Patricia had died.

When he was finally released from hospital, his thoughts were still on Danny. He kept thinking of their time in the home, and decided to go back and see it again. He had not been there since he and Patricia had collected a sullen Danny. Bob brought his family with him, wanting them to see where he had lived; he thought of the irony of being with his wife and children in this place where he had first come because he no longer had a family.

It was Christmas, so most of the children had been sent to distant relatives or foster homes; the place was empty. When he explained that he had once been a student there, the superintendent gave him a tour a round the dormatories and grounds.

He walked into the large ward where he and Danny had spent their first night. The ward looked clean, painted white, beds made expectantly for when the boys would return after the Christmas holidays. The room seemed smaller than he remembered it, almost cosy. He remembered how Danny and he had slept together in the same narrow bed for warmth and comfort, younger then than his own children were now. He looked down at his daughter. Never, he thought, would I have imagined then that I would be able to create something so remarkable as children — little Kingsley standing with his mother near the door, and Candice standing loyally beside him.

"This is where Uncle Danny and I slept when we first came here. I would sneak into his bed to keep him warm. Well, I guess it was also to console myself, I was so scared," he said to her.

While many things had changed — no more chicken coops and no cows for milk — some things were exactly as they had been thirty years ago. He could see the toilet block still standing and he remembered that behind the bricks was the place where he had kissed Annabel Stewart. Even now he could remember how good it made him feel to have Annabel be his friend, and the desire to touch his lips to hers. It was the same feeling he had the first time Carole had agreed to go to a movie with him, something he had not felt since Patricia died.

Walking back to his car, Bob looked at what remained of the stone wall. He stared, imagining a row of young boys seated there, looking hopefully down the road. He wondered what happened to them — Annabel, Benny Miller, Thomas Riley, Charles Wainwright, and Frank Phillips. Did they have families? Were they still waiting for someone to come along? Or were they like him, somewhere in the middle?

On the drive home, with so many memories swimming around him, one in particular seemed to haunt him. He kept thinking back to the day when Danny had stormed off the cricket field, hissing "I hate you" as he passed him.

Bob had no leads on where Danny might have gone, did not even know who his friends were when he disappeared. He had been travelling a lot with the Navy then, but when he was in Sydney, Patricia would be so worried about Danny, fretting that he was going out late, not coming home. Just as Daisy had done before she ran away. And Danny always seemed to be on one of his wild sprees when Bob was visiting, as if he could not stand being in the same house as his brother. He remembered the punch to the stomach Danny had given him, winding him and leaving a bruise. He had never understood that anger in Danny. But, Bob reasoned now, Danny would be an adult, and those boyhood tensions would be far behind them both.

Bob thought the best way of finding Danny would be to start at the post office. Painstakingly he looked through the phone books of every Australian state and territory for listings under 'Brecht'. It was over thirty years since he last saw Danny, but it took him only an hour to look through the directories of the major cities. Bob found listings for 'D. Brecht' in Marrickville and Turramurra in Sydney, Subiaco in Perth, Toorak in Melbourne, and Townsville.

The first number was a David Brecht. The second number was a Darren. The Perth number was another David. The

Melbourne number did not answer. The fifth number was answered by a woman.

"Is Danny Brecht there?"

"Hang on," she said, and Bob could feel the sweat rising on his palms as he held the phone. "Honey, telephone."

"Who is it?" Bob could hear a voice yelling. He felt a chill of familiarity.

"I don't know," the woman said patiently.

"Hello?" the voice asked abruptly.

"It's your brother," said Bob excitedly.

The line was silent.

"Danny, it's Bob. Your brother."

"What do you want?"

"Well, nothing. I was just ringing because I was wondering what happened to you. Wanted to get in touch with you. I've married with two kids since I saw you. My hair has turned grey." Bob gave a nervous laugh. "I — I thought you would like to know that Patricia passed away about a year ago."

"Why didn't you call a year ago, then?" Danny said.

Bob could feel the antagonism in his brother's voice. *He still hates me*, he thought glumly.

"Look, I'll give you my number. If you're ever down this way and want to get in touch with me, give me a call. If you need anything, you know where I am. Just ring and ask."

"Well," said Danny after a pause, "there is something you could help me with. I'm a bit short. Could you lend me some money?"

Bob was quiet for a moment. He wrapped the telephone cord around his finger. "How much do you need?"

"Well, five hundred would tide me over."

"Five hundred," repeated Bob. It might as well have been five million. With the medical bills from his bypass surgery, his lowered income while he was on sickness benefits and the usual pressures of maintaining a mortgage and raising two children, he had no spare cash. In fact, he was in the worst shape financially that he'd been in since he joined the Navy.

"Look," Bob said, "It's not a good time." There was silence from the other end, so he added, "I will send you up something to help out, though."

"Yeah, thanks," said Danny curtly.

Bob felt hollow after his phone call, as though his healing heart was numb. Danny had all but told him that he didn't want Bob in his life, saw him only as a possible source of money. He sat down in front of the television, the cricket on but the sound down, and opened a can of beer. He stared at the screen but thought of the dream that had come to him since he had been a small boy.

In his youth, the dream used to frighten him and the figure on the other side of the fire seemed threatening. The dream was a nightmare. But over the years, he'd become familiar with the figure and, although he would not cross the fire, he felt simply unable to move rather than rigid with fear. Since he had the heart attack, he had wanted to cross the fire — the figure was almost familiar to him and offered him somewhere to be safe. And in the dream, the man now spoke to him. "No matter which way you turn, there is something you are not facing," the old man had said to him. And that is how he felt, more so after the phone call to Danny. So he left Carole, Candice and Kingsley to go and find out what it was.

Carole was unable to get out of bed for the first few days after her husband packed a few bags and drove away — "To find myself," he had said to her. When she finally raised herself from her bed and focused on her children, her disappointment and hurt started to brew into anger.

She hadn't realised how Patricia was the heart of their family until she passed away. Patricia had always assisted her in minding Candice and Kingsley, had been her confidante as she tried to navigate Bob's moods, one of the few friends that she had whom Bob approved of. With Patricia's passing, she'd lost her best friend. Bob had been too consumed with his own sense of loss to notice his wife's grief.

Carole studied the job section in the newspaper and soon found herself a position as a secretary at a real estate agency, answering phones and writing receipts. Because she had not been in the workforce for such a long time she could not find work that paid well. She looked at the self-confident young men who worked as real estate agents in the office. She frowned upon their lack of ethics and their rudeness to her and the other women. She thought, I could do a better job than them. So she signed up for a course to become a real estate agent.

The shift in their circumstance was hardest on her children, who had been used to pretty clothes and new games and toys. Kingsley was growing so fast he needed new clothes every six months, while Candice needed new clothes all the time to keep up with her friends. Saying 'no' to Candice was hard for Carole; to a fourteen-year-old it would seem like the end of the world not to have the latest fashions. It was at these times that her fury with Bob would rise for abandoning her, for leaving her, after all his promises, without adequate means to support herself.

While she was trying to get qualifications for a better job and continuing to work during the day, the housework would fall behind. She had to leave the children on their own from when they arrived home from school until she returned. The gate would be left open, the house a mess, the laundry left on the couches waiting to be folded, dinner needing to be cooked. Carole sighed. She remembered how, when she was first married, there had seemed to be too many hours in the day. Now, there were never enough and so much work that the house and garden were always an embarrassment.

She laughed inwardly to herself at what the wives of Bob's friends would think if they could see how she was living now. She could make the kids do more to help, she thought, but she'd made a deal with them that if they were doing their homework, they did not have to do housework. They were getting good reports from school despite the changes with their father gone. As she looked around the mess in her kitchen, she thought wryly to herself that her ingenious plan to keep her children excelling at school seemed to have backfired.

"Candice," she told her daughter, "never trust a man who says 'Trust me'."

When Christmas came and the children's lists of wants grew lengthy, she rang the Aboriginal Medical Service and asked for the name of a family in need, and how many children they had. She then had Kingsley and Candice ask the neighbours for donations of food and toys while she asked her colleagues from work to contribute. The children took their task seriously, going through their own belongings for items that could be given. Carole felt a swell of pride as Candice and Kingsley sat on either side of the hamper on the train as though guarding something valuable.

When they arrived at the tiny tenement house in Redfern, her children turned shy. The woman who opened the door was skinny with long black hair. There was a black bruise around her eye. There was no furniture in the house except a table and three small chairs. This gave Candice and Kingsley some pause for consideration of their own situation. They were quiet on the train ride home, while opening the presents Carole had bought them, and during the hot dinner they sat down to that night.

At these moments she hated Bob. This was his first Christmas away from his children, away from her. She hadn't understood when she married him how deep-seated his lack of self-esteem was. She would sometimes say to herself that if she had known, she never would have married him — except, she would quickly remind herself, she could never be sorry for having Candice and Kingsley.

Carole had seen the impact Patricia's passing had on Bob.

It was she who had noticed the bump in Daisy's stomach at the funeral, nudging Bob. Carole had shared his disgust at the way in which Daisy had moved in, taking Patricia's husband and her house and enjoying the spoils of the restaurant Patricia had helped Pasquale build. Unlike Bob, Carole did not despise Pasquale. She felt pity for him. It was Patricia's children she felt sorry for, sent off to boarding school while Daisy set about redecorating her new home. Carole struggled to explain the situation to Candice and Kingsley, why it was they did not see their cousins now.

Carole obtained her real estate licence and started to earn a good income. She was honest and approachable, and buyers and sellers, landlords and tenants respected her. She enjoyed the renewed independence of having her own income and making her own decisions about how things should be done in the house. The more she regained her ability to do things her own way, the more she liked it. It was two years since Bob had left, since she could not face getting out of bed because of her despair at his leaving. Now, she had to admit, there was a part of her that was happier with him gone, even though a bigger part of her missed him every morning she woke up and he was not there.

Bob wished that he had asked Patricia what she knew, what conversations she may have had with their mother that could unlock the secret of who they were. Bob had never forgotten his father's response to his question about their dark hair and eyes, the question about what they were: "You are as white as anyone else."

He was reluctant to make contact with Daisy after cutting her out of his life when she became pregnant to Pasquale. But the more he thought about what information she might have, the more he wanted to call her.

She was frosty about the subject. "I don't know why you want to open that one. It would be best if we left it alone."

So like her, he thought as he replaced the receiver. Daisy had said nothing of Pasquale or the children. She had spoken as though it were a usual thing that Bob should call her to ask about their family history; yet it had been twelve years, since he had last raised the topic with her, just after Patricia's funeral. He shook his head.

Bob's next step was to call his father. The last time he'd seen him was their encounter in Strawberry Hills, when Bob still worked for the post office. Bob spent an afternoon looking through phone books, but there was no listing for a 'G. Brecht', not in Lithgow or anywhere else. He decided to try a different course.

Bob had applied for his parents' marriage certificate. It stated that his mother was born at Dungalear Station in 1905 and that her maiden name was 'Boney'. He could find no birth certificate for her. He then applied for his mother's death certificate. It noted her place of birth as Walgett, and the year of her birth as 1904.

He began to look at maps of all of the pastoral leases. Dungalear Station sounded like a farm property. He looked on maps around the town of Walgett, to see if he could find the connection. As he searched, he was trying to make sense of what he knew. Somehow he had always known that he was Aboriginal, knew it just as the children in his class at school had known it, even though his mother had never told him and his father would not reveal it.

He began to search the Mitchell library for histories of Walgett and any mention of a Dungalear Station. He'd taken a small studio flat in Liverpool Street in Surry Hills, but he spent so many hours in the quiet book-lined caverns of the library that he began to recognise the faces of other regulars, obsessed with solving mysteries of their own.

His break came not from the books but from a conversation with another man similarly haunting the library's halls.

"Writing a PhD?" he asked Bob.

"No — it's the beard, isn't it?" Bob laughed, rubbing his stubble. "Actually, I'm not really sure what I'm looking for."

"Makes it kind of hard, doesn't it?"

Bob found he was talking to an historian, Peter Read, who was writing a book on what he called 'the Stolen Generation'. Peter told him about the Aborigines Welfare Board and how they removed children from their families and regulated the lives of Aboriginal people across New South Wales. There were documents, he explained, in the government archives of the Board's activities. "A lot of their documents have been destroyed, but you may find something in there."

Bob had few clues when he went to the NSW Archives. Dungalear Station and Walgett. 1904 or 1905. Boney. He began searching every year from 1903 for a trace of Elizabeth Boney from Dungalear Station. After two-and-a-half months of filling out request forms and waiting for copies of old documents to arrive, he unrolled a scroll to see a certificate from the Aborigines Protection Board that showed an Elizabeth Boney had been removed from Dungalear Station. Date of birth was listed as 26 June 1904. 'Removed at Girl's Own Request.' The certificate also listed one brother, Sonny Boney. Lines on paper, like a map, all pointing the way home.

28

1982

BOB PULLED UP OUTSIDE the neat weatherboard house in Walgett. There was a wire fence and gate and a path that led straight to the front door. Bob could feel his heart pumping as he took the two steps up to the front porch, opened the screen door and knocked. He heard a dog bark and the sound of footsteps. The door clicked open. Standing before him was an Aboriginal woman with short dark hair and curls around her face. She looked at Bob, arched one eyebrow and waited for him to explain himself.

Bob began, "I am looking for a Sonny Boney."

"You are, are you? And who might you be?"

"Well, I think I am his nephew. My mother was Elizabeth Boney, his sister. That is, if I have the right Sonny Boney."

Bob had been expecting some sign of delight, some recognition or an invitation into the house. Instead he was met with silence. He started to feel his stomach tighten.

"Why didn't you come knocking on this door three months ago?" the woman demanded. "He was looking for his sister his whole life. His whole life. You are three months too late."

Bob felt weakness wash over him and tears pricking his eyes. He was about to turn and head back to the sanctuary of his car when a tall, dark man came to the door.

"You'll have to excuse Mum," he started.

"I don't need anyone making excuses for me, Henry. Not here in my own home." With that the woman retreated into the house.

"She took Dad's passing rather hard. I'm Henry. Henry Boney. And if you're who you say you are, well, that'd make us cousins."

"I'm Bob Brecht."

"Well, I reckon, since your reception here hasn't been so jovial, we should adjourn to the Royal and you can shout your cousin a drink." Henry slapped Bob on the back as he walked towards Bob's car.

Bob was counting the number of drinks he'd been buying for Henry. He wouldn't normally pay for so many rounds without getting one in return. The news of Sonny's death had been a disappointment, but he was elated to have found a connection, to find part of what he was looking for.

"It was true what Mum said. Dad was looking for his sister his whole life. My eldest sister is called Eliza after her. He was a quiet man, my Dad — not like Mum. Well, you've seen her." Henry shot Bob a wink. "He used to tell us some funny ones. When Mum ran out of bread, he's say it didn't matter 'cause he only ate toast.

"They met when he moved down to Narromine in the thirties. There was no mission there, see, so he lived by the riverbank with a mob of them, Mum included. Worked in the orchards and the wheatfields. Did some cotton picking too, when they got the irrigation. But he moved back here when he married Mum. She's a Morgan from Brewarrina. They were married in '44, yeah, that's right, '44. Story goes that when he arrived in town he saw this woman giving the shopkeeper what-for for overcharging on their food. Apparently it was love at first sight for Dad. They didn't spend a night apart the whole time they were together. Here's me with my third missus and I'm younger than you by the looks of it. But they seemed to mate for good back in those days." He paused, looking into his beer.

"Mum was always fired up. She's on the Housing Board and works up at the Medical Service. She was one of them fighting to get the Foundation up and running. Her latest thing is to get a bus for the school. No one takes on my Mum." He grinned. "I'm always apologising for her."

Bob could believe that no one would take her on. He wouldn't.

"Loved his music though, my Dad. All that old American stuff — Bessie Smith, Billie Holliday, Louis Armstrong, Ray Charles. Loved it. Mum used to scoff at him and make him listen to it in his shed. But she'd take him cups of tea and chocolate slices. Used to pretend that she wouldn't let him in the house to play that depressing music. But she really wanted to give him time alone with his thoughts. She's tough, but she loved him. Hasn't thrown a thing of his away since he died. Plays those records now herself. Puts them on in the shed and goes into the house to do her work so it seems like he's down there listening to his music, waiting for a cup of tea. She's sweet really, our Mum."

Bob arched his eyebrows at Henry.

"No. Really she is, Cuz," Henry continued. Bob felt the warmth of the term 'Cuz' swim over him.

"Look, come 'round tomorrow and talk to her. I'll have a word to her tonight and make sure she's smoothed over. Just don't expect her to apologise," Henry added with a laugh.

Bob knocked again on Marilyn Boney's door. The morning air was cool but hinted at the searing heat that would follow in the next few hours.

"Alright, I heard you," Marilyn muttered from behind the door as she opened it. She held the door open, sweeping her hand towards the back of the house, directing Bob through.

"Sit down," she said, and he pulled out a chair at a blue laminated table in a spotless blue kitchen. She slammed a cup of tea with milk in it before him. Bob was too nervous to tell her he preferred it black.

"Well, what do you want to know?" she asked. But before he could answer, she continued, "He was the most decent man I ever met, I can tell you that. Not like those ones around here who drink too much and hit their women and kids 'round. Always worked hard to provide for us.

"We had the six kids," she continued, turning her wedding band. "Sonny always thought that if you had six kids, even if bad things happened to them, chances were you'd be left with at least one. That might sound a bit pessimistic but that's how it was when we were younger. Between the Welfare and the sickness."

Her eyes turned from her hands to look into Bob's eyes.

"You wouldn't know how tough it was for blacks out here in those days. During the war, there was work around, men like your uncle could leave the reserves and work for real wages. As soon as it was over, they were pushed back to the margins — shearing, branding, fencing. He even tried opal mining for a while. Didn't like handling the stones. The old people always told us not to touch them. But he would always put food on this table." She tapped the laminated surface with her finger, making the whole thing shake. "Even if it was possum. I hate possum. Tastes like gum tree. He remembered the old ways, but our kids weren't much interested in learning them. What do they care about being able to find water in the roots of gum trees when the riverbed is dry. They just get a bottle of it from the store."

"And the missions. I grew up at Narromine where there was no mission. My parents moved us there from Brewarrina for that reason. You can't imagine the conditions people had to live in. They kept anybody off the mission who started trouble and 'trouble' was just complaining about the conditions. And if you lived there, the stores sold everything at inflated prices and the managers kept all the money. Did things like keep two docket books to rip off the little money the blacks living there had. They were dreadful places — frequent fights, too much alcohol even though there wasn't supposed to be grog there."

Bob heard the front door open and footsteps in the hall.

"You took your time gettin' back," Marilyn said to Henry as he entered the kitchen.

"Can I have a cup of tea, Mum?"

"Get it yourself. I'm not the housemaid."

Henry rolled his eyes. "Want another one?" he asked Bob. Bob shook his head. As Henry busied himself with the kettle, Marilyn turned her attention back to Bob.

"Many white folks didn't like having blacks in the town. Always needed us to work for 'em but didn't want to live with us. You don't know what it was like back then. There was violence in the street and curfews to control us, especially the men. It was an offence to be drunk if you were black, and we were arrested whether we'd been drinking or not. I've seen men handcuffed and beaten with batons for no other reason than that they were black. Beaten until they died.

"When the Welfare Board was shut down, they just wouldn't rent houses to us. Here in this town there was a Whites Only toilet and they would never let our kids in the swimming pool. Separate church services, separate playgrounds at the public school, separate seating in the picture show. Wouldn't let us inside the hospitals either — put us on the back verandah.

"But Sonny wasn't one to complain. Not like most of this mob, sit on their bum, do nothing and expect it all to happen for 'em. He kept his sense of humour. He told me once that he didn't want to leave his eyes to science 'cause he couldn't read ... so they wouldn't be no good to anyone."

Henry chuckled. "Yeah, Dad would say a thing like that."

Marilyn shot him a look to let him know who was telling the story. "And he was a smart man, too. Intelligent. We weren't given the education back then. Not given the opportunities our kids were." She levelled a stare at Henry. "But we both believed that we had the same rights as everyone else. Sonny wasn't like me. He wasn't involved with the medical service and the legal service. But he'd worked hard all his life and he knew what was fair and what wasn't. He used to read a lot about what was going on. He used to read anything he could about Aboriginal people looking for their rights. 'We do not ask for charity, we ask for justice,' he'd say.

"You wouldn't know where that came from. It was something that Jack Patton and William Ferguson wrote. He liked that. Always believed that if we had citizenship rights, everything else would follow — you know, equal wages and equal education opportunities."

"Dad was always saying 'It's not charity, it's justice'," Henry added.

"You should have spent more time listening to him," Marilyn snapped. "Stop interrupting and go out and mow that lawn before the sun gets too hot. When I'm finished here, you can take your cousin over to see Granny."

Henry left the kitchen through the back door. Marilyn returned her attention to Bob.

"We were both here when the Freedom Riders came through. Got a picture of me with Charles Perkins. You should have seen the reception they got." Marilyn started laughing. "I don't know what those white kids were thinking when they hopped a bus to come here. Met with hostility, tomatoes and eggs. Punched and heckled. Got the wind up the white folks who thought they were just snotty-nosed uni students coming from Sydney to stir up trouble on issues they knew nothing about. But," she added more seriously, "it meant a lot to your uncle to know that people outside of here cared how we was being treated.

"I never had much time for those other uni types who came out here. They'd sit down and take our stories. Give the old men wine and cigarettes. Then piss on off back to the city, publish their papers and never give anything back to the people here. Old Reggie Green used to just make up stories so he could keep gettin' drunk. I tell my kids they should get an education. Help us keep our own stories. Not give them to anyone else. Especially not people who don't put anything back into our community."

Bob could see the tears welling in her eyes. He stared at his cold milky tea. "Do you mind if I look at some of the pictures you have in the hall?"

Marilyn waved him in that direction. He walked through the lounge room to the hallway where the papered walls were covered in photographs — weddings, debuts, family portraits and a younger Henry dressed in a football jersey, arms folded across his chest, chin jutting towards the camera, eyes sparkling.

Marilyn walked into the hallway and, after quickly dabbing her eye, said, "Yep. Six children and nine grandchildren. Be hard on 'em this Christmas with their Pop gone.

"He missed your mother every day, he did. You could see it in his eyes, the sadness." She was looking at the photographs as Bob glanced sideways at her. She seemed softer now.

She turned to Bob and tilted her head. "You know, he told me once that he sometimes felt that she was within his reach, that sometimes he could swear she was standing behind him, and only by turning around to face the thin air could he prove himself wrong. He wasn't a superstitious man but he told me she used to visit him in his dreams."

Marilyn was quiet for a moment. Then she snapped, breaking her own thoughts, "That's why you should've knocked on our door three months ago."

Henry kept telling Bob that they should go to see Granny. After Marilyn made them a lunch of curried-egg sandwiches and more milky tea, Henry walked Bob the three blocks to Granny's little house. The afternoon summer sun beat down on them. Bob waved flies away as they walked. "You'd think they'd be too hot to bother," Bob said.

Henry smiled. After a pause he looked at Bob. "How was Mum?" he asked.

"I got a good picture of what my uncle, your father, would have been like. I'm sorry I didn't know him. He sounds like he was quite a character."

"He was. He was gentle, but a hard worker. Real patient and honest. I don't know how someone could go through all that Dad did and not end up bitter and angry. Not that he was happy about it. But I don't know how I would do it. Things aren't fair in this town but it's much better now than it was when Mum and Dad were growing up. This town hides a lot of hate."

Bob looked at him. "Your mother told me about the segregation and the violence against blacks."

Henry stopped walking and looked at Bob. "I'll tell you how deep it goes. If you walk out to Temperance Creek — I'll take you there tomorrow — there's a tree there called Butcher's Tree. In this country, there are very few places to hide — everything is open. Dad said that as a kid he had seen the skeletons, bones and teeth, all sizes, like they were just waiting to be found. Skeletons lying over each other. And he could see the lead musket balls in the trunk."

Granny was sitting in the shade of her porch when they arrived. Her house was the last in the street. Beyond it the road turned to dirt and the grass was long. She looked at Bob as the men approached and Henry spoke.

"You won't believe who this is, Granny. He's my cousin. His mum was Dad's sister. Elizabeth."

Granny peered at Bob. "I was wondering when you'd show up." She waved him to a seat beside her, leaving Henry to stand. "So where did she end up, our little Garibooli?" Granny asked him.

"Elizabeth?"

"We called her Garibooli. Means 'whirlwind'. We're Eualeyai, us Boneys. In our language, Garibooli means 'whirlwind'."

"Garibooli," Bob repeated to make sure he was saying it right. Granny gave him a quick nod as if to say "I told you so."

"I didn't know that Garibooli meant 'whirlwind'," said Henry.

"You never asked," snapped Granny.

Bob came to Henry's rescue. "My mother, Elizabeth ... Garibooli, married my father and moved to Lithgow. She had six kids. I'm the second youngest."

Granny nodded her head as Bob spoke, as though she was agreeing that what he was saying was correct. "She always liked little ones. You should have seen how she used to fuss over her brother. Broke his heart when she was taken. Never got over it. Blamed himself. And it killed his parents, losing her. If Sonny hadn't had Marilyn — she's a Morgan, you know — I don't know how he would have done it. He loved his kids too, even though they mostly gave him grief." She gave Henry a piercing look.

"She was a fast thing. Loved to run and was always up in the trees."

Bob could not imagine his mother, whom he remembered as being so large, running and climbing trees. He had very few memories of her, but he did recall trying to put his arms all the way around her and not being able to reach. And that she smelled of lemons.

"And she was always looking at the sky, that girl. Liked looking at the stars," Granny added.

Bob felt a longing for something and he whispered the first word that came to his lips: "Carole."

He wanted to be home with her, feel her in his arms, smell her hair. She didn't, he realised, make him feel white. She had, all through the years, made him feel complete.

29

1982

DANNY HUNG UP the phone.

"Who was that?" asked Gloria.

"No one," Danny sneered at her.

"Oh, you're in one of *those* moods," she retorted, lighting a cigarette and returning her attention to the television.

"I'm going out," Danny said as he opened the front door.

He walked into the street and turned towards the pub. Townsville was hot this time of year and even at seven-thirty in the evening it would wrap around you.

When he left Sydney with the takings from Pasquale's restaurant in his pocket, Danny had intended that his family should never find him again. Trust Bob, he muttered to himself, to interfere and upset his plans. He'd felt a pang of sadness on hearing that Patricia had passed away. His leaving the way he did, knowing that she had always cared for him, never sat well with him. Many times in the last twenty years he'd thought about giving her a call. Just to see how she was. Now she was gone and the things he wanted to say to her would never be said. It had seemed too hard to face her and risk rejection. She was the only person who had been there for him no matter what. He could still remember how excited he'd get when he could make out her figure on the horizon, walking towards him as he sat on the stone wall, with the other boys, all hoping for a visitor. And he still remembered the panic he felt when she left, disappearing into the distance.

When he came to live with her, he never seemed to be able to settle down, sit still. He tried the jobs Patricia had helped him secure, but was never able to stick with any of them. Something or someone always seemed to trip him up. He met a gang of kids from Redfern and would stay in abandoned warehouses with them at night, breaking into shops when there was the opportunity. It was a world that revolved around petty thieving — bicycles, tools, machinery — a world inhabited by con artists and fast talkers. But in the simple code of loyalty amongst the street toughs — Aboriginal kids from all over the state — he found a place where he was respected. And making money their way was easier than working hard for it.

The police would target them. Danny got used to being picked up, beaten up and held in the gaol cells. Once they got to know him, the police couldn't spot him without trying to start something with him and his mates. Danny sought out the violent conflicts. He could unleash his aggression and found that once he started hitting, he couldn't stop until he was exhausted or beaten unconscious. His nights in the gaol cells only sharpened his resistance to authority and increased his skills for breaking locks; he also picked up useful tips about possible future 'business partners'.

The money sitting in Pasquale's till was just too tempting. His plan was to make for Brisbane where some of his friends had moved after the police kept targeting them in Redfern. When Danny arrived there, he found that Brisbane was a more racist place than the one he'd left. In Sydney the police would lock them up overnight for no reason, but the stories of police brutality in Queensland often had a more deadly ending.

In Brisbane he met Alison Dawson, a social worker from Bourke. She took him in, put up with his moods and his drinking. He'd been so angry — not at Alison, but at life —

that he lashed out at her. She took it, his beating her, several times until she told him that he had to stop thumping her or go. So he left, and blamed her for it.

He moved further north to the hot, sticky cane fields where people did not ask questions. In Townsville, he finally married Linda Dillon, a waif-like woman, fragile as a breath. After the backbreaking work of cutting cane, the softness of Linda seemed to be the answer to the restlessness and the running that was exhausting him. In the summer nights that grudgingly gave hours of dark, he would hold Linda tightly in his arms, feeling as though he had at last found the kind of love that people wrote songs about.

When Linda became pregnant, Danny had at first thought that this was the beginning of his life. But the pressures of work, the pressures of fatherhood and the lack of sleep made his feet itch to take the first step out of the door. He stayed, but rather than leading to a life of stability, this only increased his frustrations, his moods, his anger.

Then he met Gloria, Gloria Davidson. She was the barmaid in the pub where he frequently ended up drunk. He moved in with her when he lost his job. She was one of those women, Danny knew, who thought that they could change him. All he needed was a good woman and Gloria thought she was that good woman. He knew Gloria was fighting a losing battle. He had lost his ability to respect those who loved him, to feel comfortable with their trust in him, when he was in the home. He blamed Bob for that.

Bob. His brother. Bob always conformed, tried too hard to please everyone around him. It was easier for him, with his lighter skin, to pretend that he was as normal as everyone else. He was always trying to get Danny to do what was expected. "Try to fit in," he would say to him. Danny tried, but he knew that it didn't matter what he did, people would always look down on him because of the colour of his skin. In a way he could not explain, he had always been jealous of

Bob's ease with others, the way people seemed just naturally to like him. No one ever liked Danny that way.

Bob's friends, Charles and Benny, would corner Danny in dark places and punch him, telling him Bob had said he didn't want him hanging around them, that he was spoiling all their fun. Danny didn't believe that Bob would say what his friends claimed. He never mentioned the taunts to Bob for fear that he would say that what his friends had told Danny was true. This made him feel the way he did when the time stretched to three on a Sunday afternoon and he was still sitting on the stone wall.

But it was the day of the cricket match that changed everything between him and Bob. He had been called 'out' by Bob's friends and he hadn't been; they had cheated. He could still feel the rage of the unfairness and when he looked over at Bob he could see the look on his face, nervous that Danny was going to embarrass him by making a scene. "I hate you," he'd spat at him as he skulked off to the dormitories.

The large ward where he slept was empty. The summer day lunch time meant that everyone was outside playing. He was shaking with his anger. Bob had once always been there for him but now he was more concerned with making sure his friends were happy rather than his brother. As he stood there, so angry he was breathing hard, Mr Spencer, his house father entered the ward. He walked over to Danny, placing a hand on his back.

"Danny, I have been looking for you."

"Am I in trouble, sir?" he asked, his voice quivering.

"No. No. Not this time," he said with a smile. "In fact, quite the contrary. Come with me into my office. I want to show you something."

Danny wondered what it was that was so special. He was never singled out for good things. He hoped it might be a present, something that would make all the other boys jealous. Something that would make Bob sorry he hadn't stood up for him, sorry for his betrayal.

"Now Danny," Mr Spencer said as he closed the door, "you can't tell anyone about what we do here together, just the two of us. It will be our secret." Mr Spencer started to unbutton his pants and Danny felt a cold fear begin to freeze into his bones. "And if you do tell, no one will believe you."

Ever since that moment, he had resented every kindness that Bob tried to show him.

Looking to the sky

30

1995

THERE IS A SCENE in *Sons and Lovers* where Gertrude Morel walks out in the fields in the twilight almost before midnight. For the longest time I was convinced that D.H. Lawrence had made a mistake: where I live, it never gets dark later than 8 p.m. I didn't know about the way the sun lights other parts of the planet differently. As I grew older and reread the book, I realised that D.H. Lawrence knew exactly what he was talking about.

Growing up means looking at things differently. Sometimes that's a good thing; it means you understand the world better. I used to think the sky was Coca-Cola and the planets were the aerated bubbles. Black holes were people sucking through straws. Drinking a glass of soft drink, I was gulping down a whole universe.

Growing up in the cocoon of a loving family meant that finding out that there were children who did not have parents, parents who did not love and care for their children and people in the world who were hateful towards others without much good reason for it all came as a surprise to me when I was a teenager.

Kate didn't need books to see beyond her fences the way I did. Kate, with her wild curly black hair, her green eyes and sea of freckles, always believed that we were destined for better things. She was waiting patiently for her childhood to pass so that she could begin her adventures, almost as if she were counting the days. She could see so far beyond all she had inherited. "Just imagine," she would say, "when I'm travel editor for *Vogue* magazine and can send you postcards from all over the world. And then we can meet up for holidays at some place we've picked on a map ..." When we were growing up, Kate's ideas fascinated me as much as they seemed to put other children off. She saw the bigger picture and the possibilities beyond.

It was only when people started to bring it to my attention that I began to realise I was different. When Kate and I were in Grade One at school, Natalie Fletcher stepped in front of me as we were sitting on a bench in the school yard. Her face was so close to mine that I could see the patterns in the pupils of her blue eyes. "You're an ugly black spider. Black and ugly. Black and ugly," she said, her two friends trailing after her, laughing. It sounds inconsequential when I tell the story now, but children know hate when they see it, can sense emotion better than they can decipher words. I sat stunned, looking after her as they retreated, before I burst into tears. Kate put her arm around me with the comfort that only another outsider could offer.

That was when I first noticed that my skin was darker than my mother's, and it was the first time that I noticed it mattered. Mum said I should not be upset, that people just teased me because they were envious, because I had a cultural heritage that they were jealous of, and that I wouldn't burn in the summer sun. I should have pity for them, she told me. These explanations gave me little comfort when I was being called 'black arse' or 'black cunt'. Anything 'black' was an insult, which is why I say that Aunt Daisy is the "white sheep of the family". Some people try to make you feel bad because you're different — or because they think you're different — but when they realise that you are actually proud of those things, they try to take it away from you, tell you that "you're not a real one" or "you're an exception". It's as though they wanted to enjoy the power to taint you and then attempt to deprive you of the identity they tried to make so shameful. After I read Michel Foucault at university I could better articulate the power to name and then dispossess. And the more I thought about it, the more I concluded that the ones who win always win. George Orwell would have agreed with me, though he would have added something about the corruption that accompanies power.

I knew there were stories that we didn't hear at school, stories beneath the stories we were being told. Local Aboriginal people who had been travelling across the mountain range for thousands and thousands of years aided Blaxland, Lawson and Wentworth in their crossing. In this light, all the fuss about their crossing the Blue Mountains as though it was some kind of superhuman feat seemed absurd, unless it was their propensity to suffer sunburn that set them apart from the thousands who had crossed in the centuries beforehand. The Aboriginal people were probably amused at how long it took them to get over the hills.

I always knew we didn't just disappear into the ether, as the victor's version of history would have it, and I always knew that our replacement was not passive. I could see the way that my own history was overlooked and overwritten. When we looked at 'settlement' at school, we didn't learn about Pemulwuy, who had speared Phillip's gamekeeper for cruelly mistreating Aboriginal people. This retaliation triggered the wrath of reprisal from Governor Phillip, who gave orders to his men to bring back six Aboriginal heads. He didn't mind whose 'Aboriginal heads' they were. This was evidence that white people saw Aboriginal people as all the same. Pemulwuy did resist the Europeans. He made life hell for those who sought to stake a claim over what is now Toongabbie and Parramatta. No disappearance into the mists of time for him. When he was finally caught, shot by two men, he ended up a trophy. His head was sent off to London to sit with other trinkets from faraway colonies. The tales of the settlement of Australia and the expansion of the colony attempted to build over the stories of invasion and resistance. When stories of violence and conflict are told, like shifting sands they can bring buildings down. No point in telling the stories of Pemulwuy to high school students learning about settlement and the discovery of a populated mountain range. That would start the sands shifting.

I could understand why people were frightened of those counter-stories, but in my youth I always thought that if people heard them, they would understand the world better and their cruelty to other people, their hatred for no reason, would disappear. I was wrong about this because the sand-shifting stories are better known now than they were when I was at school and it hasn't changed the way people think about Aboriginal people as much as I would have hoped.

So don't think I sat there and let them tell me a version of history that I didn't agree with. Kate would let me get it off my chest. She wouldn't try and reason me out of my rage or find excuses for others. I'm not sure she always understood what I was mad about, but then neither did I. Sometimes I just got all worked up by things I couldn't properly explain, but she would listen until I had spent my words, agree regardless, then set my mind on something that made me happy. I would confide in Kate in the hours after school. "That sucks," she would say, and that would be all I needed to hear as she would drag me to my feet. I'd follow reluctantly, walking towards her swimming pool, happy to be in someone else's hands. Another reason why I liked her so much was because she had seen some of the worst things that had happened to me and she shared those secrets, so there was no need to explain.

Kate's mother had left her father — and Kate — for life with a man in Melbourne. Her father had suddenly found himself a girlfriend who was somewhere between his ex-wife's and his daughter's ages and spent most of his time at her house. Kate was left alone most of the time. This abandonment by her mother and holding the fort for her father embedded within her a sense of responsibility and maturity that both her parents lacked. Deprived of the freedom that comes with youth, she became restless to travel the world and reinvent a place for herself in each new location she discovered. Kate loved travel writing, especially from the nineteenth and twentieth centuries. For hundreds of years European women were forbidden to travel without a husband, their family or an escort. Some women who could not be contained by the physical and supposedly moral dangers of travelling used to travel incognito, disguised as men.

Kate especially loved a book by Lady Mary Wortley Montague who went to Turkey in the early 1700s with her husband. In her letters, Lady Montague thought that Turkish women enjoyed more freedom than she did laced up in corset and stays. Hiding beneath a veil, she wrote, a woman could walk the streets anonymously and visit her lovers without being discovered. Kate would sigh and say that "a little freedom can be a dangerous thing". I think she meant it as much about the way that women travellers had forged pathways for other women upsetting the men folk, as she did about her wish that her parents would give her a little less of it. I admire Kate. She always does exactly what she says she will do. She knows no fear.

Kate always looked to the future, dreaming further ahead than seemed real, past the year, past high school. Yet she would do so with such conviction that I never doubted what she saw was true. When I started making plans for university, it was because Kate had implied that was where we'd been headed all along. I followed her in much the same manner as I had followed her to the swimming pool. I was busy enrolling in my law degree at about the same time my father came home again.

I barely knew my father until the summer when he had his heart attack. I had just finished my first year of high school.

Before then he had been a distant figure, almost mythic, compared to the easy familiarity of my mother. It is not surprising he changed so much after his near-death experience. He had never spoken about his childhood before and I had almost assumed he didn't have one. I knew that he had a family because we used to play at Aunty Pat's house until she passed away and my cousins were sent to boarding school.

I first began to understand the life that he had led before I was born when we visited the orphanage he'd grown up in. I was twelve then. Even without knowing what he had lived through there, I could sense from the corridors and the walls what it must have been like for him. You know how you can stand in a place and it just speaks to you with its atmosphere? The thing that struck me, that made me feel nervous and cautious, was the stillness and quietness of the place. It was near Christmas and the children had been sent to visit remaining family or billeted into foster homes. We walked through a section that was part of the dormitory for boys. Dad stopped and, looking around the room, said, "This is where Uncle Danny and I were when we first came here. I would sneak into his bed to keep him warm. Well, I guess it was also to console myself, I was so scared."

If you knew how distant my father was before, you would know that for him to speak of something so personal showed how much he had changed. I guess almost dying from a sick heart is bound to change a person.

After leaving the dormitories, we passed a staircase. Sitting halfway up the flight was a girl about the same age as Kingsley with freckles across her nose, long, straight brown hair and deep brown eyes. The couple giving us the tour went over and spoke to her briefly and then she went up the stairs. I overheard the woman telling Mum that the girl had nowhere to go this Christmas, no family and no foster family. I looked back, curious to catch another glimpse of this girl that no one wanted, but she was gone. I linked hands with my mother, squeezing her fingers tightly, and did not let go until we were back in the car. The girl haunted my thoughts during the long drive back to my home on the other side of Sydney.

The trip to the orphanage had been the start of Dad's reconnecting with his past. He and Mum were separated then. During school holidays we had to stay with him during the day while Mum worked. Kingsley and I just tagged along when he went to the library and archives, but we were too distracted with inventing ways to break the boredom and not disturb the silence to notice what Dad was doing. He was happier, less angry, when he found his family in Walgett. He changed his name then from Brecht to Boney, and it was as though he had been two different men in one body.

When Dad came back home again, he had to take my mother on her own terms. He had to put up with things he would never have stood for before — cats, dogs, bonsai, her work, her study. I admired him for realising that she was worth all the compromises. He valued her more now that she needed him less. It must be hard to admit that you were wrong and say that you are sorry and live with someone who has seen you at your worst. I forgave him a lot because of his courage to come home again.

University was liberating and disillusioning. I had the freedom to do as I wished and people did not dismiss my criticisms of the way history was told. But the conservatism and insularity of the Law Faculty — from the students much more than the staff — had distressed me and I chided myself for thinking it would have been any different. I was relieved and comforted when Kingsley arrived at the same law school the next year. He had already made the transition from carefree young boy to serious and reserved young man.

In class we skipped over *Milirrpum v Nabalco Pty Ltd*, a 1975 case also known as the *Gove Land Rights* case. This was taught to us to provide concrete precedent that there was no native title held by Indigenous people. But, if you read the case you will see that Justice Blackburn wrote so much more. He may have found that there was no native title, but he did recognise that Aboriginal people had a set of laws. In his judgment he said the evidence he looked at showed "a subtle and elaborate system highly adapted to the country in which the people led their lives, which provided a stable order of society and was remarkably free from the vagaries of personal whim or influence" existed. He said that "if ever a system could be called 'a government of laws, and not of men', it is that shown in evidence before me."

So he saw a government, a system of laws. One could even say he saw sovereignty. But he felt he was held prisoner by the weight of legal precedent, his hands tied by colonial law, and said that "it was beyond the power of this court to decide otherwise than that New South Wales came into the category of a settled or occupied colony". So these laws and customs that Justice Blackburn described would be treated by the law as invisible. All *terra nullius*, vacant. Law is like history in that there are dominant, almost mythical ways of talking about it, but when you scratch the surface, you will find many subversive narratives, overlooked, forgotten, smothered by the dominant story.

That's why, when the High Court overturned the doctrine of *terra nullius*, Chief Justice Brennan spoke about fracturing the skeleton of the law. He had to explain when the courts can and can't move away from what they have said in the past and then determine how far they can go if they want to take the law in a different direction. But this reversal of law and history would not come until after I had finished law school.

You might think that today it doesn't matter, that people never worry about skin colour the way they used to. But it does in ways that you may not see and in lessons that are humiliating. I will tell you just one lesson I learnt at university: no matter how many degrees you have, how clever you are, how well you speak, how many books you read, you cannot get away from the skin thing.

I was taught this lesson by Toby Mitchell who was in my Evidence class and with whom I had several conversations in the law library during study sessions devoid of any mention of the rules of evidence. I thought he was handsome with his sandy brown hair and blue eyes and I found his confidence attractive. I felt happy when I saw him and thought about him every night before I fell asleep. I would recount our conversations word for word to Kate, analysing evidence of hidden meanings and messages. His upbringing had been different to mine, with private schools and ski trips and holidays to Europe. I felt the difference between us acutely when I first visited his parents' expansive house in a wealthy eastern Sydney suburb. Mum's house could have comfortably fit in his garage. I was nervous just walking on the perfectly polished floors. As I stood in the kitchen while Toby was out of the room, I started talking to his mother. I was trying to be friendly as she worked in the kitchen, cooking a meal that looked more elaborate than anything my mother would prepare. When Toby returned he whispered to me, very politely, that I shouldn't distract the staff when they were working.

I had been waltzing the courtship dance of movies and dinners with Toby for about a month when we went to a video evening at a friend's place, where the conversation turned to the recent bicentenary of European invasion. There had been scores of protests from Aboriginal people all over mainland Australia, culminating in a large march in Sydney to show we will never be silently folded into a more convenient telling of history. Many Australians supported this display of resistance and survival, but there were others who resented it.

"They're all half-castes," Toby's friend Justin said. "Trouble stirrers. Most of them are dole bludgers who like living in filth. Feral. The real ones don't behave like that. Give them some metho and they'll be happy." Toby's friends giggled at the comment in a carefree manner as I felt myself freezing up with hurt.

"They're always complaining. They want handouts. Want something for nothing. Think that just because they are black that they can take things away from honest and hard-working people."

"They should thank us," Justin said. "We saved them from a stone-age existence."

"I feel sorry for them. It must be hard to go from being primitive to being civilised. It is no wonder that many of them can't make the transition," interjected Francesca, Justin's girlfriend.

"Those bleeding-heart attitudes are part of the problem. You're too soft. But you'll change your tune when they make a land claim on your house," replied Justin. I looked to Toby for consolation but he was smirking in agreement.

And then the topic changed to something else.

I was distressed by Toby's attitude but said nothing until we were in the car on the way home. He noticed that I was quiet and obviously upset. "What's wrong?" he asked, genuinely concerned. Not knowing quite how to put all the questions I wanted to make him answer and all the facts I wanted to lay before him, I simply said, "How can you have those views about Aboriginal people?"

"What do you care?" he asked. But as soon as he asked, his eyes seemed to indicate that he realised the answer. You can see a lot in people's eyes. And he knew what I saw in his eyes. He said, "I thought you were Spanish. You look Spanish. I didn't know you were a coon." After a painful silence, all he could think of to say to console me was, "Don't worry, you can't tell." And his words took me back to the classroom, all those years ago: *Good. There are too many of them.*

Toby never got over the shock of finding out that I was Aboriginal. My exoticness had suddenly turned itself into traits too tainted for him to deal with. He never called me again. He avoided me around campus for nearly a year, too embarrassed to speak to me. I can't tell you how dirty he made me feel, how untouchable. It was the first time I really felt that my skin was made from dirt since Natalie Fletcher had called me an ugly black spider. But this time I felt too humiliated to tell anybody so they could give me a pep talk. And you can see why encounters like those with the woman in the post office, who in my mind looks like Nancy Kerrigan, are just everyday occurrences. Like Kate said, the things you learn at university are never the things you think you are going to learn.

I often felt that my boyfriends thought my Aboriginality was a symbol, of rebellion or tolerance. Like Phillip Knight who saw it as a way to rile his father up at Sunday family lunch when he wanted to know why Aborigines should have land rights. Or Keith Duncan, who kept telling me it didn't matter to him so often that it was obvious it did. Others, like Chris Anderson, saw it as a way of getting into a culture that they romanticised, always wanting to go to Aboriginal plays and see Aboriginal bands as though holding my hand was a pass to get in. I grew suspicious of any importance given to my ancestry.

When I left law school, I began working at a law firm that specialised in land claims. In New South Wales, legislation had been put in place that allowed Aboriginal people to claim back Crown land. Even though it was promoted as recompense for lost land, these legislative schemes made clear there was no Indigenous right to land independent of the statutory entitlement. And they often masked further acts of dispossession. Although in New South Wales it was said that the Land Rights Act was for the benefit of Aboriginal people, it only gave access to about six thousand acres. At the same time it became law, another piece of legislation was passed to remedy a bureaucratic mistake. Since 1969, the Lands Department had acted for the government when it continually took away Aboriginal reserve land and gave it to white farmers. It turned out it wasn't the Lands Department's to give; the title belonged to the Aborigines Protection Board so all those transfers of land were illegal, all twenty-five thousand acres of it.

Land rights fostered great antagonism within the non-Indigenous community, who resented what they saw as Aboriginal people 'getting something for nothing' and a threat to their own title to land (even though land rights legislation ensured that this would not happen). For example, the Western Australian Chamber of Mines ran a virulent campaign against land rights legislation which in that state ensured its defeat. It was an anti-land-rights campaign focused on creating fear within the general population by implying — erroneously — that people's homes would be at risk. "Your right of ownership could be under threat," their propaganda thundered. A television commercial, playing on this fear, showed black hands building a brick wall across a map of Western Australia with an accompanying sign: "Keep out — this land is part of Western Australia under Aboriginal land claim." These fears and phobias resurfaced in the debates around recognition of native title. They certainly seemed to work on the Tobys and Justins of the world.

In the cases I worked on we claimed vacant Crown land for our clients. The Minister then objected to the claim, saying that the land was ineligible to be given to Aboriginal communities because, although the land wasn't being used, it was needed for an essential public purpose. He would give us a list of reasons — defence, environmental protection, housing. Then we would have to show that his decision was not based on good faith, that land could not be used for environmental protection and housing at the same time, especially when it was basically swamp.

Having said that, the communities that got land back could do good things for their community with it. Build houses on it. Set up community centres. And as we started to try to implement and expand the findings in the *Mabo* case, we found that the case was not the trigger to get land — and water and fishing rights — back for Aboriginal people that we had first thought it would be. I was coming to the conclusion that the land rights system, with its secure tender, was a better outcome than native title. Kingsley is far more meticulous in his thinking, weighing up the pros and cons before making a decision. I tend to go with my gut feeling. With me, it's hit or miss. With Kingsley, it is a carefully calculated aim; but that is why he is such a good lawyer. At the time I am writing this, I do not know whether the courts will continue to narrowly define native title and whether, in the years to come, a federal government will pass amendments to the Native Title Act that will extinguish and erode native title rights across the country. I cannot see into the future like Kate can.

Kate did write her travel books. I received my signed copy of *Single in Shanghai* on the eve I was leaving for Paris. *Not Another Humorous Falafel Story* on her travels in the Middle East has recently been sent to her publishers. Kate followed the paths of the women travel writers she so admired. Her view of the world is outward looking, analytical, perceptive. She is still seeking to draw me out of my thoughts and into the world around me. She was proud of me when I went to study in Paris. "I was beginning to think you would never leave Sydney," she wrote from Prague.

I didn't know that moving to another country would change me so completely. And I have to confess that the first meal I ate was at McDonald's, to see what it would taste like, whether it would be different or similar to what I was used to. So you see, in many ways, I am a person who fears change.

But it was as though, in new surroundings, in streets crowded with disjointed houses, almost crushed together, I became a new Candice. I didn't decide that I was going to change myself, "reinvent myself" as Kate would say, yet I transformed into some new kind of me. When you travel you feel closer to the things you leave behind. It was as though there were some things, deep inside me, that were waiting to come out but couldn't while I stayed in familiar surroundings. No wonder Kate is never ready to come home.

In France, I never could understand why the balconies of the quaintly squat houses were all on the first floors. If it were my house, I would want to live on the top storey, where I would have a view across the tile and terracotta roofs. Christoph, my boyfriend, would tell me that the preference would be for the floor of the house that would require the least effort to walk through. When we travelled across the Channel, he used the English word 'preference' a lot. He'd say: "I prefer the steak," when ordering from the menu. It was true; he preferred the steak to all the other things listed. Or he would say, "I will take the steak," as though it were going to accompany us on the trip back to Paris. But he would laugh almost every time I spoke French. "*Trés charmant*," he would laugh.

Christoph says that we were destined to meet even though it seemed like the strangest of coincidences. He was studying on the same program as me. We got to talking about books and it turned out he had never read *Wuthering Heights*. And so I arrived at our next class together with a copy as a present for him. I thought nothing of buying it — I had never worked out how much I was spending. I could never make the exchange in my head, and the amount of francs always seemed so high that it never seemed as though I was spending real money. It turned out it was his birthday. He must have known that this was a coincidence because he had never told me when his birthday was. But Christoph read this special symbolism into the whole thing and seemed to think there was some kind of destiny surrounding us. It is the old story where two people live the same events but tell them differently.

I've always wanted to be loved by someone. I wanted what was in the novels I read. I wanted my own Mr Knightley, Mr Darcy or Colonel Brandon. I don't think you can love the books that I loved as much as I did and not want the romance and the passion inside their covers for yourself. And yet, when Christoph came into my life, I seemed to do nothing but resist him. He never thought of me as 'other', exotic. Being Aboriginal didn't mean the same things to him that it mean to Toby Mitchell. He could see past my skin, just like I felt when I put myself in my favourite stories. It was the situation I had for so long dreamed of finding myself in and I don't understand why I try to deny myself the happiness of having him in my life, why I am so afraid to let him make me whole.

I came back to Australia without Christoph but with a restlessness, abuzz with all the things I had experienced in a year away. I was frustrated that people at home were exactly where they were before I had left, stagnant, while I had changed so much. I felt I needed to find something to make me feel like I was back again, that I fitted in. So when my father said that he was travelling to visit Uncle Henry, I thought I might find some of that stability if I went back to the place where my Aboriginal family lived. That maybe I would find the same sense of self and confidence my father had found there.

31

1995

I LOOK TO THE SKY. Its sea and cornflower blues remind me of the flecks of colour in Christoph's eyes and my thoughts and feelings float as they touch on him. I suddenly feel overwhelmingly happy, liberated from all my denials and resistance to his offers, as though I have surrendered to him and accepted him with one pump of my heart, one squint of my eyes at the sparkling sun. As I stand here, all I have inside me is so strong, so much a part of me, that it could never be erased. No matter where I live or who I live with. That for all the things that change in a different context, there is always a part of me that remains untouchable. I needed to come here to realise that.

As I walk slowly across this remote edge of Dungalear Station, I feel fated to have come to this place with the same assurance that Kate has when she looks into the future. I sense that after my grandmother left this spot the land just waited patiently for me to arrive. This place seems full of history, of lingering moments. Too sleepy for progress, it feels as though everything has collapsed in on itself, as if everyone who has been here throughout time now exists side by side.

So it is that I come to stand on the same spot where my grandmother, Elizabeth Boney, had last seen her brother. The bitterness of what was wrong, what had been cast upon my family, is softened by a sense of triumph. Here now stand three generations of my family, aware of how much has been dislocated and lost, yet still standing on our land, at the place where the rivers meet.

And that's how history can tell a story. I can tell you a story of triumph: that to this spot, where my grandmother was torn from, I return, nearly ninety years later, educated and successful. But this history of winners masks the history of losses. For the story of my success is also the story of all that is missing, all that cannot be claimed back. There are the lost members of my family whose lives, thoughts and love I will never know. I can only imagine what has happened to all those who share my blood. All those loves lost to racism.

Danielle has taken Granny out of the car and given her a seat under the shade of the tree. I feel guilty because I had not thought to help her. I have no older relatives in my life so I do not know what to do to help her. I walk to where Granny is seated and sit beside her. Every time she looks at me, I avert my gaze, pluck at a blade of grass bent in the breeze or look up at the overhanging canopy of leaves as it sways in the wind. It is many stretched minutes until she begins to speak.

"There," she says. "That is where Elizabeth's place was." I look at the ground where, under the blades of bending grass, there are sticks, bark and pieces of metal firmly planted in the soil, remnants of a home and family.

"Your grandmother and I were both Dinewan. Garibooli, we called her. Her brother used to call her Booli," remembers Granny, "back in the days when they used my other name, Karrwi*. Karrwi and Garibooli."

"Garibooli," I whisper into the wind.

As we rest under the shade of the trees, Granny tells me the story of the Dinewan:

Dinewan was acknowledged as being the leader of the birds by all the other birds.

* *Karrwi* = Eualeyai word for sandalwood

The Goomblegubbons were jealous of the Dinewan. The mother of the Goomblegubbons was especially jealous of the mother of the Dinewan. She was also jealous of how high the Dinewan could fly. Dinewan would irritate Goomblegubbon by making a great fuss every time she landed. Goomblegubbon thought that Dinewan was showing off.*

Goomblegubbon used to wonder how she could put an end to the supremacy of the Dinewan. Goomblegubbon had cunning; Dinewan had strength. If Goomblegubbon tried to fight Dinewan, she would lose, but, she thought, if she could injure Dinewan's wings, Dinewan would not be able to fly.

One day, Goomblegubbon saw Dinewan coming towards her. Goomblegubbon squatted down into the dirt and folded her wings to make it look like she didn't have any. She spoke in a friendly way to Dinewan and after a while suggested that Dinewan imitate her. She said: "Every bird can fly. If you are the leader of the birds, you should be able to do without your wings. When birds see that I can do without my wings, they will think that I am clever and make me the leader."

Goomblegubbon spoke so persuasively that Dinewan, in her vanity, decided to sacrifice her wings. She spoke this over with her mate and he decided to do the same. They did not want to see Goomblegubbon rule. They also cut the wings off all their children.

Dinewan went to see Goomblegubbon to tell her that her advice had been followed. Goomblegubbon started laughing and dancing with joy at the success of her plot. "I still have my wings," she cried. "I tricked you. You are not very good leaders if you can be fooled so easily." Goomblegubbon flapped her wings, gloating, and flew away.

Dinewan brooded and vowed to get revenge. She thought of a plan. She hid all her babies in a bush, except for two. She walked to see Goomblegubbon with her two little ones. She found Goomblegubbon feeding her twelve babies.

* *goomblegubbons* = bustards

After a friendly conversation, Dinewan suggested to Goomblegubbon that she should only have two children. "Twelve are too many to feed. That is why your children never grow big like Dinewans."

Goomblegubbon did not answer but thought this over, impressed by the idea that her babies would grow big like the Dinewan. But she was hesitant because she remembered the trick she had played on Dinewan. So she studied Dinewan. She was tempted because she thought that if her young grew as big as Dinewan and still had their wings, they would be the leaders.

So Goomblegubbon killed all her young except two. When she saw Dinewan she told her what she had done. "The two that are left will have plenty to eat now and grow as big as your children."

"You are a very bad mother," Dinewan replied. "I have twelve children and they all have plenty to eat. I would not kill any of my children, not even to get my wings back."

"But you only have two children," the surprised Goomblegubbon responded.

"That's what you think. I have twelve," said Dinewan and she went to get her young to show them to Goomblegubbon. She presented her twelve children to Goomblegubbon and cooed. Then she said seriously, "I have twelve babies. You can look at them all and think of the children that you have slaughtered. You will be reminded of what your ambition and jealousy have made you do. By your trickery and deceit you made the Dinewan lose their wings, but for as long as we cannot fly, you will only ever have two children at a time. You can have your wings, but I will have my children."

When she finished her story, Granny paused before adding, "Whatever tricks people play on you, whatever they do to you out of jealousy and spite, we will always have our children. They will always be ours." She seemed to be talking not to me, but to the grass blades that answered her with a gentle sway, urged on by the breeze.

History is a narrative of events. The word 'history' has French (*histoire*), Latin (*historia*) and Greek (*istoria*) roots. It used to mean 'inquiry' but now it also implies a story, 'His Story', as some feminists have dubbed it. In English, the words 'story' and 'history' mean different things, but they were originally both used to describe an account of events either imaginary or true. It was only in the fifteenth century that the term 'history' was used to describe the telling of *real* past events and 'story' used for imagined ones. The German word *historie* refers to the telling of past happenings. The Germans have another word, *geschichte*, which refers to the processes of past, present and future. Thinking of history as a future process is a relatively modern notion. The Enlightenment concern with progress and development, Hegel's world-historical process, and Marx's belief that the products of history are part of our present and will shape the future in a predictable manner, have all profoundly influenced our understanding of the concept of 'history'.

As we head back to town, I recognise the landmarks we drove past to reach the place where the rivers meet.

Granny turns to me. "You are too uptight," she says bluntly. "Where's all that going to get you?"

"And one more thing," she says curtly before I can answer. "It's what's in here that matters," She taps on her skeletal chest, "Not how dark this is." She pinches the limp skin on her arm. "You'd do well to remember that," she says, peering into me and at all of my shortcomings — my insecurity, my seriousness, my inability to trust. I know that she has cut into truths, yet I feel as though the worst parts of me, the weakest, most confused and insecure parts of me, have been shed on the soil, on a spot where grief had begun to bleed generations ago.

My thoughts turn to Christoph and I suddenly feel the urge to call him, to tell him to catch a plane to Sydney as he has wanted to do since I left Paris almost a year ago.

I look out of the window and watch the landscape fold into its now familiar landforms. "Garibooli," I whisper. I like the way the word sounds on my tongue. "Garibooli. Garibooli. Garibooli."

Acknowledgments

With deepest thanks to Sue Abbey; Geoff Scott; Kate Sutherland; the Jumbunna Indigenous House of Learning; the University of Technology, Sydney; and Raema, Jason and Paul Behrendt.

The stories of Eualeyai that appear here belong, as they always have, to the Eualeyai people. I heard these stories from my father.

Sources

Lawrence Binyon, from *Poems for the Fallen*, on p. 66.
Kenneth Clark, *Civilisation: A Personal View*.
A.G.L. Shaw, *The Story of Australia*.
Kenneth Slessor, "Beach Burial", (on pp. 137–8) from *Kenneth Slessor: Collected Poems*, Angus & Robertson, 1994.
F.L.W. Wood, *A Concise History of Australia*.